D1581530

Peter Duck

*Other books by Arthur Ransome
in Red Fox*

Swallows and Amazons
Swallowdale
Winter Holiday
Coot Club
Pigeon Post
We Didn't Mean to Go to Sea
Secret Water
The Big Six
Missee Lee
The Picts and the Martyrs
Great Northern?

ARTHUR RANSOME

Peter Duck

(Based on information supplied by the
Swallows and Amazons and illustrated
mainly by themselves)

ST. COLUMBA'S HIGH SCHOOL
LIBRARY
CLYDEBANK

RED FOX

A Red Fox Book

Published by Random House Children's Books
61-63 Uxbridge Road, London W5 5SA

A division of The Random House Group Ltd
London Melbourne Sydney Auckland
Johannesburg and agencies throughout the world

First published by Jonathan Cape 1930
Puffin edition 1962

Red Fox edition 1993

This Red Fox edition 2001

Copyright © Arthur Ransome 1930

5 7 9 10 8 6 4

This book is sold subject to the condition that it shall not, by way of trade or otherwise, be
lent, resold, hired out, or otherwise circulated without the publisher's prior consent in any
form of binding or cover other than that in which it is published and without a similar
condition including this condition being imposed on the subsequent purchaser.

Printed and bound in Great Britain by
Bookmarque Ltd, Croydon, Surrey

Papers used by The Random House Group Ltd are natural, recyclable products made from
wood grown in sustainable forests. The manufacturing processes conform to the
environmental regulations of the country of origin.

THE RANDOM HOUSE GROUP Limited Reg. No. 954009

ISBN 0 09 96310 8

www.arthur-ransome.org/ar

NOTE ON THE PICTURES

When we began to do these pictures we decided that each of us was to put her (or his) name to her own works of art. But this was hopeless. Everybody wanted to help with every picture, even passing natives who saw what we were doing. So we had to leave all names out except in the case of Roger's two pictures which anybody would know anyhow.

CAPTAIN NANCY BLACKETT

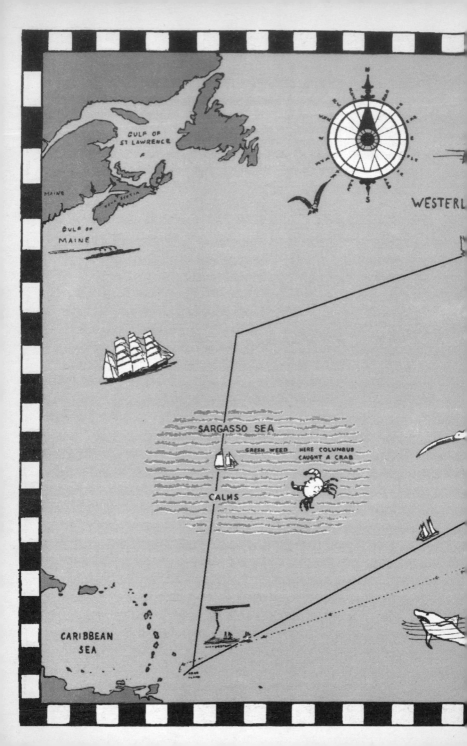

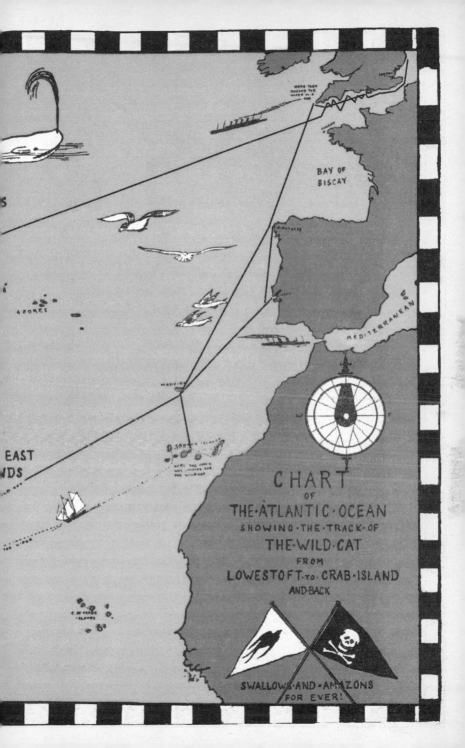

SWALLOWS·AND·AMAZONS·FOR·EVER

To
Mrs Robert Blackett
and Mrs E.H.R Walker

A humble apology for the ungrateful
brutality with which their children
eliminated them from these adventures.

CONTENTS

BOOK ONE

BOOK TWO

ILLUSTRATIONS

THE ADVENTURERS SET SAIL

BOOK ONE

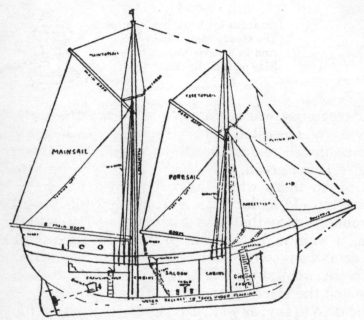

THIS·IS·TO·SHOW·THE·NAMES·OF·THE·SAILS·ETC.·AND·A·SIDEWAYS·VIEW·BELOW·DECK.

THE *WILD CAT*

CHAPTER I

QUAYSIDE

He turns his head, but in his ear
The steady trade-winds run,
And in his eye the endless waves
Ride on into the sun.

BINYON

PETER DUCK was sitting on a bollard on the north quay of Lowestoft Inner Harbour, smoking his pipe in the midday sunshine and looking down at a little, green, two-masted schooner that was tied up there while making ready for sea. He was an old sailor with a fringe of white beard round a face that was as brown and wrinkled as a walnut. He had sailed in the clipper ships racing home with tea from China. He had sailed in the wool ships from Australia. He had been round the Horn again and again and knew it, as he used to say, as well as he knew the crook of his own thumb. But for a long time now he had left the sea. He lived in an old wherry on the Norfolk rivers, sailing this way and that between Norwich and Lowestoft and Yarmouth and Beccles, sometimes with a cargo of potatoes, sometimes with a cargo of coals, and sometimes with the deck of his wherry piled so high with reeds for thatching that the sail would hardly clear them. But he had not very much to do and every now and then he used to leave his old wherry in Oulton Broad and slip down to Lowestoft to look at the boats and the fishermen and to smell the fresh wind blowing in from the sea. And for two or three days now he had been coming along to smoke his pipe on this particular bollard because he liked the looks of the little green schooner that was lying there moored to the quay.

There was a queer thing about this little schooner. There seemed to be only one man aboard her, a big fat man with a bald head. Peter Duck knew what his name was, for there were two girls helping him, and Peter Duck heard them calling him sometimes "Uncle Jim," but more often "Captain Flint." And he heard this Captain Flint calling the girls "Captain Nancy" and "Mate Peggy," but that, he thought, was probably his fun. The thing that puzzled Peter Duck most was that there didn't seem to be a crew. Yet anybody could tell that the little schooner was getting ready for sea. Captain Flint and those two girls were for ever running to the ships' chandler's in the town and coming back with new canvas buckets, and tins of paint, and marlinespikes, and spare blocks, and what not. And as for the stores that had gone aboard her, Peter Duck had heard from a friend in the Custom-House at the end of the quay, you would have thought she was bound twice round the world and back again. And old Peter Duck looked down at her from the top of the quay and wished he was going too. "Going foreign, she is, to blue water," he said to himself. And he thought of other little schooners he had known, on the Newfoundland Banks and in the South Seas. He thought of flying-fish and porpoises racing each other and turning over in the waves. He thought of the noise of the wind in the shrouds, and the glow of the lamp on a moving compass card, and tall masts swaying across the stars at night. And he wished he could go to sea once more and make another voyage before it was too late.

That morning Captain Flint and his two nieces had been even busier than usual, tidying up their ship, throwing chips and shavings over the side, swabbing down decks and paintwork and sweeping the dirty water out through the scuppers. And every now and then they kept looking up to the quay and along it towards the Custom-House and the harbourmaster's office and the road from the railway station. Old Peter Duck, smoking his pipe on the quay, twisted himself round and scratched his head and wondered what they were looking for. And then a telegraph-boy had come along the quay on a red bicycle, and Captain Flint had run up the ladder to meet him, and torn open the orange envelope of a telegram, and given the boy a sixpence and said there was no answer. "Well, that's done it," he had said to those two girls. "He can't come. He can't come at all. And we can't start without him. And it's too late to send a wire to the Swallows. They'll be here any time now." All three of them aboard the schooner looked very glum after that. But it was clear that they were expecting someone else besides the telegraph-boy, for Captain Nancy and Mate Peggy still hung about on deck, and kept looking up every two minutes. Perhaps, thought Peter Duck, they were waiting for that crew of theirs. And suddenly, round the corner by the Custom-House, came two boys and two girls, helping a porter to push a handcart

along and keeping the luggage on the handcart
from tumbling off. On the top of the luggage was
a green parrot in a cage. A monkey, on a lead, was
hurrying along after the smaller of the two boys.
Peter Duck had a look at them and thought they
must have taken the wrong turning.

*

The four were all talking at once. Something
had just happened to startle them.

"Did you see he had gold ear-rings?" asked
Able-seaman Titty.

"Why did he look so angry?" asked Roger, the
ship's boy.

"Why shouldn't old Polly say 'Pieces of eight!'
if he wants to?" said Captain John.

"Probably it was just a mistake," said Mate
Susan.

"Lucky for you it's not his vessel you're looking
for," said the porter.

"Why? Has he got a ship?"

"Black Jake's not the sort of chap it's safe to
quarrel with," said the porter. "'Pieces of eight!'
your bird said. Well, there's many a boy in this
town got a sore head for shouting that after
Black Jake. You mustn't speak of treasure to
Black Jake. No. Nor yet of crabs. Look, that's his
ship. That black schooner over there on the other
side. This'll be yours. What did you say her name
was?"

"*Wild Cat*," said Titty.

"She's called after our island," said Roger.

"There's no name on her that I can see," said
the porter. "They've been new painting of her."

But at that moment Nancy and Peggy looked up and saw them coming along the quay.

"Here they are," Peggy bent and shouted through the skylight to Captain Flint, who was busy down below.

Peter Duck had another look at the Swallows. So they were for the little schooner, were they? They hadn't taken a wrong turning after all.

Nancy and Peggy ran to the ladder and climbed up to the quay from the deck of the schooner.

"Here you are at last," shouted Nancy. "Swallows and Amazons for ever! Come on. She's a beauty, the *Wild Cat*. Real bunks in the cabins, one above another. The ones with longest legs have the top bunks. And Captain Flint's been building a cage for Gibber. It's the best cabin any monkey ever had."

"We've got a gorgeous galley to do the cooking in," Mate Peggy called to Mate Susan. "On deck, too, so there won't be any smells down below."

"Swallows and Amazons for ever!" John, Susan, Titty, and Roger shouted back, remembering how they had shouted that over the water to each other as their little boats, the *Swallow* and the *Amazon*, were sailing home on the last day of those holidays on the lake in the north. There was great shaking of hands. Nancy and Peggy shook hands even with Gibber, and had their fingers nipped a little by the parrot, for old time's sake. The parrot had been in high spirits ever since the railway journey had come to an end. "Pieces of eight!" he screamed, "Pieces of eight!" just as Nancy had taught him ever so long ago.

"He hasn't forgotten," said Nancy.

THE SWALLOWS JOIN THE SHIP

The four Swallows were waving their hands to Captain Flint, who had just come on deck. But at this Titty turned round.

"Of course he hasn't," she said. "He's got a splendid memory. He was shouting it like anything just now, when we were coming out of the station, and there was a man with gold ear-rings . . ."

"'What's that? What's that?' the man said," Roger interrupted. "The man went on saying 'What's that? Whose is that bird?' and he pushed his horrid face at us, and tried to take hold of the cage. Titty wouldn't let him, but he came with us all the way until the man by the bridge stopped him and told him to leave us alone . . ."

"How do, Mr Duck?" said the porter, as the old sailor nodded towards the opposite quay where a handsome black schooner was lying. "Aye, it was him. Getting worse then he used to be is Black Jake. We'll be well rid of him when he gets away. They say he's off to have another look at them crabs of yours. He's got the scum of the place with him in that hooker of his."

Captain Flint came climbing up the ladder to the quay.

"Hullo, Captain John," he said. "Hullo, Mister Mate. Glad to see you, Able-seaman. Hullo, Roger, not yet tired of being a ship's boy? Hullo, Polly. And how's Gibber?"

"We were most awfully afraid we were going to be late," said John. "The train got held up by something or other. Have you been waiting for us? When are we going to start?"

Peter Duck saw Captain Flint and his two nieces look suddenly grave.

"That's the whole trouble," said Nancy.

"We can't start," said Peggy.

"We've just had the telegram," said Captain Flint. "The man who was coming with us can't get away. We've got to begin looking round for someone else."

"We may be days and days," said Peggy.

"We just can't help it," said Captain Flint. "Anything breakable in these bags?"

"No," said Susan. And Captain Flint and the porter carried four long canvas kitbags to the side of the quay and dumped them over so that they fell on the deck of the schooner.

"Anyway, it's very jolly just being here," said John.

"Did *Swallow* get hurt on the journey?" asked Titty.

"Not she," said Captain Flint. "Go along and see if you can find a scratch on her. There she is in the davits.[1] A fine ship's boat she will make. And we've a good dinghy as well."

"Good old *Swallow*," said Titty, looking down at the little sailing boat that Captain Flint had brought in a crate all the way to Lowestoft from that far-away lake in the north. There she was, hanging from the davits on the starboard side of the schooner, with her oars and her mast and her old brown sail neatly stowed away in her, all ready to be lowered into the harbour. "Good old *Swallow*."

They had cleared the handcart by now. Susan

---

[1] The davits are a pair of little cranes for hoisting and lowering a boat. – CAPT. NANCY.

had taken her tin box, black, with a red cross on it, full of iodine and things for colds and stomach-aches and sticking-plaster to put on people's knees. This had been the best of Susan's Christmas presents and ever since Christmas she had been almost pleased when anybody fell down (it was usually Roger), sorry for him, of course, but pleased to have the chance of patching him up again. John had a small tin box with a compass in it, and a barometer, and a few other things best not stuffed into a kitbag. Roger's things had all gone into his kitbag, but Gibber had a box of his own, with his blanket in it and a tin mug he particularly liked. Nancy had taken charge of it and was laughing at seeing the monkey's name in capital letters on the outside of his trunk. Titty had a box full of things for writing and drawing. She also had charge of the little telescope that really belonged to John.

One by one they went down the ladder and aboard the *Wild Cat*.

"Look out for Polly below there," called Captain Flint, and Titty was just in time to take the big parrot-cage as it came swinging down on the end of a rope Captain Flint had borrowed from the porter. Roger and the monkey were down already. Roger had started first, pulling Gibber after him, but Gibber was quicker on a ladder than his master, and was pulling at him from below long before Roger reached the deck. John was waiting on the quay to settle with the porter for bringing the things from the station.

"That's all right," said Captain Flint. "It's the ship's affair, bringing the crew aboard."

"Dinner's all ready in the saloon," said Peggy, as John and Captain Flint joined the others on the schooner's deck. "I didn't cook it," she added hurriedly. "It came from the inn. But we'll cook the next one ourselves."

"Come on," said Captain Flint. "This way. Leave the kitbags on deck for now. Let's get at dinner and talk things over. Look out. Mind your heads. Oh, I was forgetting that there'll be plenty of room for most of you. I get a fresh bump or two every time I go below."

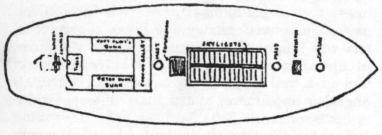

DECK PLAN

They crowded down the companion-way and a moment later, but for the laughter that kept coming up through the open skylights, anybody might have thought the schooner was deserted. The Swallows and Amazons and Captain Flint were all below deck. Gibber the monkey had gone below with them. Only the parrot, in his cage, had been left on the roof of the deckhouse to enjoy the sunshine. He was preening his feathers after the journey, and talking to himself, saying sometimes, "Pretty Polly" and sometimes, "Pieces of eight."

Up there, on the top of the quay, Peter Duck sat on his bollard alone. The porter had trundled

his handcart back to the station, but Peter Duck
was still sitting on his bollard, smoking his pipe,
and thinking. After all, he was thinking, why not?
He laughed to himself. He could just hear what
his daughters would say to their old father. His
mind was almost made up. And he began looking
carefully at the masts of the schooner. There were
one or two things up there that could do with some
little attention.

*

Hungry as they were, for the first few minutes, they could not settle down at the saloon
table. There was so much to admire below decks.
Nobody had really thought that Captain Flint
would keep the promise about taking them to
sea in a real ship. And yet here they were, all
together once more, and actually afloat, aboard
a little schooner. She had been a Baltic trading
schooner with a deckhouse with a couple of bunks
in it, and a fo'c'sle with a couple more. But Captain Flint had decked over the hold and given it a
long skylight. Where, once upon a time, had been
cargoes of firewood and potatoes, he had made a
saloon, with four cabins opening into it. There was
a cabin for John and Roger, one for Susan and
Titty, and one for Nancy and Peggy. The fourth
cabin was to be a hospital, if necessary. "But, of
course," said Captain Flint, "if anybody is really
ill, ill enough to be a nuisance, we'll put him
overboard." Captain Flint himself was sleeping
in the deckhouse, to be within easy reach of
the wheel, and the charts. The fo'c'sle had been
changed too. He had turned part of it into a big

cage for Gibber, so that the monkey had his own
bunk, like everybody else, but had it behind bars,
so that he could be locked in there if he was
getting too much in the way. On either side of
the saloon, and in the fo'c'sle, and everywhere
else where there was room for them, there were
lockers and store cupboards crammed with every
kind of tinned food.

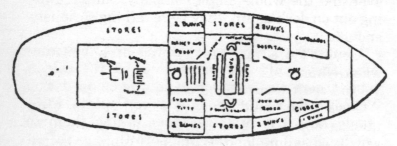

LOOKING · DOWN · THROUGH · THE · DECK

Susan stared with surprise when Captain Flint
and Peggy proudly flung open one cupboard after
another.

"Pemmican," said Peggy. "We've pemmican for
a year at least and jam enough for ten."

"But isn't it rather a waste?" said Susan.

"It'll keep," said Captain Flint. "And what do
you think we've got under the floor?" he asked.

"Ballast," said John.

"Water tanks," said Captain Flint. "You can't
have better ballast than that, and you never know
when you won't be glad to be able to drink it."

"It isn't that he means to go very far," said
Nancy, "but he just likes to feel he could."

"And now, thanks to Sam Bideford not coming

we can't start at all," said Captain Flint. "But
there's nothing against having dinner. I don't
know about you people, but I'm ready for it."

*

Every now and then shouts of laughter floated
up through the skylights, but as time went on
there were not so many, and when dinner was
over and the whole ship's company came crowding out on deck again, they were talking seriously
enough.

"Couldn't we manage by ourselves?" Nancy
was saying.

"You could show us what to do," said John.

"Look here," said Captain Flint, "it's no good
talking about it. You and John are a couple of
very good sailors, and no one could ask for better
cooks than the two mates, and I've nothing whatever against the able-seaman and the boy, but the
Wild Cat is a very different ship from the *Swallow*
or the *Amazon*, and if we're to do anything with
her worth doing I must have another man aboard
who can take watch and watch about with me . . . ."

And at that moment Peter Duck tapped his
pipe out on his bollard, got up, walked to the
edge of the quay and said, "Cap'n!"

Captain Flint looked up at the wrinkled, brown
old sailor.

"Cap'n," said Peter Duck, "can I have a word
with you?"

"Why, yes," said Captain Flint. "There's the
ladder."

Peter Duck climbed quickly down to the deck
of the *Wild Cat*. The others stood there watching

him, and wondering what it was he was going to say.

"It's like this, Cap'n," said the old sailor. "The last few days I've been thinking a deal of your little schooner, and the more I looks at her the more I likes her. Now I'd like well to be seeing blue water once again, and I've been turning it over, as you might say, and I'd like to ask you plain out if it's in your mind to be shipping a crew?"

John and Nancy looked at each other with a flash of hope. But it seemed too good to be true. What would Captain Flint say?

"A crew?" said Captain Flint. "Why, we've got three captains counting myself, and two mates and an able-seaman and a ship's boy and a ship's parrot and a monkey."

"I seen them," said the old sailor. "Now me, I'd be glad to sign on as an A.B. It wouldn't be a bad thing to have an able-seaman to each mate."

Captain Flint laughed. "As a matter of fact," he said, "we *are* one man short. But are you an able-seaman? I know nothing about you, you know. You haven't yet told me your name."

"Duck's my name," said the old man. "Peter Duck, and Duck's my nature, and I've been afloat as you might say, ever since I were a duckling. I've been on inland waters these last years, but I'm a deep sea man properly. Sailed in the *Thermopylae* . . ."

"Sailed in the what?" Captain Flint eagerly caught him up.

"The old *Thermopylae*," said Peter Duck. "There's few A.B.'s with as much experience as what I have. Sixty years of it, and maybe then a bit more."

"A fine ship," said Captain Flint.

"If you be thinking it over, Cap'n," said the old sailor, "and if it's all the same to you, I seen a block up there that's like to come adrift, and, sign on or not sign on, I might as well be putting a whipping on it." His hands were already on the halyards and before they guessed what he was thinking of doing he had begun climbing up the mainmast. A minute later he had hitched a leg over the cross-trees. Then he pulled a knife and some twine out of his pocket and they could see him busy up there far above their heads.

"Well?" said Nancy. "How about that?"

Captain Flint said nothing. He was shading his eyes against the sunshine, looking up at the mast-head to watch what Peter Duck was doing.

Just then Roger, who had been exploring under the deckhouse, trying to get a look at the little engine that was tucked away down there, came rushing up for fear he was missing anything on deck.

Like all the others he looked up at the mast-head. "Hullo," he said, "what's he doing?" but did not wait to be answered. His eyes were all over the place. There was such a lot to see in this harbour. He looked at the swing bridge, closed now, with carts and motor cars and people going across it. He looked along the quay to the Custom-House with the big crest over the doorway, and beyond it the tall masts of the fishing vessels. He looked up the inner harbour towards the dry dock, where a steam trawler was being repaired and there was a great noise of men chipping rust and riveting. And then his eyes rested on that other schooner on the opposite side of the harbour, the black schooner that was tied up against the south quay. There were men taking stores aboard her, or cargo, Roger thought, and suddenly he caught sight of a man he knew on the black schooner's deck.

"Hullo," he said. "There's the man who tried to be beastly about Titty's parrot. The man with the ear-rings."

"Where?" said Titty.

"Over there. On that ship. He's seen us. He's looking at us with a telescope."

"He's wondering what's being done to our mast," said John.

But Peter Duck was coming down now, hand over hand, faster than he went up, with his legs about the mast to steady himself.

"Good enough," said Captain Flint. "In the *Thermopylae*, I think you said? There've been few ships to touch her. I think we might fix something up together. But you'd better meet the rest of us. This is Captain John. This is Captain Nancy. Both have commanded their own vessels. This is Able-seaman Titty. This is Roger, the ship's boy. Where are the mates? Great hands at cooking are our mates. Ah, here they are. Mate Susan of the *Swallow* and Mate Peggy of the *Amazon*. This is Mr Duck, who's thinking of coming down Channel with us . . ."

"Down Channel, sir?" said Peter Duck. "But I made sure you was going foreign."

"No reason why we shouldn't," said Captain

Flint, "if we all get on together. We've got no plans as yet."

"It was blue water as I was thinking of," said Peter Duck.

"You think we're fit for it?"

"She's a tough little packet is yours," said Peter Duck, "and two men and a boy could take her anywheres."

"What about girls?" said Nancy rather fiercely.

"I don't count captains girls," said Peter Duck, "nor mates neither, nor yet able-seamen. And I've three girls myself, all proper sailormen, though they're settled down now and got families."

Nancy laughed. "That's all right," she said. "Some people don't understand."

"How soon could you join?" asked Captain Flint.

Everybody listened. Peter Duck thought for a moment before answering.

"It's like this," he said. "I've a vessel of my own to lay up before I can sail with you. Lying at Oulton she is, my old wherry, and I must sail her up to Beccles and leave all snug with one of my daughters for to keep an eye on her while I'm away. All that takes time. And then there's my things to put together. It's a good while now since I last went to sea."

Faces fell once more. Perhaps after all it would be days and days before they could be starting.

Peter Duck went on. He looked up and sniffed the air and glanced at the vane over the Custom-House. "But there's a right wind for Beccles now, and she's a flyer is my old wherry. *Arrow of Norwich*, they call her. Everybody knows of her. I don't say but what I might be back here with

my dunnage tomorrow morning, and you'll hardly
be sailing before then. There's best part of a day's
work to do on the rigging, seems to me."

Captain Flint laughed. "I thought you were
going to say the week after next. That's all right.
You're the man for us, if you think you won't mind
cramming into the deckhouse with me. You and I
ought to be handy for the wheel . . . ."

A few minutes later Captain Flint and Peter
Duck were walking off together along the quay
to the harbourmaster's office.

"Well, that's just saved us," said Nancy.

"And isn't Peter Duck a lovely name?" said
Titty.

"That man's still got his telescope," said Roger.
"But he isn't pointing it at us now. He's watching
Captain Flint walking along the quay."

They looked across the water to the black
schooner. The man who had been angry with the
parrot was standing on the deck with a telescope
to his eye, watching Captain Flint and Peter Duck,
who were just turning into the harbourmaster's
office.

Captain Flint came back alone. He was in
the highest spirits.

"We simply couldn't have done better," he was
saying. "The harbourmaster tells me that that old
man's the best seaman that's ever shipped out
of Lowestoft. The *Thermopylae*! We shall know
something about sailing when that old fellow
has finished with us. And now we can start the
moment we're ready. Trial trip tomorrow. Well,
anyway, the day after. I was thoroughly bothered
when I heard Sam Bideford couldn't come. What

a bit of luck. An old sailor from the *Thermopylae*! Good enough for anybody."

"What is the *Thermopylae*?" asked Roger.

"A fine clipper ship," said Captain Flint. "She was named after a battle, a land battle, though, not like Salamis. Oh yes, Roger, we heard all about your picture of that, of Salamis, I mean, and how you put funnels on all the triremes. You'll be an engineer before ever you'll be a sailor. You've been at the engine already in this ship . . . ."

Roger grinned a little shyly. "How do you know?" he asked.

"One large smudge of grease on your left cheek," said Captain Flint. "There's nowhere else you could have got it. Simple, eh? Well, come along now and have another look at it. And get your things stowed in your cabins, you others. We've a lot to do before Mr Duck comes aboard in the morning."

The rest of the day was busy for everybody. The old sailor, Peter Duck, was sailing the *Arrow of Norwich* up to Beccles, and wondering what his daughter there would say when she heard that her old father was going to sea once more. Aboard the green schooner Roger had been appointed engineer. He was oiling the engine, and Gibber the monkey was following him round with an oil-can, copying him in everything, and dripping oil on likely places. A board had been slung over the stern, and John was sitting on it with a tin of white paint and a brush, painting in the name "WILD CAT LOWESTOFT" in good big letters. Peggy and Susan were going through the stores and getting things into working order in the little galley at the forward end of the deckhouse, where they were to cook. Nancy and Titty were polishing up the brasswork and talking of old times. Captain Flint was lending a hand here, there, and everywhere. The parrot was practising his words. And away there on the black schooner at the other side of the harbour, Black Jake, that dark, scowling man with the black ringlets and the gold ear-rings, was watching all that was going on through his long telescope.

SWALLOWS·AND·AMAZONS·FOR·EVER!

CHAPTER II

RED-HAIRED BOY

"WELL," said Nancy, "how did you sleep?"

"Very well, thank you," said Titty, who was just bringing the parrot up on deck. Every one of them could have said the same. They had all slept very well, though they had been long in getting to sleep that first night. Voices had called from cabin to cabin. Top bunk spoke to lower bunk. Lower bunk had something urgent to say to top. Then there had been the creaking of the fenders between the schooner and the quay. There had been the noise of a passing tug. There had been the noise of someone in a rowing boat going home late at night to one of the ketches moored higher up the harbour. It had seemed almost wasteful to go to sleep, but, once they slept they had slept well, and waked up fresh and eager for their life aboard ship.

Peggy and Susan were busy in the galley. Peggy had already been ashore for a quart of new milk. Captain Flint was shaving in the deckhouse. John was looking into *Swallow*, to see that all was ready. Captain Flint had promised that if there was time, they should lower her into the water and go sailing in Lowestoft harbour. John and Titty had been wanting to do that from the moment they saw her, but had hardly liked to suggest it when there was so much to be done in getting the *Wild Cat* ready for sea. Roger was prowling round the decks, looking at one thing after

another. Gibber, the monkey, was up at the top
of the foremast looking away towards the fishing
vessels. So many masts all together reminded him
perhaps of forests at home. Titty put the parrot's
cage on the roof of the deckhouse, and went round
with Nancy to have a look at the little sailing boat.

"She looks lovely in her new paint," said Titty.

"He's given her new halyards, too," said John.

"There's that man," said Roger.

They looked across the water to the black
schooner. The man whom the porter had called
Black Jake was leaning over her bulwarks and
watching them.

"Hullo! There's a boy up the mast there. He
isn't as high up as Gibber though."

There was a red-haired boy, not as big as
John, but a good deal bigger than Roger, halfway
up the black schooner's mainmast, and busy with
a scrubbing brush and a pail.

"He's a cabin-boy or something," said Nancy.
"We've often seen him before."

"I bet he has a horrid time," said John. "The
porter said we were lucky not to be joining that
ship."

But just then, there was a sudden stir on the
black schooner's deck. A man doing something
at the foot of the foremast shouted something
and pointed across towards the harbourmaster's
office. Black Jake started up and stared in that
direction. Then he climbed up to the quay and
set off, running, towards the swing bridge.

"What's the matter with him now?" said Roger.

The next minute there was a general rush
along the deck of the *Wild Cat*. John, Nancy,

Titty, and Roger, as well as Black Jake, had seen the old sailor with a huge canvas kitbag on his back, who was hurrying along the quay past the Custom-House.

They banged on the deckhouse door.

"He's back! He's here! Mr Duck's back again!"

Captain Flint came out in a hurry, drying his chin.

"Good for him," he said. "Where is he?"

Peter Duck came to the edge of the quay and rolled his kitbag off his shoulder. It fell with a thud on the deck, and was followed by a bundle of oilskins. He came slowly down the ladder in his big sea-boots, that he was wearing to save having to carry them.

"Come aboard, sir," he said.

"Fine," said Captain Flint, shaking hands with him. "We're all very glad to see you."

"You're just in time for breakfast," said Susan, putting her head out of the galley. "At least, it'll be ready in two minutes. The water must be just going to boil."

Outside there, on deck, nobody, not even Captain Flint, could take his eyes from Peter Duck's kitbag. It was an ordinary canvas kitbag, but it had a large coat of arms painted on it. There was a shield divided into four quarters. In one were three ducks swimming on curly waves. In another was a Norfolk wherry under full sail. In the third were three flying-fish, and in the fourth were three dolphins. Above the shield, by way of a crest, there was a capstan with a turn or two of rope about it, and below the shield in big clear letters was written "Admiral Peter Duck."

The old sailor laughed when he saw what they were looking at. "It's a long while ago since that was painted," he said. "We had three days' calm in the China seas and all the fo'c'sle took to painting coats of arms, because the fish wasn't biting."

"And are you really an admiral?" asked Titty.

"Why not?" said Peter Duck. "The cook in that vessel was a rare good hand at dragons. So he painted dragons in all four corners of his shield and called himself the Emperor of China."

Just then Roger pulled at Titty. "There's that man again," he whispered. "He's come right round."

Titty looked up, startled. The others, seeing her, looked up, too.

A man was standing on the edge of the quay, right above them, a dark man, with black hair and big gold ear-rings that showed below his hair. He stood there glowering down at the little group on the deck of the *Wild Cat*. Peter Duck glanced up at him. The man opened his lips, but he did not say a word.

"Pieces of eight! Pieces of eight!" screamed the parrot in the sunshine.

The man scowled, turned sharp round and walked hurriedly away.

"What on earth's the matter with that man?" said Captain Flint.

"It's the sort of man he is," said Peter Duck.

"Roger's quite right," said Titty. "He *is* the man who tried to grab the parrot when we were coming from the station."

"He didn't exactly grab it," said John. "He just got angry and wouldn't leave us alone."

"He was watching us from the boat," said Roger.

"He owns her," said Peter Duck.

"Hullo, is she still there?" said Captain Flint. "The harbourmaster told me she was sailing last night."

"There he goes, over the bridge," said Roger.

A minute or two later they saw him come out on the south quay and speak to some men who were busy with the schooner's warps. They saw him pointing across at the *Wild Cat*.

"Why do they call him Black Jake?" Titty asked. "Is it because of his hair?"

"Because of his heart," said Peter Duck.

"Queer sort of cove," said Captain Flint. "Now, Mr Duck, will you come along and stow your dunnage in the deckhouse. There's a good big locker under that starboard bunk. And then we'll see what sort of a breakfast these mates of ours are going to give us."

At that first breakfast with Peter Duck at one end of the long narrow table and Captain Flint at the other, everybody was rather shy. Captain Flint and Peter Duck talked a little, mostly about the *Thermopylae* and old days in sailing ships, while everybody else watched and listened. As soon as it was over, work began in earnest. Every rope in the ship was to be overhauled, for one thing. "You don't want gear going bad on you at sea," Peter Duck had said, and Captain Flint agreed. There was no point in going out even for a trial trip until everything was as right as they could make it. He had got rid of the carpenters a month before. Then there had been all the painting and varnishing. Then there had been the storing of the ship. He had stored her so well that he had the happiness of knowing that nothing was out of his reach, the Mediterranean, America, or the South Seas. And yet, it seemed there was still a tremendous lot to do before he could even take his ship outside the harbour.

"No. No. Wait to see how we get on," he had said when Titty had asked about the launching of the *Swallow*. "We shall want help this morning, but if all goes well we'll put her over in the afternoon."

All that morning they worked, and, all morning, people passing along the quay stopped to look down at the little schooner and up at Mr Duck, who spent most of the time at the top of one or other of the two masts. Everybody seemed to know him. Everybody had a word for him. Even the harbourmaster, the greatest man of the whole port, with gold on his cap and on his dark blue coat, strolled up and stopped for a minute or two.

"Quite like old times for you, Mr Duck," he called up.

"And old times were good times," Mr Duck called down from the mainmast cross-trees.

Roger and Gibber had vanished soon after breakfast. Everybody knew they must be in the engine-room. Susan and Peggy went marketing. John, Nancy, and Titty were helping on deck, passing things up at the end of a line to Captain Flint or Peter Duck when they were up the masts, or just hanging on to a rope here or a rope there when they were told. They were being very useful, but they had plenty of time to look about them, and they could not help seeing that all morning they were being watched from the black schooner at the other side of the harbour. The men over there had stopped shifting her warps. She was clearly not going to sea that day.

Everybody aboard the *Wild Cat* was very hungry when Susan and Peggy, after coming back laden from the market and trying what they could do with the galley stove, decided that the potatoes had been boiled long enough and that the mutton chops would be burnt if they tried to give them another minute's cooking. When Peggy banged the big bell just inside the galley door there was a cheerful rush from all parts of the ship. There was no hanging back. The cooks of the *Wild Cat* did not have to complain that people let their dinners get cold. Indeed, Roger was very unwilling to go and wash some of the dirt off first, when he came crawling out from the dark engine-room, round the companion steps and into the saloon.

Work had gone very well.

"We'll be going to sea tomorrow, eh, Mr Duck?" Captain Flint said as they sat down at the saloon table.

"There'll be nothing to stop us by the time we knock off tonight."

"Where are we going?" Everybody shouted at once.

"Trial trip," said Captain Flint, "and if all's right, we'll be off down Channel next day."

"What about *Swallow?*" asked Titty, when things had quietened down again after this bit of news.

"You can take her sailing this afternoon," said Captain Flint.

*

For an hour after dinner John and Nancy were still wanted on deck, and Titty was helping the mates with washing up and the cleaning of an obstinate frying-pan. But the moment to which they had been looking forward came at last. Captain Flint and Peter Duck stopped work for a minute or two while they lowered the little sailing boat into the water, and fixed a rope ladder over the side of the *Wild Cat* so that the crew could go down her side into the *Swallow* like a lot of pilots going down into a boat at sea.

"Are you all right?" called Captain Flint, when John and Nancy had stepped the mast and everybody was aboard.

"Quite all right," said John, though he was feeling a little nervous at sailing *Swallow* in strange waters and for the first time for nearly a year.

"Catch!" Captain Flint dropped the end of the painter. Roger coiled it away before the mast. Nancy pushed off from the *Wild Cat*'s green side. Susan and Peggy were hauling up the old brown sail with its well-remembered patch. Titty's little flag was already fluttering at the mast-head. They were off.

The wind was coming down from Oulton, and for a moment or two John tacked up against it, just to get the feel of the tiller, but as soon as he was sure that *Swallow* was still the same old *Swallow* and that he had not forgotten how to sail

her, they decided they would go through the swing
bridge to have a look at the outer harbour.

"The *Wild Cat* does look fine," said John.

"I should think she does," said Nancy. "That
green paint just suits her. And all the new halyards. I say, John, let's have a look at the black
schooner."

"She's rather a beauty, too," said John, as
they slipped across towards her.

"Much too good to belong to a man like that,"
said Nancy.

"Sh!" said Susan.

"There he is," said Peggy.

They were close to her now and looking up
they saw Black Jake scowling down at them over
the stern of his vessel.

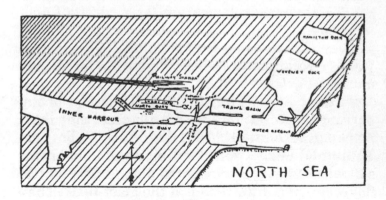

The wind freshened a little, and *Swallow* felt it.
She was moving very fast. They had just time to
read the name painted in big white letters across
the stern of the schooner, "VIPER BRISTOL," and
then they were slipping away towards the bridge

and hoping that the puff of wind would last them through it.

"What a funny name for a boat," said Roger.

They had a fine sail round the outer harbour, looking into one basin after another. They saw the Government fishery vessel, with the reindeer horns from Lapland fastened up on the bridge. They watched one of the fishing ketches sail out between the pier heads. "That's where we'll be going tomorrow," said Nancy. Then John gave Nancy the tiller, and she sailed the *Swallow* into Hamilton Dock, where they saw the steam trawlers. By that time Susan and Peggy were thinking they ought to be putting a kettle on to boil, so they sailed back, though they had to use oars in getting through under the swing bridge. They put the cooks aboard, and then John, Nancy, Titty, and Roger went off for a last half-hour of sailing.

They tacked away up the inner harbour, past the dry dock and the vessels being repaired, past the grey dredgers at work getting up the mud from the bottom. They did not go very far before turning back. With Captain Flint and Peter Duck working so hard they did not want to be even a minute late. They were on their way home sailing with the wind down the middle of the Channel, and John was just going to turn across to the *Wild Cat* when Titty, looking at the *Viper*, suddenly said, "There's that boy."

"What boy?" asked Roger. "Where?"

"There," said Titty, but she did not point. "The boy with the red hair. He's fishing. Fishing from the *Viper*. Look!"

Everybody saw him now, sitting on the *Viper*'s bulwarks, with his feet over the side. He was holding the end of a fishing-line that went straight down into the water below him.

After what they had heard of Black Jake, and after what they had seen of him, they were inclined to be sorry for any boy who served aboard his ship. It must, they thought, be pretty awful. Not at all like being aboard the *Wild Cat*. Every time they had seen the red-haired boy that day he had seemed to be at work or on the run. But now, as they looked at him again, they thought better of Black Jake. At least he allowed his ship's boy time to fish over the side.

They were about twenty yards from the *Viper* by that time, and John was hauling in the sheet to change course. Nobody saw exactly what happened, but there was a sudden squeak and the red-haired boy somehow shot forward off the bulwarks and dropped with a splash into the harbour.

"What a duffer!" said Nancy.

"Did someone push him in?" said Titty. "It looked like that."

No time was wasted in thinking what to do.

"Jibe!" shouted John.

He turned *Swallow* round almost in her own length. The boom swung over and a moment later the little boat was shooting up into the wind close under the side of the black schooner.

"Stand by to lower sail!" said John quietly.

Close by the *Swallow* a tangled red mop came to the surface.

"Lower away," called John, and Nancy and

Titty brought the sail down just as John let go
the tiller, leaned over and took a firm grip of the
red mop.

"Yow! Yow!" squeaked the boy, spluttering and
blowing as his head came above water. "Don't you
go for to pull my hair like that. And take hold of
this line. It's the only one I got. I can get aboard
if you take a grip of the belt of my breeches. But
let go my hair. Don't take a hold of it again. Hoist
away, now."

"Up she raises!" said Nancy, getting a hold of
the red-haired boy by the collar. Between them,
she and John hoisted him in over the stern of
the boat, though long afterwards he used to say
he could have got in easier himself.

Titty, meanwhile, had taken the line and was
coiling it in.

"Was he going to be drowned?" asked Roger,
almost as if saving him had been a mistake.

"That's all right," said John, as the boy landed
head first in the boat, soaking his rescuers with
dirty water. "You'll be aboard again in a minute."
He looked up at the steep black side of the schooner. Nobody was looking down. There was nobody
there. Nobody seemed to have heard the splash or
to know that they had just lost a man overboard.

"*Viper*, ahoy!" called John.

"*Viper*, ahoy!" called Roger shrilly from the
bows.

There was no answer.

"That's rum," said Nancy, after giving a hail.
"What's become of that man with the ear-rings?
Oh well, come on, John. Let's take him across to
the *Wild Cat* and then he can run round. It's no

good his trying to get up here without a ladder."

She shook some of the wet off her, lugged
the oars out from under the jumble of sail, and
pulled across towards the green schooner. Titty
had not quite done coiling in the fishing-line. She
was going slowly towards the end. She knew the
sort of things boys used for fishing in harbours.
Far worse than worms. But when she came to
the end she found nothing but two bare hooks.

Captain Flint had heard the splash and seen the
rescue. He was waiting for them at the top of the
rope ladder. Peter Duck was there too, and caught
the painter which Roger, showing off a little to the
red-haired boy, coiled and threw up to him.

"Up you go," said John.

The boy took hold of the ladder and went up as
easy as a monkey. It was clear that rope ladders
were nothing new to him. Water dripped from him
as he climbed. Titty went up next, not very easily,
because she was carrying the fishing-line. Then
Roger, who was beginning to tell the story of the
rescue before he even got his head level with the
rail. Nancy and John unstepped the mast, made
all fast, and hurried after him.

On the deck of the *Wild Cat* the red-haired
boy was standing in a pool of water from which
little rivers trickled over the clean white planking
to find their way into the scuppers. Peggy and
Susan had come out from their galley, hearing
that something was happening. Peter Duck was
making fast the *Swallow's* painter, and looking
over his shoulder at the boy.

The red-haired boy was shifting uneasily from
foot to foot, with all this crowd looking at him.

THE RED-HAIRED BOY GOES OVERBOARD

"Why, it's young Bill," said Peter Duck. "Everybody knows young Bill. Born on the Dogger Bank, he was. He ought to know enough not to fall overboard."

The red-haired boy blushed hotly.

"He was fishing," said Roger.

"And a big one pulled him in," said Captain Flint. "What do you catch in the inner harbour? What sort of baits do you use?" His eye fell on the hooks and sinker at the end of the line that Titty was still holding. "What have you done with his baits, Titty?"

"There were none," said Titty.

The red-haired boy looked more uncomfortable than ever.

Peter Duck laughed. "It's the first time in his life young Bill's fished without bait," he said. "That I'll be sure."

"Let him have a mug of hot tea, somebody," said Captain Flint. Susan was off into the galley and back in a minute with a mug of steaming tea and a hunk of cake.

"Look here, my lad," said Captain Flint. "What's the trouble? You needn't be afraid of anybody in this ship. You've nothing to worry about. It's no crime to go bathing . . . ."

Peter Duck was looking carefully at the hooks.

The red-haired boy burst out. "Well, I tell him there was nothing on them hooks, and he threw the line himself and made me get up on the rail, and then he tell me to tumble in natural . . ."

"Oh, look here," said Captain Flint.

"It's all along of Mr Duck there," said the red-haired boy miserably. "They wants to know if he's shipping with you, and where you're bound for. And they'll wallop the life out of me if I don't find out."

"That's all, is it?" said Captain Flint. "No trouble about that, though you've taken a funny way of asking. But we've got no secrets. I'll tell you, and you can tell them. Mr Duck is shipping in the *Wild Cat* as able-seaman and acting bosun. And as for the rest of our crew, you can say we've three captains aboard and two mates, to say nothing of the others."

"Oo," said the red-haired boy.

The Swallows and Amazons looked at each other, but nobody even smiled.

"Drink that tea while it's hot," said Susan. "It's not too hot. There's a lot of milk in it. And you ought to have something hot at once after going in like that."

The red-haired boy drank it up, gulp after gulp, while the others watched him do it.

"As for where we're bound for," Captain Flint went on when the mug seemed to be empty. "We don't yet know ourselves. Now then, my lad, you skip along, get into some dry clothes, and tell that skipper of yours that if there's anything else he wants to know, he'd better come and ask. Got another slice of cake there, Susan? And give him his hooks and line, Titty."

The red-haired boy grinned for the first time.

"Thank you, sir," he said.

"Skip along," said Captain Flint. "You know as much as we do now. And you could have learnt it all without going swimming."

"And take a word from me, young Bill," said

Peter Duck. "You'll come to no good shipping with
Black Jake."

The boy looked round the little group. "I must
go to sea somehow," he said. "And if the others
won't take me . . ."

"Well, skip along," said Captain Flint. "We're
busy. Sailing in the morning."

And with that the boy, munching one hunk of
black juicy cake and carrying another, given him
by Peggy, for future use, climbed up the ladder to
the quay and went slowly off towards the bridge,
on his way round to the other side of the harbour
and the black schooner that lay there without a
sign of anybody being aboard her.

*

"As for where we're bound, we don't know
ourselves," and "Three captains aboard and two
mates . . . ." If Captain Flint had been trying to
find the very words that would make Black Jake
more curious than ever, he could not have chosen
better.

*

"I'd think twice about jumping in like that just
for the sake of asking a question," said Captain
Flint when the red-haired boy had gone.

"But he was pushed in," said Titty. "I'm sure
he was."

"Oh, rubbish," said Captain Flint, but a minute
or two later he spoke to Peter Duck. "Who does
that boy belong to?" he asked.

"He don't belong to anybody, properly speaking," said Peter Duck. "He was born in a trawler.

His mother died when he was a baby. His dad was lost in a gale a year or two back and young Bill looks after himself mostly. There's hardly a vessel out of Lowestoft that hasn't found him stowing away to get to sea."

"H'm," said Captain Flint, and glanced across the harbour. "I wonder if we ought to have let him go back."

But there were many other things to think of in the *Wild Cat* that night. *Swallow* had to be brought inboard again and lashed down under a canvas cover. Many a long day was to pass before she would be afloat again. After all that day's work on the rigging, there was a lot of rubbish, scraps of rope and wire, to be cleared off the decks. Then there were one or two more last-minute purchases to be made. John, Susan, Nancy, and Peggy went off into town to make them. Captain Flint took Titty and Roger with him to the harbourmaster's office. He wanted to make sure that the *Wild Cat* should not lose her berth by going out for a trial trip. He wanted to be able to come back to the same place after the trial trip. Roger took his chance and told the harbourmaster the story of Bill's tumbling overboard and the rescue. Titty once more said she thought Bill had been pushed in. The harbourmaster laughed. "Well," he said, "I wouldn't let a boy of mine ship with that fellow. He's in with every bad lot about the place. Not that I think he'd push a boy into the harbour. There's no sense in that, no sense that I can see."

By the time they got back, supper was ready, and soon after that, knowing that they were to start with the morning tide, Captain Flint hurried his crew to bed.

CHAPTER III

TRIAL TRIP

NOT one of the crew had thought sleep at all possible that night and all of them were surprised when they heard a bumping on the deck above their cabins, and woke to find that it was already daylight. They had forgotten to put out the hanging lantern in the saloon and it swung there looking like a ghost. There was very little washing done below decks before Susan hurried up the companion and found that someone had already been ashore and brought a milk-can full of fresh milk, and also that someone had lit the oil-stove for her in the galley. The kettle was close on boiling. The others, after a lick and a scrub, came hurrying on deck, some by the companion, some up the ladder through the forehatch. They found that it was not only in the housekeeping line that a good deal had been done that morning. The *Wild Cat* somehow looked altogether different. The topping lifts had been set up and the booms lifted. Mainsail and foresail, lovely new creamy canvas, were cast loose ready for hoisting. The staysail was at the foot of the forestay, held in a bunch with a bit of thin twine that would break at the first pull on the halyards. The jib had been hoisted already, but in stops, rolled up, that is, and tied, so that a pull on the jib sheets would be enough to break it out.

"This looks like business," said Nancy.

"I should just think it does," said John.

The other vessels in the harbour were all asleep. There was still dew on the rail and on the top of the deckhouse. But, early as it was, someone was already awake about the quays, for the pier head lights had vanished, and the thin morning sunlight was falling on a red flag hoisted on the flagstaff by the swing bridge to show anybody who might want to know that there was a depth of ten feet at least between the heads. Everybody looked across to the *Viper*, but the black schooner lay there beside the opposite quay without a sign that anybody was aboard her.

Breakfast was almost as much of a scramble as washing. They had it on deck – just thick bread and butter and steaming mugs of cocoa. As soon as that was done, indeed, while some people were still eating their bread and butter, they crowded into the deckhouse to look at the chart already spread out on the table. Everybody leant over it while Captain Flint pointed out the way they were going.

"The wind's almost due east just now," he said. "We'll use that to throw her head off, but we won't try going out under sail, not the first time with a new crew. We'd have to tack out against the wind and I'd like to be sure you all of you know your ropes before we start that sort of thing. No thanks, Susan. I've had enough, for now anyway. All hands on deck, and let's see what sort of a job we make of getting up the mainsail. We'll have it up now, though we're going out with the engine. All right, Roger, we'll be going down to look at it in a minute." Roger was already lifting the trap-door in the floor of the deckhouse where there was a short ladder down to the stuffy little engine-room.

"Throw her head off?" said John.

"Hoist the staysail and hold him to wind'ard to force her head off the quay," said Peter Duck.

Everybody hurried out on deck.

"Now," said Captain Flint. "Mr Duck and I can hoist that mainsail between us. But we have to take one halyard at a time, and belay the peak[1] while we're hauling on the throat. Let's see 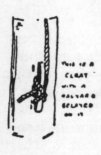 what we can do with the lot of you tallying on. Come on, then. Nancy and Peggy haul away on the peak with me. John, Susan, and Titty haul away on the throat with Mr Duck. All right, Roger. Room for you here. Titty's shantyman. Pipe up, Able-seaman. Let's have 'A Long Time Ago.' Mind everybody hauls together at the right words."

"Here you are, Cap'n John," said Mr Duck. "Get a hold here, below my grip. You, too, Mister Mate."

Titty piped up:

"A smart Yankee packet lay out in the bay,
    To me *way* hay, *o-hi-o*.
A-waiting for a fair wind to get under way,
    A *long* time ago."

[1] "Belay" means make fast. The throat is the end of the gaff nearest to the mast. The peak is the other end. – NANCY.

At the *way* and the *hi* and the *long* everybody hauled down with all their weight, and
then shifted their hands up ready for another
pull.

> "She was waiting for a fair wind to get
>   under way,
>   To me way hay, ohio.
> She was waiting for a fair wind to get
>   under way,
>   A long time ago."

Titty got the verses in the wrong order, but
that made no difference. The gaff swayed up,
lifting the canvas after it. A trail of wooden hoops
climbed slowly up the mast after the gaff jaws.

> "If she hasn't had a fair wind, she's lying
>   there still,
>   To me way hay, ohio.
> If she hasn't had a fair wind she's lying
>   there still,
>   A long time ago."

"You've forgotten the lime-juice," panted Roger.
Titty went back a verse or two.

> "With all her poor sailors all sick and
>   all sore,
>   To me way hay, ohio.
> For they'd drunk all their lime-juice and
>   could get no more,
>   A long time ago."

Their pulls were perhaps not quite as long as they would have been if they had had longer arms. But Titty, with hardly any breath left for singing, managed to get the verses out somehow over again in a different order. The others had more breath and easier words, just singing out "A *long* time ago" and "To me *way* hay, *o-hi-o*" as they pulled. It took time, but there was the sail spreading up and up far over their heads.

"Chockablock," said Peter Duck at last, and belayed the throat halyard, while John, Susan, and Titty got their breath again.

"Belay," said Captain Flint, and Nancy and Peggy stood puffing and blowing and feeling the palms of their hands. "We won't have the peak right up till we're in the outer harbour. Well done, everybody. That's the hardest job there is aboard a schooner. You'll be able to get the staysail up yourselves. Now then, Roger, come along and let's have a look at that engine of yours." Roger and Captain Flint disappeared into the deckhouse.

John and Susan coiled the throat halyard and hung the coils out of the way. That rope would not be wanted again until the time came to lower the sail.

"What about washing up?" said Peggy. "Shall we just put all the mugs in a basket and do the washing up afterwards?"

"You'll have time now," said Peter Duck. "Skipper and I'll be a minute or two, what with all the warps to shift and the little donkey to get a-going."

"What little donkey?" asked Titty.

"Sailorman's name for the engine," said Peter Duck. "Engines and donkeys is all one. One day they'll pull and another day they won't, do what you will with them."

"Sails won't pull in a calm," said Peggy, over her shoulder as she went off to the galley.

"That's not their fault," said Peter Duck. "Give them wind and they'll work right enough. But you can drown one of these here little donkeys with oil and paraffin, and it'll do no more than cough and spit at you. Got no gratitude hasn't donkeys. Listen, though, to that. Skipper's got this one a-going."

There was a sudden chug, chug-chug from below. Then silence. Then chug, chug-chug again, and another silence. There was no more thought of washing up.

"We'll have time later," said Susan.

Peter Duck was up on the quayside, hurrying from bollard to bollard casting loose the warps. John and Nancy hauled them aboard. Peter Duck took one of the stern warps forward round a bollard on the quay and back again, throwing the end to John who made it fast.

"We'll be wanting to cast that loose in a minute," said Peter Duck, seeing that John was making fast as if for ever.

The noise below began again. "Chug, chug, chug, chug, chug," and settled down till it was as regular as the ticking of a clock. Captain Flint and Roger, both very red in the face, climbed up into the deckhouse and out on deck.

"All ready?" asked Captain Flint. "Good. Now

then, Roger, you stand by this lever. When I say, 'Full ahead,' shove it as far forward as it will go."

"Aye, aye, sir," said Roger, his eyes sparkling, taking his place by a little brass lever just inside the deckhouse door.

"Come on, you two captains, and hoist the staysail. The two mates stand by the wheel. Keep it just as it is, and hand over to Mr Duck as soon as she starts moving. All ready with the spring, Mr Duck?"

"Aye, aye, sir."

Captain Flint hurried forward. John and Nancy had picked out the staysail halyard, seen that all was clear up the mast, and were ready to hoist the sail. Titty was with Peter Duck at the stern. He had given her a fat rope fender to hang over the side to save the *Wild Cat*'s green paint.

Captain Flint sang out, "Up with the staysail," and hand over hand, John and Nancy hauled it up. It flapped idly in the light wind coming straight in from the sea. Captain Flint hauled in for a moment on the port sheet, so that the staysail stiffened on the port side, and the wind, taking it aback, began slowly, ever so slowly, to force the bows of the *Wild Cat* away from the quay.

"Haul in on the spring, Mr Duck!" Peter Duck hauled on the warp that he had led forward from the stern. The *Wild Cat* headed out from the quay.

"Chug, chug, chug, chug, chug, cough, chug, cough, chug, chug," went the little engine down below, and Roger, at the deckhouse door, was holding on to the lever and waiting for the word.

Captain Flint let fly the staysail sheet. "Full ahead, engineer!"

Roger pushed the lever forward, and the tune of the engine changed as the propeller began to do its work. Peter Duck let go one end of the warp, and Titty, who had brought her fender in now that it was no longer needed, hauled in the slack of the warp as it slipped round the bollard and fell between the *Wild Cat* and the quay. She soon had it aboard. Peter Duck took the wheel and spun it round. The *Wild Cat* moved slowly out of the inner harbour between the grey walls and out. The swing bridge was open for the *Wild Cat* to pass, and a milk-boy with a tricycle was waiting for it to close again, looking down at the little schooner and whistling as if to make up for the general quiet at that time of the morning. The *Wild Cat* moved slowly on, the little engine coughing away inside her, and spitting out of the exhaust pipe at the stern. She moved down between the long piers, and into the outer harbour.

Captain Flint came aft, bringing John and Nancy at his heels.

"Mr Duck," he said, "I think you and I might be getting the foresail up now. John'll keep her going straight for the pier heads."

John was on the point of saying he would rather wait to take the wheel until she was outside with plenty of room, but he was too late. He found himself with his hands on the spokes of the wheel, while Peter Duck and Captain Flint were already hurrying forward. Nancy was looking at him almost with envy. There was nothing for it

but to hope that he would manage not to do
something dufferish by mistake. He turned the
wheel just a little first one way and then the
other. The *Wild Cat* was moving slowly under the
little engine, which was only just strong enough
to shove her along. She seemed, however, to steer
quite easily. John hoped Nancy had not noticed his
experiments. Now he looked far ahead to the outer
piers, with their queer little pagoda-like shelters
with the lanterns on the top of them, set himself
to steer exactly between them and almost came
to believe that he had been doing this all his life.
He saw Captain Flint take a sharp look round and
then, as if quite at ease, turn back to his work.
That was comforting, too.

Peter Duck and Captain Flint were at the
foot of the foremast. Peter Duck took the throat
halyard, Captain Flint took the peak. They hauled
away and the gaff of the foresail moved slowly up
above their heads. Then there was Peter Duck
swigging on his halyard till he had it bar taut,
throwing his weight forward and pulling in the
slack, and then making fast and taking a look
up the mast to see that the blocks were all but
touching. Captain Flint was still hauling on the
peak halyard. The gaff cocked itself up, and the big
creamy sail no longer swung loose, but stiffened
until the crinkles in it ran up and down instead
of across. Captain Flint belayed his halyard. Then
they slackened away the topping lifts, so that the
weight of the boom made itself felt, and the crinkles straightened out.

They hurried aft to the mainmast, and the
peak that had been left not fully hoisted rose

up and up. It stopped. Again topping lifts were slackened away and there was the mainsail really looking like a sail at last.

"Setting nicely," said Peter Duck.

John had been thinking of nothing but the steering. The little group of the others had been watching every detail of the setting of the sails.

"It's just like setting sail on *Swallow*," said Susan, "only everything's heavier."

"And you don't have to haul down the boom," said Nancy. "Come on. They'll be sailing in a minute. They'll be wanting someone to haul on the staysail sheet and the jib sheet. Let's be there."

When Captain Flint turned from squinting up at the mainsail into the morning sunlight to see that all was really well with mainsail and foresail, he saw Nancy and Susan all ready, with the sheets of the headsails in their hands. "That's right," he said. "Stand by for a minute or two."

The *Wild Cat* passed out between the pier heads into the North Sea. On the pier heads a couple of men gave a cheery wave to her as she slipped out and lifted to the slight swell. Titty waved back, and so did Peter Duck. Roger did not even see them. Everybody aboard the *Wild Cat* was a little out of breath, except Peter Duck, though there had been no accidents and everything had been easy enough. Another time, things would be easier still.

Captain Flint and Peter Duck were coming aft.

"She's clear enough now, sir," Peter Duck was saying. "There's the buoy. She'd lay the course now, lay it under sail."

"Now then, John," said Captain Flint. "Let's see you head her North-north-east. That'll clear the buoy. Staysail and jib sheets there, forrard. On the port side. That's right, Susan. A hard pull to break it out."

Things were happening fast.

John twirled the wheel, and the compass card inside the little window just before him moved round. East . . . East by North . . . East-north-east . . . North-east by East . . . North-east . . . The mainsheet tautened with a jerk. Peter Duck was hauling in a little on the sheet of the foresail. The staysail was pulling. Nancy was making fast. The big jib was fluttering loose. Nancy turned to help Susan. It quietened and was pulling too. North-north-east. The *Wild Cat* was sailing.

"Stop the engine, Roger," called Captain Flint.

Roger swung his lever to its middle position and then dived into the deckhouse.

"I say, Rogie, do you know how?" asked Titty anxiously.

"Of course I do," said Roger. "He showed me."

He was gone. A moment later the chug, chug, chug of the engine came to an end. John and Titty looked at each other. The deck was certainly on a slant. There was the beginning of a noise under the forefoot. She was not moving slower but faster. Titty put her hand on the wheel and felt the tremor of the little ship. John was moving the wheel this way and that, meeting her as she yawed, and coaxing her to lay a steady course. Titty looked back at the lengthening wake astern. This was like sailing *Swallow* only somehow better. A touch on the wheel and this whole ship obeyed with the whole lot of them aboard, a regular house of a ship, with towering sails higher than lots of houses. There was a lump in Titty's throat, and John's lips were pressed tight together.

Roger came up again from below, with a very dirty happy face, wiping his oily hands on a bit of cotton rag.

"She went awfully well with her engine," he said.

John and Titty were almost glad to be able to laugh at him.

Captain Flint and Peter Duck were hurrying about the deck, slackening away this rope, hauling that a little harder in, trying one thing and another, until they were satisfied with the set of the sails.

And then, after passing the black and white bell buoy clanging away in the lonely morning, after passing the Newcome Spit buoy, striped red and white and round as a football, Captain Flint came aft and stood by, while John spun the wheel round and put her about. Peter Duck, Nancy, and Susan let fly the headsail sheets and then again they had to be hauled in on the other side, and once more there was careful trying until Captain Flint and the old seaman were thoroughly pleased with them. With all four sails drawing, the ship was beautifully balanced and she could be steered with a finger.

This time they went well out to sea, before going about and heading northward up the coast until they brought Yarmouth abeam, and looking through the telescope could see the tall brick tower on Brush Quay, and the Britannia Pier, and the long spreading town. They held right on towards the red light-vessel with a thing like two spinning tops with their points meeting up at her mast-head. Most of the time John and Nancy took turns at the wheel, though everybody, even the engineer, was allowed to feel it. Titty brought the parrot on deck after a time, to enjoy the sunshine, and to have a real look at the sea. Roger let Gibber have a run, too, but Captain Flint said that the monkey was not to be allowed near the engine just now, because they would be wanting to use it again going into the inner harbour, and with monkeys you never really knew what might happen. At last Captain Flint put her about once more, eased off all the sheets and steered for the Corton light-vessel, with its ball cut in half and another ball on the top of it ("They have to have these things to tell one lightship from another"), and so for the Newcome Spit buoy and home again to Lowestoft Harbour.

"Well?" said Captain Flint.

"She's just perfect," said John. And all the others said so too.

"Well, Mr Duck?" said Captain Flint again.

"Fit to go anywhere, she is."

"Down Channel and across the Bay?"

"Down Channel?" said Peter Duck. "I'd take her round the Horn."

"We've to carry our sail till we're well inside the heads," said Captain Flint. "Will you take the wheel while we go in? We'll jibe her now, and bring the booms across."

There were a few minutes of frantic bustle,

while John brought her head round and Captain Flint and Peter Duck eased the booms over and Nancy and Susan tended the headsails. Then, Peter Duck took the wheel and the *Wild Cat*, with a fine flurry of foam under her forefoot, and the wind almost dead astern, headed in for the harbour.

Just as the *Wild Cat* was coming to the pier heads, she met a schooner shooting out, a black schooner, bigger than the *Wild Cat*, and carrying a great spread of sail.

"Isn't that the *Viper*?" said Captain Flint.

"That's her," said Peter Duck.

"There's Black Jake steering her," said Nancy.

"There's the red-haired boy," said Titty. "And what a lot of men!" There were three or four grown men busy on deck.

The two schooners passed within a few yards of each other, the *Wild Cat* coming in and the *Viper* going out.

As they passed they saw that Black Jake, who was at the wheel, was staring hard at them, as if he knew them but for some reason found it hard to believe that they were there.

But there was no time then to wonder about Black Jake and the *Viper*. There was too much to do aboard the *Wild Cat*. The moment she was in the outer harbour, Captain Flint luffed up into the wind and began taking sail off her. He dived below and started the engine, but had a few fathom of chain ranged free on the foredeck in case the engine played them a trick and they needed the anchor in a hurry. He took in jib and staysail, lowered foresail and mainsail, and then, at half speed, the *Wild Cat* moved slowly up the harbour through the inner piers, and back to her old berth. The man at the swing bridge waved to them as they passed through and the cheerful, kindly harbourmaster shouted a "Good day" to them.

"It'll be quite lonely with no *Viper* to look at," said Titty when they had turned right round in the inner harbour, and at last were once more tied up to the quay.

"Jibbooms and bobstays but here she comes again!" exclaimed Nancy.

The black schooner was even then gliding through into the inner harbour.

"What's she come back for?" said John.

"Must have forgotten something," said Peggy.

"Our red-haired friend looks a little worried," said Captain Flint.

Roger waved to him, but Bill did not wave back. Black Jake was close to him, and perhaps Bill thought he had better not. There seemed, too, to be something of a quarrel going on among the *Viper*'s crew. Presently she was tied up once more alongside the south quay.

"We've looked at her enough," said Captain Flint. "Come on, all of you, and help to stow sails, or the *Viper*'ll be neat and tidy first in spite of the start we've had." But the *Viper* did not seem just then to care about being neat and tidy. Her crew went off along the quay, and left her just as she was. As for the *Wild Cat*, everybody was so proud of her after that trial trip, that even Roger forgot to remind Susan that it was rather late for dinner until all the sails had been stowed and ropes coiled

and the whole ship so neat that no one could have
known she had been at sea that morning.

CHAPTER IV

WASHING THE ANCHOR

THAT night, after supper, the whole ship's company were on deck enjoying the quiet of the evening after the busy day. During the afternoon, they had filled up the tanks with fresh drinking-water, so that they had enough for a long cruise. "With all the water ballast we've got under the flooring we could sail round the world," said Captain Flint proudly. They had taken aboard a lot of fresh meat, butter, eggs, vegetables and bread. There was no point in using the tinned things if they did not need to. They had bought a grand lot of fresh fruit and half a dozen of those big Dutch cheeses, red as giant cherries, because they happened to see them in a window. Everybody knew that tomorrow they were going to set sail in earnest and now, with the ship so well provisioned, feeling that they could go anywhere, and were already no longer dependent on the land, they were all gathered together up in the bows of the ship talking of places to visit.

Polly, the ship's parrot, was singing out "Pieces of eight" and reminding people that he was a Pretty Polly, and crawling beak over claw up the forestay and down to the bowsprit and along the top of the rail. Gibber alone was below decks. He had been given a bag of monkey nuts that Captain Flint had bought in the town, by way of a little extra for him, and as he did not quite trust the others, he had taken the bag down below and was eating the nuts in his bunk. Captain Flint was sitting on the capstan smoking his pipe. Peter Duck was smoking his, and putting a whipping on the end of a new warp. The others were hanging about and dropping in a word or two now and then and mostly all at the same time. Captain Flint had a chart of the Channel with him and he was showing them how they would be going across the mouth of the Thames and between the Goodwins and the coast, and past Dover, and within sight maybe of Cape Gris Nez. It grew dusk, and hard to see the names on the chart, and, as nobody seemed to want to go in, he sent Peggy to the deckhouse to bring the hanging lantern. Far away, beyond the bridge, from one of the boats in the Trawler Basin, came the noise of an accordion. Someone over there was playing "Amsterdam." Everybody in the *Wild Cat* was so much interested in the chart and in Captain Flint's plans for visiting the Channel ports and then perhaps crossing to Brest and going down across the Bay to Cape Villano and Vigo, and perhaps even to Madeira if they got a spell of fine weather, that nobody was thinking about the *Viper* and Black Jake, though there had been some talk a little earlier about the oddness of her returning to port.

*

At the other side of the narrow inner harbour lay the *Viper* in her old berth, and Black Jake was sitting on a hatch, looking across at the *Wild Cat* in the gathering dusk. He was alone on deck. Bill, the red-haired boy, was curled up on some sacking in the forecastle, forgetting in sleep the aching of his bones. Black Jake had taken it out on Bill that morning when he had come on deck and found the *Wild Cat*'s berth empty and the *Wild Cat* nowhere to be seen. He had been surly with his crew, too, when he had got them together in a hurry from their lairs in the town. And they had all turned furiously against him when, after all the work of hoisting sail and warping the ship out, they had met the *Wild Cat*, with Peter Duck at her wheel, coming back to Lowestoft, and Black Jake had turned about and brought the *Viper* in again. They had tied up to the quay once more, but then had stumped off back to their taverns leaving the whole ship in disorder, with sails lowered and not stowed. And Black Jake sat there alone on deck, biting his nails, and staring over the water at the *Wild Cat*.

What were they talking about, over there, on the foredeck of the little green schooner? Could he be mistaken, when he himself had seen Peter Duck bring his dunnage aboard? What else could it mean when Peter Duck, after sticking to his wherry for so many years, had made up his mind to go to sea again? "Three captains aboard and two mates." That fool of a boy had learnt that much anyhow, and what could it mean but the one thing. It was no ordinary voyage when so many officers were shipping together. That a voyage was planned he was sure enough. He had seen the stores going aboard, steadily, day by day, and such masses of them. As much as he had thought necessary for the *Viper*. No wonder, if they were bound for the same place. And then he thought of Peter Duck again. Black Jake bit his nails and scowled. The beauty of the evening meant nothing to him. He did not hear the old tunes played on the accordion in the Trawler Basin. He did not hear when the accordion-player rested, and some Irishman with a fiddle set sea-boots dancing on the decks of the trawlers. There was no room in his mind for anything but the one question: What was it that was being planned between old Peter Duck and that fat man who owned the little green schooner? Was Peter Duck after all these years going to tell that fat man over there what he had always refused to tell to Black Jake, or indeed to anyone else? What was that chart they were looking at? If he could get a sight of that it might be the answer to his question. If he could only hear what was being said as they crowded round the capstan head and peered into the chart. And then the great anchor caught his eye, hanging from the bows of the *Wild Cat*, its chain disappearing into a hawse-hole on the level of the deck. Black Jake stopped biting his nails. He stood up and walked to the stern of the *Viper*. Below him the *Viper*'s dinghy was lying. He looked up and down the deserted quays. He took one more glance across the harbour to the little group in the twilight on the foredeck of the *Wild Cat*, looking at the chart by the glimmer of a lantern. Then he swung himself over the side, lowered himself down the warp into the dinghy, cast off, leaving the warp dangling in the water, and rowed noiselessly away.

He did not row straight across to the *Wild*

Cat. Someone might have seen him. He rowed
up the inner harbour as if to visit one of the
moored ketches. No one saw that dark figure
in the dark boat slipping silently along in the
shadow of the quay. No one saw him work his
way across to the other side among the anchored
vessels. No one saw him paddling slowly, idly, as
if for no purpose at all, under the quay where the
Wild Cat was moored. He passed close under the
bows of a rusty black trawler, waiting her turn on
the slip. Above him in the twilight was the square
green stern of the *Wild Cat*. He shipped his oars
and, more quietly than ever, clawed his way along
her steep, green side. The anchor was above him
at last. He took his dinghy's painter, made a loop
in it and hooked it over a fluke of the anchor. The
tide was flowing in and the slight current kept the
dinghy steady where he needed it. He took a hold
of the anchor, as high as he could reach. Quietly,
quietly, he pulled himself up. A knee was on the
anchor. He took a higher grip. A foot was on the
anchor. He gripped the chain above. Slowly he
raised himself. His head, at last, was level with
the hawse-hole. What was that they were saying?
Under his breath he cursed the chattering parrot.

*

Something like four fathom of anchor chain
had been ranged on deck. The anchor had not
been used after all, but it had not seemed worth
while to stow the chain again as it was likely to be
wanted in the morning if it seemed best to anchor
while making sail. Nothing makes more noise

than getting chain up from below, and perhaps
Captain Flint, knowing how early he would have
to be to catch a helping tide down the coast, had
already made up his mind not to wake the younger
part of his crew before he could help it. Anyhow,
there was the chain on deck ranged forward of the
capstan. Two turns and a half hitch had been tak-
en round the samson-post,[1] and besides, a small
belaying-pin had been stuck through a link of the
chain when it ran between small bollards on deck
on its way to the hawse-hole. There was no danger
of the anchor slipping before this pin had been tak-
en out and the chain unfastened. Some very small
noise made Peter Duck look down at the chain. It
may have been that a link shifted and clanked
against another as Black Jake hoisted himself up.
It may have been, as Titty still believes, that Black
Jake's ear-rings jingled. Anyhow, something did
catch the attention of Peter Duck and made him
look at the chain. And something did catch the
attention of Titty, so that she noticed that something was wrong with the parrot. The parrot was
on the rail along the top of the bulwarks, flapping
his wings and chattering and looking down. He
had stopped saying "Pieces of eight." He was not
even saying "Pretty Polly." He was just chattering,
as if he were afraid or angry.

"What's the matter with . . .?"

But Titty never finished her sentence. She
caught the eye of Peter Duck. That was enough.
The others went on talking.

---

[1] The samson-post is a very strong post that goes right through
the deck and down to the keel. – NANCY.

"Yo, ho, ho for the Canaries," said Nancy.

"Or the Azores," said John.

Titty, with her mouth open and her sentence unfinished, saw Peter Duck bend quietly and unfasten the chain from the samson-post. She saw him pick up a mallet. And still the parrot chattered and flapped its wings.

She saw Peter Duck swing the mallet and strike the belaying-pin out of the link. Four fathom of chain flew with a roar through the hawse-hole. There was a crash of breaking wood and a tremendous splash, as the anchor, with Black Jake upon it, dropped, smashed the dinghy and plunged to the bottom of the harbour.

*

Everybody rushed to the side and looked down. Bits of broken dinghy showed in the dusk. And then a dark head came to the surface.

"Black Jake again!" cried Titty.

"Who else?" said Peter Duck.

They watched him swim across to the *Viper*. They saw the dark figure, dim in the dusk, swarm up the warp over the *Viper*'s stern.

"Gosh!" said Nancy.

Captain Flint spoke as quietly and calmly as if someone had dropped a teaspoon. "What happened, Mr Duck?" he said.

"Anchor went with a run, sir," said Peter Duck. "It just seemed to me it could do with a bit of washing. So I knocked the pin out and let it go. Black Jake was on it."

"On it?" said Captain Flint, looking, for the first time, a little astonished.

"He was listening through the hawse-hole," said Peter Duck.

"There's something very funny about all this," said Captain Flint.

"You may well say that," said Peter Duck. "Worse than funny, you might say."

The others were staring first at Captain Flint and then at the old sailor.

No one else in the harbour seemed to have noticed that anything had happened. The fiddler was still scraping out a jig tune in one of the vessels over by the market. Foot passengers were crossing the swing bridge. A light showed for a moment on the *Viper* and then vanished.

"He'll have to change everything he's got on," said Susan.

"And then he'll come charging round with a policeman or two because of our anchor smashing his dinghy," said Peggy.

"What a galoot you are," said Captain Nancy to her mate. "How can he go to the police? He'd have to explain how he happened to be on our anchor and squinting through our hawse-hole . . . ."

"Then he'll do something else," said John.

"It's as if he'd got something against us," said Susan.

"Well, he has now, even if he hadn't before," said Nancy cheerfully. "He must have got a nasty shock when he went down with the anchor."

"But, but, but . . ." said Roger, but got no further.

"What's the fellow after?" said Captain Flint.

"It's a long yarn, is that," said Peter Duck.

"Let's have it," said Captain Flint.

Peter Duck looked up at the quay above them, dark in the gathering dusk.

"You never know who might be listening," he said.

"Come along to the deckhouse," said Captain Flint. "We can take a look out now and again to see that no one's near enough to listen."

"Better so," said Peter Duck.

"Come on," said Titty eagerly. There was almost a stampede along the decks, as Captain Flint, taking the lantern with him, walked aft with Peter Duck.

"What about your bedtime, Roger?" said Susan.

"Oh, I say," said Roger. "Just this once . . . ."

And so it happened that the whole ship's company were crowded into the deckhouse when Peter Duck, sitting on the edge of his bunk, began to spin his yarn.

CHAPTER V

PETER DUCK SPINS HIS YARN

Everyone had grown accustomed to Peter Duck. He seemed, somehow, to be part of the ship, and they themselves seemed to have lived in the *Wild Cat* for a long time. They would have been startled if anyone had suddenly reminded them that the Swallows had come aboard for the first time only three days before, and the Amazons less than a week before them. But now, as they waited for the old sailor to begin, and he sat there on the edge of his bunk, pushing the dottle of tobacco into his pipe with a horny thumb, he seemed different. The light of the lantern hanging under the beam fell on the same old kindly wrinkled face, but it was as if those shrewd old eyes of his were looking at them out of another world. This, perhaps, was because he was remembering things that had happened a very long time ago

"By my thinking," he said at last, "there's nothing there to make much of a do about. A little money maybe, and if any man were to have it in his own pocket he'd find it burning a hole there, and he'd spend it likely on what he'd be sorry for, and he'd be worse off than if he'd never had the handling of it. By my thinking that's what it is, and I've been sorry enough that ever I tell that yarn to my wife that's dead now, and my three daughters when they was little girls, thirty years ago maybe or more. It's been a plague to me ever since, not but what most folk know by now that I'm not going to do a thing about it . . ."

"About what?" said Roger.

"Treasure?" said Captain Flint.

"About whatever it is," said Peter Duck. "Whatever it is I saw buried down at the foot of a coconut palm, fifty, sixty, or maybe seventy years ago."

"But where were you?" asked Roger.

"In the coconut tree, of course," said Peter Duck, "in the coconut tree, just waking out of my night's sleep."

Another idea struck Roger. "Did you snore then, too?" he asked.

"Roger," said Susan severely.

"He does now," said Roger. "Beautifully."

"I reckon I didn't then," said Peter Duck slowly, "or they'd have heard me and buried it in some other place. And maybe they'd have buried me too," he added after a pause.

"Who?"

"Shut up, Roger," said Captain Flint. "You'll hear if you keep your ears open and your mouth shut."

"I'd better begin at the beginning," said Peter Duck, "and tell you how it all come about. You see I'd slipped my cable out of Lowestoft, and gone to London in a coaster. And I'd run away from her at Greenhithe, and then in the docks I shipped aboard a fine vessel trading to the Brazils, shipped as cabin-boy I had, when I was no bigger than this ship's boy that keeps wanting me to crowd on topsails before my anchor's fair out of the ground. We'd a fair passage across the Western

Ocean but it ended over soon. Struck a pampero
or a Sugar Coast hurricane or one of them other
big winds she did, and lost both her sticks and
broke her back, and we took to the boats and she
smashed one of them, and the other one, the one
that I was in, didn't last long, but a seaman in her
lashed me to a spar, and the next I knew was that
I was washed up, beached good and proper on a bit
of an island. There was a big surf roaring along
that shore, and if I'd chosen any other place I'd
have had the life pounded out of me at once, but
I'd had no choosing in it, being lashed to the spar
and half drowned anyways, and I was washed up
between some rocks into a narrow little hole of a
place where the surf that didn't run though the
spray was spouting over from the swell that was
rolling in against the rocks outside. I never see
any of the others again off that ship. The first
thing I did see was crabs."

"Big ones?" asked Roger, and Titty nudged him
with her elbow.

"All sizes," said Peter Duck, "but mostly small.
And these crabs they wasn't the sort of crabs you
know. They look at me greedy-like, and come on,
waving them clippers of theirs and opening and
shutting them. It wasn't above a minute or so
before one of them crabs was taking a hold of the
calf of my leg. Well, you may lay to it, I wasted no
more time than I could help in getting free from
that spar, and then I fetched that crab a kick and
threw a stone at the others. I got one, too, and he
fell over. And his friends was on him in a minute,
and their clippers clacking like a watermill, and
waving over him, and they had him to pieces and

into their mouths and crunch, crunch . . . horrible sight it was . . . and them crabs looking greedy at me all the time.

"And then when I walk up that beach to have a look about me and to see if there was any others of us saved, I might have been a drum-major, the way that regiment of crabs come following after, running sideways, and lifting themselves, and clapping their clippers, and goggling at me with them eyes of theirs, set on their faces like them martello towers you see along the south coast. I hadn't the tonnage of Roger there, and I didn't like the look of them crabs.

"But in the end I was glad of them. I couldn't find a thing to eat, not at first. And then, after I'd killed a few more of them crabs, I was listening to the others cracking them and crunching them, and I didn't see why I shouldn't have a share. So the next one of them crabs that come too close to me, I killed him with a stone and grabbed him up before them others could get at him, and pulled his clippers off, and smashed his shell with the stone, and found him pretty good eating, particularly the handle end of them clippers of his. The stuff I sucked out of them was good and tasty and there was a bit in there that was decent chewing too. I was hungry, of course, to begin, but the taste of them crabs was a long ways better than what you might think it might be. I ate three or four of them right away.

"And my eating them crabs seemed to do me a bit of good with the others, for pretty soon they'd slither away in a hurry if I stepped sharply, and I had only to pick up a stone to send them scuttling

PRACTICE WITH THE HALYARDS

all ways at once. But the worst as you might say
was to come. For them crabs that was running
about in the daytime was as harmless as lambs
beside them that showed up at night. Just as
night come down these other crabs come up, and
they was the sort that if I threw a stone at one of
them he'd just think nothing of catching it in them
clippers of his and heaving it back. That was the
sort of crabs these was, and they seemed to think
as I was just what they was wanting. They was
tired of eating them small crabs and I reckon they
think I was something new, with a softer kind of
shell.

"I legged it just in time, and the biggest of them
had a clipper full of the starn of my breeches and
I hope it choked him. Them breeches was no good
after, no protection at all. But, as I was saying,
I legged it, and swarmed up one of them young
coconut palms as was growing along that shore
a bit above high-water mark. And up in the top
of that tree there was some young coconuts, and
I cut a hole in one with my knife, and the milk
came trickling out, and I found just a little meat
in it too. And I slept up in the tree all that night
and come down in the morning and took it out
of them smaller crabs, and did well enough what
with them and the coconuts. But when night come
there was them bigger crabs again, and I knew
enough now not to let one get a hold of me. I was
shinning up that tree with time and to spare.

"And so it went on, day after day and night
after night, and I got into a regular way of living,
always shinning up that tree at fall of night and
coming down again when I felt hungry and the

sun was up. It was a lazy kind of life, and the
winds used to rock them coconut palms. It was
like sleeping in a cradle, or a hammock, an easy
kind of motion. It wasn't no kind of blame to me
that I come to sleep long hours. There wasn't no
bells striking, and there wasn't no bosun after
me with a rope's end. It all come as a kind of a
holiday. And then one day when I'd slept maybe
longer than usual, I waked up in a hurry with the
sound of folk talking under my tree."

"Who was it?" asked Titty breathlessly, and
Roger might have nudged her with his elbow,
but he didn't think of it.

"Lucky for me I looked to see before shouting
out," said Peter Duck. "I looked down through
them palm leaves, and there was two men at the
foot of my tree, digging a hole in the ground with
a long knife."

"Pirates?" said Titty.

"They looked all that to me," said Peter Duck.
"And they sounded all that, the way they was
talking. One of them was crouching and digging,
while t'other one of them was looking round. And
then that one would dig away and the one that
had been digging before would stretch his arms
and take a turn at looking round.

"'I'd be sorry for the one that sees us at this,'
says one of them.

"'There's not one will have thought of following
us, not with that keg I let them take ashore,' says
the other.

"No boy gets brought up at a rope's end, as
you might say, without knowing when to keep
his mouth shut, and I see quick enough this

was no time for talking. So I kept still up there among the leaves at the top of that palm and looking down on them and watching what they was doing. Pretty soon one says he reckons the hole's deep enough, and the other one says there's none likely to come seeking for it on this side of the island where there's no shelter for ships. 'And it isn't as if we was going to leave it for long,' says the other. And with that they takes a sort of a square bag they had from right under the tree where I hadn't seed it before . . . Square all ways that bag was . . ."

"Couldn't it have been a box that they'd put in the bag for easy carrying?" asked Captain Flint. He dropped a match that had burnt all the way to his fingers. He had lit it meaning to light his pipe but had somehow forgotten about it.

"That's just what it likely was," said Peter Duck. "You could see the corners of it sticking through the canvas. Well, they took this square bag and lowered it down into their hole, and then they scraped the sand and earth in again with their knives and their hands and stamped it down and smoothed it over till they was satisfied, and with that they slapped each other on the back and went walking off again among the trees.

"I was down out of my bedroom quick enough after that. You see, it come to me clear that pirates was humans, which crabs is not, and that them two had a ship somewheres, and that maybe I'd see Lowestoft again, which I'd given up all thought of. So I went legging it away through the trees after them two. And they went clean across the island, with me not so far from them among

the trees, over the shoulder of the big hill there
is there, and sure enough, looking down the other
side, I see a smart brig lying to her anchor. So I
hurried me on down on that side of the island, and
there was a boat drawn up there by a stream I'd
known nothing of, me not daring to go in among
the trees before. And there was a fire burning,
and half a dozen men singing and laughing round
a keg they had there chocked up between a couple
of stones. I had sense enough to slip away through
the trees till I could come at the men from along
the shore, and then I set up yelling and shouting
till they see me."

"What happened then?" said Peggy.

"Shut up, you galoot," said Nancy. "He's just
going to tell you."

"They ask me how I come there, and I told
them about the shipwreck and how I'd been eating crabs and drinking coconut milk, and one of
them give me a hunk of bread and another give
me the first swig of rum that ever I had in my life,
which near took the skin off my gullet. 'You're all
right now,' says one. 'Captain's luck holds. You'll
be welcome. It's as if you knowed we was short of
a cabin-boy since the old man threw the last one
overboard to teach him swimming one day when
he was playful like.' I can tell you I begin to think
I'd have done better to stay by them crabs.

"But just then them other two come, the two
that buried that square bag under my bedroom.
That's what I used to call that tree of mine.
They was the captain and the mate. They asked
me sharp enough where I'd come from, and I
told them I didn't know, but I'd been wrecked

out of a London ship and wanted to get home to Lowestoft where I belonged. They took me aboard in the end. Sailing for London they was, and a rare passage they made of it. All the way home across the Western Ocean they kept me on the run fetching tots of rum for them to the state-room aft. I've often wondered since how we got as far as we did. And all the time while they was drinking they'd be talking one t'other and t'other back again, secret-like, about something they'd left, which I took to be that square bag. But likely it wasn't . . ."

"It couldn't have been anything else," said Captain Flint.

"'Let 'em lie,' they'd say, 'let 'em lie. And then when all's clear, and they've no line on us about the ship, we'll call for 'em and bring 'em home and sell 'em gradual, and ride in carriages we will and nod to princes when they lifts their hats to us.'"

"What was the name of the ship?" asked Captain Flint suddenly.

"The *Mary Cahoun*," said Peter Duck. "But that wasn't the vessel they were talking of. They'd but new got the *Mary* and they'd come up from round the Horn in some other ship. I knew that from their talk, for when they was meaning this other ship they'd call her 'the old packet,' and they called the *Mary* by her name. And from what I heard, the captain and the mate of that other ship had died something sudden, and it's come to me since that this precious pair I was with had taken their papers and their names at the same time. Captain Jonas Fielder they called one of them, the one that was skipper, but he'd R. C. B. tattooed on his forearm. Many's the time I see it when he was sitting there in his shirt-sleeves lifting his glass of grog. There was something wrong most ways, it seem to me. They knew it too. The nearer we come to England the more they'd drink. They kept on lifting their glasses and swilling their grog and choking with it, and banging each other on the back as if they was afraid of something and wanted to think of something else. And then other times they would pull out a chart and look at it, and wore a hole in it they did, marking one of the islands with pencil and then rubbing the marks out. And when they'd swigged an extra lot of rum they'd just sit and wink at each other and show each other bits of paper where they'd written down some figures. And then in the morning when they was sober, more or less, they would go hunting round the cabin floor for them scraps of paper and wondering how many they'd left there, and if the crew had found them. And if they found one of them scraps of paper they'd lay into me with a rope's end for not tidying it overboard. And if they didn't find one they'd lay into me and say I'd picked it up for myself. Well naturally in the end I come to know those scraps of paper pretty well, and I see they all had the same figures, and I sewed up one of them in the inside of my jacket thinking whatever it was I'd paid for it in rope's-ending anyways."

"And those were the bearings of the island?" Captain Flint dropped another burnt but unused match on the floor and put his foot on it.

"Longitude and latitude they was. No more. Them two reckoned to find that island again, and

needed no more to help them find their square
bag, for they'd buried it themselves, and I dare say
they'd taken all the bearings they needed. They
knew those figures by heart, did them two, and
before we come to the end of the voyage I knew
them too, with seeing them so often. Anyhow the
figures was no good to either of them chaps, for
they come home with a westerly gale and full skin
of rum apiece, and they piled the *Mary Cahoun* on
Ushant rocks. There was nobody saved out of her
but the bosun and me, and the bosun had his ribs
stove in and his skull cracked, and he was dead
when some of them French fishermen come by
and take us off the rock we was on just before
the tide rose high enough to sweep us off. Another
ten minutes and they'd have been too late for me.
They was too late for the bosun anyway.

"That's the yarn. That's all there was to it, and
you never would have thought it'd have sent half
the young lads of Lowestoft crazy when I come to
tell it thirty years after, and maybe more than
that."

"But I don't see what all this has to do with
Black Jake," said Captain Flint.

"I'm coming to that," said Peter Duck.

CHAPTER VI

AND WINDS IT UP

THERE was a short breathless pause. Everybody stirred a little and looked round at the others. This story of wrecks and pirates and distant islands had taken them all a long way from the snug little deckhouse of the *Wild Cat* lying comfortably against the quay in Lowestoft inner harbour. Peter Duck lit his pipe, took a puff or two, and then once more rammed his thumb into the bowl.

Titty leaned forward and looked eagerly up at him.

"What happened when you got home?" she asked.

"I didn't get home," said Peter Duck. "Not that year nor many a year after. I worked for my keep with them French fishermen, and then one day off Ushant there was a fine clipper becalmed near where they was fishing and they rowed up to her and put me aboard in exchange for a bag of negro head . . ."

"What's that?" asked Roger.

"Tobacco," said Captain Flint. "But let Mr Duck go on."

"I reckon they sold me cheap," said Mr Duck. "That clipper was short-handed and they could have got more if they'd asked for it. As much as two bags, maybe. Anyways they put me aboard her and I was further than ever from getting home to Lowestoft. She was a Yankee clipper, the *Louisiana Belle*, and she carried skysails above her royals when other folk was taking in to'gallants. Hard driving there was in that ship. Round the Horn westaways I sailed in her, and left her in 'Frisco, and stowed away in a tea ship bound for the Canton River. And after that I was in one ship and another, here today and gone tomorrow, as you might say. There's not many ports about the world but what I've been into in my time. And I copied out them figures from that bit of paper I was telling you about, one time, and I learned that way whereabout that island was, out of curiosity, mind you, for I never had a mind to go there. And I learnt what its name was too, for it had a name. 'Crab Island'[1] they call it, and a shipmate of mine pointed it out to me once, when we was up on the fo'c'sle head together, two hills showing but the island itself hull down, and he told me he'd watered there from a spring on the western side. That'd be where I found them with the boat that day when I was taken off."

"But did you never find a way of going back there?" asked Captain Flint.

"I'd a horror of them crabs," said Peter Duck. "And more than that I'd a horror of them drowned men of the *Mary Cahoun*. What had they done, them two, that they was afraid to take that bag with them but buried it out there with none but them crabs to watch it? It brought them no good. And what did I want with it either? The sea was enough for me. It wasn't cluttered up with screw

[1] Not to be confounded with the much larger Crab Island east of Porto Rico.

steamships. There was great sailing in them days,
and whenever I did come ashore paid off, I couldn't
so much as see a vessel going down river outward
bound without wishing I was aboard her. Money?
I'd all I wanted and spent it quick enough so as
not to waste time ashore. But I did keep that scrap
of paper with the longitude and latitude of that
island written on it, though I knew them figures
well enough by heart. Couldn't forget them if I
tried. But I cut out that bit of jacket when I
throwed the jacket away, that bit where I had
the paper sewed, and I kept it and the paper in
it, until the day come when I wished I hadn't.

"You see the years was passing and I'd brought
to in Lowestoft at last, paying off in London River,
and going down to Norfolk in the railway train,
thinking I'd like to see the old place now I was
a man, and not so young neither. There was a
good few remembered me, but none of my own
folk. They was all gone, but no matter. It's no
good looking for the dead. And I met a young
woman there, clipper built, you might say, with
a fine figurehead to her, well found, too, and her
dad kept a marine store, no, not the one where
you was fitting out, but another, cleared away
long since from where the new market is. And
we got married, and I put to sea again, coming
home when I could, and she went on living along
with her old dad in the marine store, and we had
three daughters. And then one day when I was
home from sea, she was turning things out of this
and that, and she come on that bit of old pea-jacket
sewed up square with tarred twine, and she asked
me what it was. And I telled her the yarn that

I've been telling to you, and my three daughters
sitting there listening with their mouths open.
That was the beginning of it. They couldn't be
tired of hearing that yarn. And they telled it to
others, and them others telled it to some more,
and it come so in the end that I could never put
my foot ashore in Lowestoft without some fancy
man or other getting at me to tell the yarn again
and to give him that bit of paper and set him up
rich for life. That square bag I telled you about
was growed into cases of gold dollars and casks
of silver ingots from the mines. They was at me
all the time to sail across there with them to fetch
the treasure, as they call it, when I'd talked of no
treasure but only of a square bag with something
in it that likely didn't belong to the two that buried
it, and they buried, too, now, forty years back in
a hundred fathom of blue water."

Captain Flint opened his mouth to speak, but
said nothing. Peter Duck went on.

"My three daughters grow up, proper young
clippers like their mother, and folk was beginning to leave me alone about that scrap of paper
that I wished I'd lost off Ushant all them years
before, and then Black Jake come along. My old
wife she was dead then, and I was away from
the sea, sailing my wherry between Norwich and
Lowestoft, me and my three daughters. Knitting
needles and quants[1] was all the same to them.
They was good at both. It was a pretty sight to

[1] A quant is a long pole for poling ("quanting") a wherry along
when there is no wind to help her or where the channel is too
narrow for sailing against the wind.

see them taking that old boat upstream against the wind by themselves with me sitting on the hatch, smoking my pipe and drinking my pot like any admiral.

"Well, Black Jake come along with his long hair and them ear-rings of his, and always plenty of money in his pockets that nobody knows how he come by. He'd heard that yarn in the taverns in Lowestoft and he waited his chance to get at me. I could never be quit of him. No matter where I tied up, there he'd be, and talking always of the one thing. Nothing else would suit him. I must draw him a picture of that island, a chart, to show him just where my tree was and where I see that bag buried, and then I must give him the sailing directions to find the island and he would be off there to make my fortune as well as his own. You've seen Black Jake. He don't look the sort of man it's safe to share a fortune with, now does he? And I wasn't wanting a fortune anyway. Well, naturally, I wouldn't tell him nothing at all.

"And then he tried to marry my daughters, thinking he'd get one of them to wheedle what he wanted out of me. He had a try at one and then at another. But my daughters has more sense than to be marrying Black Jakes, and they married farmers, one at Beccles, one at Acle, and one at Potter Heigham. And that's just right for me. Gives me three ports of call, where I can tie up my old wherry, and have a pipe by the fireside."

"And which of them do you like the best?" asked Roger.

"Depends which way the wind is," said Peter Duck. "A south wind takes me up the Thurne

River, and then I always think most of Rose, that's the gal that lives at Potter Heigham. An east wind blows fair for Beccles, and my daughter there has a good little farm and a sheltered mooring just above the bridge. And if there comes on a south wind while I'm there, or a north wind while I'm at Potter Heigham, why it's a right wind for Acle, and when it comes so, why, I just naturally think that Annie's the best of the lot and I take my chance of the tide to go and have a look at her."

"I see," said Roger, and he really did a little later when Peggy had explained it to him.

"But their marrying didn't stop him," said Peter Duck. "When he knew he couldn't get what he wanted that way, Black Jake started hanging round my wherry whenever he come home from sea. Again and again I found my cabin rummaged when I'd been ashore. And in the end I found that bit of paper sewed up in the square of old pea-jacket was missing. Missing it was, that bit of cloth with the paper with them figures on it sewed up inside. I searched for it high and low, not but what I knew them figures. It wasn't that. But I didn't like letting Black Jake get it after all. And the next thing I hear was that Black Jake was missing and two others with him. That was the first time I'd had a kind thought for them crabs. I knowed where he'd gone, of course, and I hoped they'd make a meal of him.

"Best part of a year he was gone, and I'd begun to hope we'd seen the last of him, when he come back alone, and I knowed he'd found nothing. How could he, without he'd dug the whole island. Them

two that went with him died of fever, he said,
and as they was the same sort as himself nobody
minded. He come back raging mad, worse than
before. For Lowestoft folk knew how I'd missed
that square of old pea-jacket, and what was in it,
and they knew the old yarn, and there wasn't a
boy that met Black Jake in the street, and had a
door handy to bolt into, that didn't ask him how
much treasure them crabs had left him. Raging
mad he was, and folk did tell me I should keep
a watch for flying knives at night. But ever since
then he could never see me down at the harbour
without thinking I was shipping foreign to go to
the island, and he's sworn that what I wouldn't
tell him I should tell no man else ... Five year
ago it is now since he come back, and these last
four months he's been fitting out the *Viper* for sea,
and some rare bad lots he's taking with him. He's
likely going to have another look. And then when
he see me come aboard here, shipping along with
you ..."

"That was why he was spying round in the
dark," said Captain Flint. He laughed aloud. "And
I told that red-haired boy we were carrying three
captains and a couple of mates. That was why he
hurried out after us, and turned sharp round and
came in again when he met us in the harbour
mouth."

"He thinks you're bound for Crab Island sure
enough," said Peter Duck.

Captain Flint for a moment seemed hardly to
see Peter Duck or the others, crowded together
in the little deckhouse. Sitting on the edge of the
chart-table, his head bent under the roof, he was

seeing things very far away. "It stands to reason," he said at last, "there's something in that bag, and if no one's been there and picked it up, it's the safest, surest thing in buried treasure that ever I heard of. I crossed the Andes, travelling day and night, on much less of a hint than that."

The old sailor looked up at Captain Flint, leaning forward to look at him without being dazzled by the lantern.

"I don't care who digs up that bag so long as Black Jake don't," he said. "But whatever it is it's best let lie. You don't want it, not with a tidy little schooner like this fit to take you anywheres. I don't want it, not with my old wherry that'll last my time and a bit more."

Captain Flint looked away, and tapped the tobacco out of his pipe.

"I can't help thinking it's wasted on those crabs," he said. "I don't wonder Black Jake wants to go and have a look for it."

"He don't want to go looking for it," said Peter Duck. "He wants to walk straight to it on that island, and pick it up. He can't do that without me. He'll stick at nothing, will Black Jake. You've seen enough to know that. And if you want to have no more trouble, you'd best put me ashore and get another able-seaman for your trip down Channel, and you'll find Black Jake won't be bothering you at all."

"No, no! Oh, I say! What!" There was a sudden startled chorus of protest. Captain Flint hit the top of his head on a beam under the deckhouse roof. He took no notice of the bump but spoke at once.

"I thought you said you wanted another voyage?"

"And so I do," said Peter Duck.

"And the ship and the crew suit you?"

"Couldn't ask for better."

"Then stow this talk of leaving us. If we suit you, you suit us. And if you think I'm the sort to leave you ashore because of a scowling, crook-eyed son of a sea-cook with a fancy for gold ear-rings, you're mistaken."

"That's the stuff, Captain Flint," said Nancy delightedly.

"Of course you mustn't go," said Roger.

"Mr Duck!" said Titty.

"We'll sail tomorrow, Mr Duck," said Captain Flint, "and if your Black Jake is fool enough to follow us, we'll lead him a bit of a dance."

"He'll follow, sure enough," said Peter Duck.

"Let him," said Captain Flint. "Anyway, we'll sail. And you'll sail with us. Below decks, you others! Below decks and into your bunks and sharp about it. We're sailing first thing."

"But what about the anchor?" asked John.

"It'll be clean enough by now," said Peter Duck.

"Man the capstan then," said Captain Flint. "Man the capstan and heave it up, and then below decks without waiting another minute."

He took the lantern, and the whole ship's company went forward along the dark deck. There was silence in the harbour. They peered across at the *Viper*, but all was dark where she lay. The capstan bars were ranged handy along the bulwarks, and in a minute the Swallows and Amazons, all six of them, had fitted their bars into the slots in the capstan head, and, walking steadily round and round, were walking the anchor up as if it were a feather. It is astonishing what six people, even small ones, can lift with a capstan, all working together.

Captain Flint flashed a pocket torch over the side. The anchor had come up clean. The dinghy's painter must have slipped off it before.

There was a sudden squawk of annoyance in the darkness.

"I'd forgotten all about him," said Titty, rather ashamed.

The parrot had fallen asleep, perched on the bulwarks, and was not pleased to be waked. Titty picked him up and took him down with her into the saloon and put him into his cage for the night. Roger was nearly as sleepy as the parrot. But the others were for some time too full of talk to sleep. They undressed, talking. And, when they were in their bunks, they talked still from one cabin to another. Treasure. Black Jake. Crabs. Peter Duck. That red-haired boy who was sailing with Black Jake. They had enough to talk about.

And then, long after they had stopped getting answers from each other when they spoke, long after they had stopped talking and fallen asleep, they woke again, listening to steps going to and fro overhead, along the *Wild Cat's* decks.

"It's Mr Duck," said Susan quietly.

"Yes," said Titty. "It was Captain Flint before. I heard him tapping his pipe."

"They must think Black Jake may come again in the night," said John.

"Keeping watch," said Titty.

"Who?" A voice came now from the Amazons' cabin.

"Mr Duck and Captain Flint," whispered Susan. "Listen."

"Let's all go up and help," said Nancy.

"No, no," said Peggy. "Stop here."

"What's happening now?" This was Roger's squeak in the dark.

"Nothing. Go to sleep," said Susan. "We all ought to," she added. "If they want help they'll thump on the deck for us, or call down through the skylight."

They slept again.

But all night long, watch and watch about, Captain Flint and Peter Duck walked up and down above their sleeping crew.

CHAPTER VII

OUTWARD BOUND

"Hullo! What's happening?" Nancy was the first to wake as a heavy warp slapped on the deck above her head.

"My engine's going," said Roger half-asleep. He woke, feeling the throbbing of the hull and hearing the chug, chug, chug of the little engine that already he looked on as his own, rolled out of his bunk, reached up to tug at John, and then, in his pyjamas, ran out of the cabin, through the saloon, and wriggled round the companion stairs.

"She's moving," said Titty.

"Keep your head out of the way. I'm coming down," said Susan.

"Listen." John, sitting up in his bunk, called out from his cabin. "There's a headsail flapping."

That noise stopped and there was a sharp creak and the groan of blocks.

"That's the boom going over," called Nancy.

"She's slanting the other way," said Peggy.

"Heeling, you mean," said Nancy. "Yes, she is."

"They must have got the sails up without us," said Titty.

"Somebody's started my engine," said Roger indignantly, coming back after having a look at it.

There was a general rush and scramble below decks. John, Susan and Roger came up on deck through the companion out of the saloon. Nancy,

Peggy, and Titty came up the ladder out of the forehatch. They came on deck in the summer morning, to find sunshine and a strong north-easterly breeze clearing away the light morning mist. The *Wild Cat*, with her engine running in case of trouble, was tacking out of harbour under jib and mainsail.

"Why did you start without us?" said Roger. "Who's engineer?"

"You are," said Captain Flint, "and in another minute or two you can stop her. But keep out of the way now. Stand by to go about, Mr Duck."

"Aye, aye, sir."

Captain Flint spun the wheel, and the *Wild Cat* swung round, while Peter Duck let fly the port jib sheets.

"Smart enough," he said, finding Nancy all ready to haul in on the other side as the sail blew across.

"Well, but why did you start without us?" said Nancy.

"Ask the skipper," said Peter Duck. "But you ain't got left behind."

"We thought we'd take our chance of a little practice without you," said Captain Flint. "Tide served. And it seemed a pity to waste any of this wind."

"We heard you walking up and down all night," said Titty.

"Ready to repel boarders," said Nancy.

"But that man didn't come again," said Peggy.

"No. He didn't," said Captain Flint, glancing back over his shoulder towards the inner harbour. "And if he wants to come now, he's too late. And

now, you scallywags, what do you think our ship
looks like with all of you slopping about in pyjamas all over the place? A floating dormitory. All
pyjamas go below. Get dressed as quick as you
can. We shall be in fairly quiet water going down
the Pakefield, but after that we'll probably catch
it. Much more wind than yesterday."

"We must stay on deck just till we're outside
the harbour."

"Tally on to the foresail halyards then, and
help Mr Duck."

"Smartly now, my hearties," cried Nancy, as
they ran forward to help Mr Duck hoist the
foresail.

"Slack away foresail sheet," said Mr Duck,
seeming almost to forget that the six Swallows
and Amazons in their pyjamas were not some
sort of native crew. "Handsomely now. Belay.
Now then. You three on the throat. T'other
three on the peak. Hoist away. Up she goes.
Hoist away. Belay peak halyard. Haul away on
the throat. Swig away there. Let me get a hold.
So. Belay. Haul on the peak. Handsomely now. So.
Belay. Slacken away topping lifts. Not that, Cap'n
Nancy. That's right. Coil down halyards. Haul in
the sheet . . . ."

As he spoke he hauled in the sheet himself, with John and Nancy tallying on to help
him.

"Staysail halyards!" he called, and Nancy and
John flew forward again. In a very few moments
the staysail was up and drawing.

"A year or two of practice and you'll be a
goodish crew," said Peter Duck.

"Ready about!" came Captain Flint's voice from the wheel.

There was a bit of a bustle for a moment, letting go sheets and hauling in again on the lee side as the sails came over. Then all was quiet once more, and the crew gathered aft by the wheel where Roger and Titty were already, Titty watching the jetty slip by as the *Wild Cat* headed for the harbour mouth, and Roger hopping in and out of the deckhouse, waiting to be allowed to shut down the engine, or move the lever to full ahead, or do something else that really mattered in the engine line.

"All right, Roger," said Captain Flint. "Stop her!"

The chug-chug of the little engine came to an end. Roger came on deck again.

"The engine wants some more cleaning," he said.

"Job for you and Gibber," said Captain Flint. "But get dressed and let's have breakfast over first."

Roger was gone.

"Hurry up, you others," said Captain Flint. "We're hungry. Besides, I want to be free to look at charts and things, and some of you will be wanted to take the wheel."

Nancy, John, Susan, and Peggy disappeared in a bunch.

"What are you waiting for, Titty?"

Titty was looking back at the harbour they were leaving. Far away there, beyond the swing bridge, in the inner basin, loose grey canvas was climbing up among tall masts and rigging.

"The *Viper*'s hoisting her sails," said Titty. "I do believe she's coming after us."

Captain Flint glanced over his shoulder.

"It may be some other vessel," he said. "You can't tell from here. What do you think, Mr Duck?"

"Able-seaman's right, sir, seems to me. Aye, they're getting their sails up." He took the telescope from the rack close inside the deckhouse, and looked through it towards the inner harbour. "Aye," he said, "they're setting their sails, sure enough. They've a halyard unrove, I reckon. I can see that young Bill up at the mast-head."

"Good luck to them," said Captain Flint. "They can set them and welcome for all we care."

But Peter Duck kept the telescope to his eye, watching that fluttering grey canvas, until the *Wild Cat* was well outside the pier heads.

"Skip along, Titty," said Captain Flint, and Titty disappeared below, to change from pyjamas into something more fitting for an able-seaman to wear on a schooner bound down Channel.

*

Below decks things were very unsteady. Dressing was not so easy as it had been when the *Wild Cat* was tied to the quay. Slap. Slap. Bang. The waves hit the bows of the little green schooner in a cheerful, welcoming manner, as she came out of the sheltered harbour to meet them. There was a good deal more noise than there had been during the trial trip, and members of the crew, dressing in the cabins, looked at each other doubtfully. Then, suddenly there was a sharp change in the motion, and, as the *Wild Cat* heeled over on the starboard side, shoes, clothes, hairbrushes and human beings slid unexpectedly across the floor. Roger sat down. Captain John had forgotten that he was not in harbour, and had stood an enamelled mug of tooth water on the little shelf that served as a table. It went flying. John tried to save it, tripped over Roger, and fell head first into the lower bunk.

Susan was farthest on with her dressing, and did not seem to mind the motion. She just leant back against the bunks and went on brushing her hair. Titty slipped sideways. The floor of the cabin sloped uphill. Titty seized some clothes and a pair of canvas shoes. "I'm going to finish my dressing on deck," she said hurriedly, climbed up the slope of the floor, got out of the door and stumbled up the companion-way.

Nancy, in the cabin of the Amazons, said nothing. She just looked at Peggy. A queer expression came into her eyes, as if she were looking not so much at Peggy as through her. She picked her shoes up out of the muddle on the floor, then dropped one of them, tried to catch it, slipped, recovered herself, made up her mind she would get that shoe later, and almost fell out of the cabin door and round on the stairway of the companion. She felt better as soon as her head was above deck. This would never do, she thought. She must have been mistaken in thinking she felt so bad. She put on the shoe she had with her, took two or three good sniffs at the wind and then went back after the shoe she had left. She found Susan and Peggy side by side on the bottom step of the companion-way, putting on their own shoes with difficulty and laughter, but talking quite happily of cooking on the swinging stove because the other would be on too much of a slant. It was bad enough having to step over them. But she did it, worked herself round into her cabin, found her shoe and came out again, grabbing at the saloon table to steady herself. "Hullo, Nancy!" said Peggy. "Isn't this jolly?" But Nancy did not answer. She had meant to get her shoe, and she had got it, but this talking would have been too much. She got across the saloon, and through into the fo'c'sle, to get her head up through the fo'c'sle hatch into the fresh hard air. For once, Nancy, the Terror of the Seas, did not feel at all like a captain. She hardly felt it would be safe to say, "Shiver my timbers!" Her timbers felt a bit shivery already. And the funny thing was that Peggy, who was afraid of thunder and things like that, seemed not to be bothered at all by the unusual motion.

On deck things settled down quickly. Old Peter Duck was moving here and there, seeing that everything was as it should be. Coiled halyards that had shown signs of straying had been recoiled and stowed in places where they were willing to stay. The anchor had been brought inboard and secured in its place. He was busy now lashing down the little rowing dinghy. The fenders that had been used to protect the new green paint of the *Wild Cat* from the dirty quays of Lowestoft were all inboard, each in its place, ready for next time it would be needed, but not one of them left hanging over the side to make good sailors laugh. Peter Duck, busy about this and that, seemed happy to have his feet once more

on a slanting deck, lifting and swaying along at
sea, after so many years on the level deck of his
old wherry moving steadily along smooth inland
waters.

And the land was slipping by. The *Wild Cat*
was off at last and making the most of the good
north-easter, running down inside the shoals, past
Claremont Pier, and the hospital and Kirkley
Church. Pakefield Church was abeam. Out to
sea a coasting steamer was hurrying south, from
Newcastle or Grimsby or Hull, hurrying, but not
moving as fast as her own smoke which was blowing before her in a long low dirty cloud. Fishing
ketches were leaving the harbour, and some of
the trawlers, and far away on the horizon there
were two or three little plumes of smoke, showing
where there were steamers so far away as not to
be in sight. One by one the rest of the crew climbed
up on deck, hung on to anything that came handy
and looked about them. The trial trip had been
in smooth water compared with this. Now they
were off at last and learning what it was like
to be at sea. Today there was a real wind. The
land seemed to sway up and down as they rushed
along. Sometimes the *Wild Cat* would lift to an
even keel as a sea passed under her, and then
the land would drop to the bulwarks. Then over
she would go again, and the land seemed to leap
up the sky, and in the place where it had been
a moment before there would be the grey water
sweeping along by the lee rail.

Presently Captain Flint called John to the
wheel.

"Take over, will you, while I deal with that

Primus for them? Steer for that buoy. Black and white, with a cage on the top of it. Steer close by it, leaving it to port."

John gulped, but said "Aye, aye, sir," as stoutly as he could. A moment later he was feeling the ship, meeting her as she yawed, looking anxiously back at her rather waggly wake, and trying to do with a real ship at sea what he had learnt to do very well with the little *Swallow* on the lake in the North. But it was not easy in this hard wind and uncertain sea. There she was again, heading the wrong side of the buoy. Oh, bother it, and now too far the other way! And there was Nancy watching. This would never do. He must keep that piebald chequered buoy just showing on her port bow. Gradually the *Wild Cat* steadied down and John grew confident enough to look at Nancy who, he feared, had all this time been looking critically at him.

But Nancy was not thinking about him, or about the steering, or even about the *Wild Cat*. She had a queer staring look, as if she were trying to do some difficult sum in mental arithmetic. John could hardly believe that this was the same Nancy who was always so free with her "Hearties" and "Shiver my timbers!" and so ready to call other people tame galoots and to teach them all there was to be known about the sea.

"Come and look, Nancy," called Peggy's voice from inside the galley in the forward part of the deckhouse. Nancy pulled herself together, and clinging to the bulwarks worked herself along to the galley door. It opened.

"Come in, but shut the door quick. It's too

blowy from that side," said Peggy. "Just look at the Primus, swinging in rings, like the compass, so that the kettle keeps steady whatever the ship's doing."

Nancy let go the bulwarks and fell against the deckhouse. She pulled the galley door open again and put her head in, but quickly drew it back. In the tiny galley there were Peggy, Susan and Captain Flint. Captain Flint had been showing them how to deal with the Primus, and he had used rather too little methylated spirit, besides pumping a little too soon, so that the Primus had smoked a bit. It was burning all right now, and the kettle was boiling and the galley was full of steam and the smell of paraffin. And there were Peggy and Susan in the middle of that smelly fog, cheerfully cracking eggs into a bowl and making coffee in an enormous coffee-pot.

Nancy shut the door quickly and dragged herself back to the bulwarks, throwing her head up to get all the wind on it she could. This was terrible. Everybody seemed to be all right except her. Right forward she could see Roger eagerly asking questions and Peter Duck as steady on the slanting deck as if he had grown there and had roots, explaining something about getting the anchor inboard. Was the sea always like this? She could hardly bear the thought of going below, and yet she desperately wanted something hot to drink. When at last she saw Peggy and Susan, shouting with laughter, dodge out of the galley door and round to the companion taking damp towels to lay on the saloon table, Nancy began to wish she was back at home.

The damp towels, of course, were spread on the saloon table to keep plates and things from slipping about, and a minute or two later the two cooks were carrying down a great mess of scrambled eggs and the coffee-pot and a big can of milk. Damp towels, however, were not enough, and Captain Flint went below to fit the fiddles to the table. Fiddles for tables aboard ship are wooden frameworks that divide up the table into small partitions so that if things slide they cannot slide far. "Feeding-boxes," said Roger, "and one for each of us." Then, when everything was ready, Peggy came up on deck to bang mercilessly on a big bell. Peter Duck came aft and took the wheel from John. John hurried down the companion to join the others. Roger had come down by way of the forehatch. Captain Flint was sitting in the arm-chair at the port end of the table. Nancy, feeling as if someone had hit her on the head with a club, somehow found her way to her place at his right hand. Breakfast began.

"Hullo, where's Titty?" said Captain Flint.

Titty had been looking over the stern towards Lowestoft, watching to see if the *Viper* came out. It had been a hard job to hold the telescope steady. At last she had given up trying and had put the telescope back in its place in the deckhouse. That had been enough to make her quite sure she did not want to leave the deck again, even for breakfast. All she wanted was to stay still and breathe as much air as possible. Even the sunshine seemed to her to have turned a queer unpleasant colour.

NANCY AND TITTY SHARING THEIR MISERY

"What's become of Titty?" said Captain Flint, between mouthfuls, down in the saloon.

"I'll go and tell her," said Nancy.

"I'll go," said John.

"I want to go," said Nancy fiercely, and she staggered up off the bench and somehow got out of the saloon and up the companion. Captain Flint looked gravely after her but said nothing.

Nancy came out on deck and found Titty in the stern, still watching the sailing vessels come out of Lowestoft.

"Come down to breakfast, Titty," said Nancy bravely, and then suddenly gave up. Titty, looking round, saw Captain Nancy struggle forward round the lee side of the deckhouse, grip the bulwarks and hang her head over the rail.

In a moment Titty joined her. If Nancy, the Captain of the Amazons, that notable timber shiverer, could be seasick, then anybody could be without shame, and for some minutes a captain and an able-seaman, sharing their misery, hung over the side together.

Peter Duck, his grey beard blowing in the wind round his weatherbeaten old face, an old stocking cap crammed down over his ears, gripped the spokes of the wheel, moved them this way and that, and, with his eyes looking far ahead, seemed to see nothing and to hear nothing that did not concern the steering of the ship. The whole crew of captains and mates and everybody else could have been seasick over the side without disturbing him in the least. But he did, now and then, look back at a group of sailing vessels leaving Lowestoft, that was already far astern.

Presently Captain Flint came up the companion with a mug of hot coffee in each hand. He found the sufferers and told them that some of the most famous of sailors were always sick at the beginning of a voyage in spite of spending most of their lives at sea. Nancy cheered up a little. Titty said she didn't believe it would have been so bad if she hadn't been looking the wrong way trying to see if the *Viper* was coming after them or not.

"And what about the *Viper*, Mr Duck?" asked Captain Flint, going aft to take the wheel and send Mr Duck down to breakfast.

"There's several vessels come out," said Mr Duck. "All in a bunch. It'd be hard to say if one of them's the *Viper*. But if she isn't out yet, she'll be coming. You may lay to that, sir. Black Jake wouldn't come in after us yesterday and not come out after us today. He ain't going to lose sight of us, not if he can help it."

"Oh, come, Mr Duck, these things don't happen nowadays."

"Black Jake's his own law," said Peter Duck. "He knows I'm aboard here, and if he's got it in his head that I'm taking you to that place I told you of, he'd sail round the world after us."

"Well," said Captain Flint, "if one of those vessels is the *Viper*, and she's after us, she'd have turned south by this time."

"Look you there," said Peter Duck, and Captain Flint snatched up the telescope from the rack inside the door.

One vessel had left the little group of sailing craft heading eastwards from Lowestoft. This vessel was now alone and heading south.

"Schooner," said Captain Flint. "All lower sail set. Main topsail just going up. It's our old neighbour."

"I'd be surprised," said Peter Duck, "if you was to say it wasn't so."

CHAPTER VIII

FIRST NIGHT AT SEA

ALL that day they sailed on with the north-east wind driving them southwards, past Walberswick, with its church tower and windmill, past Aldeburgh and Orfordness, and then from one lightship to another across the wide mouth of the Thames estuary. They passed the Shipwash lightship, with its ball at the mast-head, and the Long Sand, with its diamond, and then changed course a little so that they passed close by the Kentish Knock, which had a small ball on the top of a large one. They passed so near the Kentish Knock that they waved their hands to a man on the deck of the light-vessel and he waved his hand to them. Then they changed course again, steering a little west of south, for the Elbow buoy off the North Foreland. It was not a very clear day and for a long time they had been out of sight of land, and when they saw the North Foreland, with its steep chalk cliffs and the white lighthouse above them, they felt already like ancient mariners making a landfall after a long voyage.

They had had a fairly rough passage, too, but as the day wore on, Nancy and Titty had begun to feel better. The others had said nothing to them about their misfortune. None of the others had been seasick, but they could not be sure that they would not be, later on. Gradually, during the day, they had learnt how to keep their balance on the swaying deck of the little schooner. They had learnt the whereabouts of all the best things to which it was possible to hang on while moving about. Captain Flint had divided them into watches, too. He was taking the port watch, because in the saloon he sat in the arm-chair at the port end of the table and Peter Duck, who sat in the arm-chair at the starboard end, was to take the starboard watch. Lists were made by John and copied out on a sheet of paper pinned up inside the deckhouse:

Port Watch	Starboard Watch
CAPTAIN FLINT	MR DUCK
NANCY	JOHN
PEGGY	SUSAN
TITTY	ROGER

These lists looked all right, but Titty and Roger were not to keep regular watches, but to make themselves useful when wanted, and, as Captain Flint said, they couldn't expect the mates to do the cooking and be on duty at the same time and half the night as well. But it was a good thing to have the list so that all knew their proper places.

"But aren't we going to stop somewhere for the night?" asked Peggy.

"What for?" said Captain Flint.

"Sailing in the dark?"

"Why not? It's a grand night and a fine wind, and we're lucky to have it."

It was just about Roger's bedtime, and a late

bedtime at that, when they had the North Foreland abeam. Roger wanted to be allowed to stay
up, but Susan and Captain Flint would have none
of it, though it was agreed that Roger should be
waked if the engine was wanted during the night.
Titty, too, was sent off to bed, but she did not
mind because she had got well enough to have
some Yarmouth bloater for supper (she had only
sucked an orange for dinner, like Nancy, though
the others were eating hot mutton chops) and she
thought that if she lay down at once she might be
able to keep herself from being sick. At dusk she
took a last look round on deck, and a last look at
the black schooner that had followed them down
the coast all day, and then, determined to be better in the morning, hurried down below and was
lying flat in her bunk just as soon as she had been
able to get there. Susan and Peggy were allowed to
stay up some time, partly on the excuse of doing a
little washing up, but when they had had a good
look at the rows and clusters of flickering lights
that marked Broadstairs and Ramsgate, they too
were urged to go below.

"I'd send the whole crew to bed," said Captain
Flint, "but four eyes are better than two, and we'll
be sailing through the Downs to the bottle-neck of
the Channel, and there'll be a lot of shipping. I'm
taking the first watch tonight, and Mr Duck and
John'll be wise to get all the sleep they can now,
for they'll be on duty at midnight when Nancy and
I'll be going to our bunks. How are you, Nancy?"

"Quite all right," said Nancy stoutly.

"Fine," said Captain Flint. "Put an extra sweater on and keep the rest of this watch with me."

The four of them went below, Susan and Peggy to settle down for the night, Nancy to get some warm things, and John to lie down after borrowing Susan's alarm clock, setting it to go off at ten minutes to twelve and putting it under the pillow of his bunk.

Mr Duck had lit the side lights some time before they were needed. He had gone forward to have a look at them, to see that they were still burning brightly, green to starboard, red to port, to show any other vessel she might meet in the darkness which way the *Wild Cat* was going. He was busy now making sure that the lamp inside the deckhouse should throw its clear light on the compass so that the steersman, from outside, could see it plainly through the little window. As soon as he was satisfied with that, he put his head out of the deckhouse door and looked aft, as Titty had, to see if the following schooner was still there. There were a good many lights about, and he did not stay to make sure.

"You'd better get your sleep, Mr Duck," said Captain Flint. "You've only an hour or two."

"Aye, aye, sir," said the old seaman. He took his old head in again, laid him down on the starboard bunk in the deckhouse and began to snore, an easy, comfortable, mellow snoring, as soon as his head touched the rolled-up coat that he always liked better than a pillow.

Nancy came on deck with a scarf wound round her neck and an oilskin coat over her sweater.

"Hullo," she said, as she came round the deckhouse to the wheel and heard that steady snore, "Mr Duck's asleep."

"Good man he is," said Captain Flint. "That's
the way to do it. Waste no time in counting sheep
but go to sleep as you hit the pillow and wake up
ready for any job that offers. That's the sailor's
way."

"What's that light over there? Playing tricks."

"Over where?"

"Broad on the port side," Nancy chuckled.

"That's better," said Captain Flint. "North Goodwin lightship. Three flashes together once a minute. We're going inside the Goodwins. Come along
now and take the wheel and see what you make
of compass steering in the dark. South by west's
the course."

"Sou' by west it is," said Nancy, taking over
the wheel.

"That's the style," said Captain Flint, and
though Nancy could not see his face, she knew
he was smiling. "Keep your mind on the compass
card and on steering a straight course and you'll
have no time to be seasick." And with that he
left her to it and went forward along the deck, to
listen to the water under the *Wild Cat's* forefoot
and the wind in the rigging and to feel that he
too, like Peter Duck, was glad to be at sea again.
"Go anywhere," the old man had said. And why
not? He came aft again.

"And what did you think of that yarn of
Mr Duck's last night?" he said.

"Jolly good story," said Nancy.

"Yes," said Captain Flint rather tamely.

But Nancy did not notice his disappointment.
She had quite enough to think of with the steering wheel in her hands, and the compass card in

its bowl behind the window restlessly swinging.
The line at the back of the bowl never marked
the same point of the compass for ten seconds
together. Now south, now south-south-west, and
Nancy busy with the wheel trying her hardest to
steady it on a point between the two. And Captain
Flint had much to think of, besides the strange
tale of buried treasure. Every now and then he
would dive into the deckhouse, make a mark on
the chart on the table there and hurry out once
more. Every time he opened the deckhouse door
Peter Duck's snoring sounded louder.

"There's something grand about that snoring,"
said Captain Flint at last.

"We hardly need those foghorns," said Nancy,
"not if we can count on him to be asleep at the
right moment."

On and on through the summer night, the
Wild Cat hurried on her way. It was as if she, too,
were glad to be out of harbour at last and bound
for somewhere or other. Her green starboard light
glowed on the foam that churned away to leeward.
The cool wind plucked at the steersman's hair
under her stocking cap. She turned to Captain
Flint who was standing beside her, dimly lit by
the light from the compass window.

"I should never have thought she'd go so
fast with such a little wind."

"But it isn't a little wind," said Captain Flint.
"It's a rattling good one, and you would think it
half a gale if we were going the other way and
had to beat against it."

On and on the *Wild Cat* hurried through the
Downs. Here and there were the riding-lights of

coasters anchored in shelter, waiting to go north with the change of the tide. Through the Gull Channel the little schooner passed, and Captain Flint and Nancy saw how the Brake lightship, straining at her anchor, pitched as the seas passed under her, so that the red light flashing from her mast seemed to be trying to scratch half-circles in the sky. Other light-vessels were in sight for a time. There was the East Goodwin flashing out once every ten seconds away on the other side of those dangerous sands. There was the South Goodwin with its two flashes twice a minute. There was the blaze of Deal town, and the South Foreland light, high above the cliff, flashing ceaselessly, urgently, once every two and a half seconds, was unmistakable away there on the starboard bow. Each lightship and lighthouse had its own message to give in the language of flashes, and Captain Flint, checking the flashes with his stopwatch, knew where he was as well as if it had been broad daylight. Then, besides these lights, which were the signposts of the sea, there were all the moving lights of the traffic making use of them, white mast-head lights above red and green sidelights showing the steamships, and reds and greens with no mast-head lights showing the sailing vessels. The nearer the *Wild Cat* came to the Channel the more lights there were to be seen as big and little ships crowded together entering or leaving the North Sea. A huge liner bound for the East out of London river came racing southwards towards the Channel, a tremendous mass of lights like a runaway town in the dark.

Now and then Captain Flint took over the

wheel, and left Nancy to count flashes and watch the moving lights, but she felt safer from seasickness when she was thinking of the steering of the ship.

At midnight the South Foreland light was abeam. There was no sign of John, and they had only to listen to hear the steady snore of Peter Duck still sounded from the deckhouse.

"What do you say, Nancy," said Captain Flint. "Time to call the starboard watch. But we can carry on a bit longer without jibing, and when we do jibe we'll want their help and they'll want ours. Shall we let them sleep till we're fairly round the Foreland?"

"Shiver my timbers," said Nancy, "I'd like to carry on all night."

"Another half-hour'll be enough," said Captain Flint. "But I'm glad to hear you shivering timbers again."

*

The little alarm clock had done its best and John, fast asleep, had dreamed a bee was buzzing near his ear. But, tired though he was, he had gone to sleep thinking hard of the time when he would have to go on watch. He knew he had to wake at midnight, and in spite of sleeping through the buzzing of that bee, he did indeed wake not many minutes later. Had that alarm gone off? He reached under the pillow for the clock. A faint light came through the door from the saloon, but it was not enough to see the time by. He ought to have thought of that and put a pocket torch in his bunk. He lowered himself down so as not to wake the sleeping Roger in the lower bunk, and slipped through into the saloon. The lantern was swinging wildly over the table, but one glance at the clock was enough for John. Peter Duck must have gone on watch without him. He slipped back into the cabin, grabbed from behind the door the oilskin coat that he had been looking forward to wearing, dodged back into the saloon, round the table, up the companion stairs, and almost tumbled round the deckhouse in his hurry.

"I'm awfully sorry I'm late, Mr Duck." He had begun to say it before he saw that Nancy and Captain Flint were still at the wheel.

"You're not the only one," said Captain Flint.

"Listen," said Nancy.

John listened. There was the noise of water, the noise of wind, but close at hand there was a very different noise, a steady, contented, confident snore.

"Shall I wake him?" said John.

"May as well now," said Captain Flint.

John went into the deckhouse, hesitated just a moment, and then plucked respectfully at the figure in the starboard bunk.

In one single second the snoring stopped, Mr Duck was awake, was sitting up, and had a foot already on the deckhouse floor.

"Isn't it our turn?" said John.

"You may be sure it is that," said Peter Duck, as he hurried out of the deckhouse door, pulling an old muffler round his neck, cramming on a sou'wester, and shuffling an oilskin round his shoulders. "Been too long ashore," he said. "Don't keep watches on the *Arrow of Norwich.*

You shouldn't have let me sleep, sir. What's the course, Cap'n Nancy?"

"Sou' by west."

"Sou' by west it is," said Peter Duck.

"We'll be changing the course in another ten minutes," said Captain Flint, "and we'll have the booms to shift over."

For a few minutes they were all four together by the wheel. Peter Duck took a look about him. "Doing well, she is. There's the Varne. Opening up Dover lights. Fast little packet she is and all."

Then came the bustle of changing course.

"Will you handle her, Cap'n John, while we look after them booms?" said Peter Duck.

"You've done it in daylight," said Captain Flint.

"It feels a bit funny in the dark," said John.

"Don't worry about the dark. You watch the compass. Keep her south by west a minute or two longer."

"What'll the new course be?"

"Sou'-west by west."

"I steered nearly all our watch," said Nancy.

"Don't talk to the man at the wheel," said Captain Flint. "You come along forward with me to tend jib and staysail sheets."

"I'll never find them in the dark," said Nancy.

"You'll have to learn," said Captain Flint. "Come along. Any time you like, Mr Duck."

"We might get them over now," said Mr Duck.

Nancy and Captain Flint disappeared. John, with his eyes fixed on the glowing compass card inside the window, was yet aware of Mr Duck busy with the mainsheet. Captain Flint came aft again to help him.

"Luff," cried Peter Duck, and as John brought the *Wild Cat* a little nearer to the wind he heard the creaking of blocks as the sheets were hauled in.

"Bear away now."

"South-west," said John aloud. "South-west by west. West-south-west." Over went the boom with a great creaking, but none of the violence he had expected, and John, putting her now on the new course, knew that Captain Flint and Peter Duck were letting the sheets out again and making them fast.

"South-west by west," said Peter Duck sharply.

"South-west by west it is," said John.

Captain Flint had hurried forward again to help Nancy with the sheets of the headsails.

"Well, that's that," said Captain Flint a few minutes later, as they came aft. "She'll do unless the wind changes."

"It's not going to do that," said Peter Duck.

"Skip along down, Nancy," said Captain Flint. "You've done jolly well. Go and get your sleep now."

No one would have guessed from Nancy's cheerful "Good night" that she had been seasick all that day.

"Good night," called Captain Flint. "Well, Mr Duck, I'm turning in, too. I'll take on again at four." He went into the deckhouse and John and Peter Duck had the ship to themselves, just as Captain Flint and Nancy had had her before them.

*

It was pitch dark now, but the Narrows were

ablaze with lights, and Peter Duck was checking them over as if he were an old hen counting chickens. Anybody would have thought he had invented those lights, it was so clear that he was pleased to be seeing them again.

"There's France that is. Cape Griz Nez. Aye, and there's Folkestone. Now you see them Dover lights. Last time I were past here there were the *Prooshian*, five-masted German, piled up under the cliffs just east'ard of them lights."

Peter Duck was looking all round him, recognising in the darkness the places he had known twenty years before. But presently he remembered something else.

"Cap'n Flint say anything about the *Viper* when you come on deck?"

"No," said John. "I forgot about her. I wonder where she is now."

"I wouldn't say no to you if you was to tell me that was her," said Peter Duck.

"What?"

"Over the starboard quarter now. Them lights."

John looked round. Away there in the dark were a red and green light close together. As he watched them, the red light disappeared. The green light was left alone. John glanced down at the compass, and when he looked back again the green light was showing on the port quarter.

"Sailing vessel, that's certain," said Peter Duck. "And I'm just a-wondering if that ain't the *Viper*. One green light's much like another, and you can't tell t'other from which, but seems to me that vessel's got her eye on us. She's not steering a course. See! There's her port light, red again. Now

it might very easy be that Black Jake was holding
of her wheel. Well, skipper's set a course, and it's
not for us to change it, but I doubt he wouldn't
mind us finding out if that vessel ain't following
us and not shaping no course of her own. Just you
let me have the wheel."

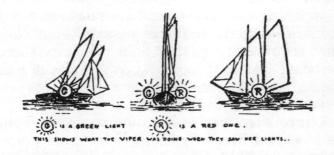

:G: IS A GREEN LIGHT   :R: IS A RED ONE.
THIS SHOWS WHAT THE VIPER WAS DOING WHEN THEY SAW HER LIGHTS.

Peter Duck spun the wheel and suddenly headed the *Wild Cat* in, as if for the lights of
Folkestone.

"You tell me what lights she shows us."

"Red and green," said John.

"Heading down Channel same as us. Now then?"

"Green light's gone," said John.

"I thought so," said Peter Duck. "She's headed
in to see what we're going to do in Folkestone."

Once more he spun the wheel and put the
Wild Cat back on her course. "Aye," he said,
"and now he'll show his green and come after
us again." As he spoke the green light shone out
again beside the red, the red disappeared, and
the other vessel was once more heading down
Channel.

"The *Viper* sure enough," said Peter Duck. "Plain as talking that was."

"But why?" said John.

"He thinks I'm taking you to Crab Island," said Peter Duck. "That's what it is. He'd better have left me in Lowestoft, had the skipper." And then suddenly he spoke of other things. "You and me's got this vessel in charge," he said, "and ought to be watching our course, and keeping a look out, and picking up the lights as they falls due. Now, what should you say that light was, over there, starboard bow, flashing away as if it was in a bit of a hurry about something?"

"I don't know," said John.

"Dungeness, that is, and if it was daylight, we'd see the fine black tower of it, a proper candlestick, a black tower with a white belt about its middle and a white lantern and gallery to it overhead, a good mark from anywhere, and we'd be seeing Lloyd's signal station, and the red house where they make the fog signals, and the little white tower that holds a low light down near the end of the point. There's more than one man taken his ship into shoal water for not knowing Dungeness and mistaking a water tower there is inland for Dungeness high light. And then beyond Dungeness we'd be seeing Fairlight Church, another good mark for poor sailormen coming up Channel with their stomachs sickened of salt pork. I've come right up Channel before now and known that be the first land we sighted, that and Beachy Head and before we sighted them nothing at all but the noise of foghorns, and us groping our way in blind and

wishing all steamships was at the bottom of
the sea."

Roger, of course, would have gone on asking
questions about Black Jake and the *Viper*, but
John knew at once that Mr Duck did not want
to talk about them just then, so he asked no
more, though now and again he glanced over
his shoulder to see the green light belonging to
the sailing vessel that had altered course when
they had, still not very far away over the port
quarter. The other vessel, whatever she was, was
keeping her distance and following the *Wild Cat*
down Channel. John wondered if Black Jake was
at the wheel and if that red-haired boy they had
fished out of the harbour was watching for the
Wild Cat just as he himself was looking away into
the dark for the green starboard light of the *Viper*.
If indeed that vessel was the *Viper*. Well, morning
would show that, and John put most of his mind
into steering a straight course. This was better
than that night when he had sailed *Swallow* in
the dark and all the lights had gone out, and he
had so nearly run her on a rock.

And then, at last, a faint light began to
lift in the eastern sky. Looking north, John
could see once more where the sea ended and
the land began. The water was no longer black
but a dull grey. White tops of waves showed in
the dark, moving splashes of white long before
the shapes of the waves that carried them could
be seen. Away there, over the port quarter, a
green starboard light was still showing, but they
could see now that the vessel that carried it was
a dark schooner, shadowy in the dim light before

the dawn, swaying along down Channel, not more than half a mile off.

Captain Flint, yawning and rubbing his eyes, came out of the deckhouse, pulling an old tweed hat down over his head and buttoning his jacket over his muffler. It was four o'clock in the morning.

"Dungeness abeam, sir," said Peter Duck.

"Wind's holding well," said Captain Flint. He looked round the sky until he saw the shadowy shape of the sailing vessel over the port quarter.

"That schooner," he said. "But where's her topsail?"

"She didn't want to pass us," said Peter Duck. "Took it in for the night."

"You're sure she's that neighbour of ours."

"I do think just that," said Peter Duck.

"Sou'-west by west," said John as Captain Flint took the wheel.

"Sou'-west by west," repeated Captain Flint. "Down you go now and get all the sleep you can."

"Shall I call Nancy?"

"No. It's light enough now. I shan't want her."

"Good night," said John. "At least it's good morning really."

"See you at breakfast," said Captain Flint. "You too, Mr Duck. I'm all right. Your watch below."

John went off round the deckhouse and down the companion. If anybody had been awake to see him come down they would have wondered why he was smiling to himself, a broad, happy smile. John was extremely happy. He had kept his first night

watch at sea. And most of the time he had been
steering. Nancy was not the only one who could
say that. He went into his cabin. A little light from
the saloon showed him Roger fast asleep in the
lower bunk. John caught himself almost laughing
from happiness. This time he slipped quietly out of
his clothes and into his pyjamas before he climbed
into his bunk. It was sloping the other way now.
For a moment or two he lay awake. The water
creaming along the side of the ship sounded quite
different down here, where you heard it just the
other side of the planking. Quite different. And
up on deck it must be getting lighter and lighter.
The night was over. John pushed his nose into his
pillow and fell asleep.

CHAPTER IX

BEACHY HEAD TO THE WIGHT

Down below everybody overslept again, and when they woke and came running up on deck in their pyjamas, they found Peter Duck at the wheel, and Captain Flint waiting for his breakfast, looking a little sleepy, but enjoying a morning pipe, sitting on the roof of the deckhouse, dangling his heels, and watching a black schooner, her grey canvas almost white in the sunshine, sailing along on the port quarter, just where John looked for her the moment he came up out of the companion.

"Still there," said John.

"The *Viper*," said Titty.

"Perhaps she wants to race," said Nancy.

"She can outsail us if she wants. Carries more canvas," said Peter Duck.

"We'll get breakfast over," said Captain Flint, "and then we'll set topsails and see what she does. What have you two mates to say for yourselves? Here are us poor sailormen starving for something hot."

"Sorry, sorry," said Susan. "Come on, Peggy. I put some quaker oats to soak last night. Will you broach two tins of milk? We'll give them boiled eggs and do our getting up afterwards. You fly down, Titty, and get dressed."

"Go ahead then," said Captain Flint, "and John and Roger can have a bit of a bath. There's a canvas bucket with a rope to it."

"I'll just go down and let Gibber out," said
Roger. "I'll get the towels at the same time."

"Bring them up the forehatch," said John.
"What's that lighthouse right under the cliff?"

"Beachy Head. We're getting along. We couldn't
have had a luckier slant of wind."

A minute or two later, the forehatch was
pushed open from below. Gibber came out, shivered a little, and then, making up his mind that
things were not so bad, climbed up the capstan and
sat there making faces at the wind. Roger pushed
the towels up and came after them. Then John and
Roger took their clothes off, tossed them down the
forehatch, and closed it to keep them dry. John
went to the lee side, threw his bucket forward at
the end of its rope and hauled it up again as the
schooner swept him past it. The first time or two
he got very little water. Once he waited too long
and had the bucket nearly pulled out of his hands.
But he soon learnt the trick, more or less, and he
and Roger took turns, emptying buckets of water
over each other. At the first splash the monkey
leapt from the capstan, ran to the foremast, and
raced up the wooden hoops of the foresail to the
gaff jaws and above them to the cross-trees,
where it stopped, leaning down and chattering
with anger, while John and Roger sluiced the
water about on the deck far below.

Cold water, bright sunshine and the clear
green and white of Beachy Head somehow made
it hard for John to believe the sort of things he
had found easy to believe last night. This morning
the black schooner over there looked in no way
different from other sailing vessels. She was the

Viper all right. There was no doubt of that, but sunshine and cold water made it hard to believe that it was not mere accident that brought her down Channel in such close touch with the *Wild Cat*. After all, they had left Lowestoft very soon after each other.

But when John and Roger had dressed and cleaned their teeth (Susan had put her head out of the galley to remind Roger not to forget to clean his) and they came on deck again and found Titty and Nancy waiting about very ready for their breakfast, John told Nancy what had happened while he and Peter Duck had been keeping watch together. Nancy seemed to think it real enough.

"He wants to do something beastly," she said, "after being ducked in the harbour like that."

"He's probably a real pirate," said Titty. "Not like Captain Flint. A bad one. He looks it, with those ear-rings."

They hung on to the shrouds and looked across the waves at the black schooner that was so steadily keeping pace with them.

"He's probably going to have another look at those crabs," said Roger.

"That's what Mr Duck thinks," said Nancy.

They looked aft at the broad back of Captain Flint, sitting on the roof of the deckhouse. Just then the bell was banged suddenly and close behind their backs by Peggy, and they looked round to see Susan, also dressed, disappearing down the companion with a great saucepan of steaming porridge.

"How did you get dressed?" said Nancy. "You can't have washed."

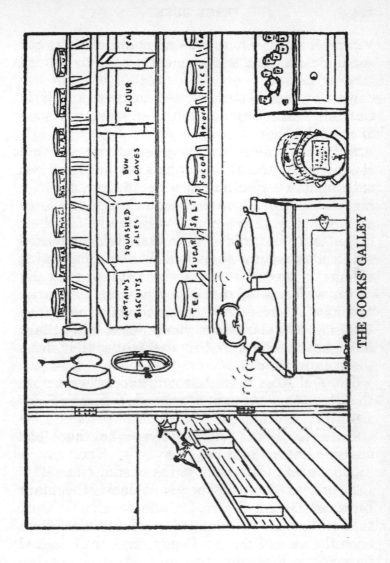

THE COOKS' GALLEY

"We took turns," said Peggy. "I stirred the pot while Susan went below and then she stirred and I bolted down."

"Never was better pleased to hear a bell in my life," said Captain Flint, slipping down off the deckhouse roof and sweeping them with him down to breakfast. "Hurry up now, and let me get it over, so that Mr Duck can come down. Take him up a mug of coffee, Titty, to be going on with."

*

Sunshine and cold water had made John doubtful for a moment if he had really seen those lights change in the dark as the *Viper* followed exactly the movements of the *Wild Cat*. But now, after breakfast, in broad daylight, something happened that made it clear to everybody aboard that Black Jake was indeed watching everything they did.

Captain Flint let John and Nancy take the wheel and steer the schooner, heading west now, to pick up the Owers lightship, while he and Peter Duck brought out the topsails, and presently set them, after Roger with some monkey nuts had coaxed Gibber down out of the way. The topsails made a great difference to the speed of the *Wild Cat*, and at once she began to leave the black schooner astern.

"This'll settle it," said Captain Flint, coming aft with the old seaman and taking up the glasses to look at the *Viper*.

Almost as he spoke, Peter Duck said, "Can you see what they're doing by the foremast?"

Up to the foremast head of the *Viper* loose canvas climbed, opened, spread out, and presently filled all the space between mast-head and gaff. The *Viper* lost no more ground.

"She could leave us hull down if Black Jake were to set both topsails," said Peter Duck, after watching to see if the *Viper* was going to set a topsail above her main. "But it isn't that he had in mind."

"It certainly looks very queer," said Captain Flint.

"It'll look queerer yet," said Peter Duck.

"Well," said Captain Flint, "the sea's free to all, and if that fellow likes to waste his time running down Channel after us, it's no concern of ours."

"He'll make it ours before all's done," said Peter Duck.

"He'll be sorry for it if he does," said Captain Flint.

*

All the rest of that day everybody aboard the *Wild Cat* was watching the *Viper* and wondering what it was that Black Jake hoped to do, following them like this. That first day, coming out of Lowestoft and sailing through the Downs, the *Viper* had been little more to them than another vessel sailing in the same direction. Besides, they were at sea. They had begun their voyage. Nobody can think of everything at once. And that day it had been enough for them to learn to keep their footing on slanting decks, to watch the land slipping by, and buoys, the lightships and the traffic. Black Jake had somehow belonged to

Lowestoft harbour and that they had left behind.
They hardly thought of him. Peter Duck's yarn,
too, had been a splendid story but it had been a
story of the distant past. It had explained why
Black Jake had been inquisitive. It was only
today that they began to understand that perhaps the story was not over and that perhaps
Black Jake and Peter Duck, the *Viper* and the
Wild Cat, and even they themselves were at that
very moment taking a part in it. It was a grand
day and perfect sailing, white tops to the waves,
a blue sky and a steady north-east wind from off
the land. Land was always in sight to the northward, the south Downs showing green behind
the coast-line and its watering-places, Shoreham,
Worthing, Littlehampton, Bognor. But the Swallows and Amazons saw little of it. They were
shaking down into the routine of life aboard ship,
and dinner that day was at the proper time, but
when they were not actually cooking, or steering,
or swabbing down decks, or showing each other
that they had not forgotten the names of all the
ropes, they were watching the *Viper*, thinking of
Black Jake's voyage to Crab Island, remembering
his angry face when the parrot, knowing nothing
about it, had blurted out its hint of treasure in the
"Pieces of eight!" that Nancy had spent so long in
teaching it, and wondering what life was really
like for the red-haired Bill; and if, indeed, he had
been pushed overboard or had simply fallen in,
that time when they had fished him out.

And then, towards evening, after tea, when
they had passed the Owers lightship and were
steering for the Nab Tower, something happened

that changed their feelings yet again. It was simply this, that Black Jake set a topsail over his
mainsail and the *Viper* at once drew level with
the *Wild Cat* and began to run away from her.

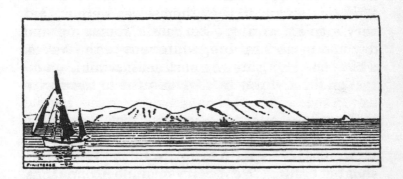

"She's winning like anything," said Roger.
"Hadn't we better start the engine?"

"Just call Mr Duck, somebody," said Captain
Flint, a little later. The old seaman was getting
some sleep, but he came out of the deckhouse in
a moment, and, as usual, looked astern for the
black schooner.

"She's passed us," said Captain Flint. "What
do you make of that?"

"Crowding on sail," said Peter Duck. "Both
topsails. Black Jake's not the man to do anything
without he has a reason for it. What's he think's

coming?" He looked round the sky and sniffed the wind. Then he looked again at the black schooner, already far ahead of them.

"Looks to me," said Captain Flint, "that she's setting a course to pass outside the Wight."

"Maybe he thinks we're going to do the same, with us so far south."

"But crowding on sail?"

"Seems to me like he might be thinking the wind's going to drop and he's clapping on sail to come to an anchorage where he can hold on while the tide's running east against him."

"You don't think he's given up his game with us?"

"That man plays no games. We've not seen the last of him."

"Well," said Captain Flint. "We'll put him wrong about one thing. We'll carry on and let him think we're heading to pass outside the Wight and then we'll turn north by Bembridge Spit. He'll have to beat back then if he doesn't want to lose us. We've had a good run so far and if we can get to Cowes before the tide turns against us, there's no harm in all hands having a quiet night at anchor there, if you really think the wind's dropping. Not that it looks like it."

"If it wasn't for the *Viper* hurrying on I'd be thinking the wind would hold for a week. But he's one for knowing, is Black Jake."

Indeed the wind seemed to freshen. It drew a little towards the north, and the *Wild Cat* rushed along with the water foaming under her lee, while the *Viper*, under her press of canvas, was heeling over like a yacht and fairly racing for the shelter of the island. When at last Captain Flint and Peter Duck hauled in the sheets, and the *Wild Cat* changed course to pass north of the island, the *Viper* held on under all sail and was presently out of sight behind the Bembridge point.

"It seems almost funny without her," said Peggy.

"I wonder if the red-haired boy is thinking it seems funny without us," said Titty.

"There won't be much seems funny to him while he's sailing along of Black Jake," said Peter Duck.

And then he began pointing out the Warner lightship, and Spithead and the forts, and Portsmouth. And Captain Flint ran the ensign up to the peak of the mainsail and let Nancy dip it, just to see if anything happened, when a destroyer rushed by in the usual dreadful hurry about something or other. And something did happen. Although the destroyer was in such a hurry the ensign at her stern fluttered down for a moment and up again. And then there was a liner coming out, but somehow she did not notice the *Wild Cat's* salute. "Too proud, that sort," said Peter Duck. Generally, once the *Viper* was out of sight, they found it hard to believe they had been followed by her all the way from Lowestoft. The evening was just an ordinary summer evening, and they were enjoying their first sail in famous waters. They had passed Ryde and were nearing Cowes, and Susan and Peggy were thinking about getting supper, when suddenly the burgee dropped at the mast-head, the ensign dropped at the peak, the sheets slackened and the *Wild Cat* began to lose her speed.

The wind came again in a moment, but, some-how, just to know that Black Jake had guessed that the wind was going to drop, and that now it was actually dropping, made the chase seem real once more, and they began to wonder what was the anchorage Black Jake had had in mind when he had begun to hurry on. The *Wild Cat* was still moving fast through the water, but she was mov-ing slowly past the land. They knew that the tide had turned against them and that the wind would not for long be strong enough to carry them over it. The wind grew fitful. There were a great many yachts in the anchorage at Cowes and the little green schooner picked her way through them, moving more and more slowly.

"Let fly staysail sheets. Get the headsails down."

The *Wild Cat* stemmed the tide no longer.

"Let go starboard anchor." Down it went, and John and Nancy grinned at each other, both remembering Black Jake's ducking at the same moment.

"Give her fifteen fathom, Mr Duck."

There was hurried work on deck lowering the sails.

"We won't put the covers on," said Captain Flint.

"We'll be getting the wind again in the morn-ing," said Peter Duck.

And so, temporarily, and as if unwillingly, the *Wild Cat* brought up at Cowes, ready to sail on when the wind would take her. Her crew looked at each other. There was still a steady swirl of water past the ship's sides, but that was only the tide. Close by were the houses of Cowes, the inns with gardens above the water, the old grey building of

the Squadron, the houses up the hill, the yachts
at anchor with dinghies and launches going busily
to and from the landing places. For the first time
since leaving Lowestoft, the *Wild Cat* was at rest.
The houses were not moving. She was not moving
past the houses. John, Nancy, and Titty looked at
each other. Yes, they were all feeling it. It was as
if something had gone out of the ship.

Captain Flint, busy with Peter Duck putting
tyers round the sails, was still thinking of the
Viper. "I almost wish we had him still in sight,
Mr Duck," Nancy heard him say. "I hate to think
of him going off to have another dig at your
island."

Just then Peggy rang a bell at the door of the
galley, and at the same moment there was the
noise of oars close alongside and a voice hailed
them from the water, "Anybody for the shore?"

Captain Flint jumped up. "Why, yes," he said.
"I think there is. Who wants ices?"

"Supper's ready," said Susan.

"Let's have it later," said Peggy. "It's a cold
supper."

"It'll seem beautifully hot after the ices," said
Roger.

"I'm going, anyway," said Captain Flint. "Anybody else can come who wants. What about you,
Mr Duck?"

"Too old for ice-creams," said Mr Duck, "and
I'm not that set on shore. I'm staying by the ship."

"We shan't be long. Hurry up, you others. What
time do the shops close here? What? Already?
Hurry up then. Just as you are."

He threw the ladder over, and everybody,

except Peter Duck, crowded down into the shore boat. Peter Duck was busy with the big hurricane lantern getting ready to hoist it on the forestay. The boatman pulled away for the landing, and as they looked back towards the *Wild Cat*, they saw a white riding-light climb slowly up her forestay. Peter Duck was putting her to sleep.

Almost all the shops of Cowes were shut, as Captain Flint had feared, but he found a confectioner's open, with a notice in the window to say that Chocolate and Vanilla Ices were For Sale.

He ordered a round of each, told the shopkeeper to keep the crew supplied, and said he had something to look for in the town. He hurried out of the shop. Half an hour later, when they were beginning their third round of ices, chocolate ones, he came back looking very hot and bothered.

"There isn't an ironmonger's open in the whole of this place."

"What was it you might be wanting, sir?" asked the shopkeeper.

"Spades," said Captain Flint, to the astonishment of his crew.

"You won't get them, not as late as this," said the man, "and I don't suppose what I've got would be any use to you."

Hanging up under the ceiling were a lot of the sort of toys that sweetshops keep in seaside towns. There were model boats, some of them, as Roger noticed, with quite a decent lot of lead on their keels. There were buckets with "A Present from Cowes" painted on them. There were string bags full of coloured indiarubber balls. The shopman half closed the door to get at the things that were hanging up behind it, and took down a toy spade, an iron one with a varnished wooden handle.

"Would this be any good, sir?" he asked.

Captain Flint tried the blade of it, between his finger and thumb.

"All right for digging in sand," he said.

"That's what it's meant for," said the man.

"Better than nothing," said Captain Flint. "How many have you got?"

"Only these two," said the man, taking another down from behind the door. "We're expecting a new stock next week, if you could call again."

"I'll take the two of them," said Captain Flint.

"And buckets to match, sir?"

"Eh? Buckets? No, thank you."

The man tied the two spades together, wrapped them up in paper, and used a lot of string on them, as if they were really good.

The crew finished up their ices, and said, "No, thank you," when they were offered another round.

"What do you want those spades for?" asked Roger, when the ices had been paid for, and they were all hurrying out into the street.

"There isn't a spade in the ship," said Captain Flint. "And I've only just noticed. Ridiculous. And I thought I'd fitted her out with everything." And he strode down the middle of the road, carrying his paper parcel.

"These aren't very good ones," said Roger, when they were getting into the boat to be rowed back to the ship.

"I know that," said Captain Flint. "I hope the ices were better."

"The ices were quite all right," said Roger. "And the glasses weren't half as thick as they are in some shops."

CHAPTER X

CAPTAIN FLINT'S FIDGETS

"UNCLE Jim's got it again," said Nancy. She was sitting on the top of the capstan on the foredeck of the *Wild Cat*, watching the yachts at Cowes reflected in the smooth oily water. They had had a good night below decks, though in the deckhouse Captain Flint and Peter Duck had been talking still, when the last of their crew had fallen asleep. Breakfast was over, a very early one. Roger was sitting on the edge of the forehatch, playing with Gibber. Titty was hoisting the parrot's cage on the forestay in place of the riding-light that had hung there all night. Peggy and Susan were peeling potatoes, John was leaning over the bulwarks watching the anchored vessels, which were heading all ways in the slack water, and wondering when they would begin to show that the tide was turning west.

"What's he got?" asked Peggy.

"Just look at him," said Nancy. "He's just like he was the last time he went off to the Malays. Or was it Java? Don't you remember how he used to prance up and down the houseboat? It's a sort of fidgets."

They all looked aft. Peter Duck was sitting there on a little canvas stool he had brought out of the deckhouse, busy putting a shine on the sidelights and the riding-light that he had on the deck beside him. He was working hard but with no hurry, enjoying his pipe and the morning sunshine, content with everything. But Captain Flint was walking up and down the deck from the wheel to the mainmast and back, lighting his pipe again and again and throwing the matches overboard. He looked as if he did not know whether the sun was shining or not. Suddenly he stopped short, as if he had made up his mind about something, but then he shook his head and went on walking up and down with his pipe in one hand and a matchbox in the other.

"It was just the same before he went to South America," said Nancy.

"He looks awfully Captain Flintish," said Titty.

"That's what he's feeling like," said Nancy. "He's just bursting to go off somewhere and do something."

"To show that he hasn't quite retired?"

"Something like that. When he feels too retired he always tries to dash off."

"So he could with a ship like this," said Titty. "I heard Mr Duck say so."

"It's Mr Duck's story that's stirred him up so. And then knowing that Black Jake was going off to have another dig. I knew what he was thinking of when he went and bought those spades last night."

"I say," said John, who had been listening, but saying nothing. "Anybody been into the deckhouse this morning? Did you notice the chart they had on the table?"

"The English Channel," said Nancy.

"It wasn't," said John. "It was a chart of the Caribbees."

"Pheew!" said Nancy. "But I might have guessed it."

*

Captain Flint walked forward and joined them. At least, he had a look over the bows at the anchor chain which was hanging straight up and down. Then he shifted one of the capstan bars in its place in the rack against the bulwarks. Then he had a look at all the halyards on the foremast. Then he said "Pretty Polly" to the parrot, but turned away sharply when the parrot sang out "Pieces of eight!" in reply. Then, for a minute or two, he stood looking down into the two buckets that stood between Susan and Peggy, one half full of potato peelings and the other with a lot of large white shiny potatoes in it just covered with water. Then, for the hundredth time that morning, he lit a match and was going to light his pipe with it, but stopped, looking at his pipe and thinking of something else, until the match burnt his fingers and he had to throw it overboard in a hurry.

"Spit it out, Uncle Jim," said Nancy, kindly enough. "We're all waiting."

"He's Captain Flint when he's afloat," said Titty.

"Jibbooms and bobstays!" said Nancy, "then what's he humming and hawing about?"

Captain Flint glanced aft. Peter Duck was comparing the two big copper sidelights and giving a last shine to the one he thought needed it most. Captain Flint made up his mind to speak.

"It's Mr Duck's story," he said at last. "You heard it, all of you. Well, what do you think about it?"

John and Nancy looked at each other, but said nothing.

"It's a fine story," said Titty, "especially that part about the crabs."

"If crabs are really as big as that," said Roger. "Have you ever seen crabs as big as that?"

"I wasn't thinking of the crabs," said Captain Flint. "It's the treasure. Mr Duck saw it buried. Saw it, mind you. That's Point One. Miles better than any old tale about a chart all covered with skeletons and red ink that one old sailor had from another who had it from his great-uncle who thought that his grandfather had been a lively fellow on the Spanish Main. Mr Duck saw the stuff buried. That's Point One . . ."

"He didn't say it was treasure, did he?" said Susan. "I thought he didn't know. It might be anything."

"I've been thinking about that," said Captain Flint. "It's so jolly hot in those West Indian islands that no man ever walked even half a mile there to bury something that he didn't think was well worth while keeping to himself. No. It stands to reason it was treasure. And Mr Duck himself saw it buried. Point One. Now. The two scoundrels who buried it were both drowned. No rival claims. They had no time to tell another soul about it. It's still there. It's as good as if Mr Duck had buried it himself. We know it was buried. Point One. We know that nobody knows where it was buried except Mr Duck. That's Point Two. It's the surest thing that ever was waiting to fall into anybody's mouth. It's like a bit of Euclid. Two things equal to the same thing are equal to each other. Q.E.D."

"What about Black Jake?" said Nancy.

"He knows where the island is, because he stole the bit of paper Mr Duck had sewed up in a scrap of old jacket," said Peggy.

"Right," said Captain Flint. "Black Jake is Point Three. He knows where the island is, but he doesn't know where the stuff was buried. Here's a man who sailed to Crab Island to look for it, didn't find it, because Mr Duck hadn't told him where to dig, and came back still thinking it such a likely place that he's off to have another try. Here's a man who goes half mad when he sees Mr Duck shipping with us, for fear he's going to show us where that stuff was buried. Black Jake's Point Three. He's seen the island and he's keener than ever."

"Perhaps he'll find it this time," said John.

"Not without Mr Duck to help him," said Captain Flint.

"Look here, Uncle Jim," said Nancy, "what do you want to do about it?"

"Well, I can't help thinking it's almost a crime to leave it there. A sure thing like that. I've been treasure-hunting all my life, but I've never been after a thing as sure as that. I must say I should like to bring it off, just for once."

"You know he never really has," said Nancy.

"It seems such a pity not to," said Captain Flint, "with a ship like this fairly stuffed with stores . . . and Mr Duck himself aboard her."

"But Mr Duck doesn't want to go to Crab Island ever again," said Titty.

"I know," said Captain Flint unhappily. "But he might change his mind."

"He wouldn't like Black Jake to have it, whatever it is," said Nancy.

"That's just it," said Captain Flint.

"But Black Jake's started probably already," said Roger. "We ought to be using our engine."

"Mr Duck thinks he's waiting for us."

"Well, let's go anyway," said Titty.

"Yes, let's go," said Susan. "Some time or other, when we've had a bit more practice. Let's go next year. It's the sort of thing that wants a lot of planning."

"I suppose you're right," said Captain Flint dully, after brightening up at the first words Susan had said. "And anyway, it's Mr Duck's treasure, and we can't very well go after it if he doesn't change his mind. But . . ." He stopped short.

Peter Duck had put the sidelights away and was coming along the deck.

"Vessels is beginning to swing," he said cheerfully, "and I feel a breath just now. And then another. It's coming down out of the north-east again. See that ripple yonder. If we was to start hoisting sail we'd be ready for it. There's no sense wasting an easterly when bound down Channel. Easterlies is rare."

They looked across towards Southampton Water. Vessels anchored by Cowes were beginning to swing, showing that the tide was turning. The *Wild Cat* was swinging, too, and, with the turn of the tide, a gentle breeze came out of the north-east, strengthening to a steady sailing wind.

"You're right, Mr Duck," said Captain Flint. "We'll make all the use we can of it. No harm

in that, anyway. All hands to make sail. You'll
have to shift that parrot off the forestay."

The potato peelings went flying over the side.
That strange green-feathered riding-light was
lowered and, shrieking "Pieces of eight!", was
carried below decks, like Gibber the monkey, in
order to be out of the way. Susan ran with the
potatoes to the galley, and put both buckets inside
the door. John, Nancy, and Peggy fitted capstan
bars, while Captain Flint and Peter Duck together hoisted up the sails. In a very few minutes the
crew were walking round the capstan to the old
tune of "Amsterdam," while Peter Duck was looking over the bulwarks to see the anchor come up,
and to sign to them when to stop. The *Wild Cat*
was off again.

When the bustle of getting under way was
over, and ropes were coiled down and the deck
cleared, Nancy went forward once more to her
seat on the capstan, taking Susan with her. The
others were all at the stern watching Peter Duck
at the wheel. Captain Flint was in the deckhouse,
looking at the chart.

"It's almost a pity we can't let him do it,"
said Nancy.

"Well, it's such a tremendous way," said Susan.

"It isn't really that that matters," said Nancy.
"It never matters how far you go. Exploring's only
going next door, but it's going on going next door
without turning back. But if there aren't any
shops on the way, what are you going to do? It
really all depends on you and Peggy making the
food and water last out."

"Of course there's an awful lot of food," said

Susan, "but we don't really know how much. Peggy and I have only just begun to go through the lists."

"If it wasn't for having all of us on board he'd be going," said Nancy.

"Yes," said Susan, "I suppose he would."

*

With wind and tide to help her, the *Wild Cat* soon passed Egypt Point. Cowes was no longer to be seen. A big liner with four funnels was coming up the Solent. "In from New York," said Captain Flint, who had come out from the deckhouse and was looking at the liner through binoculars.

"Water all the way," said Titty.

"What *do* you mean?" said Peggy. "Of course it's water all the way."

"That's the lovely thing about water. Salt water, I mean. It's not like the lake. Once you're on it, there's nothing to stop you going anywhere."

Captain Flint looked at her hopefully.

"There really isn't," he said. "Titty's quite right."

"May I look through the glasses?" said Roger.

The others came aft, and crowded into the deckhouse to look at the chart, to see just what was happening, and then crowded out again to look at buoys and landmarks and to make sure that they had seen right. It was a grand day now, of bright sunshine, with a steady, cool wind. It was enough to make anybody happy, just to be afloat and sailing, to see the green shores racing past, to see the bubbling wake slipping away astern, to see all the sails drawing, to hear now and then a gentle, low thrumming in the shrouds, to see the sunlight sparkle in the spray thrown out to leeward by the bows of the little schooner.

"I wish this was going on for ever," said Titty.

"No sense in stopping while this wind holds," said old Mr Duck, who was at the wheel, steering her so easily, so steadily that her bowsprit end drew only the tiniest of circles on the sky, and the compass seemed stuck in its bowl, and the wake the *Wild Cat* left astern might have been drawn with a ruler. There was need for careful steering now, for she was heading south-west through the Needles Channel, and the wind was dead aft.

"We seem to have lost Black Jake all right," said Nancy.

"He's probably gone back to look for us," said John.

"He's racing us," said Roger. "Miles ahead."

But just then, as the Needle Rocks, dark above the blue sunlit sea, drew into a line with the lighthouse on the last of them, and the little group in the stern of the *Wild Cat* could see past the point and behind the white, green-topped cliffs, Captain Flint gave a startled grunt. Peter Duck glanced over his shoulder.

"It's a rare bad anchorage that in most winds," he said, "but good enough in north-easterlies. He knew what was coming. Nothing to do but to lift his peaks and be after us again."

"Is it really the *Viper*?" asked Peggy, looking at a schooner that seemed to be airing her sails, anchored under the lee of the land.

"Of course it is," said Nancy. "There's his headsails going up. He's been waiting for us."

The sails of the black schooner filled, and slowly, sheltered by the land, she gathered way. The *Wild Cat* was no longer alone.

"But why did he wait for us?" said Peggy.

"What a galoot you are," said her sister. "Don't you see now? He thinks Mr Duck's sailing with us to show us where the treasure is. He means to come too."

"Well, it's waste of time for him," said Susan. "Won't he be mad when we turn round to go home?"

"But," said Titty, "if he doesn't want to lose us, why didn't he come to Cowes with us last night and anchor close by?"

"Why should he?" said Peter Duck. "That's not his way. He don't want to lose his men ashore, for one thing. Then he's told them he'd pick us up this morning coming out by the Needles. Well, here we are. That sort of thing sets a skipper up with his crew. You see, he's dead certain he knows the port we're bound for."

"I wish he was right," said Captain Flint.

CHAPTER XI

WORDS IN THE DARK

ANYBODY who had not known the truth and had just seen the *Wild Cat* and the *Viper*, sailing down Channel that bright summer morning, would have thought that they were friendly ships cruising in company. For the black schooner no longer kept its distance from the green, but sailed nearer and nearer, coming up first on one side and then on the other, luffing into the wind and waiting for the *Wild Cat*, and then swooping after her again. It was as if Black Jake wanted to show them that his was the faster vessel and that he did not mean to leave them.

Nobody liked it. Until that morning after leaving Cowes it had not occurred to any one of them, except, perhaps, to Peter Duck, that there was anything in the *Viper* of which they might have reason to be afraid. After all, what was she but another vessel, bowling down Channel, and sharing with them the same good wind? The English Channel is one of the great highways free to all the world. The *Viper* had as much right to be sailing down it as the *Wild Cat*. If she followed the *Wild Cat* from curiosity, why, as Nancy said, "A cat may look at a king, and why shouldn't a viper look at a cat?" "Specially a wild one," said Titty. But when it came to Black Jake's being so sure of them that he waited for them by the Needles, and then came sailing after them without any pretence that he was doing this by accident, nobody liked it at all.

It was like being followed about by some stranger in the street. The thought of it spoilt altogether what should have been a delightful bit of sailing. They had a grand run across the bay past St Alban's Head, far enough off shore to keep outside the race, but just not too far to let them see, through the glasses and the telescopes, the old ruined chapel on the top of the hill. Then, from a long way out to sea, they saw the long, low wedge of Portland Bill. Here, too, they passed outside the race, where, sometimes, the sea goes almost mad, flinging itself all ways at once, so that even in calm weather little ships keep clear of it if they can. But always, close to them, sailed their strange unwelcome consort, so near that they could see Black Jake at the wheel, and three or four other men, and once caught sight of the red-haired boy hurrying along the deck.

"This is a bit too much of a good thing," said Captain Flint at last. "I'll show him we don't want his company."

"We might try it," said Mr Duck, and he called all hands on deck.

Next time the *Viper* was a little ahead of the *Wild Cat*, Captain Flint suddenly put the helm down and luffed up under the *Viper*'s stern. The crew rattled in the sheets. Up she came into the wind. Jib and staysail were let fly. The *Wild Cat* paid off on the other tack and was heading back up Channel, for Portland and the Wight.

"He couldn't have a plainer hint than that," said Captain Flint.

"She's coming round," said Titty.

The *Viper* was doing exactly what the *Wild Cat* had done, and was heading up Channel in pursuit of her.

"We can't go back because of him," said Nancy. "Let's just take no notice at all."

"Hang the fellow," said Captain Flint.

"In Execution Dock," said Nancy.

"Jangling," said Titty, "in a lot of rusty chain."

And again they flung themselves on the sheets, and the *Wild Cat* went about once more, and settled down on her course for the Start. The *Viper* instantly came up into the wind and, as they passed her, they heard a jeering laugh. Black Jake was not to be shaken off by hints.

They were well on their way across the wide mouth of Lyme Bay, with the *Viper* still in close attendance, when the wind suddenly freshened. They saw the *Viper* heel right over as the first squall struck her, and even in the *Wild Cat* Susan and Peggy came up from the saloon in a hurry to know what was happening.

"What are you two doing down there?" Nancy asked, hanging on to the windward shrouds as the startled mates put their heads out of the companion-way.

"Counting up the stores," said Susan.

"Good for you," said Nancy. "I'd been hoping you would."

"Well, try to keep her a bit steadier," said Susan. "It's lucky everything's in tins."

For a minute or two the mates stayed on deck. It was as if some sudden miracle had been worked with the smiling blue sea of the morning. The wind was still coming from the north-east, but, after two or three fierce squalls, it had settled down to blow much harder than they had yet known it.

The sky had clouded, the waves were dark but for the white tops that blew across in white spray from one wave to the next.

"What about the engine now, Roger?" said John.

"I don't want to use the engine when she's really sailing," said Roger.

"Will she stand it?" said Captain Flint.

Peter Duck looked up to windward, and looked up at the bending masts, and aft at the long wake of white foam.

"She'll carry what she's got and not a stitch more," said Peter Duck. "Nine knots she'll do with this, and maybe ten. Aye. She'll stand this. Stiff enough. And we'll get the shelter of the Start."

"I'd been thinking of Brixham," said Captain Flint.

"We'll be down by the Scillies tomorrow if this holds. We'd best be making the most of it. Blowing itself out. That's what it is. And after that we'll likely get it hard from the west."

The *Wild Cat*, after those first squalls, settled down to run like a scalded cat as well as a wild one. With this great wind blowing over her quarter, Captain Flint held her steady on her course, and she fairly tore through the water.

And with the strengthening of the wind, the *Viper* seemed at first to have enough to think of without attending to the *Wild Cat*. She, too, seemed to be settling down to make the most of it. She raced away, a splendid sight, with the white spray leaping high from under her bows. The sailors of the *Wild Cat*, watching the *Viper* flying along like that, almost forgot how much they hated her. At dusk, she seemed to change her course, and they saw her heading northward, and then the dark came down and they saw her no more.

It was not until the middle of that night that they had news of her again.

It was just at the beginning of Peter Duck's watch. John and the old seaman had come on deck sharp at midnight, to take over, and Nancy and Captain Flint should have been on their way to their bunks. But Captain Flint had taken Mr Duck with him into the deckhouse again, to have a look at the chart and the barometer. They had gone in only for a moment, and with the wind that was blowing, Captain Flint had thought it as well that there should be two at the wheel. So Captain Nancy and Captain John were holding the ship on her course. It was a pitch dark night and they could see nothing outside the bulwarks except the flashing lights on Start Point and the Eddystone Lighthouse. Sky, land, and sea were all black, though patches of star-sprinkled sky showed now and then between the black clouds overhead. But there was nothing to worry about. Far away over the water, there were the lighthouses flashing their cheerful messages. The two captains knew where they were. They had a course to steer. The compass card glowed bright inside the window, and beyond it, if they stooped, they could see Captain Flint's hand, with a pencil in it, pointing to something on the

A·NIGHT·SCENE

WHEN·IT·IS·PITCHY·DARK·YOU·CANT·
SEE·ANYTHING·AT·ALL. Roger

chart. The sidelights were burning steadily. The shrouds were thrumming in the wind, and the *Wild Cat* was churning along at a really splendid pace.

And then, suddenly, a new noise came out of the darkness. It was the noise of water under the bow of another ship. It was a noise very close at hand. There was a shout somewhere to windward.

"Call them," said Nancy, and John thumped hard on the deckhouse door. Peter Duck and Captain Flint came tumbling out in a moment.

"There's a ship," said John, "close to us."

"Without lights," said Nancy.

At that instant, the *Wild Cat* came suddenly on an even keel. Her sails slackened and flapped dully. The green glow of her starboard light gleamed dimly on canvas where had been nothing but the blackness of the night. For one moment they all saw the glimmer of a light, not more than a dozen yards away. Another vessel, larger than theirs, was racing beside them in the dark.

"Keep your course," said Peter Duck, and John and Nancy felt his firm hand on the wheel.

"*Wild Cat*, ahoy!" A voice came out of the darkness, so near that it almost seemed that someone was talking just across the starboard bulwarks.

"Don't answer," said Peter Duck.

The voice came again, a jeering, lilting voice, like the voice of a chanty-man singing his words before the crew join in.

"Peter Duck! Peter Duck!"

"Don't say a word to them," said Captain Flint.

The voice came again, a hard voice, jeering as before.

"Where are you bound for, Peter Duck?"

John felt Nancy grip his arm.

The voice came again.

"Better ship along with us, Peter Duck."

And then from among that little group at the wheel of the *Wild Cat* came a voice that John and Nancy had never heard before, though it was the voice of Captain Flint, whom Nancy had known all her life. It was a roar more than a hail.

"Haul your wind there! Haul your wind, or, by crumbs, I'll sink your ship!"

There was a noise of sudden quarrelling in the other vessel. A deckhouse door swung open, and then closed again, throwing for a moment a light on struggling men.

"Look out," cried Peter Duck. "Her stern'll swing aboard us."

"Where's that fender?" said Captain Flint half under his breath, groping along the bulwarks.

Luckily it was not needed. Almost the vessels touched, but not quite, as the *Viper* drew ahead and hauled her wind. Voices came again, already farther off.

"Away to Rio. Away to Rio. Oh, fare you well, my bonny young maid, for we're bound for Rio Grande!"

"They've been getting at the rum," said Peter Duck.

Nancy loosened her grip on John's arm, and John, in the darkness, knowing that she could not see, allowed himself to rub the place.

"I say, Uncle Jim," said Nancy, "would you really have sunk them?"

"How could I?" said Captain Flint.

How could he, indeed? But, from that moment, John and Nancy knew that something had changed aboard the *Wild Cat*. Something had happened to bind Peter Duck and Captain Flint together. The *Viper* was an enemy now, for both of them, and not for Peter Duck alone. Captain Flint was not the sort of man to stand Black Jake's playing monkey tricks in the dark, tricks that might easily have damaged the *Wild Cat's* new paint, and, if there had been any nervousness in her steering, might even have ended in a serious collision.

"Time you went below, Nancy," said Captain Flint.

"All right," said Nancy, "but I'm coming up when it's our watch, and anyhow you'll call me if they come again."

"You shall have your whack at them if they try to board," said Captain Flint. He said it with a laugh, but anybody could tell from the way he said it that he no longer thought of the English Channel as so safe a highway that nothing of that kind was likely to happen.

That was the last they saw or heard of the *Viper* that night. She raced off again into the dark, and though Captain Flint took no more rest, so that there were three of them on deck keeping a keen look out, not knowing what next might come into BlackJake's dark mind, they saw no lights nor any other sign of her. It was not until Nancy came on deck again, sleepy-eyed, but eager for news, that they saw the black schooner again. She must have crossed their bows in the dark and waited for them, for when they first caught sight of her, in the first pale light of a grey morning, she was a couple of miles away to the south-east or perhaps rather more.

That great wind had swept them along at a tremendous pace. They had seen the flashing light on the Lizard first over the starboard bow and then abeam, and now it flashed out for the last time when they had already passed it and looking astern could see the steep cliffs of the Head, cold and grim against the dawn.

"Where are we going now?" said Nancy.

"To have a look at the Land's End and the Scillies," said Captain Flint. "And then, if the wind holds and that fellow won't leave us alone, we'll give him a run up to Ireland."

"We'd best get quit of him," said Peter Duck.

But the wind had blown itself out, as Peter Duck had thought it would. After sweeping them down from one end of the Channel to the other, it dropped to nothing. They had hardly steerage way through the water when the tide, running out of the Channel, carried them past the Land's End. The mates, the able-seaman, and the boy were dawdling over breakfast, hearing from Nancy of that wild business of the night that they had missed by being asleep. Captain Flint, Peter Duck, and John were on deck, looking at the lighthouses at the Longships and on the Wolf Rock, and at the black schooner which seemed, in spite of the lack of wind, to be creeping up to them again when, with only a few minutes' warning, they lost sight of everything in a thick blanket of white fog.

CHAPTER XII

BLIND MAN'S BUFF

In fog, mist, or falling snow . . . a sailing ship under way shall make with her foghorn, at intervals of not more than two minutes, when on the starboard tack one blast, when on the port tack two blasts in succession, and when with the wind abaft the beam three blasts in succession.

BOARD OF TRADE REGULATIONS

THE fog came suddenly, and with it a slow swell from the Atlantic, lifting the *Wild Cat* lazily up and dropping her gently down smooth hills and valleys of greenish-grey water. There was still a faint breath of wind from the north-east. The moment he had seen the fog closing in, Captain Flint took a bearing of the Longships and another of the Wolf Rock and went into the deckhouse to plot the position on the chart, and to set down the time, 8.57 a.m. At 8.57 a.m. they knew exactly where they were, south-south-west of the Land's End, south by west from the Longships, north by east from the Wolf Rock. They knew where the *Viper* was too, at that moment. Before the fog blotted her out they had seen her, heading west and about a mile south by east from the *Wild Cat*.

Just before the fog hid her, Peter Duck had changed the course of the *Wild Cat*.

"We couldn't ask for nothing better than this fog," he said, and without waiting a moment, spun the wheel, and headed the *Wild Cat* due north.

"Now," he said, "will you and Cap'n Nancy rattle in them sheets? There's no weight in the wind. But I'd like him to see us aiming for Dublin . . . ."

For a minute or two, before the fog hid the two vessels from each other, the *Wild Cat* was sailing close hauled as if to round the Longships, bound north for the Irish Sea.

John went into the deckhouse and asked for the foghorn.

"Better take the big one," said Captain Flint, who was busy with his calculations, and John came out again with a huge foghorn of the old sort that has to be blown through but makes almost as much noise as the steam syren of a small tug. He was just gathering breath to blow it, when Peter Duck stopped him.

"No," he said quickly. "Leave that and bang the bell. Quick, while he knows where we are. Let him think we've got no horn. Lost it overboard, maybe. Anyway, don't let him think we've one of them bull-roarers that'd scare the life out of a liner's fourth officer and give him something else to think about than berthing in Southampton on time. Let him think we've nothing but a bell. Cat's eyes that man's got. Dark's like day to him. But I don't know but what we may give him the slip in a fog." And with that he gave one hard blow on the ship's bell, just outside the deckhouse door, within easy reach from the wheel. "Starboard tack[1] we're on, heading north."

---

[1] Better get this clear. Starboard is right hand, when facing forward. Port is left. A vessel is on the starboard tack when the wind is coming from the starboard side. Port tack is when the wind is coming from the port side. Now you know. – CAPT NANCY.

Captain Flint shot out of the deckhouse.

"What's that bell?" he said.

"Against regulations, sir," said Peter Duck. "And Black Jake'll likely report us to the Board of Trade for not having what they call an efficient foghorn."

"But we've got a couple," said Captain Flint. "One of the new horns you work with your hand, and the old thing I gave John just now, that makes four times the noise."

Peter Duck reached forward and gave one more sharp stroke on the bell.

"It'll carry a fair way, that bell," he said, "and we may need the foghorn later."

Three hoots on a foghorn came dully through the fog.

"There's the *Viper*," said Nancy.

"Aye," said Peter Duck. "Heading west she was. Still got the wind abaft the beam."

"But what are you thinking of doing?" asked Captain Flint. "Anything you like, of course, if we can get rid of that fellow."

"There'll be a wind coming behind this fog," said Peter Duck. "There's all but no wind now, but if Black Jake had his eyes on us these last few minutes he'll have seen us heading north and heard our bell."

"But why north?" said Captain Flint.

"If the wind comes out of the nor'-west, and it will, by the smell of the fog and the way the swell's moving, we can take our choice, close hauled up the Irish Sea or running free for Spain, while the *Viper's* butting into it across the Bristol Channel. Sound that bell again, will you, Cap'n John?"

"The dinner bell's louder," said John.

"Lay into that then," said Captain Flint. "One stroke every two minutes. We're on starboard tack. It can't do any harm. Spain, did you say, Mr Duck? Why not Madeira?"

"There'll be no lack of sou'-westerlies to bring us home," said Mr Duck.

Bang. Bang. Two dull reports sounded somewhere not so very far away over the starboard bow. A long-drawn-out hoot, four whole seconds of it, sounded somewhere to southward.

"Lighthouses taking a hand," said Captain Flint. "That's the Longships and the Wolf Rock. I've just been looking them up. Every five minutes we'll be hearing those bangs, and the Wolf does its howl every thirty seconds. Precious little wind there is now to get us out of this."

The booms were swinging across with the swell. The gaffs swung overhead. The sails flapped heavily.

"It's coming," said Peter Duck.

"Well, I wish it would come soon," said Captain Flint. "We don't want to lose our reckoning and go drifting about here, between Land's End and the Scillies, with the Wolf Rock and the Seven Stones too near to let us feel comfortable."

"It's coming," said Peter Duck. "Lay into that bell again, one good whack. Now listen."

Out of the fog to the south of them came three blasts on a small foghorn.

"He's keeping his way," said Peter Duck. "Or wants us to think so."

The others came up on deck, laden with breakfast things for the galley and washing up, thinking that the bell they had heard was to tell them to hurry up, but wondering what the other noises were.

"Hullo," said Nancy. "A real fog. What were those guns?"

"Fog signals," said John.

"This is just like a fog on the fells," said Peggy.

"It's very coughy," said Roger.

"I'll let Polly stay down in the saloon," said Titty. "And, Roger, you'd better not bring Gibber up to let him catch a cold."

"Both of you go below at once and dig out your mufflers," said Susan. "You too, Peggy. Bring up mine at the same time, somebody."

"And mine," said Nancy. "I left it below when I went off watch to have breakfast."

An astonishing cold had come with the fog.

"You'd almost say it was icebergs," said Peter Duck, half to himself. "I've felt the cold of them through fog many a time. But it ain't. It's a nor'-westerly blowing up behind it. We'll likely have a gale before night. It often comes hard from nor'-west after an easterly."

Almost as he spoke jib and staysail flapped and were held aback.

"Let go jib and staysail sheets," said Peter Duck. "Now then, haul in to starboard. So. Don't bring that jib in too flat, Cap'n John."

The wind, a light wind, sweeping the fog with it, but not lifting it from the water, was coming from the north-west. The *Wild Cat* was now on the port tack, though still heading north as if to round the Longships and make up across the Bristol Channel.

"Well, sir," said Peter Duck. "We've a chance now of giving him the slip and leaving him guessing, if the fog stays with us, as it likely may."

"No harm in trying," said Captain Flint.

"Ready about," said Peter Duck. "And quietly, now. Will you help her round with the staysail to windward if she needs it. There's but a light air to go about in."

Captain Flint hurried forward. The *Wild Cat* slowly, almost unwillingly, came up into the wind, seemed for a moment to hang in stays, and then paid slowly off again on the starboard tack. Round she came, until she was heading a little west of south.

"Fetch that bell two smart strokes, Cap'n Nancy."

"But oughtn't it to be three?" said Nancy. "We've got the wind abaft the beam."

"Two strokes, Cap'n Nancy. We want him to think we're on port tack now and still heading north. You see, the wind's changed."

"Giminy," said Nancy, "this is war." And she gave the bell a couple of blows that fairly made it ring.

"Now, listen," said Peter Duck.

"Boom. Boom," came from the Longships, and again the long-drawn-out howl from the Wolf Rock.

"No. Not that. Listen."

Somewhere away to the south of them they heard a single blast on a small foghorn, the same that up till then had been giving three hoots at a time.

"Starboard tack now, and still going west," said Peter Duck, and looked round at Nancy with a smile. "Or not. I wouldn't put it past him to be trying the same tricks on us we're going to play on him. Now then. We wants no noise. It's my belief he'll be coming north after us this very minute. Who's got good eyes? Cap'n John. You're in my watch. Will you go forrard, right up to the stem-head, and keep your eyes skinned. If you see anything, sing out sharp. If you hear anything, keep quiet, but let us know. Cap'n Flint, sir, how'd it be to have the whole crew right along the deck so's we can send messages without no shouting?"

"Right," said Captain Flint who was busy streaming the log.[1] He knew just where they were at the moment, but it might be some time before they saw land again.

John and Susan went up to the foredeck. Peggy and Roger sat, one each side of the *Swallow*, on the skylights between the two masts. Titty leant against the side of the deckhouse. Nancy waited by the galley door ready to give the bell another couple of whacks.

"No more, Cap'n Nancy," said Peter Duck, just in time. "She's moving now, and Black Jake'd know at once the sound was nearer."

Just then the parrot, indignant at being left alone in the saloon, sang out, "Pieces of eight! Pieces of eight!" at the top of its voice.

---

[1] The log is one of the finest dodges in a ship. It works rather like the speedometer of a motor car. A thing like a propeller spins in the water at the end of a long line, and the spinning of the line twirls the wheels inside a little dial where a pointer shows just how far the ship has moved. – ROGER, SHIP'S ENGINEER.

"Lucky I didn't bring him on deck," said Titty as she hurried down the companion to suppress the parrot by putting his blue cover over his cage. "It's in a very good cause, Polly," she said, as she left him and ran up on deck again in time to hear that same short, single blast on a horn, somewhere in the fog in the direction in which the *Wild Cat* was now heading.

"Due south," said Peter Duck quietly to Captain Flint. "Pretty near due south that foghorn's bearing now."

Very slowly, hardly leaving a wake, slipping silently over the smooth Atlantic swell before that breath of wind out of the north-west, the *Wild Cat* moved south in the fog. Titty looked up and found she could not be sure whether the burgee was at the mainmast-head or not. John and Susan, up in the bows, looked like ghosts, and the white jib beyond them seemed to be made of fog, not canvas. Outside the ship she could see nothing at all except a few yards of grey-green water.

There was a gentle squeak as Peter Duck turned the steering-wheel. Titty saw the old seaman say something to Captain Flint, who moved into the lee of the deckhouse to speak to Nancy. Nancy slipped forward to whisper to Roger, who was sitting on the skylight. Roger, on tiptoe, hurried to the companion and disappeared below. He was up again in a minute with Gibber's oil-can, which he gave to Mr Duck. Mr Duck put a drop or two of oil in the right place and the steering-gear squeaked no more.

The fog signals from the lighthouses, the double boom from the Longships every five minutes, and the howl from the Wolf every half-minute came regularly, but they were all listening for something else.

The *Viper's* foghorn presently sounded again.

"Still bearing south," said Peter Duck under his breath.

"A bit odd that, if he's been sailing west on starboard tack with the wind from nor'-west."

"It's more'n odd," said Peter Duck.

Roger slipped as he made his way forward on the decks, wet with the fog.

"Sh!" whispered Peggy.

Everybody looked that way, and then at each other, listening.

The *Wild Cat* made hardly any noise at all, hardly as much noise as the wind blowing over soft grass.

But suddenly John, in the bows, held up his hand. Susan signalled to Peggy. Peggy to Nancy. Everybody froze. There was no doubt about it. Somewhere in the fog, close to them, was the creak of steering-gear. Everybody knew that it was not the steering-gear of the *Wild Cat*. Then, away to leeward, came the noise of a wooden block on a slack rope, tapping a mast. Then the noise of men's voices, angry, muffled.

Titty looked at Peter Duck. He was not so much steering as holding the steering-wheel so that it should not move the millionth of an inch. He was not going to trust to oil alone to keep it quiet. The *Wild Cat* moved on, slowly, slowly. The muttering that, when they had first heard it, had sounded near the bows, sounded now astern.

"Them," Titty whispered to herself. "It must be them."

Everybody except Peter Duck was peering away into the fog. Peter Duck was looking at nothing but the compass card inside the deckhouse window. He leaned forward and wiped the window with a red and green speckled handkerchief.

And then that same short blast on a foghorn sounded ahead of the *Wild Cat*, as it had sounded before.

Everybody stared forward, except Peter Duck. Peter Duck stuffed his speckled handkerchief into his pocket and went on watching the compass card, keeping a firm, steady grip on the wheel.

"Was that the *Viper*, or wasn't it?" whispered Captain Flint.

"We'll soon know," whispered Peter Duck. "Still bearing south, that foghorn of his."

"If it wasn't them, who was it?" thought Titty, and Captain Flint and everybody else aboard was thinking the same thing, except perhaps Peter Duck, for whom nothing seemed to matter but the compass card inside the deckhouse window.

The deep booming of an Atlantic liner's siren startled them.

"Far enough," whispered Peter Duck, "and her course is a long way south of this. She'll be ten miles west of the Scillies before we cross her wake."

Again, and nearer now, came the single hoot on exactly the note of the horn they had heard from the *Viper* soon after the fog had rolled over her and hidden her.

RUN DOWN IN THE FOG

"Still south?" asked Captain Flint, who had slipped into the deckhouse for a moment, to look at the chart, and now came out again after seeing for himself that Peter Duck was right and that they had nothing to fear from the liner.

"South," said Peter Duck. "If she's been sailing all this time on the starboard tack she must have got an anchor out over her stern. Stand by, sir, now, with that big foghorn of ours, the bull-roarer, not that Board of Trade toy."

Captain Flint brought the big foghorn out again, and rested it on the roof of the deckhouse.

Again there was the hoot of a foghorn, close ahead of them.

"Let fly now, sir," said Peter Duck. "Three blasts to stir old Davy out of his bed."

Captain Flint took a long breath, set his mouth to the bull-roarer and let fly, and if Davy Jones had been sleeping anywhere within a mile or so, the noise would surely have tumbled him off his locker. It was a long, tremendous roar, so loud that Titty was almost deafened by it, and Nancy, who was by the door of the galley and had not seen what was going on behind her, looked as startled as if an Atlantic liner were at that moment looming over them out of the fog. Peggy and Roger were startled almost into squeaking, though they instantly hushed each other. Susan and John, up in the bows, turned round wondering what was happening, just as Captain Flint, taking a second long breath, let fly again.

Before his second blast was finished, they heard the foghorn ahead of them. Weak, plaintive it seemed after that tremendous roar. It sounded this time not a single short blast, but one after another, in quick succession, as if it were afraid to stop.

Captain Flint let fly for the third time.

The other foghorn hooted desperately now from close under the very bows of the *Wild Cat*.

Titty saw Captain Flint look questioningly at Mr Duck. Mr Duck did not stir.

Suddenly there was a yell from John.

"Boat right ahead! On the port bow."

"Guessed as much," said Mr Duck.

There was a wild scream, from close under the bowsprit as it seemed to Titty and the others in the stern. But they saw Susan running aft along the port side.

"Throw him a rope," she cried. "Quick! Quick!"

Everybody hurried to the port bulwarks. Drifting by close under the *Wild Cat* was a small ship's gig, tarred black. In it was a smallish boy clutching a mechanical foghorn, and looking up with terrified eyes at the *Wild Cat* gliding past him and at the faces looking down at him over her rail.

"Catch," called Captain Flint, picking up the loose end of the mainsheet, which was hanging in loose coils on a belaying-pin in the rail, and dropping it neatly across the boat as it slipped by.

The boy did not hesitate. He dropped the foghorn, grabbed the rope as high as he could reach, threw himself clear of the boat, and scrambled up. In another moment Captain Flint was hauling him over the rail, while the boat, empty except for the foghorn, drifted away into the fog and disappeared astern.

The boy, trembling all over, stood on the deck, looking round him and holding to the bulwarks.

"Why, it's Bill," said Peter Duck.

"It's the red-haired boy," said Titty.

The boy's wet red face broke into a smile.

"Come aboard, I have, Mr Duck."

CHAPTER XIII

DECISION

"BARBECUED billygoats," cried Captain Nancy, "but . . ."

Peter Duck interrupted.

"Sound carries in a fog, Cap'n Nancy," he said, "and we've made enough noise already, what with shouting and getting him aboard. Cap'n John, I'm ashamed of you. What's the look-out doing, hanging round the poop? Mate Peggy, I thought you was amidships. Mate Susan, wasn't you up on the foredeck with Cap'n John? Tidy mess it seems to me with the whole crew aft. Time enough we'll have to settle with Bill when we're farther out of this. Cap'n Flint, sir, would you mind now giving another three blasts on that bull-roarer? Just in case they're listening for it in the *Viper*. I wouldn't like to set them wondering too soon why they only heard it once. Three blasts, sir, as before."

Captain Flint leaned forward again over the deckhouse roof and blew three more great blasts on the old horn.

"Oo," said Bill. "Sounds better like this than it does when you hears it coming down on you out o' the fog. I thought I was a goner just now."

"Less lip," said Peter Duck. "We ain't begun to think of you yet. And why hain't you coiled the mainsheet as you come aboard by? No. Begin at the right end, where it's made fast. You ought to know as much as that."

Everybody had hurried back, each to his post.

"And what now, Mr Duck?" said Captain Flint.

"That's for you to say, sir," said Peter Duck. "Maybe we ought to pick up that little dinghy and go and look for Black Jake to give it him back and his cabin-boy as well. He'd be sorry to lose that little boat, and the foghorn too . . ."

"I'll see him fried first," said Captain Flint, and there was a laugh, instantly choked, from Nancy, who was near enough to hear.

"I'd rather stay," said Bill.

"You wasn't asked," said Peter Duck.

"I'm only sorry we didn't sink the boat," said Captain Flint. "He may find her again when the fog lifts."

"Then we'd better be shifting," said Peter Duck. "Fog may last an hour or two yet, or it may not. But the wind's nor'-westerly, right enough, and that's a grand wind for Spain. Sou'-sou'-west half west's the course, to put us outside Cape Villano coming from the Longships. And topsails would help her along."

Just then the liner's siren sounded, and Captain Flint reached for the bull-roarer.

"No," said Peter Duck. "We're a different vessel altogether. We're not that one with a bull-roarer, no, nor yet the *Wild Cat* that had nothing but a dinner-bell to clatter on, the vessel Black Jake's seeking away there between Land's End and the Seven Stones. We'll sound on the Board of Trade horn if we sound anything, but it don't matter for a bit if we do keep quiet."

"I'll be getting those topsails up then," said Captain Flint. "Give me a hand, Nancy."

He brought up the topsails from the sail locker, gave Titty the bundle of the foretopsail to look after while Nancy and he hooked on the halyard sheet and downhaul, mousing the hooks with twine so they should not slip open. And then, just as the little jib-headed sail was up at the mast-head, the sheet jammed. Nancy tugged. Captain Flint tried it. No. The thing was stuck somewhere or other.

"Have it down again," said Captain Flint.

It would not come.

There was a sudden patter of bare feet on the wet deck. A small figure ran forward. A mop of red hair, two red feet, a ragged coat, a pair of old blue trousers with a black patch across the seat of them, shot between Captain Flint and Nancy, and leapt at the mainsail's wooden mast-hoops. The blue trousers and the black patch faded upwards into the fog.

"All clear, sir." A hoarse whisper sounded above their heads. A small figure dropped hand over hand down the halyards to the deck, and as Nancy and Captain Flint hauled again on the topsail sheet, the clew of the sail moved out along the gaff and all was as it should be.

"That's not a bad boy," said Captain Flint, as Bill bolted back again to stand by in case he was wanted by Mr Duck.

"He and Gibber are two for a pair," said Nancy. "But what was he doing in that dinghy, all by himself with a foghorn?"

"I've a pretty shrewd idea," said Captain Flint. "But we'll hear presently. There's the foretopsail to set now. Thank you, Titty. Out of the way,

you two. Peggy, what about scaring up a mug
of hot cocoa for the passenger? But don't rattle
your pans in the galley."

Peggy on tiptoe went off into the galley, closing the door carefully behind her. She knew, like
Captain Flint, and all the others, that Peter Duck
was right. There were more urgent things to think
of than the red-haired boy. They were still in the
fog. They had heard the *Viper* pass them, going
north to look for them, but for all they knew she
might have turned again and might be no more
than a few yards away hidden in that loose choking blanket of fog that made it all but impossible
to see from one end of the ship to the other. The
wind was getting up, though as yet it blew the
fog in thick curling wisps through the rigging
and across the decks instead of lifting it up and
driving it away. With topsails set, the *Wild Cat*
was moving fairly fast through the water. All to
the good, to get away from Black Jake, but, at the
same time, with every minute they were coming
nearer to the great thoroughfare of shipping. And,
bad as it would be to be found by Black Jake and
his men, it would be not much better to be run
down by some big steamship hurrying on its way.
They had heard the howl of the Wolf every half-
minute, and knew that it was no longer south of
them but north. They had passed it, and, steering
south-south-west, were heading as it were into
the middle of the road, with traffic that they could
not see coming both ways at once. Peter Duck was
right. This was no time to ask the red-haired boy
questions. The only thing to do was to keep quiet,
to keep a sharp look out, and to hope at the same

time that the fog would last and they would be able to sail through it without being run down by someone else. How right Peter Duck was they were not very long in finding out.

Captain Flint and Nancy were looking up at the foretopsail, trying to see if it was setting properly, when a steam siren sounded somewhere away off the starboard bow. It was a shriller noise than the booming note of the big liner, which, as Peter Duck had said it would be, was already far away to the west. It sounded again, a long, shrill blast.

"Steamship," said Captain Flint.

"That one seems a bit nearer," said John quietly. "The big one's much farther away."

"Quite near enough," said Captain Flint, and turned to go aft.

Just then a foghorn sounded from close by the deckhouse. Three clear hoots it gave, loud, but not so loud as the horrible noises made by the bull-roarer.

Captain Flint and Nancy hurried aft, in time to see the red-haired boy sounding the Board of Trade foghorn, that works like a pump. Roger was standing watching him open-mouthed and envious.

"Three times," said Peter Duck. "Put some beef into it. We're getting into the track of the Channel shipping."

Again that shrill siren sounded, close on the starboard bow.

Everybody stared into the fog. A minute passed. Another.

"Let them have the horn again," said Peter

Duck. But the red-haired boy had only time to get a single blast out of it.

"Something right ahead," shouted John at the very top of his voice as the steam siren sounded again, this time as if out of the sky immediately above him.

The white fog turned suddenly black before them. Peter Duck spun the wheel, putting the helm hard aport. The *Wild Cat* came sharply round into the wind, with her sails all shaking. Her bowsprit end just cleared the towering, rusty walls of an ocean tramp feeling her way in from the Atlantic. From high above the *Wild Cat* faces looked down out of the fog on the startled group at the stern of the little schooner.

"What are you playing at down there?" sounded an angry voice.

"Aye, it's you to shout," said Peter Duck, "when as near as nothing you sent us to the bottom."

"I thought steamships had to keep out of the way of sailing vessels," said Nancy.

"So they have, by law," said Peter Duck, "and there's a whole town full of good sailormen at the bottom of the sea for thinking the same. They have to keep out of our way, the clumsy, racketty, bangetty bundles of scrap-iron, but do they, I asks you? Do they ever? And least of all in fog."

The big tramp steamer lurched on her way. Her propellers beat the water as the Atlantic swell lifted her stern. Her wash, cutting across the line of the swell, sent small, steep waves to run amuck, one of which, all unexpected, heaped

itself up and slopped over the *Wild Cat's* waist,
sluicing aft past the galley door just as Peggy
came out with a mug of cocoa.

"What's happening?" asked Peggy, seeing the
startled faces, the sails slack and flapping, hearing
the noise of the tramp's engines, and the splash,
splash of her propeller, going off into the fog.

"Narrow shave of being run down," said Nancy.

"And there wasn't nobody handy with ropes
to haul us aboard like you hauled me," said Bill,
who had been so much afraid of being run down
when he was floating alone in a dinghy that he
was almost cheered at the thought of being run
down with so many others to keep him company.
"Thank you kindly, miss."

"Look out. It's pretty hot," said Peggy.

"You may well be thankful for that," said Peter
Duck. "There's plenty as would have drowned you,
fooling about in a boat trying to make us think you
was the *Viper*."

"But I didn't, Mr Duck," began Bill. "I really
didn't."

"Sound that foghorn," said Mr Duck. "We'll
have the truth out of you when we're ready for
it."

He swung the *Wild Cat* back on her course
again. The sails filled and everything settled
down; settled down that is, as far as anything
can be said to have settled down when a little
ship is sailing in a dense fog across the mouth of
the Channel. The big tramp steamer had scared
them, towering above them suddenly, out of the
fog, and though everybody was bursting to find
out what the red-haired boy had been doing alone

in a boat, everybody knew now that the most important thing of all was to listen and to keep sailing. The whole crew were on deck, excepting the parrot and the monkey. Peter Duck never left the wheel, and every two minutes, at a word from him, the red-haired boy was sending out three blasts on the foghorn, while Captain Flint kept walking quietly fore and aft, listening for noises, and now and then slipping into the deckhouse to have yet another look at the chart that by now he almost knew by heart.

The *Wild Cat* was steadily moving faster and faster through the water, and she had left the Wolf Rock far astern, and long out of hearing when, at last, Titty, who had been with Roger in the stern looking at Bill, wondering what he was really like, and watching him pump at the foghorn when Mr Duck nodded to him, saw that the jib no longer seemed to be made of fog, and that John and Susan up in the bows could no longer be mistaken for ghosts.

"Fog's lifting," said Peter Duck suddenly. "We could do with a bit longer, barring them screw steamers."

"We can't have it both ways," said Captain Flint. "I'd like to let Black Jake go cruising up to Ireland looking for the *Wild Cat*, and that's likely enough if the fog holds. But I wouldn't mind it if we met no more of these blundering tramp steamers, not as near as that one, anyway."

"Was Black Jake going up to Ireland?" said Bill. "What about me? He'd have had to pick me up first."

"Likely he would," said Peter Duck. "Valuable

you are. He might have come back for his boat or
his foghorn, but I reckon he'd made up his mind
to be losing the both of them, and you think he'd
be coming back for you. Not likely."

"Lucky I caught your rope," said Bill.

"Lucky for you," said Peter Duck. "What about
us?"

"With all them cap'ns aboard," said Bill, "one
of em's bound and sure to want another boy."

The fog did indeed begin to lift. It was soon
possible to see a hundred yards or so from the deck
of the schooner. It was as if she were sailing in the
exact middle of a round pond, shut in by a high
wall of fog. Only, though the pond was so small,
a swell was rolling across it of that tremendous
kind that does so often come sweeping out of the
Atlantic down into the Bay of Biscay. Beyond that
wall they could hear faint, distant sirens. Within
it they were alone.

"What do you think about it, Mr Duck?" said
Captain Flint at last. "Nobody's going to run us
down now. Titty, run along forward and tell John
and Susan they can come aft. And Nancy's there
with them. I want one of them to take the wheel
from Mr Duck, while we're hearing what the passenger has to say for himself . . . ."

Bill looked suddenly grave.

Titty hurried away forward. She hurried because she did not wish to miss a word of what was
coming. How had it happened that the red-haired
boy had been drifting alone in the fog? Was he
on Black Jake's side or theirs? Had they rescued
him or made him prisoner? What had been going
on last night when the *Viper* had nearly crashed

into them in the dark? What had been happening
in the fog, while Peter Duck had been pretending
the *Wild Cat* was heading north for Ireland when
really she was heading south for Spain?

"Come on, Susan," she said, almost as if Black
Jake were listening out on the bowsprit end.
"Come on, John. Come on, Nancy. Captain Flint
thinks it's all right now; the fog's not so bad. He
wants somebody to take the wheel. They're just
going to decide about the red-haired boy . . . ."

They all hurried aft together, in time to hear
Captain Flint say: "We'll do better for him than
that, if we think he's worth keeping at all."

"But you can't throw him back," said Titty.

"Why not?" said Captain Flint.

"I've got a spare toothbrush he could have,"
said Susan. "I brought two for each of us."

The red-haired boy looked doubtfully, first at
Peter Duck then at Captain Flint, then at the
children of whom this schooner seemed so full.

"Sou'-sou'-west, half-west," said Peter Duck,
giving up the wheel.

"Sou'-sou'-west half-west it is," said John, taking it over. Peter Duck turned sharply on the
red-haired boy.

"And now, young Bill," he said, "let's hear what
you was doing in a dinghy letting on with a foghorn as you was a sailing vessel on the starboard
tack. What have you got to say about that? Don't
let's hear nothing but the truth."

"It wasn't my fault I shipped along of he,"
said Bill.

"Never mind that," said Captain Flint. "Let's
hear what you were doing with that foghorn."

"Black Jake he send me down into the dinghy
with the horn, and then he tell me to sound it, once
at a time, every so often, so he'd know where I was
and pick me up when he come back."

"Back?" said Captain Flint. "Where from?"

"He was going to lay aboard you in the fog
and get a hold of Mr Duck."

"H'm. Was he? And how many did he think
would be enough for that?"

"Five of 'em there was. There was Black Jake.
Then there was Simeon Boon, that's just come out
after two years' hard. Then there was Mogandy,
the nigger, blacker'n Black Jake. Then there was
a brother of Black Jake that was hiding in the
fo'c'sle till we'd sailed. Police wanted him for
something. Then there was the man that was
chucker-out at the 'Ketch as Ketch Can' . . ."

"That's a fishermen's tavern in Lowestoft, sir,"
said Peter Duck. "It's got another name. You'd not
know it."

"And then there was me."

Captain Flint threw back his head and laughed.

"There was six of us altogether," said Bill.

"All right," said Captain Flint. "So the five who
stayed in the *Viper* were going to board us, were
they?"

"Black Jake tell 'em it'd be easy. There'd be
no more'n two of you on deck, and if one of 'em
was Mr Duck, why that was all he wanted. If
Mr Duck wasn't on deck, Black Jake he reckoned
to hold down the hatches and offer to blow you up
with dropping something down if you didn't send
Mr Duck up quick."

"Pleasant," said Captain Flint. "But if that

was what he was thinking, why didn't he try that game last night, when he ran up alongside us with all lights out in the dark?"

"Half of 'em was drunk last night," said the red-haired boy, "and some of 'em was frightened. And Black Jake was letting fly at 'em all night for the chance they'd missed, and then, when the fog come on this morning, he fair drove 'em to it. 'Cap'ns and mates and all,' he says, 'I've that here as'll send 'em squealing. Give up Peter Duck,' he says, 'they'll throw him overboard to us and be thankful.'"

"And so you were to sound the foghorn while they were to creep up to us in the fog?" said Captain Flint.

"I didn't have nothing to say neither way," said Bill. "They'd all had a go at me about one thing and another ever since we was clear of Lowestoft pier heads. I'm all one bruise, I am. What could I do when Black Jake drop me over into the dinghy. 'Pass up them oars,' he says. 'You won't want 'em. And now,' he says, 'if you don't sound that horn regular you'll be run down and sunk.' 'And what if he is?' says Mogandy. 'There's no name on the boat,' says Black Jake. And he throw down the painter into the boat and let her drop astern, and the next I knowed they were gone into the fog, and what could I do without oars? Swim ashore? What could I do but sound that horn?"

"Well, there's something in that," said Captain Flint.

"And then you come right down on top of me and throw me a rope and I come aboard. I'll work my passage, sir," he added eagerly, "if you'll let me stay with you back to Lowestoft."

"What if we aren't going there?" said Captain Flint. John and Nancy looked anxiously at Susan.

"What if we aren't going there?" said Captain Flint again. "What do you think about it now, Mr Duck? Eavesdropping wasn't enough for him. Kidnapping he was up to. Piracy. The fellow'd stick at nothing. Why not spike his guns for good by lifting that treasure of yours, Mr Duck, and bringing it home? Once he knows it's gone, you'll have a quiet life."

"I've never said yet there was a treasure in that place," said Mr Duck, "and I've always said I'd never go there. But after what's happened since yesterday I'm with you, sir. I'll show you the place as near as I can. If it's anything you fancy, well and good. Even if them crabs have scoffed the bag and all that's in it, it'll be a grand bit of sailing down the Nor'-east Trades."

But it was Susan who, in the end, gave the deciding vote.

"Whatever it is," she said, "Black Jake ought not to have it. And Peggy and I were counting things all yesterday, because of what you said at Cowes. We've got enough for a very long time."

"Six months' stores," said Captain Flint. "And if there's anything short we could fill up in Madeira."

"I think we ought to go," said Susan. "Black Jake's almost a murderer. He oughtn't to be allowed to get it after this."

"Susan," said Captain Flint, "shake hands. You're fifteen kinds of trump."

"Well done, Susan," said Nancy. "I thought you'd agree in the end."

"What about you, John?" said Captain Flint.

"Susan's quite right. We ought to go," said John.

"Swallows and Amazons for ever!" cried Nancy.

"Don't shout, Nancy," said John, and Peter Duck looked northwards over his shoulder.

"What's going to happen?" said Roger. "What's it all about? What? What?"

"We're going to Crab Island to get that treasure," said Titty, who had been listening open-mouthed.

"Then we'll really see those crabs," said Roger.

Bill stared first at one and then at another.

Captain Flint walked hurriedly forward, right up to the bows and back again. He came aft chuckling in his excitement. "We'll bring it off," he was saying. "Nothing's going to stop us. Black Jake did a bad day's work for himself when he set his ship's boy afloat in a dinghy. As for you, you young pirate," he added, turning to Bill, "where did you sleep aboard the *Viper*?"

"Sail locker," said Bill.

"We'll do a bit better for you than that, if you're to sign articles with us."

"I'll do whatever Mr Duck says," said Bill.

"We'll fix you up a bunk in the hospital cabin," said Captain Flint. "There's nothing in there but tinned food. Take him below, you others, and introduce him to Gibber and the parrot. Matter of fact," he added, turning to Peter Duck, "I've been feeling a bit uneasy about that boy, ever since we sent him back to the *Viper*, that day when John and Nancy fished him out of the harbour."

Bill, hearing this, bobbed up again into the highest spirits.

"Come on, Bill," said Nancy.

"Come along," said Roger, "Gibber'll be pleased to meet you."

"Where's all them cap'ns and mates of yours?" said Bill. There was a general laugh.

Bill looked from face to face with surprise.

"Come on," said Roger again, and Bill, nerving himself to meet a whole saloon full of officers, followed him down the companion.

*

"You'd better go down with the others to fix him up," said Captain Flint to John. "I'll take the wheel. Ask Susan and Peggy if they can't give us something to eat."

"Sou'-sou'-west, half-west," said John.

"Sou'-sou'-west, half-west."

"Blue water sailing after all," said Peter Duck, looking round at the thinning fog.

And Captain Flint watched the compass card, smiling happily, as he kept the *Wild Cat* on her course for Finisterre, and thought of Madeira and the distant Caribbees.

CHAPTER XIV

QUIT OF THE *VIPER*

THE message about food was given and at once forgotten. What with Bill and the decision just taken, not even Roger at that moment could think about such things as dinner.

"Well," said Nancy cheerfully, as they crowded into the saloon and Bill looked round in surprise to see no officers about. "We're in for it now. I knew he'd never be content just hanging about near home. Three cheers for Christopher Columbus."

"It's a good thing we've been careful with the water from the very beginning," said Susan.

"This is going to be a real voyage," said Titty.

"What do you mean?" said Bill.

"Mr Duck's island," said John.

"Those crabs," said Roger.

"I'm jolly glad we ran you down," said John. "You know, it was just that that settled it, our going, I mean."

Bill stared.

"Why," he said, "we knew in Lowestoft you was going there. We was sailing the night you first come aboard, only Black Jake see Mr Duck a-talking to your skipper. And then next day when he see Mr Duck bringing his dunnage aboard, why then he knowed. And then when he pushed me overboard and I told him what your skipper said about all them cap'ns and mates . . ." Bill lowered his voice, and looked round at the cabins.

"He did push you overboard that day?" said
Titty. "I was sure he did."

"Course he did," said Bill. "I ain't no natural
diver. When I come back and tell him what your
skipper said, Black Jake he telled the others and
I got more'n half a rope's-ending next morning
when he come on deck and find you'd cleared out
of harbour and given us the slip. And then when
you come in again as we was going to look for
you I got it worse from the others. We knowed
you was going well enough. And Black Jake telled
Mogandy and Boon and the rest they'd nothing
to do but to get hold of Mr Duck and they'd be
rich men for life. They reckoned to do it, too, this
morning."

The Swallows and Amazons looked at each
other. With Bill so sure that from the beginning
they had been bound for Crab Island, it began to
seem odd, even to Susan, that they had really
set sail from Lowestoft without meaning to go
treasure-hunting at all. When Captain Flint left
the wheel to Mr Duck and came hurrying down
after them into the saloon, just for a moment, to
spread the big chart of the Atlantic on the saloon
table and to show them where they were going
(he, too, had already forgotten about the food)
they could see that Bill simply did not believe
that they were looking at it now for the first
time. It may seem a queer thing, but perhaps
it was just because Bill took it for granted that
they had set out on that tremendous voyage that
the others so quickly grew used to the idea of it.

Indeed, they almost forgot to think about the
voyage in the interest of fitting Bill out as a

member of the crew. Nancy had a white canvas hat for him. John offered him a pair of shorts, but Bill preferred his long trousers, patch and all. His feet turned out to be about the same size as Peggy's, and luckily she had a pair of sandshoes to spare as well as an old pair of sea-boots. As for oilskins, there were a lot of spare ones. "And, anyway," said John, "we're never all wearing oilskins at once." Susan and Peggy cleared a lot of tins out of the lower bunk in the hospital cabin for him, and Titty pinned up a picture postcard of Lowestoft harbour on the wall, to make him feel at home. They decided where he was to sit at the saloon table, and remembered, with horror, that Captain Flint had asked for food. Susan and Peggy left the others and bolted up the companion, to get to work in the galley. Roger showed Bill where the engine was stowed. John and Nancy took him into the fo'c'sle. Roger introduced him to Gibber, who let Bill tickle him behind the ear. Titty introduced him to the parrot, who gave him a terrible nip in the finger.

"But where *are* all them cap'ns and mates?" asked Bill at last, lowering his voice. "Sleeping, are they?"

"There just aren't any," said Titty.

"We're them," said Nancy.

And they tried to explain to Bill about the adventures they had had in the *Swallow* and the *Amazon*, but somehow it didn't seem much good. Bill just roared with laughter. "And me creeping on my toes," he said, "for fear of 'em." Suddenly his face grew solemn. "Lucky for you your skipper telled me what he did. Why, if Black Jake had

knowed ... If he'd knowed that, why he'd have
had Mr Duck out of here before you was halfway
down Channel. He wouldn't have waited for no
fog ...."

*

Just then Captain Flint, with a new confident
ring in his voice called down through the skylight.
"Come up and have a look round, you people.
Fog's gone. We've done it!"

They crowded up on deck. The lurching of the
vessel had already told them that there had been
a complete change in the weather, just as Peter
Duck had guessed there would be. They found
the wind blowing hard from the north-west and
strengthening every minute. Besides the ocean
swell there were waves now, hurrying so fast
that their tops tumbled head over heels in a
smother of white spray. The wind thrummed in
the rigging, and the *Wild Cat* left a long troubled
wake streaming away astern of her. There was no
fog. There was no land in sight. And there was no
sign of the black schooner.

"We've done it all right," said Captain Flint.
"That's one, two, three steamers, two cargo boats
and a tanker ... more of them hull down ...
there's another of those French fishermen ...
Not a sign of the *Viper*. No. We've done it."

"Hope he'll like Dublin," said Nancy.

"Or the North Pole," said John. "The farther
he goes the better."

"Aye," said Peter Duck, after a slow careful
look all round the horizon. "Seems we're quit of
him, right enough."

"Thanks to you, Mr Duck. We've got clear from him, and we've got one of his crew instead of him having one of ours," said Captain Flint gleefully. "Well, Bill, I wonder if Black Jake's missing you much?"

"There's nobody aboard the *Viper* what anybody can lay into now."

"So you think they're cruising round the Wolf Rock looking for you with a rope's end?"

"Well, I ain't there, anyhow," said Bill.

*

Dinner that day was hours late, a joyful but a most unsteady meal. The sea was getting rapidly worse and worse. They had had a taste of wind that last night coming down Channel, but then the wind had been off the land. Now, running south for Spain, they were exposed to the full drift of the Atlantic. Old Peter Duck was enjoying it. "I knows this bit of water," he told the mates, while they were giving him his dinner. "By Ushant right down across the Bay I knows it. I were in them Frenchy boats fishing round here when they give me to the skipper of the *Louisiana Belle* for a bag of tobacco. But I told you that yarn before. First an easterly, then a fog, and then a blow from the nor'-west. We'll be hove to before night, but we'll be getting better weather in the morning." He had his dinner, lit his pipe, and went up again to take the wheel while Captain Flint came down.

Captain Flint had been the first to ask for food, but Susan said it was waste of time cooking for him if he would talk instead of eating. He came down with two volumes of Hakluyt's *Voyages* from

the shelf in the deckhouse, and he had brought the
big chart down again, and nothing would stop him
from using plates to keep the chart spread out over
the fiddles while he was looking first in one of the
books and then in the other. But in the end he
remembered that Mr Duck had been up most of
the night, and he sent John and Bill up to take
the wheel, and gulped down his food and hurried
after them.

He found them together at the wheel when
he came on deck, but Peter Duck had not yet
gone to his bunk. He was standing in the deckhouse, leaning out of the doorway, watching
the two boys at the wheel and looking at the
weather.

"Blowing up quick, it is," he said when he saw
Captain Flint. "Wind after fog. Always the way.
It's a right wind for us, if it don't blow up a bit
too hard."

"There's no shelter to look for out here," said
Captain Flint.

"We don't want none," said Peter Duck. "With
every mile we make to the southward we gets
deeper water. We don't want no better. Get her
into deep water and she'll ride out anything. It's
shoal water makes the trouble and drowns poor
sailormen. We'll best be putting a reef or two in
her sails, and then if it don't get no better, we
can heave her to for the night, and she'll lie as
snug as a gull."

Reefing was no easy job but it was done, at
last, and then, with Captain Flint on deck, the
old sailor went to his bunk and lay down for a
minute or two, but he could not stay there. He

came out again and stood there, watching the way the little schooner ran.

"Aren't you going to get a bit of sleep, Mr Duck?" said Captain Flint.

"Time enough for sleep later on," said Mr Duck.

Hour after hour she ran on, easier now under her shortened sails. But the sea was growing steadily worse, and the wind blew harder and harder. The mates tried washing up on deck after dinner, but so much water was coming aboard that it felt rather as if they were being washed up themselves. Roger brought Gibber up to have a look at things, and sat with him on the top step inside the companionway. But a bucketful of spray flew in there and soaked him as well as the monkey, and they had to close that door to keep the saloon dry. They had already closed the skylight. It was oilskins that afternoon for everybody who came on deck. Those who were not at the wheel found shelter for themselves under the lee of the deckhouse and tried to keep the water that blew across the roof from pouring down their necks. There were always two at the wheel, and all the time the spray came blowing over, slap, slap, against their oilskin backs. The motion grew worse again, and Susan and Peggy, taking turns with it, had a hard job to keep the kettle in its place when they wanted a drop of hot water. At last, just as it was falling dark John heard Peter Duck, who was at the wheel with him, shout to Captain Flint who was standing close by: "She's done very well, she has. How'd it be if we was to heave to now, for a quiet night, before anything carries away?"

"What if that fellow races us across?" said Captain Flint, who, now that he was bound for Crab Island, hated the idea of stopping even for a moment.

"He'll have to come down this way," said Peter Duck, "unless he wants contrary winds the whole way across. There's no good way but the old sailing ship track by Spain and Portugal to the North-east Trades away down by Madeira and the Canaries. If the weather's bad for us, it's worse for him. If the *Viper*'s not hove to at this minute, somewheres north of the Land's End, Black Jake's wishing she was. She's a flyer, the *Viper*, but she won't carry sail in bad weather."

"Shall we ever have it worse than this?" Nancy asked, snuggling down into her oilskins.

"We'll be having good weather when we get by Finisterre," said Peter Duck, "but it won't last as bad as this beyond the morning."

"So long as it doesn't get any worse, it's all right," said Nancy, who was very pleased indeed to find that she was not feeling sick.

"Well," said Captain Flint, "you know the Bay better than I do. And there's one thing about it. We could all do with a bit of sleep after last night."

Bill earned good marks from everybody in the half-hour of tremendous business that followed. He never quite managed to be in two places at once, but worked so hard and made himself so useful that it almost seemed as if he had. When they had done, and rested, panting for breath, they had the heavy booms lashed down in their places, stowed all the ordinary sails, and left the

Wild Cat under a tiny storm-jib and a trysail, balancing each other, so that she lay quiet, meeting the waves as they came but no longer driving on her way.

"Beautiful she lays," said Peter Duck, when all was done. Nobody on land would have thought so, but aboard the *Wild Cat* it felt like a peaceful holiday after the last strenuous hours of the evening. No more water was coming aboard. The lurching of the vessel was less violent. But the mates did not try to cook anything for supper. Everybody cheered them when they came staggering below with a huge jug of boiling cocoa.

*

Just before Titty and Roger went to their bunks for the night, they were allowed on deck for a last look round. It was a wild sight. Now and then when the schooner lifted on the top of a great sea, they caught a glimpse of a steamer's lights far away. There was nothing else to be seen but flying clouds overhead and the white rolling tops of the waves. Yet the *Wild Cat* was comfortable enough. Hove to, under her two small sails, the little schooner seemed to be at home in the midst of the tumult. She seemed to be picking her way almost in her sleep in and out among the mountain ranges of the sea. Alone in the dark, her lights burning confidently and brightly, the *Wild Cat* lay resting, as Peter Duck had said she would, easy as a sleeping gull upon the heaving waters.

Bill, too, to his surprise, had been sent off to his bunk soon after supper.

"Everybody'd better take their chance of a good

night's sleep," said Captain Flint. "Wheel's lashed. Mr Duck and I'll keep a look out. Off you go, Bill. No point in sitting up with your eyes closing. You did good work with those reef points, my lad. Off you go now. You can get up as early as you like in the morning."

In the saloon, after the others had gone, John, Susan, Nancy, and Peggy sat at the table under the swinging lamp. For a little they talked of the voyage ahead of them and of Mr Duck's island, but the talk soon turned to Bill, who, after all, was not so far away.

"He's awfully good at going up the mast," said Nancy.

"Anybody can tell he's been to sea before . . . really to sea," said John.

"It must be awful in trawlers," said Susan.

"I don't suppose he thinks anything of this," said Peggy.

"Of what?"

"Being hove to in a storm," said Peggy, grabbing the table as the *Wild Cat* seemed to pitch and skid sideways both at once.

"Well, it isn't half bad," said Nancy.

"He's going to be useful in all sorts of ways," said John.

"What would have happened to him if we hadn't picked him up?" said Peggy.

"Drowned, probably," said Nancy. "Black Jake hadn't even left him an oar."

"Sh," said Susan. "He may not be asleep."

Holding firmly to the table, the bulkhead and anything that came handy, the four of them crept towards the cabin that had once been labelled hospital, but now bore a new label, "Bill. A.B." on its half-opened door. John looked in. The others listened.

"He's gone to sleep in his clothes," said John.

"Oh, I never thought of it," said Susan. "That's my fault. He'll have to have somebody's spare pyjamas."

"I'll get him mine," said Peggy.

"It's no good waking him now," said Susan. "He's probably horribly tired."

*

Upstairs in the deckhouse, Peter Duck lay in his bunk, darning socks. Susan had offered to darn them for him, but he had said that darning socks was the sort of work he liked to do at sea. Captain Flint sat at the chart table, playing patience, swaying in his chair to meet the motions of the ship. Miss Milligan was the patience he was playing and he had brought it out twice running. After each game he had gone out into the wind and made the round of the deck to see that everything was all right.

"If I bring it out three times running, Mr Duck," he said, "if I bring it out three times running it'll show Fate's taking a hand in the game and we're going to lift that treasure of yours, eh, Mr Duck, Black Jake or no Black Jake?"

Mr Duck's darning-needle was working more and more slowly.

"Grand sailing in the Nor'-east Trades," he said.

A few minutes later, Captain Flint swung round in triumph.

"Three times running, Mr Duck," he cried. "You couldn't have a clearer sign."

But Mr Duck's sock had dropped on the floor, with the darning-needle fastened to it at the end of a long painter of grey wool. Mr Duck had slipped down in his bunk. His mouth had fallen open a little. His breathing had become more regular and was beginning to sound its usual musical note. Mr Duck was asleep.

Captain Flint picked up the sock, spiked it with the darning-needle, and dropped it into the bag-of-all-sorts that was hanging from the end of Mr Duck's bunk. Then he got up and went out once more into the night.

"Three times running," he said. "Three times running. What, it's sure as if we had the stuff already stowed aboard."

SWALLOWS·AND·AMAZONS·FOR·EVER·

CHAPTER XV

BILL FINDS HIS PLACE

Bill stirred in his bunk, and waked suddenly to disturbing comforts. What was this soft blanket at his chin instead of the hard canvas of the *Viper*'s sail locker? Bill woke all of a piece, everywhere at once, like a little animal, and with a single swift wriggle pressed himself hard against the planking at the back of his bunk. Close in the angle of wall and floor, whether in a bunk, a sail locker or elsewhere, a boy is fairly well protected against ropes' ends and such things. But no rope's end searched him out or thudded on the planking. No. He was mistaken. He had not overslept. Nobody was cursing him for not having lit the galley fire. There was nobody there. He was alone, with a couple of warm, brown blankets in a box in which he could stretch without coming anywhere near touching either end.

He remembered where he was, and a slow grin spread over his broad, freckled, red face.

"Wonder who's lighting the galley in the old *Viper*?" he thought, and then he shivered, remembering the fog of yesterday, the drifting dinghy, the noise of sirens and foghorns, the sudden shadow of a ship's bows coming down on him out of the fog, the rope thrown to him, and then the surprise of seeing Mr Duck at the wheel, and of finding what vessel it was that had picked him up. Better could not have happened to him than that.

Light came into the little cabin from the skylight over the alleyway and saloon, but Bill could
not see out. He had no need. He had not been
born on the Dogger Bank for nothing. He knew
at once, from the motion, that the *Wild Cat* was
still hove to. That was all right. No hurry. And
then Bill chuckled to himself.

"Cap'ns and mates an' all," he was thinking.
"Why, if Black Jake had knowed there was nobody
else aboard he'd have had Mr Duck out of the *Wild
Cat* in two shakes, so he would . . . Not but what
they ain't a handy lot for children."

There was no one to remind him that he himself was not as old as Nancy. He felt a hundred in
comparison with any one of the crew. The skipper
and Peter Duck seemed to him right enough. The
skipper could handle the ship and everybody knew
that a better seaman than old Peter Duck had never sailed out of Lowestoft pier heads. Common talk
that was. Everybody knew it. But the rest of them!
"Cap'ns and mates! Cap'ns and mates! Why, Black
Jake and his gang'd eat 'em. It's a good thing as
I come aboard. Makes three of us, anyway."

He reached up out of the blankets to the little
rack above his head and took down from it the
new toothbrush that Susan had given him the
night before. He looked at it curiously. "Cap'ns
and mates!" he said again, "and they don't know
how to clean between their teeth with a bit of rope
yarn!"

But just then someone stamped on the deck
overhead, and he heard John and Roger struggle
out of their cabin and race for the deck. Toothbrush in hand, he was after them in a moment.

Queer sort of clothes they seemed to have on, the
sort of thing you'd see minstrels wearing, giving a
show on Yarmouth Pier. He dashed up the companion after them, and out on deck.

"Morning, Captain Flint! Morning, Mr Duck,"
they said as they hurried, not too steadily, forward along the heaving deck. He said the same,
and hurried after them, getting a nod from the
skipper, on the way.

Captain Flint and Peter Duck were busy,
with sextant and chronometer, trying to get an
observation. The sun was showing now and then
through scurrying patches of grey cloud. There
was not quite so much white water as there had
been, and though the wind was still strong it was
no longer lifting whole tops of waves.

"Come on," shouted John, flinging his pyjamas
down the hatch and swinging a canvas bucket
over the side.

"Come on," said Roger, tearing off his pyjamas, throwing them after John's, ready for the
bucketful of salt sea water that John emptied
over him.

Those queer clothes of theirs certainly did seem
to come off easily. Bill pulled at his ragged jersey,
after wedging his jacket in a safe place among the
halyards. He struggled out of his patched blue
trousers. He pulled off the vest that for some
weeks had been keeping him warm underneath.
It was pretty cold, but if these children could stand
it, he would.

"Come on," said Bill, bracing himself to meet
the bucketful that got him full in the face.

"Come on," said John. "You take the bucket

and chuck one at me ... I say, you do know how to dip full buckets. I never get a really full one first chuck. Hullo! Haven't you got a towel? Skip along, Roger, and bring one up. Let's have the bucket. I'll try to give you a really good one, too."

A few minutes later Bill rubbed a good deal of himself dry with the towel that Roger pushed up through the hatch. Somehow or other he forced damp arms and legs into his clothes and felt surprisingly warm. He would do the whole thing properly while he was about it. He took the canvas bucket and filled it once more over the side. Then, pulling out the toothbrush, he dipped it in.

"No need for that," said John, thinking of the taste of salt water. "Susan always gives us a ration of fresh for teeth."

"I was just giving it a bit of a damp," said Bill. That was wrong, was it? Well, a fellow couldn't learn all these tricks at once. He glanced hopefully aft. Perhaps they would be making sail. If it came to sails he'd be one up on these children again. Not like toothbrushes!

But he had to wait till after breakfast for his chance, and then it did not come with sails.

Breakfast was late. But the queer thing was that there was no shouting at anybody, though everybody must have been hungry. The two mates just came pelting up, saying they were sorry, and bolted round the corner into the galley, where the skipper himself had put the porridge on to boil in the double cooker. There was no doubt about it. The *Wild Cat* was a very queer ship indeed. And later, when everybody but the skipper was down in the saloon, and Susan was ladling out the porridge, while Peggy was sluicing hot cocoa into the mugs, Bill looked from face to face and wondered. There was probably a catch about it somewhere. But old Peter Duck blew the steam off his cocoa and swigged it as if everything was perfectly usual. Well, folk did say that there was nothing about the sea that Peter Duck didn't know. Life in the *Wild Cat* was a bit different from life in a Grimsby trawler, and still more different from those days in the *Viper* which had left a fair lot of bruises on Bill but he supposed that the longer he lived the more he was likely to learn. With one eye on Mr Duck, he blew the steam off his own cocoa, and pitched the porridge into his gullet, in the same calm, business-like manner that he admired in the old seaman. As for those children . . . When breakfast was over and Captain Flint had come down for his, while Mr Duck had gone on deck, and when Captain Flint had gone, too, and the crew were alone in the saloon, Bill saw his chance of showing that he, too, knew something. It came with a word that Nancy let slip about the horrible way in which the *Wild Cat* was shaking things up. Bill felt in his pocket. Yes, he still had that quarter plug of black tobacco . . . .

*

Captain Flint and Peter Duck had been on deck for some time smoking their morning pipes in the shelter of the deckhouse and wondering how soon things would have calmed down enough to let the *Wild Cat* square away once more for Finisterre. Captain Flint tapped his pipe out on the rail and noticed that nobody except himself and the old seaman had come on deck after breakfast.

"Funny, they're so quiet down there," he said. "I suppose they've a lot to talk over with young Bill. Hullo! There's Nancy . . ."

Nancy had come up through the forehatch. She moved unsteadily to the side, and looked over the bulwarks at the grey water and at the white-topped waves that came rolling down to the *Wild Cat* one after another, threatening to come aboard but never doing so.

"Hullo, Nancy?" called Captain Flint.

Nancy looked round, but did not answer.

"What's the matter with Nancy?" said Captain Flint. "I thought she'd got over it for good, that first day."

Just then Titty, very pale and green, came out of the companion, and stood there, holding on to the mast.

"You too?" said Captain Flint. "What have you been up to below decks? You were all right last night, and it was much worse then."

Titty looked at him as if he were three yards farther away than he was. She slid and scrambled, keeping her feet but nearly falling, down to the bulwarks where she clung on by the shrouds.

"What's happened?" asked Captain Flint again.

"It's . . . it's quite all right," said Titty, and was dreadfully sick over the side.

"What can they be doing down there?" said Captain Flint, and he walked round the deckhouse and down the companion into the saloon.

*

He found no one in the saloon. But there was a noise of talking in the fo'c'sle. Captain Flint started forward. This is what he heard.

"That's two." The voice was the voice of Bill, who was sitting on a coil of rope talking to John, Susan, Peggy, and Roger.

"Well, I told them not to try it," said Susan. "And don't spit on the floor again, please, Bill. Go on using the old paint can."

"I think I've had enough for now," said John.

"Can't I try just a tiny bit?" said Roger.

"No," said Susan.

"I'm not going to try it," said Peggy.

"I can turn you all up without that," said Bill. "This seasickness, it's just nothing. Chewing tobacco ain't got nothing to do with it. Shall I tell you how they cure me? 'Don't you never hold in,' they said. 'Get it over the side and feel better,' they said. And the way they cure me was bacon fat. Have you got any bacon fat?"

"Yes," said Peggy.

"Well, you wants a bit of string," said Bill. "Then you ties the string to the biggest bit of bacon fat you can swallow. Then you swallows it, keeping a hold on the other end of the string. Then you . . ."

There was a noise of scuffling up the ladder and out of the forehatch.

Roger, with a face the colour of old mousetrap cheese, came bolting out of the fo'c'sle, was brought up sharp by a lurch of the vessel, grabbed at a bulkhead, came skidding through the alleyway into the saloon, dodged Captain

Flint, struggled round the table, flung himself at the companion steps and climbed desperately.

The voice of Bill came again from the fo'c'sle, in tones of mild surprise.

"Well," he said, "if they won't wait to be told . . ."

Captain Flint smothered his laughter, turned back, and went up again on deck. By now the whole ship's company was there, except, of course, Bill. Nancy, Susan and Peggy were up in the bows, looking doubtingly at each other. John was holding on to the capstan, swallowing hard and fast. Titty and Roger were leaning over the bulwarks together. Titty was holding Roger's head. Mr Duck was taking no notice of them at all, looking at clouds racing across the sky.

Captain Flint said nothing. He walked slowly forward, in time to see a shock of red hair come up out of the forehatch. Bill, the ragged ends of his blue trousers tucked into a spare pair of sea-boots, lent him by Peggy, climbed out.

"You keeps a hold of the end of the string," he was saying, "and you jiggles it, just so's to shift the bacon . . ."

Nancy, Susan and Peggy turned hurriedly away. John gulped.

"Look here, young man," said Captain Flint to Bill. "We can't have you aboard here if you begin the day by putting three-quarters of my crew out of action."

"I was just telling 'em how to cure seasickness," said Bill.

"Well, suppose you don't," said Captain Flint. "Those two mates are doing the cooking, and if you go on the way you've started there won't be any dinner. You'd better stop this and give them a hand with the potatoes."

"I'm a rare hand with potatoes," said Bill willingly. "Gutting herrings, too. There ain't a boy in Lowestoft can gut herrings like what I can ..."

"All right," said Captain Flint. "Get those mates to give you some potatoes to peel. But don't talk to them about herrings. Not yet."

"Don't seem as if they likes to learn about them things," said Bill.

*

Nothing more was said about Bill's cure for seasickness. Nobody bore him any malice for it, but he learnt that day that there were some things allowed in the *Viper* that were not allowed in the *Wild Cat*. After the middle-day dinner Captain Flint, impatient to be getting on, decided that under very much shortened sail she could stand what was left of the gale. Bill showed then, while they were setting the reefed foresail, that at some jobs not one of these children could touch him. Then, when the tiny headsail had been let draw, and the *Wild Cat* had heeled over and picked herself up to run, and was flying away to the south-west across the Bay of Biscay, Bill went aft, dug out once more his plug of black tobacco, cut himself a small scrap, braced himself close by the steering-wheel, and silently chewing, settled down to watch with an expert eye Captain Flint's performance as a helmsman.

"How long have you been chewing tobacco?" asked the skipper suddenly.

"I begin when I were young," said Bill. "You needn't be feared sir. I always spits to loo'ard."

"All right," said Captain Flint. "But don't waste tobacco on the others, and no chewing below decks or in your cabin."

All the rest of that day, all that night, and all the next day, no one was allowed to touch the wheel but Captain Flint and Peter Duck, while the *Wild Cat* raced for the south among rolling seas that seemed like mountains. Whenever he could, Bill was on deck, watching them. It was only on the second day when the wind began to lessen, that he was at all dissatisfied. He admitted to himself that Captain Flint could steer well enough, though not up to Black Jake. With Peter Duck's steering he had, of course, no fault to find. But he did think, that second day, that they might have shaken out a reef and carried a bit more sail.

Once, when Peter Duck sent him into the deckhouse with a message, he stopped to look at the sporting guns that Captain Flint had there standing upright in a rack, with a bit of oily rag stuffed into the mouth of the barrel to keep dirt out.

"What's this one?" he asked.

"Rifle," said Captain Flint, glancing up from the chart.

"And this?"

"Shotgun."

"Rabbits and such?" said Bill, looking with greater interest at the third.

"Elephant-gun, that," said Captain Flint. "I had it in Ceylon."

"There ain't no elephants aboard the *Viper*,"

said Bill, "but I reckon it's lucky you got them guns."

"We've lost the *Viper* all right, after that last blow," said Captain Flint, "even if he didn't go right up the Irish Sea looking for us in that fog."

"When Black Jake's got his teeth into something he don't let go as easy as that," said Bill.

"Cheer up," said Captain Flint. "We won't hand you over."

"I wasn't thinking you would," said Bill.

Queer ship, the *Wild Cat* was, and queer folk aboard her, too. They didn't seem to take things seriously. They didn't know Black Jake and his friends. Bill said no more, and went out.

But Nancy, who had been looking at the pencilled spot on the chart, that Captain Flint had just been putting there to mark their position, followed him. She found him in the lee of the deckhouse looking up at the sails.

"What's up, Bill?" she said.

"If this ship was mine," said Bill, "and I had Mr Duck aboard her, and knowed that Black Jake was after him, I wouldn't be sailing her easy. I'd crowd on sail, and carry on till her masts went or I sailed her under. That's how I'd sail, if I knowed that Black Jake was a-sailing after me."

CHAPTER XVI

THE MADEIRAS AT DUSK

ON the fourth day after the *Wild Cat* had dodged
the *Viper* in the fog and picked up the red-haired
Bill, the look out (Peggy, as it happened) got a
first sight of Finisterre. There had been a good
deal of mist after the storm, and Captain Flint
had been looking at the log every half-hour or so
and spending a lot of time in the deckhouse doing
one sum after another to find out how far they
must have sailed. He had been very pleased indeed
when Peggy had suddenly called out that she saw
land. The mist was lifting to the south-east, and
there, below it, was the long, steep-browed cape
and the rock of Centolo lying off the point, and two
or three tunny fishers with their tall sails. Captain
Flint came out and sat on the roof of the deckhouse
staring proudly at Finisterre almost as if he felt it
was his own. After all, he had left the Land's End
in a thick fog, and been hove-to for a good many
hours in the storm, and found his way here right
across the Bay of Biscay. Anyone thinks well of a
point or a lighthouse if it turns up just when and
where he has been expecting to see it. And all the
crew of the *Wild Cat* crowded along the rail and
took turns with glasses and telescopes in looking
at the famous cape.

It was a long way off, and there was no point
in going nearer to it. At least, so Captain Flint
thought, and in the end everybody agreed about

it. Some of them had at first been thinking that
it would be fun to land in Vigo and Lisbon, and
anyhow to sail close along the coasts of Spain
and Portugal. But there were good reasons why
they should not waste a single moment on mere
sightseeing.

"Suppose we go into Vigo," said Captain Flint,
"and spend a couple of days there. Those two days
may be just enough to let Black Jake get to Crab
Island before us."

Peter Duck agreed with Captain Flint, and
he had other reasons of his own. "Harbours,"
he said, "are all one and all dirt. Well enough
if we was hard up for grub or run out of water,
but a well-found ship's no need of them. Now the
Thermopylae, she'd be as much as a hundred and
twenty days out of Shanghai, and did she ever run
into a port where she'd no cargo to land? Of course
she didn't. And why should we? I'm not so set on
Crab Island, but that's where we're bound for, and
I'm all for keeping her sailing till she makes it. We
owes it to the ship."

"It ain't as if Black Jake don't know how to get
there," said Bill, talking it over with the others.
"And if he gets there first we'd best go somewhere
else."

So, though the *Wild Cat* was no racing clipper
like the *Thermopylae*, but only a little schooner
with pole masts and rather small sails for her
size, everybody agreed to waste no time that could
be saved. Captain Flint took the topsails off her
every night, because, he said, in these waters, and
with uncertain winds, you never knew when you
wouldn't be jolly glad not to have to take them off

in a hurry in the dark. But at earliest dawn he set topsails again. Everybody did the best they could for the little schooner, and the worst that ever John or Nancy or Bill said of each other was to point out that whoever of them was at the wheel had put a waggle in her wake.

South of Finisterre they found the good weather again. They sailed right down the coast, outside the Burlings and the Farilhoes, those two groups of rocks on which so many vessels have been wrecked. They passed them at night, not seeing the wretched little green light of the Farilhoes until they had long been watching the brilliant gleam and flash of the Burlings, although the Burlings were much farther away. Then, the next morning, they took their departure from Cape Roca, outside Lisbon, and their coastwise sailing was over. Captain Flint set a course for Madeira, and, as Cape Roca dropped below the horizon, they knew they would see no other land until they sighted Porto Santo, nearly six hundred miles away.

Already those four days crossing the Bay of Biscay had accustomed them to being out of sight of land. Some people would have thought it dull, but there always seemed to be something to look at. It might be the gulls floating after the ship with hardly a flap of their broad wings, swooping down to pick up a scrap of biscuit that somebody had dropped overboard, or flashing close by the bulwarks and catching scraps flung to them in the air. It might be a steamship, a big liner from South America, or a long, low tanker, carrying oil, with its funnel right aft and no derricks, so that anybody could tell at once what it was. Or it might be a school of porpoises, plunging together through the crests of the waves, as if they were swimming a sort of water hurdle race. In and out, their backs gleaming in the sunshine as they turned over and down again, the porpoises raced together, and everybody used to rush to the side to watch them until their white splashes were too far away to be seen. Or it might be flying-fish, glittering silver things shooting out of the side of a wave, their long fins whirring, looking like little bright white flying pheasants, diving into the top of another wave, coming straight through it and out at the other side, and sometimes skimming the water for a long distance before they disappeared in it again.

There was always something to see. And, besides, there was always something to do. Susan and Peggy were busy from morning to night with their cooking and housekeeping. "Shipkeeping, it ought to be called," as Roger pointed out one day when Susan said she was too busy housekeeping to knit a stocking cap for Gibber. Gibber, by the way, got his stocking cap all right, but it was knitted by Peter Duck when he had finished darning his socks. He knitted it from blue wool, on the pattern of his own, and Susan, when she saw it, let shipkeeping go hang while she made a red woollen tassel to go on the top of it.

Every day the main water tank had to be filled up from the small screw-top tanks that were stored under the flooring down below. In this way Susan was able to keep count of exactly how much water they were using. She never had

been very good at sums, and neither had Peggy,
but long before the end of that voyage nobody
could have found fault with their additions and
subtractions and divisions. They were calculating
all the time, and often Susan would wake up in
the early morning thinking that one of the sums
had gone wrong, and then she would sit up in her
bunk and work it out again, and tell Titty about
it, and Titty, in the bunk below, would also have
a go with pencil and paper, trying to help. Inside
the deckhouse door there was a card, and every
time one of those tins from down below was emptied into the main tank, Susan used to tick it off
on this card, so that Captain Flint, too, was able
to keep an eye on the way the water was going.
They were very careful about the water, doing
most of their washing in salt water, using special
salt-water soap. It did not make much of a lather,
and it left them feeling rather sticky, but anything
was better than running short of drinking water.
And in the end, Captain Flint said that it was all
due to Susan that things went off so well. If she
had not been so careful with the water they could
never have done what they did.

They kept watches, too. And in fine weather
John, Nancy, and Bill, two at a time, or sometimes all three together, had charge of the ship for
four hours in the afternoon. They had a compass
course to steer. There was no land for them to run
into. And anyhow, in case of meeting other ships,
or in case the wind played any tricks, they could
always bang on the deckhouse door and bring out
Peter Duck or Captain Flint, who tried to get some
rest during the day, because at night one or other

SUMS

of them was always on deck. Bill, of course, had been steering small sailing vessels ever since he could remember, and John and Nancy had learnt a lot about it by the time they had come so far. And, of course, all day, no matter what was going on in the way of shipkeeping, it was the duty of everybody who happened to be on deck to keep a good look out.

Peter Duck taught them how to make nets, and, taking turns at it themselves, and with a bit of help from him, they made a hammock and slung it between the foremast and the windward shrouds, and collected a good lot of bumps between them, what with trying to get into it or out of it while the *Wild Cat* went carelessly swinging along, up and down, over the ocean waves. The hammock was a great success, but nobody wanted to stay in it very long. Staying in it meant keeping still, more or less, if you did not want to roll out. They tried playing deck-quoits over the top of it, throwing rope rings (which Peter Duck showed them how to make) to and fro, catching them and throwing them back again. But so many of the rope rings went over the side that they grew tired of making new ones, and Peter Duck said there would be a shortage of spare rope if they went on with that game too long.

Then they took to skipping. Everybody thought this would be rather a childish game when Captain Flint first suggested it, but they very soon found they could collect bumps even better with the skipping-rope than with the hammock. It was no joke at all, skipping on the sloping deck of a little schooner, especially as the slope of the deck

was never the same for more than a second or
two at a time. Even Bill saw that there must be
something in it when he had watched Captain
Flint skipping most solemnly, a hundred skips
with the right foot first, a hundred with the
left, and then fifty both together, when he sank
exhausted on the skylight. Bill tried. He did not
sink exhausted on the deck, because he had not
time. The deck came up and met him very hard
before he had got through his first three skips.
In the end they all got pretty good at skipping,
and it came a lot cheaper in rope than the deck
tennis over the top of the hammock.

Everything was going like clockwork. Madeira
was in sight. They had passed the little island of
Porto Santo and were looking forward to anchor-
ing in Funchal and going ashore to do some
shopping in this foreign port, besides filling up the
tanks with fresh water, when, late one afternoon,
Roger, playing with the telescope, caught sight of
another schooner a long way astern of them.

Earlier in the day they had sailed through
a small fleet of Portuguese fishermen, and now
Roger was amusing himself by resting the big
ship's telescope on the stern rail and trying to
have a look at them. The whole little fleet of
them had hoisted their sails and were coming
after the *Wild Cat*, no doubt bringing their catch
to Madeira. Just for a moment they bobbed into
sight for Roger as the *Wild Cat*'s stern dropped
low, bringing the telescope down with it. Then the
Wild Cat's bows would go down, her stern would
go up, and Roger looking through the telescope
could see nothing at all but sky. Still, taking his

chance when the *Wild Cat* gave it him, Roger saw
enough of the little fleet of fishermen to notice that
away beyond them was another sailing vessel of a
different rig.

"There's another ship coming after the fishermen," he said.

Nobody took any notice. Everybody knew Roger and the sort of thing he was always seeing
when he had the big telescope to himself. Bill
and John were at the wheel. All the others,
except the skipper and Peter Duck, were up in
the bows, looking eagerly at Madeira, which was
fast becoming clearer right ahead. Captain Flint
was in the deckhouse, busy with the charts, and
wondering if he could manage to bring the *Wild
Cat* into Funchal without taking a pilot aboard.
Peter Duck was taking his afternoon sleep.

"It's got two masts," said Roger, "and big sails
on both of them."

Bill heard that all right.

"Let's have a look." He left the wheel to John,
squatted down, and steadied the big telescope.

The next moment he dived head first into
the deckhouse, startled Captain Flint, and shook
Peter Duck by the foot, as he lay there snoring in
his happy, contented manner.

"Wake up, Mr Duck! Cap'n Flint, sir. It's him!
He's after us again."

"Less lip," said Mr Duck, sitting up. "What's
all the noise about?"

But even he looked grave when, after they had
both had a look through the telescope, they agreed
that if this was not the *Viper* it was a vessel very
like her.

"Coming on fast, too," said Captain Flint.

The others had hurried aft when they saw Captain Flint and Peter Duck outside the deckhouse.

"What is it?" said Nancy.

"Black Jake again," said John.

"Not really," said Susan.

"Of course, really," said Roger. "I saw him first."

"What I would like to know," said Captain Flint, "is, has that fellow seen us? And, if so, what we'd better do about it."

"Well, we'd better have tea anyhow," said Susan, a little later.

They had tea, but by the time it was ready, it was clear to all of them that this schooner, coming south like themselves, was the *Viper*. They would have seen her before if it had not been for the Portuguese fishing boats.

"How did he guess what we were going to do?" said Captain Flint rather crossly, when they were all down in the saloon, except Nancy, who was steering.

"No guessing about it," said Peter Duck. "He's going the shortest way to Crab Island. That's one thing. He'd know you'd be doing the same. And he'd know you'd be putting in to Funchal or the Canaries to fill up with fresh water, same's he will himself."

Captain Flint got suddenly up out of his chair. There was a new look in his eye.

"Susan," he said, "let's have another look at all that water arithmetic of yours."

Ten minutes later they were back again.

"Thanks to Susan," said Captain Flint, patting

the mate on the back, lifting his mug of tea to her and swallowing all that was left in it. "Thanks to Susan, we'll do him yet. We'll carry right on. We've more than enough water to last. Funchal's on the south side of the island. It'll be getting dark before we turn the corner of the island and then, instead of stopping in Funchal Roads, or going into the harbour, we'll carry right on for the Caribbees and Mr Duck's island."

Peter Duck looked deep into the bottom of his mug. He was thinking.

"Well, Mr Duck?"

"I'll not say but it's a good plan, if you're right about the water, sir. He'll be bound to take in water here himself. It's not one schooner in a thousand carries all them tons of fresh water ballast. He'll be taking in water at Funchal, and he'll be looking for you to be doing the same. Now there's more places than one where you might likely do it. He'll be a couple of days before he guesses you ain't stopped. And then he's all but bound to think you're aiming farther south to call for water at Tenerife or Grand Canary. He'll never think of a little vessel like yours heading right across and stopping nowheres."

Not one of the crew could have a word to say against a plan so good, even if it did mean no run ashore to drink iced sherbet in Funchal. They would give Black Jake the slip once more, and if Peter Duck was right, and Black Jake went on to the Canaries, it might very well give them time to get to Crab Island, see what it was that was buried there under Mr Duck's tree, and be sailing home again before ever the *Viper* arrived.

So, as the early dark of the tropical evening rose over the sea, the crew of the *Wild Cat* looked astern at the black schooner racing after them, but still far away. They hoped, now, that Black Jake and his friends had seen them heading for the island. Close past the eastern end of Madeira they steered in the dusk. By the time the *Viper* had turned the corner, it had long been pitch dark. It would have been a miracle if anybody aboard the *Viper* had thought for a moment that the *Wild Cat* was not putting into Funchal. But the *Wild Cat* sailed on. She did not head in for Funchal lights that glittered down on the sea front and high on the hillside. She kept steadily on in the darkness, and at midnight was heading west-south-west into the wide Atlantic.

As the lights of Funchal faded astern, Captain Flint let fall one sentence of regret.

"Blow it," he said, "and I'd been counting on getting a decent spade in Madeira."

BOOK TWO

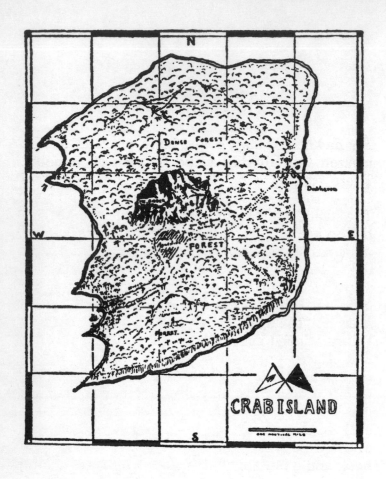

CRAB ISLAND

ONE NAUTICAL MILE

CHAPTER XVII

TRADE WIND

AT dawn next day a low bank of cloud on the horizon was all that could be seen of Madeira. There was no sign of the *Viper*, and the *Wild Cat* settled down once more to regular routine. The steady trade wind from the north-east hurried her on her way from dawn till sunset, slackening a little in the evenings, so that during this part of the voyage Captain Flint and Peter Duck agreed that there could be nothing against carrying the topsails all night. Every morning, before the sun grew hot, the whole crew came on deck in bathing things, dipped canvas buckets full of salt water, and sluiced the decks and each other by way of beginning the day. Day after day was like the one before it. Watches were kept, bells were struck, meals were cooked and eaten, pots and pans were cleaned and plates and mugs were washed. Most of the time Peter Duck had a line out with a big hook and a bundle of strips of bacon rind, hoping to catch a shark, but never catching one, though now and then on smaller hooks he did catch something that was good to eat besides the flying-fish that sometimes flew aboard by mistake and were always warmly welcomed in the galley. For real good fishing, he used to say, you couldn't beat the Norfolk Broads.

Peter Duck taught everybody a good many things about knots and ropes that are not to be found in books. Captain Flint taught both John and Nancy how to take an observation with the sextant, and together they wrestled with problems in mathematics a great deal harder than any they had met at school. At first the sums they worked out after taking their shots at the sun (and it is not easy to use a sextant on a swaying deck) ended up by making out that the *Wild Cat* was sailing in the Sahara Desert, crossing the Andes, or passing within hail of well-known cities in the Middle West. But before long they could be pretty sure of finding that she was somewhere in the Atlantic, and during the last few days of the voyage there was seldom more than fifty or sixty miles' difference between the results of their calculations and those of Captain Flint. This was perhaps the nearest thing to lessons anybody had while aboard ship. Captain Flint used to tell them all about the famous mining rushes of the past, but you could hardly call that history, any more than you could put down as natural science Peter Duck's yarns about being towed by a shark, or the truth about the sea serpent, which he had seen more than once, or about Pelorus Jack, the fish that used to pilot vessels into Sydney harbour, and had a law made in his own protection.

Every day at noon Captain Flint worked out the ship's position and marked it on the chart with a little cross of red ink and the date neatly written beside it. Everybody used to go into the deckhouse to take a look at it. That chart, and those little red crosses marking out a line that ran from the Lizard down to Finisterre, and then to Madeira, and then south-west down into the North-east Trades

MORNING SPLASHES

and then west, on and on, was almost the only thing that made it seem possible that they were really moving, and nearing the other side of the Atlantic. One stretch of sea is very like another. But for these little red crosses, each one a little farther across the chart, it might have seemed that they had been sailing in the middle of an enormous dish, sailing hard and fast but somehow fixed in the middle of it, so that they had never moved at all.

For days and days they saw no other vessels. And then one morning, as the sky lightened and the stars faded out and the sun rose over the stern, Nancy and Captain Flint, who were on watch together, saw a three-masted ship, full-rigged, under a tremendous press of canvas, far away on the horizon before them and heading about north-west. For some time they had seen, dimly, that there was something there, but now the rays of the sun, slanting low across the water, lit up her sails like pale hedge-roses. Every sail, filled by the wind, seemed curled and coloured like a petal.

"It's worth fetching Mr Duck out of his bunk to see that," said Captain Flint, and Nancy took the wheel, while he went into the deckhouse.

Peter Duck was out of his bunk in a moment, alert, ready, as if he were still on watch. He came out of the deckhouse, took the telescope, and looked at the distant vessel. The rose on her sails was paling every moment as the sun climbed higher.

"Minds me of the *Louisiana Belle*," he said. "Yankee clipper, homeward bound, that's what she is. Does me good, it does, to see a ship like that. Skysails over her royals. And main and mizen staysails set."

He looked sadly over the sails of the *Wild Cat*, wishing she could carry a little more canvas somewhere.

Captain Flint laughed.

"Can't help it, Mr Duck. There isn't another stitch we can put on her."

Mr Duck said nothing. He was thinking of the *Thermopylae*, of his own youth, of days gone by. He lifted the telescope again and watched the ship, far, far away on the horizon. Her sails shone now like white sparks in the sunlight, even to Nancy and Captain Flint, who were looking at her with the naked eye.

"Hull down she'll be in an hour," said Peter Duck at last. "We'll maybe not see another all the voyage. Rot screw steamers," he burst out fiercely, "driving vessels like her off the seas where they belong!"

When the others came on deck, the vessel was already below the horizon. Nancy told them about her.

"We really must be getting across," she said. "Mr Duck thinks she'd come up from the Horn, bound for Boston or New York."

"We ought to begin to look for branches then," said Titty, "and birds. Columbus saw lots before he sighted land."

"His course was a bit north of ours," said Captain Flint, "so he saw the weeds of the Sargasso."

"He found a crab and kept it," said Titty. "And

lots of flowers. Don't you remember reading us that bit last week?"

"We'll begin keeping a look out for them," said Captain Flint, though not as if he thought they would be seeing anything very soon.

But two nights after that, while John was at the wheel, keeping watch with Peter Duck, he heard a frightened cheeping in the dark, and when it grew light he found a little bird like a spotted flycatcher, only with green on its wings, sheltering under the dinghy. It would not eat rice, or oatmeal, or even biscuits. Everybody was afraid it would be starved. But then Peggy remembered some flour that Susan had wanted to throw away because it had maggots in it. Roger had said, "Think if we were wrecked. We wouldn't mind the maggots then." And Susan had said he could keep it if he liked, so long as it didn't get loose. Roger had put it in an old cocoa tin, and kept it in his cabin, in case of shipwreck. This was very lucky, because the little bird took no interest in any of the ordinary kinds of food, but was delighted with the maggots. It ate about a dozen, sipped some water, had a bath in a saucer, dried itself, perching on the mainsheet in the sunshine, and then suddenly flew away over the bows, on into the west.

"We *must* be getting near land," said Titty, "or he'd have stayed longer."

"Birds is foolish like," said Bill. "I've knowed 'em fly slap bang into the lantern, when we was lying to our nets out in the North Sea. Same as moths, birds are. No sense to 'em."

"Well, we must be very near land all the same," said Titty.

"I wonder if it's the right land," said Peggy.

"I never thought of that," said Roger, and went into the deckhouse to make sure. "Where are we now?" he asked Captain Flint.

"Have a look for yourself," said Captain Flint.

Roger looked.

On the chart on the deckhouse table, the red crosses had been coming nearer and nearer to the outer islands and towards a tiny speck round which a red ink circle had been drawn.

John, who was looking over Roger's shoulder, measured to see how far the red crosses were from each other, and how far the last one was from the little circle that marked Crab Island.

"I say," said John, "if we do as much today as we did yesterday we ought to get there tomorrow."

"I'm not sure about that," said Captain Flint. "We're not doing quite what we were, but unless it falls calm again, we ought to be seeing Crab Island some time before tomorrow night."

As he spoke, coming out of the deckhouse, to look round, the wind freshened a little. It was almost as if the *Wild Cat* had heard him and had made up her mind to have a good run to finish up with.

"Oughtn't we to nail a gold ducat to the mast?" said Titty, "to be given to the one who first sights land? Or was it some other bit of money? Anyway, Columbus did it."

"There isn't a ducat aboard," said Captain Flint.

Titty thought for a minute.

"I've got it," she said. "Let the first one who sights land be the first one to step out of the boat. You see it won't be quite such a desert

island for any of the others, because somebody
will be ashore already."

"That seems to be fair enough," said Captain
Flint. "And we might name the landing-place
after him, too. Or her. It'll probably be a her
in this ship."

After that people kept walking up to the bows to
look ahead into the west, although Captain Flint
had said there would be nothing to be seen until
tomorrow.

"We may have gone a bit farther than he
thinks," said Roger. Telescopes and glasses were
overworked. Everybody was wanting a turn with
them.

"Who's going to stay up all night?" said Nancy,
as she came up on deck after tea.

"Nobody," said Captain Flint. "The watch below
goes to bed tonight exactly as if we were still a
thousand miles from land."

"Pity we aren't," said Peter Duck. "There's
no good comes of land anyhow, except ship's
stores, and they're mostly not what they're sold
for."

Nobody minded. Everybody knew that Peter
Duck would have liked a clear passage, round
and round the world with no land to bother about
anywhere. He would have been a proper sailor to
join the *Flying Dutchman*, that old ship that has
been sailing on and on for hundreds of years and
will sail on for ever.

"There'll be nothing to see in the night," said
Captain Flint. "You and I'll take one watch, Nancy, and Mr Duck and John'll take the other, and if
we want anybody else on deck, we'll send down to

roust them out. There'll be hard work for everybody tomorrow, and a good night's sleep is the
way to get ready for it. Sighting land's nothing.
The real work comes after."

All the same, that evening, nobody was in a
hurry to go below. Peter Duck and John had the
first watch, but they were never really alone on
deck until just before Captain Flint and Nancy
turned out to take over at midnight. Even Susan
was not as sensible as usual. She was very pleased
with the way things had lasted out. They were
not nearly half-way through the tinned foods, and
they had a full six weeks' water supply still in the
tanks. She was feeling, perhaps, that she need
not be so careful any longer. On any other night
she would have chivvied Roger and Titty to bed,
and gone to bed herself so decidedly that Peggy
would have gone too. But, on this last night of
the ocean voyage, she was walking up and down
the deck with Peggy till nearly ten o'clock. Titty
hung about the deckhouse, looking at the path of
the moon over the sea and thinking of Columbus
on his high poop. Roger, after he had begun to
go to bed, came up again through the forehatch
to tell the others that he had been to say good
night to Gibber and had found the ship's monkey
so restless and jumpy that he was sure there must
be a smell of palm trees in the air already. Nancy,
knowing that her watch was to come, was the
only one who went to bed in anything like proper
time. Bill, of those who were not on duty, stayed
up longest. He was never one to waste any sleep
he could get, but, that last night, he did not go
to his cabin after supper. Everybody thought he

had, but he took his chance, and went up through the forehatch, and climbed out to the very end of the bowsprit, and sat there, astride of the spar, swaying on and on ahead of the ship, above the dark water in the moonlight night.

"What are you doing out there?" called Captain Flint, when he came on deck just before midnight, and strolled up forward, and saw Bill riding the bowsprit away out there under the foot of the jib. "Your watch below!"

Bill wriggled back inboard and shot down the forehatch like a startled rabbit down its burrow.

"Out on the bowsprit end, was he?" said old Peter Duck, when Captain Flint told him about it. "Many's the night I've done that when I was a lad. It's a grand place to see the stars from and to feel the driving of the ship."

CHAPTER XVIII

LAND HO!

An hour before the usual time, the crew and the deck of the *Wild Cat* were dripping with good salt water. Captain Flint and Nancy had turned in at four o'clock, when Peter Duck and John took over to watch for the last time the dark sails pale as the sky lightened, and for the last time to see the fiery ocean sunrise over the stern of the ship. But Captain Flint was up again at seven bells, and so were all the others. John, at the wheel, could hear drawers being pulled out and banged in again inside the deckhouse, and then Captain Flint came out with a hand lead for sounding and a big coil of line, with the depths marked on it with tags of bunting and bits of leather and string tied with knots. That certainly looked as if they were nearing land, although, for all that could be seen, the *Wild Cat* might have been no nearer land than she had been a week before. All round her, the sea stretched to the horizon. But there was the skipper bringing out the lead and hanging the lead line over a belaying-pin all ready for use. The dripping crew looked at the horizon in a new way, as if they expected to see something on the other side of it.

At breakfast everybody was bothering Peter Duck to tell them again just what the island would look like.

"It'll be full forty years since I see it," said

Peter Duck, "and then it was a seaman point it out to me when we was passing far out. Two hills there are, and they open out as you goes to nor'ard of 'em. The biggest of 'em's in the middle of the island. The other big one's nor'-west from it, and then there's a smaller you'd hardly notice away to south-east. That seaman as was telling me, he'd been there for water. I dare say I'll remember the place when I see it, but it's no use my telling you what I don't know rightly myself."

"You'll be staying on deck to catch first sight of it?" said Titty, when Peter Duck was going off into the deckhouse.

"We shan't sight it no sooner for my staying on deck," said the old sailor. "I'm bringing to in my bunk till it's my spell at the wheel. I'll trust it to the rest of you to keep a look out for that island."

Indeed not one of them could think of anything else. Even Gibber and the parrot, both of whom were brought on deck, were very restless. This may have been because they knew in some way of their own that land was near, or just because they felt the disturbance in the minds of all the crew. Nobody could settle down to anything, and Susan complained that that morning's breakfast plates were the worst wiped of any plates on the whole voyage.

At midday Mr Duck came on deck again and Captain Flint took observations of the sun and worked out the ship's position. Everybody, except Mr Duck, crowded into the deckhouse to see the little cross marked in pencil and then inked in in red ink. It showed how very near the island they really were.

"Any time now," said Captain Flint, "but if it's
all the same to you," he added, grabbing Peggy,
who was just going to bolt forward to get a good
place to look out from, "the cooks will let us have
our dinners just the same."

Dinner was quickly over, and for once even
Susan thought it might be as well not to wash
up right away. "We'll wash up better after we've
sighted it," said Peggy, and Susan agreed. Everybody was on the look out. Bill had been the first
to go aloft. He had climbed right up the foremast
and was standing on the cross-trees. John had
climbed up the ratlines and was waiting up there
in the shrouds, close below Bill. Nancy had gone
up the mainmast shrouds. Peggy, Susan, Roger,
Titty, Gibber, and the parrot were all up on the
foredeck. Captain Flint had let them have the
glasses. John had the little telescope. Peter Duck
was at the wheel. Captain Flint was walking up
and down the starboard side of the deck, from the
deckhouse to the capstan and back again, now and
then sweeping the horizon with the big telescope.

"Look! Look!" said Roger suddenly. "Do look
at Gibber."

Gibber was solemnly trotting along after Captain Flint. He had a belaying-pin in one hand, and
when Captain Flint used the telescope, Gibber put
the belaying-pin to his eye, and copied the skipper
exactly.

Everybody shouted with laughter, and laughed
the more when Captain Flint wondered what
they were looking at, turned sharp round and
caught Gibber at it, sweeping the horizon with
the belaying-pin in a most professional manner.

FIRST SIGHT OF CRAB ISLAND

And just at that moment, when not a single one of them down on deck was thinking of the island, there was a shout, almost a yelp, from the top of the foremast, far over their heads.

"Land ho!"

Bill had been in a tremendous hurry to get those two words out.

"Where? Where?" Shouts floated up from the deck and across from the mainmast where Nancy was eagerly straining her eyes to see something more than that unending rim of sea.

"Starboard bow!" shouted Bill. "Let's have that telescope, Cap'n John."

"I see it, too," said John. "Nearly dead ahead. Well done you for spotting it."

"Well done, Bill!" Shouts came from all over the ship.

Gibber, seeing everybody looking up at Bill, dropped his belaying-pin, raced up past him, and clung to the truck at the very top of the foremast.

Captain Flint ran up the foremast shrouds.

"I want Mr Duck to see this," he said. "Look here, John, will you run down and take the wheel a minute?"

Peter Duck, alone of all the ship's company, had not said a word on hearing Bill's shout. He had hardly glanced up. At the moment he was at the wheel. His job was to steer the ship and keep her on a compass course, no matter what other people might be shouting, hanging about in the shrouds up there, or perched on the cross-trees.

But he gave John the wheel on getting the message from the skipper, and a moment later he was going up the foremast shrouds.

"It's land all right," said Captain Flint, handing him the glasses, which he had got from Susan in exchange for the big telescope before going aloft.

"Crab Island," said Peter Duck. "There'll be two hills there, but we've got 'em in line on this bearing, so's they look like one. Maybe we'd better alter course a little to bring it on the port bow. With this wind we'll be better going round the north end to look for an anchorage. There's no place this side, only for wrecks. Well, I tell you, sir, I never thought to be seeing that place again."

Everybody could see the land now, the faint, pale hump rising out of the sea, because everybody knew exactly where to look for it. Yet it was a long way distant when it had first been sighted. Very, very slowly the *Wild Cat* seemed to bring the island nearer. It was difficult to believe that she was sailing just as fast as she had been the day before. It was not until quite late in the day that they could see the long line of white surf that marked the shore. All through the afternoon, they were taking turns with glasses and telescopes, watching that pale sketch of a hill turn into something solid and dark, with green forest spreading over its slopes. In the end Captain Flint could bear it no longer, gave up looking at the island, and went into the deckhouse to play Miss Milligan's patience, one game after another.

Towards evening they could see that there were indeed two hills, or rather three, one low one to the south, a large one in the middle with a black, rocky peak lifting above the trees, and another large one, though tree-covered, that had at first

been hidden behind the shoulder of the other.
And all along the western shore of the island
here seemed to be a continuous line of breakers
crashing in white surf upon the beach.

"And where was it your ship was wrecked?"
asked Titty.

"It was black dark," said Peter Duck, "so I
couldn't rightly say. But it's my belief she'd be
driven on the shallows on this side, and then,
with the swell lifting her up and letting her drop,
pounding her on the bottom, she'd break up in no
time at all. And there's not a boat could have lived
that night, driving ashore with a big sea running.
It's a miracle I come ashore alive. There'd have
been a lot of trouble saved, to Black Jake for
one, and maybe to our skipper for another, if I
hadn't. There's only one place along that shore
where there's a bit of quiet water. A foot or two,
one way or the other, and I'd not be looking at
the island now. The crabs or the fish would have
had me long ago."

"Palm trees," said Titty suddenly, her mind
taken from the thought of that old wreck by the
new sights before her, "Look at them against the
sky, up on that hill."

"Can you see any of the crabs?" asked Roger,
tugging at Captain Flint, who had put away his
cards by now, and was looking at the island
through the telescope.

"Not from this distance," said Captain Flint.
"Now, tell me, Mr Duck, it was somewhere by
this shore that you saw the stuff buried."

"It was under my tree I see them two putting
a bag in a hole. And that was right on the edge

of the woods, where the palm trees grow down to the beach. Yes, it was down this side they come, and I followed 'em back over the shoulder of the big hill, and down t'other side to where they'd a boat ashore in a bay there is there. They likely knowed the island well, them two, bringing their boat ashore with a stream of water handy."

"We'll use their anchorage tonight," said Captain Flint. "Mate Susan will be pleased enough to have her tanks full again."

"Fresh-water washing for everybody tomorrow," said Susan.

"Bathing," said Titty.

"Nancy's going to wash her hair," said Peggy.

"Well, aren't you going to wash yours?" said Nancy.

"The parrot'll enjoy having a good splash, too," said Titty. "He's never really seemed to think much of salt water when I've offered him a bath."

"Pretty good hills, they are," said John. "There ought to be splendid climbing on those rocks."

"We'll do some exploring once we've got the treasure aboard," said Captain Flint. "Bill's Landing, it's going to be. That's one good name. What about Mount Gibber for the big hill? We'll get no end of fun out of this place."

"It's when the anchor goes down that troubles begin," said Peter Duck, who cared nothing at all for islands and wanted only to be sailing once more.

Bill watched the island but did not say a word. He knew the North Sea as well as most people know the place where they were born, and going to sea, for him, had usually meant fishing on the Dogger Bank. This was something different. Madeira, seen at dusk, with Black Jake close in pursuit, and the *Viper* coming up astern, had meant little more to him than a lucky bit of cover to allow the *Wild Cat* to throw the enemy off her track. But to come to this green island, with its beaches of bright sand, its black, cliff-like peaks, rising out of feathery palms swaying and blowing in the trade wind, this was indeed going foreign, and Bill would not trust himself to speak lest, for once, he should let the others see he was surprised. It was better to see all he could and to say nothing. These children would say everything that wanted saying.

And then another thought troubled his mind. These children seemed to find it easy to forget Black Jake, but Bill knew him. Peter Duck had been mighty sure that Black Jake would think they had run down to the Canaries when he found that they were not in Funchal harbour, but what if he hadn't? What if somehow or other he had reached the island already? The *Viper* was a fast vessel and carried more sail than the *Wild Cat*. Bill looked eagerly enough at feathery palms and shining beach, but he looked for something else. Was anyone moving on those shores? Was anyone digging under those waving trees?

The sun was already dropping low towards the sea when the *Wild Cat* came sweeping round the northern headland. The wind was slackening. Bill, unable to hold in his fears, with all those others chattering about this and that they saw on the island shores, had gone aloft once more to the foremast crosstrees. If there were a vessel

at anchor behind the island . . . at least he would
know the worst and get it over.

Round the headland came the little green
schooner. The sails were jibed over, and she
slipped along in smoother water, sheltered by the
high ground, though Captain Flint was keeping
her pretty far out for fear of shoals and sunken
rocks. Captain Flint had taken the wheel himself.
Peter Duck was carefully searching the shore with
the big telescope. He had been thinking of going
up to the foremast-head to get a better view of
rocks and shallows, but he had seen that Bill was
up there already and had shouted to him to sing
out if he saw a shoal patch. John and Nancy were
on the foredeck ranging a dozen fathom of chain
clear. During the afternoon they had been helping
Mr Duck to get the big anchor shackled to the
chain, and all ready to let go. Titty and Roger,
Gibber and the parrot were with Captain Flint at
the wheel. The monkey was running backwards
and forwards on the roof of the deckhouse, running on all fours, as he often did when he was
excited about anything. The parrot was in his
cage.

Susan had swept Peggy with her into the galley.

"Don't let's spoil things by being late with
supper," she had said, and the two of them
were hard at it, cooking an extra good one, and
watching the island shores slip by, one strange,
wild picture after another framing itself in the
galley doorway.

The sun went down in a blaze of fire just as
Mr Duck turned quietly to Captain Flint and said:
"I can see where the stream comes out. I mind it

well enough now. The *Mary Cahoun* them fellows
took me off in was laying just south of that bit of
a head. There. Between that one and the next."

"Haul in sheets," called Captain Flint.

At the word Bill came hurrying down by the
foresail halyards.

"Black Jake ain't here yet," he said happily, as
he joined Mr Duck in hauling in the mainsheet.

"Who thought he would be?" said Mr Duck.
"You stand by now and be ready to take the
wheel if the skipper wants to leave it."

The *Wild Cat* headed in towards the shore
in the swiftly falling dusk.

"I won't take her too close in," said Captain
Flint, "though most of these islands have deep
water on the western side. Will you stand by to
take a sounding, Mr Duck?"

The others watched, breathless, while Mr Duck,
after swinging the lead in long, easy swings,
whirled it round and round and suddenly let it
fly forward so that it dropped into the water well
ahead of the ship.

"By the mark ten," called Peter Duck, hauling
the line taut and looking at a little strip of leather
with a hole in it fastened to the line. "Cap'n John,
fetch me that tin of tallow I made ready just inside
the deckhouse door."

John was back with it in a moment, and Peter
Duck pushed some of the tallow into a hold in the
bottom of the lead, using his thumb as if he were
pushing down tobacco in his old pipe.

The *Wild Cat* was slipping on. Again the
lead whirled and flew forward and dropped with
a splash.

"By the deep, eight, and sand," called Peter Duck, feeling between his fingers the stuff that had stuck to the tallow under the lead.

"Eight," called back Bill, standing beside Captain Flint.

Again a splash forward. A silence while Mr Duck was hauling taut the line and feeling that it was touching the bottom.

"By the mark five . . . And sand."

Captain Flint headed the *Wild Cat* into the wind.

"Haul down jib and staysail!"

The headsails fluttered down.

Peter Duck went on steadily sounding.

"Five."

Again.

"And a half. Five."

Again.

"Five."

"LET GO!"

There was a heavy splash, and then the rattle of chain, as John and Nancy let go, and then began playing out fathom after fathom as the *Wild Cat* gathered sternway.

"Fifteen fathom out, sir," called John.

"Give her another five," called Captain Flint.

The *Wild Cat* had made her ocean passage and was anchored in the New World.

Dark was falling fast. There was busy work on deck, as Captain Flint and Peter Duck, John, Nancy, and Bill brought down the great sails that had brought them so far. Then the davits were rigged, and the dinghy was lowered over the side.

"No, no," said Captain Flint. "No one's going

ashore tonight, but Mr Duck's going to lay out a kedge anchor while we're stowing these sails. Bill, you can go with Mr Duck. John, have you got those tiers handy? Let's get at it."

Ten minutes later, the *Wild Cat* was snug for the night. On either side of her were low headlands with tall palm trees dark against a darkening sky. There was a sudden screaming flight of parrots, that brought an answering scream from Polly, who was being given a last look round on deck before being taken below. Gibber was already in his bunk. Everybody was speaking in a whisper, so as to hear the noises of the land. Palm trees were creaking, and rustling their dry, feathery leaves. There was the whistling of tree frogs, and the sharp crac-crac of the grasshoppers. And then, suddenly, millions of lights showed along the edge of the forest, moving all the time. It was as if millions of small bright sparks were dancing there in the dusk.

"Fireflies," said Captain Flint.

"It can't be," said Titty.

"This is the real thing at last," said Nancy.

And then the silence of the ship was broken by the loud, cheerful clanging of the bell inside the galley door.

"We're a bit late after all," said Susan, "but supper is ready now."

"Come on," said Peggy. "She's made a regular thumper."

"Well, I think we deserve it," said Captain Flint.

CHAPTER XIX

ISLAND MORNING

THERE are sometimes advantages in being small. If Titty had been bigger than Susan she would have been sleeping in the upper berth in their cabin, in which case it would have been difficult for her to get up without waking the mate on that first morning in the anchorage at Crab Island. As she had the lower berth, it was easy. She slipped into her bathing things, crept out of the cabin without hitting anything on the way, crossed the saloon on tiptoe, went quietly forward through the alleyway, and, before going on deck, stopped and listened for a moment below the open forehatch. She wanted to hear things before she saw them, so as to enjoy them twice over. She had been looking forward to a desert island ever since she could remember, and she wanted to make the most of it. She stopped at the foot of the ladder and listened. She could hear wind in trees, and grasshoppers, and birds. And then, besides these land noises, there was a noise of land and sea together, the endless noise that you hear when you put one of those big twisted sea-shells to your ear, a noise of waves rolling up and breaking on the shore. She heard, too, a stir in the parrot's cage, but dared not say "Hush!" for fear Polly should choose not to understand her and should answer with a yell. Gibber, she could see, was still curled up asleep in his bunk.

Titty took hold of the sides of the ladder, put her foot on its lowest rung, shut her eyes, and, keeping them shut, climbed up on deck. She wanted to come up on deck and then open her eyes suddenly upon the island scene. But before she was half through the hatch she heard the tapping of a pipe on the bulwarks and knew that, after all, someone had got up before her. She opened her eyes and saw Peter Duck away aft, by the deckhouse, leaning over the bulwarks as if he were looking down into the water. He had not heard her. So, just for a moment, she did not call out to him but pretended to herself that she had sailed alone across the ocean and brought to in this tropical bay.

It was really there, with colours even brighter than she had seen them in her mind, the burning sky, the bright green feathery plumes of the palm trees, the black rocks of the hill towering above them. The sun was climbing up behind those rocks. They were already in blazing sunlight while the green jungle beneath them was still dark. There was sunlight now on the deck of the *Wild Cat*, but there was shadow under the hill. And out of that dark forest parrots were flying up and sparkling suddenly as their bright wings left the shadow and caught the sunshine high above the trees. Yes, the island was really there, and the smell of it drifted over the water, a musky, tropical smell, very different from the smell of tarred ropes that had been in Titty's nostrils as she climbed up through the hatch.

Peter Duck jerked suddenly upright and Titty saw that he was hauling in a line hand over hand. A moment later a rainbow-coloured fish, glittering, flashing in the sunlight, flopped on the deck. Peter Duck grabbed it, freed it from the hook, and dropped it back. Titty, who had run aft, looked over the side and saw the little fish splash into the water, hesitate for a moment, and then with quivering fins and tail swim down into a brilliant world.

"Morning, Able-seaman," said Peter Duck. "You and me's first on deck in a strange port. Two A.B.s together. That's as should be."

"Good morning," said Titty. "But why did you put him back?"

"It's not the gay ones are the best eating," said Peter Duck. "Look you here at these, now." (He pointed to a heap of great fish in an old box he was using as a fish basket, on the deck beside him.) "There's not one with a Joseph's coat like what that fellow was wearing. But there's not one ᵒf them here has half that fellow's bones. All bones he is, and a gay coat on the back of them. There's not chewing for a mouse on him. Well, we've enough now for a grand fish supper. What about turning to and sluicing down the decks?"

"All right," said Titty, looking down over the side again.

"Clear enough," said Peter Duck. "Five fathom it is here, and you'd think it no more'n a couple of feet. Well, I'll be catching one more and put the line away."

Titty stared down into the water that was clearer than good glass. Far down below, on the sandy bottom, where there were patches of green ribbon weed, a shoal of rainbow-coloured fish were swimming. They moved all together, slowly, from one underwater forest to another, and then, suddenly, like one fish, they all darted sideways, or darted forward, or changed their minds and hurried back by the way they had just come.

"That's the big-mouths feeding on them," said Peter Duck. "There. Four or five of them. Grey. Slow they comes, slow, and then, skat! and Joseph's coats go flying and big-mouth gets the one that's thinking of something else and maybe slow in dodging. Now. Watch that one. Coming this way. He's going to make a mistake."

There on the bottom between two patches of weed Titty saw the scrap of silvery fish that Peter Duck was using as a bait. It moved. She saw one of the big grey fish that Mr Duck called big-mouths turn slowly towards it. The bait jerked upwards, just a foot, like a small fish trying to escape. And then it was gone, so suddenly that Titty hardly knew that the big-mouth had pounced until Peter Duck said: "Got him!" and began hauling in the line, when she saw the flashing of the broad silver sides of the big-mouth as it flung itself about trying to shake free. Up it came to the top of the water, followed by a crowd of other fish, and then, just as Peter Duck lifted it into the air, there was a splash, the bait was swinging at the end of the line, the big-mouth was swimming down again, and all the little fish that had followed him up were paying for their curiosity by fright, and were flying in all directions.

"Lost him, after all," said Peter Duck. "Well, maybe we've got more'n enough without him.

What about getting at them decks before the sun's too hot on them?"

"Can't I have the rope ladder out and go for a swim first?"

"It don't seem fair to give a shark his breakfast before you've had your own."

"But it doesn't look sharky a bit. And Captain Flint promised we should bathe when we got here."

"Twice this morning I've had one come up after a big-mouth when I was hauling him in, aye, and bite him off neat as nothing and leave me the head of him on my hook."

"Oh, well," said Titty, "perhaps I'd better not." But she was not at all sure whether Mr Duck was teasing her or really meant it.

She did the next best thing to swimming. She dropped a canvas bucket overboard at the end of its rope, hauled it up full, and turned it upside down over her head. Peter Duck filled a bucket too, and sent the water flying over her. And then the two able-seamen, Titty and Peter Duck together, settled down in earnest, beginning up in the bows of the ship, hauling up buckets of water, emptying them on deck, and driving the running sheets of water along the planking with a couple of big, long-handled mops.

They had worked their way right aft as far as the deckhouse when Captain Flint startled them by coming out of the deckhouse door and taking a header clean over the bulwarks.

Peter Duck dropped his mop and had the rope ladder hanging over the side in a moment.

"Sharks about!" he shouted, as Captain Flint

came up and shook his bald head and wiped the
salt water from his eyes. "Look out, sir!"

Titty found suddenly that she could not breathe.
She had just seen what it was that had made
Mr Duck put so much hurry in his voice.

A big, triangular fin, above a huge dim shadow
in the water, was moving fast towards the swim-
mer. Peter Duck stooped, snatched one of the
big-mouths out of the box that held his morning's
catch, and threw it, hard, so that it hit the water
with a splash, just between Captain Flint and that
dark moving fin. As it touched the water there was
a tremendous swirl, in which the dead fish and the
big triangle of fin vanished together. Captain Flint
struck out instantly for the ship and was climbing
up the rope ladder on the *Wild Cat's* green side just
as a long grey shadow flashed white in the water,
and the shark turned over and a horrible mouth
snapped only an inch or two below his foot. For a
moment Titty thought that she was going to be
sick. She grabbed Captain Flint's wet arm, as if
he could not, by himself, climb fast enough over
the bulwarks.

"All right, Titty," said Captain Flint. "And I'm
very much obliged to you, Mr Duck. That brute
might easily have left me with a leg too few for
comfortable walking."

The others came tumbling up in their bathing
things.

"Who was first in?" shouted Nancy. "I heard
someone splashing about. I'm going to be second,
anyhow. Come on, John. I'll race you. Can you
swim ashore from here?"

"No bathing, Nancy," said Captain Flint.

"Hullo, what's the matter?" said Nancy.

"He's just this minute nearly been eaten by a shark," said Titty.

Roger ran to the side and craned his head over the bulwarks. Captain Flint laughed.

"Do you remember looking for sharks over the side of the houseboat, that day you made me walk the plank? You were afraid the sharks wouldn't be big enough to eat me."

"This is different," said Roger.

"Giminy!" said Nancy. "It really was a shark. Look!"

They all saw that three-cornered fin cutting through the water seventy or eighty yards away. It disappeared, and after that, oddly enough, they never saw another.

"It was very silly of me to go over like that," said Captain Flint. "It was just being so jolly pleased to be here. I'd been promising myself a swim. Today's the day, you know. That kind of feeling. By Jove, you two have done the decks already. Come on, let's sluice some water over the lazybones, and then get breakfast over."

*

"And now," said Captain Flint at breakfast, "the first thing to do is to get across the island, find Mr Duck's tree, and bring the stuff aboard."

"Begging your pardon, sir," said Peter Duck, "the first thing's the ship. You never know how soon we may be off again, or bothered with a bit of bad weather, and the first thing we ought to do is to have them water tanks all filled up again and be quit of all fear of running short. And then there's

the rigging to overhaul. Chafing there's bound to
be on a long passage, and I'll be taking the chance
to get things ship-shape before we sail."

"We've used forty-three tanks full from the
starboard side and forty-four from the port side,"
said Susan. "Eighty-seven altogether."

"We couldn't be having better weather for tak-
ing the tanks ashore and bringing them off," said
Peter Duck. "It's too good a chance to be missing,
I'm thinking. Barometer's as steady as a rock."

"I know it is," said Captain Flint. "But that's the
very reason why we ought to go straight across to
the other side of the island to lift that stuff. Look
here. You're going to show me where it is."

"As near as I know, I'll show you. Not that
there's anything there. Whatever it was, it's
maybe gone by now."

"That's all right," said Captain Flint. "If it's
gone, it's gone. But you can't show me the place
without coming across the island. And that means
leaving the ship. And you say yourself we can't
count on settled weather. This may be the only
chance of you and me being able to get across
there together without worrying about what's
happening to the schooner."

For a moment, it almost looked as if Peter
Duck and Captain Flint were going to quarrel.
But they didn't.

Susan said: "Why can't we be getting the
water in while you and Mr Duck go across the
island?"

"Why not?" said Captain Flint. "We must leave
somebody in charge of the ship, and with us away
Captain John and Captain Nancy take command,

and if they and the two mates can't manage those tanks as well as we can I'll be much surprised."

"Well, there's something in that," said Peter Duck, pushing the tobacco hard into his pipe. "If I got to leave the ship, better when it looks like easy weather."

And then, of course, Roger started.

"But aren't we all going to fetch the treasure?"

"It won't take long. Let's all go," said Nancy.

"Oh, look here, Nancy," said Captain Flint, "I'm counting on you and John to look after the ship and give the mates a hand with the water supply . . . ."

Bill sat there saying nothing, but looking rather glum. All he cared about was that he did not want to lose sight of Mr Duck. These children were all very well, but where Mr Duck was, there Bill wanted to be. Sailormen ought to stick together.

"All right, Bill," said Captain Flint, laughing, "he won't leave you behind."

Bill grinned and cheered up very much, though he wondered how much Captain Flint had guessed of what he had been thinking.

In the end it was agreed that John, Nancy, the two mates, the monkey, and the parrot should stop in charge of the ship. Captain Flint, Peter Duck, Bill, Titty, and Roger were to cross the island. Roger had been so sure he was going that Captain Flint felt it would be hard to leave him behind. And if he were taken, why not Titty? Mr Duck had said the going was not so bad. Susan and Peggy set to work to put rations together for the explorers. Then they were all to go ashore together and have a look at the stream.

The dinghy was already afloat. The moment things had been decided, Captain Flint and Peter Duck, with John and Nancy helping, and Titty watching anxiously for fear of damage to *Swallow*'s new paint, brought the little sailing boat to the side, hooked on the davit tackles, hoisted her up, and lowered her into the water.

"These davits'll be the very thing for lifting in the water tanks," said Peter Duck. He brought one of the empty tanks up on deck, and showed Nancy how to put a rope sling through the handles at the side of the tank, how to hoist it up with the davit tackle, and then how to swing the davit inboard so as to lower the tank on deck.

"It's not that these little tanks are all that heavy," he said, "but you may as well handle them easy as not."

At last everything was ready. The water-breaker from the galley had been lowered into the dinghy. "Whatever else happens," Susan had said, "we'll give that barrel a rinse." Two of the water tanks had been lowered into *Swallow*. John had stepped *Swallow*'s mast, and Nancy was standing by all ready to hoist the sail. Titty and Roger were sitting on the tanks. Bill had obeyed orders and taken his place in *Swallow*, not very willingly, for he had seen that Peter Duck was already afloat in the dinghy, with both the mates. He was hanging on to the rope ladder.

"Hi! Hi! Uncle Jim! Captain Flint!" called Nancy. "We'll start without you and then where'll you be?"

But Captain Flint was swinging himself over the bulwarks and coming down the ladder. In his hand was a long paper parcel, and as soon as he was in the boat he began unwinding the generous string of the Cowes confectioner. He stuffed the paper away under the thwart, and felt the bright blue ironwork of the two toy spades.

"They certainly are pretty rotten ones," he said, "but I dare say they'll do."

Bill pushed off from the side of the *Wild Cat*. Nancy hoisted the old brown sail. The little *Swallow* filled on the starboard tack and was off.

Titty drew a long breath.

"And the last time we sailed her was in Lowestoft," she said.

"And before that on the lake," said John. "We never thought when we were sailing home from Horseshoe Cove that this year we'd be landing in her on a desert island."

"I wish *Amazon* were here," said Nancy, looking at the little brown dinghy in which Peter Duck, with one of the mates behind him in the bows, and the other facing him in the stern, was already pulling for the shore.

"She's a proper little sailor, your *Swallow*," said Bill.

"The *Wild Cat* looks a beauty, too," said Titty, thinking that Captain Flint might be hurt if they spoke of nothing but the *Swallow*.

And, indeed, the green schooner, lying there at anchor, was a lovely sight.

But Captain Flint and Roger had no eyes for ships that morning. They were thinking of nothing but Crab Island and what they might find when they landed.

The *Swallow* sailed across the bay before going

about and heading back again for the strip of bright sandy shore where the little stream ran out. John found he had to tack once more before getting in because of a little spit of land that divided into two what had seemed to be a single bay. Afterwards they came to understand how this had happened when they saw that at some time the stream had shifted, leaving its old bed dry and making a new one for itself. The spit of land had built itself between the old outlet of the stream and the new.

Peter Duck and the two mates came rowing in just as *Swallow*'s nose touched the shore.

"Go on, Bill," said Titty, as she felt the scrunch of the keel on the sand. "It's really desert. You're the first to put your foot on it."

Bill splashed overboard with the painter and pulled *Swallow* a foot or two up the beach.

"What did you say this bay was to be called, sir?" he asked with a grin.

"Bill's Landing," said Captain Flint.

"Pleased and proud to welcome you," said Bill.

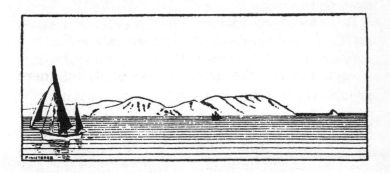

CHAPTER XX

BLAZED TRAIL

THE others scrambled ashore after Bill, and ran to meet Mr Duck and the mates, who were just coming in the dinghy. At least, they tried to run, but found that something had gone wrong with their legs, or else with the shore. There they were, on solid ground at last, after so many days and nights of rolling and pitching at sea, and yet for a minute or two they found it much harder to balance themselves on the island beach than on the swaying decks of the *Wild Cat.*

"This shore simply won't keep still," said Roger.

Bill laughed.

"I seen a man fall off the quay in Lowestoft harbour once, coming ashore after a spell at sea." He made the others laugh, too, staggering along the beach as if he were aboard ship and not yet used to the motion.

But the shore settled down presently, though all that day first one and then another of the explorers kept feeling a little uncertain and rocky. First to one and then to another it seemed that the ground was suddenly swaying up or down like the deck of a ship.

"We'll get our land-legs all right if we start work," cried Captain Flint. "Let's get going." He stuck his two little spades upright in the sand, and began hauling the *Swallow* farther up, though

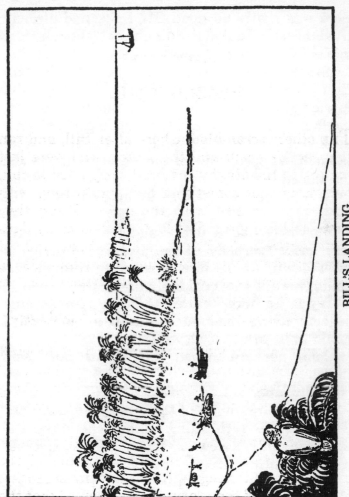

BILL'S LANDING

there was really no need. Mr Duck had already
lifted the barrel out of the dinghy and slung it from
an oar for the two mates, and they were carrying
it, pirate fashion, towards the stream. Captain
Flint lifted the empty tanks out of *Swallow*, and
hurried after them. "No. No. Higher up," he said,
and found what he wanted in a little pool between
black rocks in the very shadow of the trees. Here
he knelt, scooped some of the water in his hands,
and tasted it.

"Grand," he said. "Come along and try it, Mr
Duck."

Everybody had a drink and found the water
very good, everbody except Roger, who tried it
lower down, where it was running through the
sand. There it was decidedly brackish.

"Try it up here," called Captain Flint, seeing
Roger spitting the water out in a hurry. "It's
bound to be brackish down there."

"Come here and wash your mouth out," said
Susan.

Roger came.

"I don't think much of the crabs," he said.

He had been thinking of nothing else, and
had seen only a few of them, yellowish crabs
of disappointing size.

"Them's the day shift," said Peter Duck.
"Smaller than what I remember them over on
the other side. But you should see the night
gang."

It was a deep little pool, under the rocks,
where the stream left the trees, though only a
few feet across and not big enough for bathing.
But it was big enough to let them force the tanks

under till they filled. This was lucky, as it would
have been a long job filling them if they had had
to bail the water into the tanks with a mug.

"Come on," said Captain Flint. "Leave them
to it. Time's going on. Two captains in charge.
What more do they want? But somebody ought to
be getting back to the ship. We don't want Gibber
taking her to sea."

"All right, Uncle Jim," said Nancy. "Off with
you. We'll take *Swallow* back now for a cargo
of empty tanks. John and I'll take turns staying
aboard the *Wild Cat*. We'll have all the tanks full
and stowed long before you're back. Mr Duck's
shown us how to use the davits like cranes for
bringing the full ones aboard. Give us a hand in
pushing *Swallow* off. You pulled her up much too
high."

"Now see here, Cap'n Nancy," said Peter Duck
earnestly. "Don't forget to belay the ends of your
falls while you're hoisting them tanks aboard. You
don't want to lose one to the bottom and have a
fall unrove if you happen to let it go with a run.
And the same to you, Cap'n John. You'd be able
to reeve another, I don't doubt, but them sort of
happenings ain't seamanlike. We don't want none
of them aboard the *Wild Cat*. Now if I was to be
stopping aboard along of you . . ."

"We're starting, Mr Duck," said Captain Flint
hurriedly, on hearing these last words. "They'll
make no mistakes. And we ought to be moving."

Nancy laughed. Susan had a last look to
see that Roger had his knapsack on properly,
with both the straps the same length. Captain
Flint tucked the two little spades under his arm.

Everybody shouted, "Goodbye!" and "Good luck!" and the exploring party went off up the stream into the forest.

A sudden quiet fell on the beach.

"I rather wish we were going too," said John.

"Rubbish!" said Nancy. "It's the only chance we'll ever get of being in full charge of the ship. Give me a hand down with one of these tanks. Shove along with the other, you two mates. They aren't so awfully heavy."

A few minutes later the little brown-sailed *Swallow* was slipping out from the cove towards the anchored schooner. Susan and Peggy had settled down by the side of the stream to a thorough rinsing of the old oaken water-breaker. During the last few days of the long voyage the little barrel had certainly been giving the drinking water a remarkable smell of its own.

*

"It don't look the same," Peter Duck kept saying, as he and Captain Flint, followed by Bill, Titty, and Roger, pushed their way into the green forest. "No. It don't look the same. My bearings is all mixed with the stream coming out at a different place. Trees is different too, seems to me. But maybe we shan't go wrong if we follow the stream up the hill and then strike east over the shoulder."

Trickling along under the trees, the stream flowed in a narrow channel of dark earth and black stones, sometimes disappearing altogether under the roots of great trees. Some of the trees were very like pine trees and reminded Titty and Roger of the woods above the lake in the far-away country at home. Under these trees the ground was ruddy with burnt, brown needles, which seemed astir with the ants hurrying busily among them. There were ant-hills, too, as high as Roger and all of a tremble with the movement of the ants inside. Then there were gum trees, giant ferns, every kind of palm and many strange flowering trees the names of which they did not know. There was great delight when they came on a wild banana tree, with a heavy drooping cluster of ripe fruit. Bill, Titty, and Roger ate some as they walked along, and Captain Flint cut a big bunch and put it in his knapsack.

"What have you people got on your feet?" he said suddenly.

"Sandshoes," said Titty. "Susan wouldn't let us come barefoot."

"I've got a pair of the mate's on, too," said Bill.

"She wanted to make us put on sea-boots," said Roger.

"She was quite right," said Captain Flint. "Well, make all the noise you can while you're walking."

"It's not only snakes you'd best be looking for. There's them hairy spiders. Don't you let one of them things grapple and board."

"Look at this centipede," said Titty. "It's the biggest I've ever seen."

"Best give him a good offing," said Peter Duck. "But he's nothing by what I've seen in the Malays. You see them down there like tarred hawsers, dark as Navy Plug some of them . . . dangerous, too."

"The Malays?" said Captain Flint. "Remember

that hill above Penang, the one with all those temples?" And with that the two of them were at it, talking of things they had seen long ago, just as if this wild forest on Crab Island was hardly worth looking at.

But Bill cut a good big stick for himself, and banged on the ground and the tree stems as he walked along. Roger and Titty stamped on the ground, but soon forgot to stamp because there was so much to see.

They met nothing really dangerous, but very many things that they had never seen before. There were gorgeous butterflies, as big as saucers, and climbing plants that draped the trees with hanging clusters of red and violet flowers. And clouds of tiny birds were buzzing round these clusters of flowers, birds so small that at first Titty thought they were biggish bees. Some of them were blue, like kingfishers, and others had a sheen of purple and dark red that changed as they caught the light or slipped into shadow flitting in and out among the leaves. And then there were big birds, too, green parrots, mostly, like Polly, and noisy chatterers, that made more noise than the parrots, except when the parrots were startled and a flock of them rose together into the air above the trees, so that the explorers could not see them, but only heard the wild screaming of them high above the green feathery screen that shut out all but small patches of the sky.

It was hard going in places, with the thick undergrowth and the tangles of climbing plants.

"I don't believe we ought to have brought

you children," said Captain Flint after they had
worked slowly through a rather tough bit.

"We're not going back now," said Roger.

"We simply can't," said Titty.

"Well, I'll tell you what," said Captain Flint.
"We'll be blazing our trail as soon as we leave
the stream. We could leave you to camp by the
stream and pick you up on the way home."

But nobody liked this idea, and it was forgotten
a few minutes later when they found their way
blocked by a great mass of loose rocks and earth,
sprouting with trees and ferns, but towering above
them almost like a precipice.

"Landslide," said Captain Flint.

"Here's the water, sir," said Bill, "coming down
the hill, it is."

"Bear to the left then. Up the hill."

They climbed steeply up the side of the hill
along the edge of the landslide. Here the able-
seaman and the ship's boy could do as well as the
skipper and the bosun, dodging under branches,
and scrambling up over roots and stones. Up and
up they went, Bill leading the way, and banging
with his stick, following always the tiny trickle of
water. They came out at last above the landslide,
and could look down on the tumbled mass of earth
and rocks and young trees growing in it wherever
they had found foothold. They could see that all
this side of the hill must have slipped down across
the old course of the stream, which now trickled
along the upper edge of it before twisting down
the side of it to find its way into the valley.

"I wonder when that came down," said Captain
Flint.

"Since I were here," said Peter Duck, "but none so long since, neither . . . Ten or twelve year maybe. Look at the size of them little trees growing in it."

Above it, too, the trees were small and new, growing out of the hillside that had been scraped bare by that great sliding mass of earth and rocks.

Bill, Roger, and Titty rushed forward and upward through the trees. Suddenly there were no more trees. Above them was nothing but black rocks, hot to the touch.

But it was not the rocks they noticed when they came suddenly out there above the trees. It was the sea, that seemed to stretch for ever into the distance far beneath them.

"Hullo!" said Bill, stopping short and just saving his hat from being blown away by the wind off the Atlantic.

"This is something like being on the peak in Darien," said Titty, "only, of course, stout Cortez must have been looking the other way."

"It's the sea," said Roger. "You do see a lot of it from up here."

"Who's fat Cortez?" asked Bill.

"He was a Spaniard," said Titty. "He climbed up a hill and looked at the Pacific."

"A dago," said Bill. "But they mostly runs thin, aboard ships, anyway. There was one I knowed, shipped as fireman in a steam trawler. Skinny, they used to call him. There wasn't nothing to him. Thinner and thinner he got, shovelling coal, and he used to keep making new holes in his belt so's he could tighten it, till it wasn't worth his while to make no more 'cos all the belt was hanging loose

outside the buckle. That's the sort of dago he was.
This Cortez must have been different."

"He comes in a bit of poetry," said Titty.

"Dagos runs thin," said Bill again, "but maybe
the man what made that poetry never saw him."

Peter Duck and Captain Flint climbed up to
them. They, too, looked down over the waving
green tops of the forest to the blue, white-flecked
ocean on which for so long they had been sailing.

Captain Flint sniffed the air like a dog picking
up a scent. Somewhere down there, below him,
was the thing he had come so far to find. "Shallow
a long way out," said Peter Duck. "These islands
mostly is, on the eastern side of them. The sea
keeps piling the sand up. You can't come close in
without grounding, and there's no sort of shelter
from the trade winds. If you want to come in this
side, you must wait for a lull and be off again the
minute the wind pipes up. Even in a flat calm the
swell breaks along them eastern shores."

"Not a sail to be seen," said Captain Flint.
"Let's be getting on down."

The explorers went on again, a few yards
above the top of the landslide.

"That's the end of the stream," said Captain
Flint, looking up above them at a thin trickle of
water that came out from under precipices of black
rock that seemed almost to lean out from the side
of the hill. "I don't like the look of that," he added.
"Too steep for my liking altogether. I shouldn't like
to be up here when there's another bit of a shrug
and the next lot comes down. Most unpleasant it
would be. I remember once in Formosa . . ."

"Who blazed that tree?" said Titty.

"What tree? Where?" cried Captain Flint and a moment later was scrambling and slipping down over a slope of rock to a ragged pine-like tree, one of the forest's outposts on the mountain-side, to look at a large scar where the rough bark had been sliced away.

"It wasn't a woodman did that," said Captain Flint eagerly. "He took two blows at it from above."

Titty found herself wondering who it was who asked the executioner to sharpen his axe and cut boldly, when the clumsy fellow got nervous and took three blows to lop off a head of English chivalry or something like that. It was queer the way things came shooting into your mind just when you were really thinking of something quite different.

"It might be a ship's carpenter," said Peter Duck, picking his way carefully down.

"It was done after the landslide," said Captain Flint. "No point in blazing a tree up here unless there was something to make you climb so high. Hullo. Come on. There's another. Come on, you three, unless you'd like to wait till we come back."

"What for?" said Roger.

"Well, come along then," said Captain Flint.

"Seems to me," said Peter Duck, "that maybe it was Black Jake marked them trees. It's not five year since he was here. He'd have to anchor on the western side, same as us, and he'd know well enough it would be on the east that I was throwed up after the wreck. Stands to reason that would. Follow the stream they would, same as us, up from that side, and then from mark to mark down on this, so's to come back the same way."

"I'm sure you're right," said Captain Flint, gripping his two spades in one hand, and going down hill with big strides.

"What's this?" said Roger, tugging at something that was sticking in the second of the blazed trees. It broke in his hand, and came away.

"Old herring-knife," said Bill. "Don't you know that? You takes the herring this ways, and you slits it up, so . . ."

"It's East Coast fishermen use them knives and no others," said Peter Duck, looking at the bone handle on which rust was growing like a fungus where the steel rivets came through that held the handle to the rusty blade, broken off short where Roger had twisted at it to get it out of the tree.

"Black Jake may have stuck it there himself," said Titty, "with a message to one of his friends, perhaps."

"There's more than one of his friends have had a message from him with a knife," said Peter Duck, "but it's not in a tree he'd be sticking it."

"There's another tree marked," said Bill.

"Come on," said Captain Flint. "I'm beginning to think we owe a lot to Black Jake. If it hadn't been for him you wouldn't have told us the story. If he hadn't chased us down Channel we should never have come so far. He's given us a loan of a very good able-seaman. That's you, Bill. And now it seems to me he's made things easy for us by blazing a trail down to the eastern shore."

"You may be sorry yet you ever saw him," said Peter Duck, and then, taking a last look at the sea, through a gap there was in the trees, he plunged down into the forest after Captain Flint, closely followed by Bill, Titty, and Roger, though Roger had got the knife back and was trying to clean some of the rust off it as he went along, before putting it in his pocket.

"You don't really want it," said Titty.

"I do," said Roger. "Of course I do. To put in my museum."

In the end the rusty knife came to pieces in his hand, but he wrapped the bits of bone and rusty steel together in his handkerchief, and made Titty stuff it in the outer pocket of his knapsack.

"Pirate's knife," he said. "Jolly few museums will have got a thing like that."

Titty had to admit to herself that it sounded very well. As for Bill, he asked no questions. Things like that were for keeping until they came in handy for throwing at something else. If Bill had found it, he might have had a shot at a parrot with it. But wrapping it up in a handkerchief! Well, you never knew with these children. They were certainly a queer lot.

The blazed trees clearly marked an old track, though, if there had ever been a regular path from tree to tree, there was no finding it now. Trees had fallen across the place where the path might have been, decayed, eaten by ants or rotted into reddish fibre that crumbled when it was touched. Plants of all kinds had grown up there, so thickly that if it had not been for the blazes on the trees nobody would have thought that this could be the way to anywhere. But the blazes were plentiful and easy to see, and Captain Flint and Peter Duck, going in front, cleared a way

for the others, trampling underfoot the lower
growths, and here and there using their knives to
cut through the twisted ropes of climbing plants,
like honeysuckles, which in places made a net
that no one could have broken through by simply
pushing. The little party of explorers moved down
from the shoulder of the hill, screened from the
sun by the foliage overhead but accompanied by
a continuous loud screaming of startled parrots
and chatterers.

Besides the cries of the birds, which sometimes
made quiet talking difficult, another noise was in
their ears. All the time after they had passed the
landslide and begun to follow the blazed trees
down from the shoulder of Mount Gibber they had
been listening to the noise of surf far away below
them. They had heard it in the peaceful anchorage by Bill's Landing, but now that they were
coming down through the forest on the eastern
slopes of Mount Gibber it began to be deafening,
this endless rhythmical noise of the swell rolling
in, turning to breaking waves and crashing into
white surf that boiled along the sands. Captain
Flint, hearing it, louder and louder, could hardly wait for the others. He hurried on from one
blazed tree to the next, hoping always to see the
trees thinning before him and the open sky and
the Atlantic beating on the island shore.

"Not so fast, Cap'n. Not so fast," Peter Duck
would say from time to time, and then Captain
Flint would say he was sorry, and would hang
back and walk slowly, to let people get their
breaths again. And then the noise of the sea
would be too much for him, and, without knowing

it, he would begin to forge ahead once more, faster and faster, impatient with the undergrowth that clutched at his knees.

At last Peter Duck called out to him in vain. Captain Flint had caught a glimpse of the sea. He ran forward out of the palm trees, to look down on a steep beach of sand that threw the sunshine up most blindingly into eyes accustomed now to the cool green shadows of the forest.

Peter Duck moved no faster than before. Bill galloped forward and Titty and Roger hurried after him, leaving the old seaman to come at his own pace out through the last fringe of tall palms. He heard a shout from Captain Flint and eager cries from the others, and then, at the very edge of the forest, something caught his eye where the grass was thin and burnt in the sand. He looked out through the trees. Captain Flint and the others were bending over some old half-filled diggings along the edge of the forest. Peter Duck shook his head and looked down once more at the scattered white bones that had first caught his eye. He stooped and picked up from among them a broken clay pipe, of odd pattern, with the bowl narrow and slanting forward from the stem. Then, stirring the sand with his foot, he moved a white and broken skull. He covered it up with the sand, and, with the pipe in his hand, went out from under the palm trees to join the others.

"Black Jake's been here all right," said Captain Flint.

"He has," said Peter Duck.

"Doing some hard work he was," said Bill.

"What's that?" asked Titty.

Peter Duck held it out. "See," he said. "Stamped 1915 and 1915 that pipe is. Everybody was smoking them pipes round Lowestoft in the years after the war. There's Lowestoft men been here."

"It looks as if Black Jake's done an awful lot of digging," said Captain Flint. "You don't think he could have found it?"

"He was digging in the wrong place," said Peter Duck. "It's not here I was throwed up. Bit farther north it was. There's no rocks here. I'll know the right place when I see it, I dare say."

Bill, Titty, and Roger did not wait for another word, but ran on northwards along the beach.

Peter Duck turned to Captain Flint again.

"Black Jake's been here right enough," he said, "and someone's paid for it, too. Fighting, or murder. Likely enough they'd be fighting when they tired of digging, not rightly knowing where to dig." He took Captain Flint back under the trees and showed him the bones and the broken skull. "It wasn't no fall smashed that in," he said.

"I'm glad that able-seaman of mine didn't see it," said Captain Flint.

"We'll have no call to be going back this way," said Peter Duck, as, after covering up the skull once more, they walked out of the trees.

Captain Flint for a moment looked grave, thinking of the sort of men he would have to deal with if Black Jake and his crew were indeed to follow the *Wild Cat* to the island, as Peter Duck seemed to think they would.

He put his glasses to his eyes and searched the eastern horizon. Not a thing was moving on the sea except the white crests of the waves.

He turned to Peter Duck again. "Well," he said, "the best thing we can do is to hurry up. We've only got to find your tree, get the stuff and clear out, and Black Jake can have the island and be welcome to it."

"I've nothing against that," said Peter Duck, and they walked on after the children.

SWALLOWS·AND·AMAZONS·FOR·EVER:

CHAPTER XXI

DUCKHAVEN

CAPTAIN Flint and Peter Duck walked on after the others, who had hurried northwards along that shining beach. For a long way there were signs of old trenches and pits more than half-full of blown sand close under the trees. They stopped now and again to look at an old broken spade-handle, a rusty kettle or a battered stew-pot with a hole in it.

"This looks like the end of their diggings," said Captain Flint at last. "They seem to have got tired of it here."

"Likely enough," said the old sailor. "Digging all the way along here from where we come out of the trees. Quarter of a mile they dug up. Foolishness, seems to me, digging and digging like that with nothing to show for it."

"H'm," said Captain Flint. "I shouldn't like to count up all the digging I've done one time or another, and often in ground that looked as good as anybody could want, and with a man in the next claim shovelling the stuff out in panfuls and going home in a month with a fortune made."

"Gold-mining?"

"Yes," said Captain Flint, "and never enough to show for it to make a ring for the little finger of a monkey."

"They say custom eases all," said Peter Duck. "With all that bad luck astern of you, you won't be taking it so hard when our time comes to up-anchor and get away back to sea after digging up an old sack with maybe nothing in it worth spitting at."

"Well, Mr Duck, the sooner we get to digging up that sack the better. Hullo, what are those children up to?"

Half a mile ahead of them a rib of dark rock ran out of the forest, crossed the sand and plunged into the sea. And every now and then, as one of the big waves rolled in, it was as if a fountain shot up there, a feathery white plume of spray that blew across the beach like steam. And on the rocks they could see Titty waving to them, while Bill and Roger were looking at something on the sand.

Anybody could see that Titty was probably shouting. But Peter and Captain Flint could hear nothing, because of the roar of the surf.

"Water spouting over," said Peter Duck. "I mind that well enough. Looks to me as if they've found the place for themselves without my showing them."

"Come on, Mr Duck," said Captain Flint and hurried along the beach.

As they came near the rocks, Titty came running to meet them.

"It's a harbour," she was shouting. "A harbour. And a real wreck."

Bill and Roger were crab-hunting.

"If you'd only been a little quicker," said Roger reproachfully, "you'd have seen them. There were lots under this rock just now. Yellowy ones. But anyhow there are millions in the wreck."

"Isn't it a lovely harbour?" said Titty, and then she saw that Captain Flint was not listening to her. He had no eyes for anything or anybody but Peter Duck.

Peter Duck was looking down into a narrow gully between the black rocks. There was a little sandy beach at the head of it, a perfect boat-landing. There were rocks on each side of it, and between the rocks water rose and fell and lapped against them, stirred by the swell from outside, but quiet and almost smooth. Beyond the rocks to the north, as to the south, a long churning line of breakers rolled over and broke in foaming white surf. In this one place there was peace. The Atlantic swell broke on the reef outside, and fell over the rocks already tamed and harmless. Where the reef joined the rocks on the beach the breakers rushed along it, and it was here, where the rocks rose steeply out of the sea close to the land, that every now and then an angrier breaker than the rest flung itself up into the air in that fountain of blown spray that they had seen from far away.

"There's been some fine big crabs about," said Bill. "Look at them clippers. How's this for hanging clothes on a line with?" He picked up a fine orange-coloured pair of clippers from a lot of old bits of crab shells washed into a crevice of rock.

"But it really is a gorgeous harbour," said Titty.

"Yes," said Captain Flint. "You could beach *Swallow* in here all right." But Titty knew he was not really thinking about *Swallow*. He was looking at Peter Duck. Peter Duck was screwing up his eyes and smiling queerly.

"Well, Mr Duck? Well?" said Captain Flint eagerly.

"I never would have thought it was such a little place," said Peter Duck at last. "Shrunk it has, like them crabs. They was a sight bigger when I was here and all alone with them."

"This *is* the place?" Captain Flint was already looking up the beach towards the coconut palms along the edge of the forest.

"Aye," said Peter Duck. "This is the place. Spouting water and all." He wiped some blown spray from his face. "Funny I should remember that. Aye. This is the place. If I'd missed it and been washed up in surf I'd have been pounded to nothing, and if I'd hit the reef I'd have been smashed like them crab shells. I must have just missed the end of the reef and been swept up in the smooth water. Miracle, it seems to me. If I'd come ashore anywheres else I'd have missed sixty years of sailing. Sixty good years I'd have missed. Think of that now."

Titty stared at him. She tried to think of him sixty years ago, small and wet and wretched, tied to a spar, and washed ashore from a wreck, not like Robinson Crusoe, with lots of useful things to help him, but with nothing at all but a pocket-knife.

"Was the old boat here then?" she asked.

Just beyond the rocks they had found the remains of an old decked boat. Just the bows of it were visible, sticking up out of the sand. The caulking had rotted away and you could see between the planks. A great gaping hole had been smashed in one side of it, so that anybody not very large could have crept in between its ribs. The moment they had seen it, they had wanted to get inside, but not when they came nearer and saw that it was alive with yellow crabs that crawled in and out through the hole. Even Bill had hardly liked the idea of crowding in there with the crabs.

Peter Duck came to the edge of the rocks and looked over at the wreck on the other side.

"Since my time," he said, "but a good few years it's been here to be sanded up like that."

"But what about your tree, Mr Duck?" Captain Flint was bursting to use his little spades. He had not seemed to hear that there was a wreck to look at.

Peter Duck walked slowly up the beach, looking at the coconut palms that swayed in the fresh breeze off the Atlantic. All the others followed him. At any moment he might give the word and they would know where to dig.

"I'm beat," said Peter Duck at last. "They're as like as belaying-pins, them trees. They're as like as links in chain cable. There's no man alive could tell t'other from which."

"But it was a tree close here?"

"Close above the rocks it was. The smallest it was, and the easiest to climb. I wasn't no bigger than Roger here."

"It'll have grown since then," said Titty. "It might be the biggest of all." There was indeed one tall palm that waved its feathery crest high over the tops of the others.

"The lot of them'll have growed," said Peter Duck.

"Hang it all," said Captain Flint. "They may

have grown up, fallen down, been eaten by ants, rotted into fibre and blown away in dust before this. I don't know how long palm trees live. They may not be as tough as old sailors."

"And that's true," said Peter Duck, "and I was forgetting it. I was thinking I'd have to be picking out my old bedroom tree, and with all them trees as like as clincher nails I was feeling like a man making the Finnish coast without a chart. Ever been along the Finnish coast, Cap'n? Peppered, it is, with pink rocks as like as a lot of bollards."

"Hadn't we better have dinner?" said Roger.

Bill looked round hopefully.

"Best thing we can do," said Captain Flint. "This is going to be a longer job than I thought. I'd been forgetting there might be trouble over finding the right tree."

"Let's have dinner at the harbour," said Titty.

They walked down the beach again and dumped their knapsacks by the rocks, where they could look down towards that little sheltered sandy bay. Captain Flint dug out the bananas he had cut on the way across, and a big package of pemmican Peggy had made up after breakfast. Everybody had a packet of ship's biscuits, and a packet of sweet ones. Nancy had made Mr Duck borrow her knapsack, and among the things Susan had put in it was a big hunk of one of the Dutch cheeses they had bought that last day at Lowestoft. She knew he particularly liked it. Everybody had a waterbottle.

It was already very late for their midday dinner, and they were hungry. But, for all that, it was an unsettled meal. Captain Flint could not forget for

a moment that they were within a very few yards
of the treasure, whatever it was. He kept getting
up and walking about. He crossed the rocks with a
biscuit in his hand to have for the first time a close
look at the old wrecked boat, and came back to ask
Mr Duck if he didn't think somebody else besides
Black Jake might have been after the treasure.
Mr Duck said he didn't know, but that nobody
had come ashore in that boat on purpose. It was
nothing but an old boat stove in and washed up
in a storm.

"It might do for a hut," Captain Flint said.

"Not with all those crabs," said Titty.

"We'll have to have a tent then. We may
be digging a week."

"If we're going to stop here," said Titty, "couldn't
we bring *Swallow* round to try the harbour? It's
the best she's ever had."

Captain Flint flung himself down again.

"That's exactly what we'll have to do," he said.
"We'll have to come over here, all the lot of us,
and dig over the ground at the foot of every one
of those trees. Well, there's no road for carrying
things. We can't bring all the food and bedding
on our backs, let alone the drinking water. We'll
have to turn *Swallow* into a cargo boat and bring
the stuff round by sea. Then we'll camp here and
stick at it till we find it."

"And we'll call the harbour Duckhaven," said
Titty, "because it's where Mr Duck was washed
up. If he doesn't mind."

"It's no odds to me," said the old sailor, "and
Duckhaven sounds a good place for Ducks, and
this was that all right, barring them crabs. There's

one duckling would have died young if it hadn't been for this Duckhaven of yours. Duckhaven's a likely name, too. Look well, it would, on an Admiralty chart."

"Can I have another pemmican sandwich?" said Roger.

"You haven't finished that one," said Titty.

"I want to use the last bit of it," said Roger. "I want to use it to bring the crab out that went into that hole, and I can't unless you let me have another for myself."

"Give him two," said Captain Flint, "and tell him to eat them both at once. Look here, Mr Duck, what about bringing *Swallow* round here? Could it be done without risking her overmuch?"

"Easy as falling off a yard in a Cape Horn buster," said Peter Duck, "only you don't want to try it while the trade wind's blowing. Bring her round before sunrise or at dusk when the wind drops and comes off this shore, and there'd be nothing to it, if you bring her in at the right place."

"I'll take a mark for it," said Captain Flint, and was up again and striding up the beach. Mr Duck followed him. Titty waited a moment and then ran after them, leaving Bill and Roger still busy trying to tempt a crab out of its hole.

"What about the biggest of those trees of yours?" Captain Flint said, taking out his pocket compass. "No one could miss that. And it's bang above the rocks. Keep it just clear of the end of the reef and you want no better mark."

He walked right up to the tree and leant

his back against it, looking out to sea, and then down at his little compass.

"East-south-east the end of the reef bears from this tree. If we keep the tree bearing west-north-west when we're coming in, we can't miss the place."

"You left your sandwich behind," said Titty.

"Thank you very much," said Captain Flint. "That harbour of yours is going to be useful."

"You'll have to pick your time to come round when you've an off-shore wind," said Peter Duck. "But you'll do it easy enough."

"Hullo, what are those two up to now?" exclaimed Captain Flint, looking down the beach towards Duckhaven, where Bill and Roger were hurriedly slipping backwards down the near side of a rock.

"Help," shouted Bill, "them crabs is scoffing the vittles."

The others went to the rescue. There, where they had thrown themselves down to eat their dinner beside the quiet water of the tiny harbour, they found the crabs once more in full possession. There were hundreds of them. Roger explained.

"We were watching the bit of sandwich to see that crab come out of his hole, and he didn't come, and then we heard a noise and looked round, and there were the others all over the knapsacks, and we couldn't do anything because Bill's stick was right in the middle of them."

"Well, you are a couple of duffers," said Captain Flint, and jumped over the rock to rescue the knapsacks. Crabs, yellow and brown, scuttled in all directions. One clung to a knapsack as Captain

Flint grabbed it up. He shook it off. It fell hard against a rock, and in a flash the others had it and were pulling it to bits.

"Horrible. Horrible," said Titty, turning away.

"Them crabs ain't got no feelings," said Bill.

Peter Duck gave an odd kind of shiver.

"Quite like old times," he said. "Gives me the shakes, it does, just to see them. But they seems so small to what they was. Maybe they growed with me thinking about them and spinning the yarn so often. But at night . . ."

"I expect these same crabs seem bigger in the dark," said Captain Flint. "We'll have to deal with them some way if we're going to camp here."

"You'll have to set a watch at night, or they'll steal the skins off you," said Peter Duck.

There was still enough food left for the explorers. They were hungry enough not to mind that the crabs had been turning the biscuits over with their yellow pincers. Captain Flint poured a drop of lime juice into each of their water-bottles, and they drank to the success of the digging.

Then, just on the off chance, they went up to the big palm tree, and Bill, Titty, and Roger took turns with one of the spades, while Captain Flint dug with the other, and Peter Duck sat there on the sand looking down at the place where he had been a little frightened boy so many years before. But presently Captain Flint laughed.

"This is no good," he said. "Just foolishness. We'll have to take this digging seriously. Scratching at it is no good." He looked up at the sun, which was already dropping towards the island hills. "Come on," he said. "We've got no time to waste. Pack up. We've got to find a good way back from here, and blaze a trail so that we can find it again when we come tomorrow morning."

"Better in the evening," said Peter Duck. "You'll do nothing without a pick and it'll take me best part of tomorrow to make one. The stuff Black Jake's left's no good to you for rust. And besides that, it'll be late enough before the trade wind drops and you can make a good landing in that little boat."

They went down to Duckhaven again, chased away the crabs, and slung their knapsacks on their backs.

"No," said Captain Flint. "That wreck'll be no good to us. We'll have to make a tent."

"With a sail?" said Titty. "And oars? Captain Nancy'll be jolly pleased. She told us that was the proper way last year."

"Well, sir," said Peter Duck, as they walked up the beach. "I'm glad to have seen the place, and I never thought I should be."

"But you'll see it again tomorrow."

"And who's to mind the ship?" said Mr Duck. "No. I don't know where that bag is now, no nearer than what you do. I've shown you where it may be, and that's more'n ever I meant to do to a living soul. No. I'll be minding the ship, or maybe there'll come a buster and she'll drag, and go ashore, and be no more use to us than that old bit of a wrecked boat. We don't want to have to wait for Black Jake to come and give us a passage home. And I don't want to be eating crabs and coconuts again for want of other grub. Nor you don't neither."

By this time the little party were at the edge of the sand, and on the point of plunging into the forest. Captain Flint had already taken a compass bearing of the shoulder of Mount Gibber, where the trees ended and the black rocks rose above them. Once in the forest there would be only the compass to guide them. Now, for a moment, he stopped, under the tall coconut palms that fringed the beach.

"And to think," he said, "that we may be standing on the stuff this very minute."

Then he led the way in among the trees.

CHAPTER XXII

GOODBYE TO THE *WILD CAT*

It took them a long time to work their way back through the forest and up the slopes of Mount Gibber. Every few yards they stopped, while Peter Duck or Captain Flint made a large blaze on a tree, to say nothing of the smaller blazes made by Titty, Roger, and Bill. What was the good of having knives if you did not use them when you had a real chance? They were making sure that they would be able to find their way back to Duckhaven tomorrow without any difficulty. Captain Flint was even taking the trouble to make a clearish path for them. A clear path, no one could have made. But he lopped away a branch here and a branch there, and cut through the long, twisted tendrils of the climbing plants that hung from the trees. It was not exactly road-making, but it was all going to make things easier for the land-party next day. It had been decided already that almost everybody was to come across to Duckhaven by land, and have nothing to carry, while the food and the sails to make tents and everything else that would be wanted for the camp was to be brought round in *Swallow.*

At last, when they were already well up on the slope of the hill, Bill saw one of the old blazes left by Black Jake, and Roger at the same moment saw another, and they knew that the new trail they were making had joined the old one that they

-

had followed down to the beach earlier in the day.
There was no need now to keep on looking at the
compass. There was no real need even to make
more blazes. They could use the old ones. They
moved much faster now up the hill to the upper
edge of the great landslide. Then they scrambled
along the top of it, below the black crags of the
peak, found the little trickling stream, drank from
it, scooping the water in their hands, followed it
down on the farther side of the landslide, and,
just as dusk was falling, hurried out of the trees
at Bill's Landing.

In the outer bay, beyond the point that divided
the old outlet of the stream from the new, the *Wild
Cat* lay at anchor, a riding-light on her forestay
glowing like a pale-gold butterfly against the last
of the sunset. A small fire was burning on the
shore where John was waiting with the *Swallow*.
The little rowing-dinghy had made its last trip
long before. They could just see it, swinging astern
of the schooner. Peter Duck had lagged behind a
bit on the way over in the morning, but he had
hurried ahead as they were coming down to the
shore on the way back. He was first out of the
trees, looking carefully at the schooner, then at
Swallow, and grunted with relief at the thought
of being afloat again.

"Hullo!" called John. "Did you find it?"

"We haven't exactly found it," called Titty, "but
we've found the place where it is. We've found the
very place where Mr Duck was washed up."

"Stiff with crabs it is," said Bill.

"Good ones," said Roger.

"All well, skipper?" asked Captain Flint.

"Aye, aye, sir," said John. "We finished taking in water about an hour ago. Eighty-seven of the little tanks. Nancy lit the riding-light, in case you were late and came out on another part of the shore. I made the fire just for company."

"Jolly well done," said Captain Flint. "With the tanks all filled we've really lost no time in spite of not having started the digging."

A minute or two later *Swallow* was afloat with a cargo of footsore explorers, and John, at the tiller, was steering her out of the inner bay and then straight for the riding-light, growing brighter every moment against a darkening sky.

"Look here, Cap'n John," said Captain Flint, "what do you think about making a voyage round the island in *Swallow* tomorrow night?"

"Of course, I'd love to," said John. "I've never had her in real waves."

"I hope there won't be too much of them," said Captain Flint. "It's a question of landing a cargo in her. There's just one place on that side where we could do it."

"Duckhaven," said Titty. "It's just *Swallow*'s size, like the harbour on our island at home. It's a gorgeous little harbour. And there's the wreck of an old boat on the other side of the rocks there, a beauty, but we couldn't go into her . . ."

"Simply crammed with crabs," said Roger.

"There's just that one place where we could take her in, and it's there we've got to do our digging. It's a good place, with a reef running out and quiet water inside. I've taken bearings. I'll come with you to pilot you in."

"Couldn't we all come?" asked Titty.

"Sorry, A.B., *Swallow* holds a good many to-night, but there won't be much room to spare when we fill her up with food and bedding for the lot of us, and old sails to make a tent, and the mates' best water-breaker, and a cooking-pan or two."

"Are we going to camp there?" asked John.

"I don't see what else to do. There's about a hundred yards where that stuff might be buried, and about a hundred different trees that might be the one we want. We may have to do a lot of digging and it's no good wasting three parts of each day and getting tired out carrying stuff to and fro . . ."

There was a loud, cheerful hail from the schooner.

"Hullo, Cap'n Nancy, can we come aboard? Hullo, Susan . . . that's a precious nice smell of dinner hanging round your ship. What have you got for us?"

"We want at least eight helpings," said Roger, "so long as it isn't curry."

"It isn't," said Peggy. "We thought of it, to please Captain Flint, and then we thought of how it burnt everybody last time. We've cooked a lot of Mr Duck's fish, and besides that we've done a macaroni cheese, a walloper. We're just browning it now."

Stiffly, one after another, the explorers climbed up the ladder and came aboard their home once more.

"Well," said Peter Duck, as he stumbled down into the deckhouse, tired after the long walk through the forest and over the side of the hill.

"It's good to be back aboard. I don't hold with islands. No motion to them. I likes best to be afloat."

"This island's had plenty of motion at one time or other," said Captain Flint. "What about that landslide?"

"Wrong kind of motion," said Peter Duck. "Give me a ship."

"He didn't find it?" said Nancy to John, quietly, after the others had gone to their cabins and she had slipped down into *Swallow* to help John to tidy up.

"No," said John, "but he isn't half as sick as we thought he would be. They've found the place, and we're going to take *Swallow* round there, and make a camp and dig until we get it."

*

That night, at supper, they made their plans. Nancy was to be leader of the expedition overland, with Roger and Titty as guides.

"What about taking Polly?" said Titty.

"You'd have to carry his cage," said Susan. "If you let him fly loose he'll only be mobbed by the wild parrots. He'd be much happier aboard."

"He'd be company for Mr Duck," said Titty.

"Glad to have him," said Mr Duck.

"I'm going to take Gibber," said Roger. "He ought to be allowed to see his own hill."

"Well, he'll walk on his own feet, anyhow," said Susan. "But you'll have to look after him at night."

"He'll probably sleep in a tree," said Roger.

"I hope so," said Susan.

"He hasn't got a single flea," said Roger indignantly. "Not since that last scrubbing."

It was agreed that Gibber should go with the land party, but that on the way across Roger must keep him on a lead, just in case Gibber, not understanding that they were really in a hurry, might delay them by explorations of his own. And Susan, in spite of what she had said, set to work to make him a sleeping-bag out of a blanket, with a string to pull tight round the mouth of it so that he could be carried inside it if necessary.

Everybody was going overland, except Captain Flint and John, who were to sail *Swallow* round, and Peter Duck, Bill, and the parrot, who were to stay aboard the *Wild Cat*. Peter Duck did not want to set foot on the island again, and, anyway, he had to look after the ship. Bill wanted nothing better than to stay with Peter Duck, and Captain Flint thought it right that Peter Duck should have somebody with him for sending with a message or anything like that. Of course, every one of the others would have liked best to make the voyage in *Swallow*, but Captain Flint had to be there to pilot her in through the gap in the breakers off the end of the reef, and John was the captain of the *Swallow*, and it would be rather hard to turn a captain out of his own ship. So John was to sail her, with Captain Flint as harbour pilot to bring her into Duckhaven. And with all the cargo they had to take there would be no room for anyone else.

"Besides," said Captain Flint, "if we make a mistake coming in there, we shall have to swim for it, and when you're swimming in a place like

that, two is company but more than two is a crowd.
John and I could look after each other all right, but
it would be a lot harder if all the rest of us were
cluttering up the sea at the same time."

Everybody saw the sense of this, and there
was no more talk about it. They began to speak
of tools. They had the two spades from the Cowes
sweetshop, of which Captain Flint was beginning
to think much better. But they badly needed a
pickaxe. The old relics of Black Jake's expedition,
which they had found in the diggings, had been as
badly rusted as the knife, the bits of which had
been passed carefully from hand to hand before
being wrapped up by Roger in a bit of paper, on
which he wrote: "For the Museum. Pirate's Knife.
Pres. by R. Walker." Not one of those old bits of
iron was going to be of any use. But presently
Peter Duck got up and went into the fo'c'sle and
disturbed Gibber by lighting a lantern, and rummaged there in a cupboard that was full of old
odds and ends he had brought together from all
parts of the vessel because he had thought they
might come in handy some time. He brought out
an old boat anchor with a broken fluke. It looked
very clumsy when he brought it back with him
to the saloon, and the others had a look at it by
the light of the hanging lantern. But Peter Duck
said he thought he could make something of it, by
sharpening the points, and splicing the long iron
shank of it to a spare capstan bar. "They're good
elm bars," he said, "and they'll stand anything in
reason . . . not that there's reason in digging for
an old bag . . . and anyway there's nought much
but sand where they buried that bag. They dug

it in with their sheath knife as I telled you."

Captain Flint became more and more cheerful.

"We shan't be beaten for want of tools," he said. "How should we when the stuff's so near we can all but see it. If the worst comes to the worst we could dig it out with spoons."

*

But the worst was not to come to the worst. First thing next morning, long before the crew came up to sluice down the decks, Captain Flint was hard at work making a couple of wooden shovels good enough to shift loose sand with, and the noise of Peter Duck's file, sharpening the points of what was now a pick and had once been a little anchor, could be heard all over the ship. Soon after breakfast he had finished it, a queer sort of pick to look at, rather small, perhaps, but more than strong enough for the light sandy soil above the beach.

It was a busy morning. The two mates were making out lists of the food that would be wanted, and getting the tins out of the store-cupboards, and ticking things off on their lists, Titty and Roger were on the run carrying the things up on deck and piling them there all ready to be stowed into *Swallow*. Captain Flint and Peter Duck were searching through the sail-locker for some old sail that did not much matter and would do to make a tent. They found what they wanted in what had once upon a time been a balloon staysail, a big one, made of very light canvas that had been so much patched and torn that it was not really worth keeping. Peter Duck set to there and then to put a few more patches in it where it needed them most, while Captain Flint went off into the deckhouse to make a sketch-map of the island for Nancy, so that she could make no mistake even if the guides did get muddled. John and Nancy shifted the water-breaker out of the galley, and began the stowage of *Swallow* by lowering the little barrel over the side, and fixing it so that it could not roll about in the boat. Everybody was hard at it and it was afternoon before the land party was ready to start. They had a late and cold dinner, and then Bill rowed the first lot ashore in the dinghy: Peggy, Titty, Roger and Gibber. Gibber was nearly forgotten at the last minute, but came scrambling down the mainmast shrouds when he saw that Roger was leaving the ship. Nancy found his lead and threw it down into the boat, and off they went. From the schooner Susan and Nancy watched their landing through the telescope, and saw how Titty and Peggy sat down on the sand, while the eager monkey took his master in tow and pulled him this way and that about the beach, delighted to be on solid ground once more.

But very soon Bill was back again and Susan and Nancy climbed over the side and down into the boat. Captain Flint hung over the bulwarks giving last directions to Captain Nancy.

"You can't go wrong this side if you stick to the stream. Climb up where it comes down at the edge of the landslide. Slip along the top of the landslide till you come to the blazed trees. Then you're all right, but remember to watch out for the place where the new set of blazes join the old ones. Bear away to the left, following the new blazes we made last night, and you'll come out on the beach just above Duckhaven. One thing more. If we're not there before you are, make a fire on the beach exactly on a line between the big coconut tree and the outer end of the reef."

"For a lighthouse?"

"Yes. We can't start till the wind drops in the evening, and it might be darkish before we get in."

"Aye, aye, sir."

"Good luck to you, Nancy. Keep your men together and make plenty of noise. We didn't see any snakes, but you never know."

"See you this evening," called Nancy. "So long, Mr Duck. So long, John."

Susan, too, called her goodbyes, and Bill pulled off for the shore. But he only pulled a stroke or two before Nancy had the second pair out, and shifted Bill to the bows, after which, with two pair of oars, and Nancy setting the time, Bill and she fairly drove the dinghy through the water.

"Might be a captain's gig," said Peter Duck.

"So it is," said John.

"Aye, aye," said Peter Duck, "I was forgetting Cap'n Nancy, seeing her there pulling away with the crew."

John, Peter Duck, and Captain Flint, watching from the deck of the schooner, saw them land, saw Bill push off once more, saw the others walk up the beach, stop and wave. They thought they heard a faint farewell shout, and they saw Bill flourish his hat. Then there was nothing but the empty beach and the green forest and Bill, in the dinghy, pulling for the schooner. A cloud of parrots rose above the trees. The expedition was already on the march.

Never before had *Swallow* been packed so carefully. Spades, wooden shovels, and Peter Duck's pick were stowed on the bottom boards. Then came the food, good solid stuff and no luxuries except perhaps the chocolate. Then there were the cooking things. The water-barrel was already fixed just aft of the mast. All these loose things were wedged with the woollen sleeping-bags that they were taking instead of bedding. Then there was that old sail covering everything and shoved firmly down. There was just room left for the steersman. Captain Flint was going to lie on top of the cargo.

As the afternoon wore on, he grew more and more eager to be off, and at the first sign of slackening wind he hung his glasses round his neck, dropped his knapsack down to John, who stowed it with the bailer under the stern-sheets, clapped Bill on the back, shook hands with Peter Duck, flung a leg over the bulwarks and climbed down. John had already hoisted the little brown sail.

"Goodbye, Mr Duck," Captain Flint called. "The *Wild Cat*'ll be all right with you and Bill, and if the weather shows any signs of turning nasty I'll come right back over the hill."

"Goodbye, Mr Duck," sang out Captain John. "Cast off forrard."

Peter Duck laughed, brought the painter aft along the deck of the schooner, coiled it and dropped it down to them.

"Goodbye, Cap'n John," he said. "And a good passage!"

The *Swallow* drifted astern. Her sail filled. Passing close under the stern of the schooner, she headed out of the bay.

John glanced up at the letters, "WILD CAT LOWESTOFT" which he had painted himself in Lowestoft harbour. Lowestoft now seemed very far away.

Bill looked down over the stern rail.

"So long, Cap'n John," he said. And then, "Good luck, sir."

"So long, Bill," called John.

"Good luck with the fishing," called Captain Flint.

For some time Peter Duck and Bill stood by the deckhouse, watching the little brown ship sail away towards the southern point.

Then Bill began overhauling a fishing-line, coiled on the deckhouse roof.

"What about them hooks, Mr Duck?" he said, and, as he got no answer, said it again.

But Peter Duck, watching the brown sail now disappearing behind the point, was thinking of something quite different.

"Well," he said, "I'd be sorry for him not to find it after all this. If it's worth finding. Eh! Less lip, young Bill. What's that? Them hooks? You'll find them in the forrard end of the locker under my bunk. We might as well be putting the lines out. Bait's inside the galley door. They always do say the best fish bites at dusk. He'll be meeting a bit of wind round there, but he's sense enough to wait. What's that? Less lip, my lad. Coming. Coming . . . ."

He looked into the deckhouse, glanced at the

chronometer, then at the clock, came out and struck the ship's bell three times, two strokes close together and a single stroke by itself.

"Three bells," he said to himself, and then, as Bill looked up from his fishing-line, he added, "Quiet without them. It's like being back in the old wherry."

A minute or two later, two splashes showed that two leads with their hooks and baits had been dropped overboard. Peter Duck smoked his pipe, leaning on the bulwarks with a hand ready to feel the slightest nibble from a fish. Bill, close beside him, chewed a small bit of tobacco given him by Peter Duck.

"When'll they be back?" he said at last.

"He's not one to give up in a hurry," said the old seaman, spitting gravely into the water.

Bill spat, too. "Nor the others neither," said he. "They're good 'uns, for children."

CHAPTER XXIII

SWALLOW'S VOYAGE

THEY were off. John had enjoyed yesterday, running cargoes of fresh water from the shore to the schooner. This was better. This was a real voyage. He thought of Lowestoft harbour and of the lake among the hills at home, and then he looked at the green feathery tops of palm trees, the green forest climbing the slopes of Mount Gibber, and the open sea. And here was he at the tiller of the *Swallow* sailing past these strange tropical shores in waters where the sharks made it unsafe to bathe. Yes, it was one of the moments at which John, if he had been asked if there was anything in the world he wanted, would have had to admit that there was not. What could be better than this?

Captain Flint watched the *Wild Cat* until the neat green schooner, lying there to her anchors, with her sails furled, was hidden by the trees on the southern point of the bay.

"She'll be all right there," he said, "with those two aboard her, unless there comes on something really bad. And that won't happen without warning. There'll be plenty of time to get back."

He put the *Wild Cat* out of his mind, and, lying on the tightly packed cargo of the *Swallow*, tilted back his sunhelmet and hummed the tune of "Hanging Johnny," a most melancholy tune that generally came to his lips when he was thoroughly happy.

"Nothing could be better than this," he said at
last. "The smaller the boat the better the fun. I
say, Skipper, have you ever handled a small boat
in a big swell before? We'll be feeling it you know,
when we get out of the shelter of the island."

"Falmouth harbour," said Captain John. "And,
of course we had it pretty rough on the lake once
or twice in the summer."

"Um," said Captain Flint . . . "This is different. But nothing to worry about. She's a jolly
good sea-boat. She'll be all right if you keep her
sailing."

They were reaching fast across the southernmost of the bays on the western side of the
island. Long splashes of sparkling white on the
farther side of the point, where it ran out, bare of
trees, showed where the swell from the Atlantic
was breaking on the sand. The noise of the surf
was louder than John had yet heard it.

"We shall be in the open in another few minutes," said Captain Flint. "If you think the wind's
too strong we could hang about here for a bit. It's
still from the north-east, and we shall be beating
against it when we're round the point."

"She'll stand an awful lot," said John, "and
we've stowed all the heavy things in the bottom
of her."

"You know her," said Captain Flint. "She's your
ship. Speaking as a pilot, though, I'll just say one
thing. You'll find the easier water farther out. It's
when the seas begin to feel the shore they turn
nasty. But you know that as well as I do." And
Captain Flint rolled on his side to get shelter for
his hands while he struck a match and lit his pipe.

Then he worked himself up to the windward side, so that his weight would be useful as ballast, had a look at the way the halyard was made fast, in case he might have to take the sail down in a hurry, and saw that he would be able to get the oars out if they should be wanted.

"Mr Duck said the wind would be going down, didn't he?" said John.

"There's less already, if I'm not mistaken, and we may get it off the land as the sun goes down, though we can't count on that."

"I think we'll go right on," said John.

The waving palms on the southernmost point of the island seemed suddenly to slip away astern of them, so that they could see an ever wider stretch of sea over the low sandy spit that ran out beyond the trees. The *Swallow* began to lift and fall, as if she felt already that she was out of shelter. John was clear of the island almost before he knew it. Captain Flint, lying hunched along the top of the cargo on the windward side, pulled himself forward a few inches, and tucked in a loose bit of old sail between cargo and gunwale, as a lick of spray flew up and spattered over his face.

John bit his teeth together, sniffed the wind off the Atlantic, hauled in his sheet, made up his mind just how far he could keep it in without skimping her, leant well back, squinted up at Titty's little *Swallow* flag flying from the mast-head, felt a throbbing in his throat that was half pleasure, half fear of making a mistake, swallowed that throbbing and said, almost as much to himself as to Captain Flint: "She doesn't mind this at all."

"No," said Captain Flint. "There's no wickedness in it. These waves look big enough but they don't mean to do anybody any harm."

Big they certainly were. They came rolling down to meet the little *Swallow*, caught her on their wrinkled lower slopes, tossed her up and up until she was high on a broad mountain ridge of blue water, and then passed on, not exactly in a hurry, but as if on business that would not wait, while *Swallow* rushed down again on the other side, and it seemed a marvel that she did not somehow lose her footing and tumble over and over. But she never did. Just at first John felt that he was leaving the whole of his inside behind on the top of each big wave as it passed, but he found his inside was still there as the next wave rolled along and *Swallow* began to climb once more. He had plenty to think about. There were the big waves, that were really the ocean swell, and besides them, on their slopes, and between them and across them were smaller waves made by the wind. Presently John stopped wondering what was going to happen as he met each wave. He was enjoying himself very much indeed. After all he had had plenty of time to get used to such waves while sailing in the schooner. They seemed a good deal bigger when seen from *Swallow*, but he was delighted to find that nothing but spray came aboard. He knew now why Captain Flint had reminded him to keep his vessel sailing. Down in the trough between the bigger waves the *Swallow* seemed to lose the wind. Her little brown sail flapped as if in a calm, filling again suddenly, with a snatch at the boom, when the next wave caught her and shouldered her up and up before letting her fall once more while it rolled on towards the distant beach. John saw Captain Flint looking at him with a smile. He laughed.

"Good work, eh, John?" said Captain Flint.

"Going about's going to be a bit of a job."

"Pick your time for it and don't be in a hurry. We shan't lose anything by standing on. Simple-hearted fellows the seas out here. Nearer in, you can't count on them. The only thing to remember in going about is not to change your mind half-way."

John grinned. He had said just that, himself, to Titty, last summer, when teaching her how to sail.

He held on until he was a long way out, then waited until one of the larger waves had gone by, and went about without difficulty in the smooth that followed it. *Swallow* headed in towards the island.

"That was all right," said Captain Flint, who had wriggled across on the top of the cargo to bring his weight on the other side, and lifted his head again now that the boom had swung safely over. "Remember to luff a bit or bear away if you see anything that looks like slopping over us. By Jove, we get a fine view of Mount Gibber from out here. That's where we crossed, right up under those black rocks. Sorry, John. You look after your steering. Never mind me. You see where there's been another landslide beside the one we had to go round yesterday. More to come, too. That slope up at the top's too steep to last. Queer thing it is, the way these islands keep changing all the time."

SWALLOW AT SEA

"I wonder if Nancy and the others can see us from up there. *Swallow*'s sail must look pretty small."

"If Cap'n Nancy knows her job and hasn't let them hang about on the way, they'll have passed the landslide a long time ago and be well down the hill on this side. You can't see anything from among those trees. We never got a glimpse of the sea yesterday after we started coming down until we came right out on the beach." Captain Flint rolled over and pulled his watch from a hip-pocket. "Time's going on, you know. I shouldn't be surprised if they're not down at Duckhaven by now and wondering when we're turning up with the grub."

John stood out to sea once more. Captain Flint, who had, at first, been carefully watching what was happening while he seemed to be idly lying about on the top of the cargo, no longer troubled now to keep a hand within easy reach of the halyard. *Swallow* went switchbacking out to sea again, up and down, up and down, with a motion to which John was already growing accustomed. Just once, when John, over-confident, was glancing over his shoulder at the shore, she butted her nose into a wave, but took very little of it aboard, because her bows were tightly packed, and Peter Duck had covered things over with a bit of old tanned sail to keep them dry, and had jammed it in all round, so that it was almost as if she had a solid deck before the mast.

"No damage done," said Captain Flint, "but ease her a bit if she's meeting another like that."

"All right," said John, and Captain Flint noticed

that in *Swallow*, John was captain, and not he. Aboard the *Wild Cat*, John would most certainly have said, "Aye, aye, sir." He was as particular about it as Titty herself.

The shape of the island seemed to be changing all the time. The little hill in the south-west corner of the island, which was covered with trees to the very top of it, stood out for a time like somebody's knee pushed up under a green blanket. Then, as they came along the southern shore, it had gradually seemed to be part of Mount Gibber, and now that they were working northward it had disappeared altogether behind the green lower slopes of that strange black-topped hill. The peak of Mount Gibber changed, too. At one time it looked like a smooth black cone rising out of the forest. At another they could see the chasms in it and black precipices above the trees, where the rocks had broken away.

The sun was dropping down behind the island when, suddenly, there was no wind. *Swallow* lost way. The brown sail flapped. The little flag drooped at the mast-head. There was no more kick in the tiller. John had the horrible feeling of having no control at all over his ship.

"She won't steer," he said, trying hard by quick, desperate waggling of the rudder to make her keep her head up to the waves.

"Wind's changing," said Captain Flint. "We shall have it off shore in a minute. Mr Duck was right."

But minute after minute passed, and the *Swallow* rolled about with the yard swinging overhead and the boom tossing itself from side to side only an inch or two above Captain Flint's white sun-helmet.

"What about the oars?" said John.

"Nothing else for it," said Captain Flint. He lowered the sail, and pulled the oars out.

At once there seemed to be reason in things again. *Swallow* stopped tossing round and round like a cork. Captain Flint, taking a pull when he could, kept her head up to the seas.

"That was jolly unpleasant," said John.

"Helpless sort of feeling," said Captain Flint.

And then, before they expected it, came a faint breath off the land. John felt it on the back of his neck, and turned round as if he could hardly believe it. Captain Flint felt it on his cheekbones. They looked up at the little flag. It was lifting, dropping, lifting, and then, rippling from hoist to fly, blew straight out from the mast.

"She'd sail," said John.

A moment later Captain Flint had pulled her round to meet this new wind. The brown sail went up, and they were off again, reaching along to the north, though a good way out from the shore.

"You can see that northern hill now," said Captain Flint. "Queer to think of Mr Duck seeing those hills forty years ago and not wanting to come any nearer, in spite of knowing what he did."

"Where was it you found Black Jake's digging places?" asked John, and Captain Flint looked suddenly out to sea and round the horizon before he answered.

"Just about there," he said, pointing to the shore. "Nowhere near the right place."

"And where's Duckhaven?"

"Not so very much farther. You'll see the rocks coming down there out of the trees. Better be working in a bit. I took a bearing from a big tree there, and I'd like to get a sight of it. It's a tall enough tree, but I'd forgotten the ground was so high behind it."

"Are there any other landing-places if we can't find it?"

"Not one. It's the only place the whole way along that shore where the swell doesn't break. It's the only place where we could bring the boat in right side up."

They sailed on in silence, watching the endless line of white surf along the shore.

"What if we can't find the place?" John asked at last.

"Nothing for it but sailing back. There'd be no trouble about that, but the others would have something to say to us for leaving them without water or food or a tent for the night."

John thought of Susan. He could almost hear her telling Roger that he should have his supper as soon as *Swallow* came in. Perhaps at this moment, somewhere on the shore, the lot of them were watching the brown sail. What would they think if they were to see it turn round and go back the way it had come? And the sun was already down behind the island. And in this part of the world the dark came on so quickly.

Suddenly he saw something that reminded him of last summer. Dim blue smoke was curling up against the background of the trees. How often the smoke of the camp fire had hurried him home, when he saw it far away.

"Well done, Nancy," said Captain Flint. "Now we're all right. But we've no time to lose if we're to get things fixed up while we can see what we're doing."

"Are you going to begin piloting?"

"All right. Begin working her in." Captain Flint looked at his pocket compass and took a rough bearing of the smoke that was now a thick column pouring up from the beach. "Short tacks. That smoke's bearing just about right as it is."

A few short tacks this way and that brought *Swallow* nearer in. They could see specks moving round the fire. But they could see no way in. There seemed to be no opening at all in the long line of breaking water. It seemed a hopeless place for a landing. But, suddenly, John called out, "Is that the tree? Sticking up. Against the sky. Behind the smoke. Hullo. There are rocks between us and the shore."

"You don't seem to need a pilot," said Captain Flint. "Have you been here before? Yes. That's the tree. It's those rocks that make the harbour. We've got to go in just south of them and turn up into the smooth water behind them."

"The wind's dropping again."

"We'll have to go in under oars anyway."

As he spoke, Captain Flint brought the sail down and took to the oars. He glanced in towards the shore. "You see the end of the reef, where the water's breaking. We want to keep that in line with the big tree, or with Nancy's smoke. She's made her fire in the right place. Good girl."

"What?" The noise of the surf was getting louder.

Captain Flint shouted, and John leaned forward to catch what he said.

"You steer for the end of the rocks, and keep the smoke and the big tree in a line behind it."

Swiftly riding on the swell, the *Swallow* swooped towards the line of spray and leaping water.

John gripped the tiller and saw nothing at all but the end of the reef, a column of smoke and, where the smoke climbed into the sky, the feathery top of a gigantic palm. Nearer. Nearer.

Captain Flint glanced once more over his shoulder.

"Right," he shouted. "Keep her so."

There were a few moments when breathing seemed impossible. Close on the starboard bow, the end of the reef showed under water in the trough of the waves. Spray was leaping high in the air as the swell crashed thunderously against a long breakwater of black rock that ran out from the shore. On the port side line after line of waves rolled in to smash themselves upon the golden beach. *Swallow* slipped past the end of the reef and was suddenly almost at peace. Behind that natural breakwater were little tossing harmless wavelets. There was a strip of sand on which there was no surf. There were more rocks. Figures, well-known figures, waving, probably shouting but quite unheard, clambered on the rocks ahead. The rocks seemed to open. For a stroke or two Captain Flint was rowing in a narrow alleyway of smooth water. One of the oars touched a rock. A moment later the *Swallow* grounded in that little sheltered basin where, more than half a century before, Peter Duck, a cabin boy, lashed to a spar, had been washed up in the storm that had wrecked his ship and drowned every other soul aboard. It was a busy place today. Nancy was there, hauling *Swallow* up and steadying her, while Captain Flint stepped eagerly ashore to count his diggers and to see that none was missing. Titty, Roger, Peggy, and Susan were all talking at once. Gibber the monkey saw his chance and leapt aboard and ran along the gunwale to make sure that John, busy unshipping the rudder, was someone whom he knew.

"Jolly good thing you lit that fire, Nancy," shouted Captain Flint in her ear. "You can't see the high tree till you're fairly near in, because of the woods behind it . . . Yes . . . Woods . . . Behind it."

Everybody was shouting because of the noise of the surf, and it was hard to disentangle what they said.

"Did you put a lantern in?" That was Susan.

"Finest voyage *Swallow*'s ever done." That was probably Titty.

"Jolly good harbour, isn't it?" This was Nancy.

"Scuttled away. They all scuttled away. But they're coming back." This could be no one but Roger.

"Come on," shouted Captain Flint. "Discharge cargo and quick about it. We've got to fix a tent up. Yes. With the mast. And how are the mates to cook supper? Food, they want. YES. POTS AND PANS."

CHAPTER XXIV

DIGGERS' CAMP

THE land party, travelling light, had made very good time. They had picked up the blazed trail without difficulty, and there had been no dawdling on the way. The only delays (and those slight) had been when Nancy had not thought much of one of Captain Flint's new blazes and had called a halt while she used her pocket-knife to improve it. They had marched out on the beach at Duckhaven when the little brown sail of the *Swallow*, a mere spot showing and vanishing among the waves, was still far away, beating out to sea from the southwest corner of the island. Their guides, Titty and Roger, had shown them the little harbour, and the old wrecked boat, and the crabs, though the crabs, as Roger had complained, had been at first inclined to run away. Then Nancy had chosen a place on the shore exactly on a line between the big tree and the end of the reef where the waves were breaking, and they had all worked hard in building the fire that had been so useful in helping *Swallow's* pilot to find the way in. Afterwards, while Susan and Peggy had been busy putting green leaves on the fire to make a smoke, Nancy, with Titty and Roger, had done a little exploring on her own account, north along the beach, and had made a discovery of which, by agreement with them, no one said anything that night. Susan had served out a ration of chocolate, but, by the time the *Swallow* berthed in Duckhaven, everybody was more than ready for a meal.

All hands turned to discharging cargo, and as soon as the water-barrel had been lifted out and chocked up among the rocks in a handy place so that the kettle could be filled at the tap, Susan and Peggy hurried off to the fire with it. Captain Flint fetched them back for a moment, when he had taken all the ballast out of *Swallow*, so that all hands working together could haul her up the beach above high-water mark, in the tiny cove among the rocks. After that they went back to their cooking. They were going to heat up some pemmican. Meanwhile, Captain Flint and the others were busy with the tent. Nancy had found a good place, with a bit of smooth sand, sheltered from the north-east by the ridge of rock that ran down into the sea. Another rock, poking up out of the sand, gave some shelter on the other side, and, at the back of it, a bit of the main ridge stuck out at just the right height to carry one end of a pole. Captain Flint lashed *Swallow's* oars together to make a crutch to carry the other end.

"If only we'd had the saw with us instead of letting you bring it round in *Swallow*," said Nancy, "we'd have cut a tree to make a proper ridge-pole. We'll cut one tomorrow. The mast's a bit short but it'll do all right for tonight."

The mast certainly was rather short, because a good bit of it had to rest on the rock at one end, and some of it had to stick out beyond the oars at the other, but when the old staysail was spread over the top they had a pretty good tent, even if it was small for so many. They decided to cram into

it. Of course some of them could have slept inside
the old wrecked boat, but they had looked into it
and given up the idea, for the wreck was simply
boiling with crabs.

"Botheration," said Nancy. "How are we going
to peg the edges?"

"With these," said Captain Flint, emptying a
small bag of wooden tent-pegs on the ground.

"That was the noise I heard last night," said
Titty. "Chipping and chipping. I couldn't think
what it was."

"And Mr Duck's stitched a lot of rope loops into
the sail." Ten minutes later the tent was ready for
the night. Nancy, Titty, and Captain Flint were
all inside it, when Roger came hurrying from the
fire. He had shouted from there, but no one had
heard him, though they were already learning to
hear what they were saying in spite of the noise
of the surf.

"Kettle's boiling," he said. "Susan sent me to
tell you to bring the mugs. She and Peggy can't
leave the fire because of the crabs."

"Why, the crabs aren't trying to grab the kettle,
are they?" said Captain Flint.

"They will go sidling into the fire," said Roger.
"Peggy and I have been fending them off, but the
moment anyone looks the other way there's one
of those crabs scorching himself like anything. A
whole lot have got burnt in spite of us."

"Half a minute," said Captain Flint, "and I'll
come and see what can be done. Try to straighten
out that side if you can, Nancy. Howk up those
two pegs and shove them in again farther out."

"I say," said Roger.

SETTLING IN AT DUCKHAVEN

"What do you say?" said Captain Flint.

"Do you think these crabs can be the same sort as the crabs that bit Mr Duck's trousers? They seem so much smaller."

"They'd seem big enough if you were on the island all by yourself," said Captain Flint, "and anyhow, I bet they'll have grown a bit when you come to tell your grandchildren about them."

"Perhaps the night ones are bigger," said Roger.

"They probably seemed bigger in the dark. You see the young P.D. hadn't even got a fire to see them by, and he hadn't got a whole lot of friends to help scare them off. I don't wonder he was glad to get away from them."

It was getting dark quickly now. Captain Flint climbed over the rocks and went up the sandy beach to the fire, to find Peggy and Susan both busy heading off the yellow crabs that looked almost orange-coloured in the light of the flames into which they seemed determined to sidle. A good lot of them had reached the fire and lay scorched and dead round the edge of it, in spite of the two mates' efforts to save them.

"It's no good," said Peggy. "If I turn away for one moment there's a new one beginning to sizzle."

"They're worse than moths," said Susan, "bobbing into candle flames."

"We'll be quit of them for a bit anyhow," said Captain Flint, and taking a stick from Peggy, he raked away the dead crabs from round the fire and threw them a little way off. Instantly the other crabs lost interest in the fire and turned on the dead bodies of their relations.

Captain Flint hurried back to the tent to help Titty and Nancy to bring along the rest of the mugs.

"Here's a crab crawling into the tent," shouted Nancy, just as he was coming down over the rocks.

"Kick it out," called Captain Flint.

"Don't hurt it," said Titty.

But long before supper was over, by that bright fire in the blue dusk on the beach, even Titty's heart was hardened, in the matter of dealing with the crabs. For the crabs themselves had no hearts at all. They grabbed at each other and tore each other to pieces, and the noise of the crunching which they made was horrible in itself. The only way to be rid of them was to throw a few of the corpses away, when the others instantly fell on them, crunching them up and waving their pincers and goggling their eyes. There was nothing to be afraid of for the six Swallows and Amazons and Captain Flint. The crabs were not big enough. They were just nasty, and they would not take "no" for an answer. Nothing seemed to teach them that they were not wanted. All the same Nancy said, "Well, I wish Bill was here. He wouldn't mind batting them at all." None of the Swallows and Amazons liked batting crabs, but Gibber was the only one who learnt to be afraid of them. He was amusing himself by poking at one or two of the crabs, picking them up by their shells and throwing them away, while keeping his fingers out of the way of their pincers, when a big crab happened to crawl up just behind him, found his tail, and thinking that in spite of its hairiness it might be worth trying, took a tremendous grip of it. Gibber let loose a squeal of pain and went spinning round and round, chasing his tail, with the big crab at the end of it flying like a ball at the end of a string. It let go in the end and shot away into the dark, but Gibber, after that, was wary of crabs, and used to give warning by loud whimpering if ever one of them came near him.

The crabs made a queer, disturbed supper of it for everybody. It was not safe for anyone to put a scrap of pemmican or a bit of biscuit on the ground even for a moment while drinking. It was gone at once. There was no difficulty in getting rid of any unwanted scraps.

"They'll be much better than we are at tidying up after a meal," said Susan.

"That's all right so long as they don't do their tidying up before we've had a chance," said Captain Flint. "That was a perfectly good bit that one just got, the one with the big eyes that's chewing it up now."

"Was it a bit you were keeping till the last?" asked Roger gravely.

"I don't know about that," said Captain Flint, "but it was far too good a bit for any crab."

The crabs were a nuisance at night, too, when the diggers had settled down in their tent. But they were not a nuisance to everybody. John was much more tired than he knew after sailing *Swallow* round from Bill's Landing to Duckhaven. Careless of crabs and deaf to the noise of the surf, he fell asleep the moment he had wriggled down into his sleeping-bag. Peggy, too, slept almost at once. Susan lay awake for a time, thinking of how the feeding and cooking was best to be done while in camp, and going through the list she had in her mind of the things that she hoped had not been forgotten. Suddenly she started up and flung a small crab across the tent and out into the night. She had felt it crawling over her bag. Titty and Roger stayed awake for a little while after that, waiting to see if the crabs would not begin exploring them too. But they, like Susan, went to sleep before they meant to. Captain Flint had spent some time after supper in walking up and down the sandy beach in the dusk, disturbing the fireflies, and treading, perhaps, on the very place where Peter Duck's treasure had been buried so long ago by the captain and the mate of the *Mary Cahoun*. The others were all in their sleeping-bags, and most of them were already asleep when he came back to the tent and lay down across the mouth of it, to discourage invaders. He lay there, planning tomorrow's diggings, but was so often disturbed by small crabs, who wanted to know what he was made of, that in the end he got up and banged about with one of the wooden shovels and threw a lot of crabs down towards the water. After that there was peace. It was Captain Nancy, the Terror of the Seas, the successful leader of the land party, who lay awake the longest, listening to the noise of the surf along the shore, and thinking of crabs. She hated the thought of live crabs. She hated the thought of dead ones. Most of all she hated the feel of them. Everything she touched seemed to be crab, and she was only just in time to stop herself from waking everybody else with a wild yell when the hem of her own sleeping-bag happened to tickle her chin. "Jibbooms and bobstays!" she said to herself, "but that would never have done. Worse than Peggy in a thunderstorm!" She chuckled at her escape and soon after that had forgotten all about the crabs. The noise of the surf seemed now to come from under the bows of a great ship moving before a gale of wind. Nancy was steering the *Wild Cat* on, on, and on, among tremendous seas. She could not have had a happier dream.

CHAPTER XXV

DIGGERS AT WORK

At sunrise everybody was astir, feeling a little queer after their first night ashore when they had been so long afloat. Captain Flint was already scraping about in the sand at the foot of the palm trees. He was in such a hurry to begin digging that they were almost ashamed when Nancy asked him: "Are there any sharks in Duckhaven?" But he said they couldn't do better than start fresh with a bathe, though they must take care not to tread on the sea-urchins, of which there were many among the rocks. He went out near the mouth of the little harbour to keep watch for sharks, so that they could have a morning dip. This took time, but it was worth it, as they probably worked all the harder for having begun the day by wallowing about in the water, though Duckhaven seemed rather a small swimming-pool when they looked out beyond the rocks to the Atlantic.

The camp fire had died down and gone out during the night, but crabs had gone on crawling into it as long as there was a flicker of flame. There was a ring of dead, scorched crabs round it, and in the morning the cooks found a lot of live crabs feeding on these corpses. They swept them out of the way, live crabs and dead crabs together, while they made up the fire anew for breakfast.

After breakfast, digging began.

Captain Flint had seen when he had first come to Duckhaven that not even Peter Duck himself could have gone straight, after all those years, and pointed to the place where the bag had been hidden. But he still thought that they knew enough to be sure of finding it without having to dig very long. After all, Mr Duck had given them all the help he could.

"The only trouble is," he said, as he marched up the beach at the head of his gang of diggers, "that we don't know just which is Mr Duck's tree, if any of them is. I don't know how long coconut palms live. His may have gone long ago. Or it may be one of these. But we do know that this is where he was thrown up after the wreck, and his tree was somewhere close by."

"Let's dig the whole place up," said Titty.

"We'll take the big tree as a centre and dig from it both ways," said Captain Flint. "Yes. That's right. John and Nancy go ahead with the tin spades. You two others use the wooden ones till the mates are ready. Now, then. Stand clear. Here goes!"

He swung the queer little pick that Peter Duck had made out of an old boat-anchor and a capstan bar and brought it down close at the foot of the biggest of the palm trees. It sank into soft sandy earth. He swung it up again and brought it down.

There was a clink of something hard against the iron of the pick.

"Ha! What was that?" he cried, and worked away furiously for a minute or two, but it was only a small black stone deep in the sand.

John and Nancy waited only for a moment, and then started digging away with the two little spades from Cowes. Titty and Roger chose a likely-looking place on their own account and attacked it with the wooden spades, and then, finding the spades not much good, used their knives, their hands, and a bit of stick. After all, they had found the treasure on Cormorant Island all by themselves, and, somehow, they thought, privately, that they would have the same sort of luck at Duckhaven. And this was much more exciting. At Cormorant Island they had known that there were no ingots in the treasure, and indeed that most people would hardly have called it a treasure at all. But here, at Duckhaven, no one knew anything. The only people who had known what was buried there were the two who had buried it, and they had been drowned off Ushant sixty years before. Titty and Roger were prepared to dig all day.

So was Captain Flint, but after the first eager half-hour of working round the big tree with the pickaxe, when he was thinking that every next blow would bring the thing to light, whatever it was, he began to be sorry that there were not enough tools to go round. What was wanted was half a dozen picks, big and little. John and Nancy were doing pretty well with the tin spades, but it was already clear that the main use of the wooden ones would be to shift the earth loosened by the pick. They were no good for making a hole by themselves. And, anyhow, there were only two, even of them.

."I wish we had a lot more spades," he said

at last, stopping to mop his forehead. "And we want a pick apiece. It's all very well burying a treasure with a sheath knife. It's a very different job digging it up, with all these roots and stones all over the place."

Then he set to work with the pick again, working along in a line so as to loosen as much earth as possible and give the spades a chance. The spades were doing their best. John and Nancy were digging a regular trench, and Titty and Roger had struck a patch of loose sand and were burrowing like rabbits.

"Let me have a go with the pick," said Nancy at last. "We can't count on finding the thing at once. We're almost bound to be sleeping here again tonight. What about cutting a ridge-pole to make a bigger tent of it. It'll take us at least a couple of days to dig even half the bit you've marked out."

"There's something in that," said Captain Flint, and he went so far as to get the saw and to start the cutting down of a tall young palm to make a ridge-pole. But he soon called John to carry on with that job, while he went back and had another hard go with the pick. Susan and Peggy had joined the diggers after washing up the breakfast mugs. They were using the wooden spades, and just as Captain Flint came back to the diggings Peggy had the bad luck to break a spade through putting too much beef into digging with it. She went on working, shovelling the sand out of a hole as well as she could with the broken end of the spade.

Captain Flint watched for a while without stopping the steady swinging of his pick. Then he stopped.

HARD AT WORK

"This is no good," he said. "What we need is stronger spades. The two I made aren't worth digging with. It wasn't your fault, Peggy. I don't wonder it broke."

Just then the tall young palm came crashing down, and John, the woodcutter, came to ask what next. Captain Flint went to look at it, to see how much ought to be cut off the top of it. Near the edge of the forest, close to the palm that had been cut down, lay a much larger fallen tree. Captain Flint took the saw from Roger and set furiously to work sawing a flattish piece out of it. The others watched, wondering.

"We simply must have a decent-sized spade," he said, and in the end he had made one, all in one piece, very rough, but a good deal stronger than the one which Peggy had broken. But he had worn the saw very blunt, and kept wishing all the time that Peter Duck was there to help.

"This wood's as hard as iron," he said, "and I never thought of bringing a file for sharpening the saw."

"What about finishing up the tent-pole," said Nancy, "while the saw's still got some cut in it?"

"All right," said Captain Flint. "This job's going to be a longer one than I thought. Of course we may strike the bag any minute, but we may just as likely be digging for a week first."

So he finished cutting the ridge-pole, and carried it down to Duckhaven. Everybody stopped digging and came to help, while the new pole was set up between the rocks and the oars, and the oars were shifted farther from the rocks, so that they had a much bigger tent than the one they had rigged up in a hurry in the evening. John was very pleased to let *Swallow* have her mast again.

It was just when Captain Flint had done his part of the tent-making, and was setting to work once more at the diggings, that Nancy let out the secret of the discovery made the day before.

"What about a drink of water after all that?" she said, glancing along the beach to the north and waving a hand.

"We must go slow on the water," said Captain Flint. "I don't want to waste time sailing round to fill the breaker, and it's far too big a job to bring it overland full of water. I can hang on all right till dinner-time."

Titty slipped out from dodging along the edge of the trees. Roger was close behind. They both had tin mugs in their hands.

"I say," said Captain Flint, "I know it's jolly thirsty work, but does Mate Susan know you've been at the water already?"

"Just try it," said Nancy. "Is it fit to drink?"

Captain Flint took Roger's mug and smelt it.

"There's nothing wrong with it," he said. "There can't be. The barrel was only filled yesterday."

"This didn't come out of the barrel," said Titty.

"Where did you get it from?"

"It comes out of a rock," said Nancy, "but it isn't exactly a stream. It just disappears again."

"Well, it's fresh water, anyhow," said Captain Flint. "Good, too." He finished off the mug. "Let's have a look at the place. This looks like saving us a lot of trouble. I was really getting bothered about that water-barrel, with the lot of us coming thirsty to meals, and all this digging to do."

Nancy's spring was hardly three hundred yards from Duckhaven, but it was little wonder that Peter Duck had not found it, even if it had been there sixty years before. A spur of high land ran down towards the sea. It was covered with trees, and it was not until you were in among the trees that you could see that there was a backbone of black rock under the foliage. Nancy, Titty, and Roger had noticed a great commotion of birds above these trees when they had walked this way along the shore after looking at the crabs in the old wreck. Now usually when the parrots and other birds were disturbed by anything, they rose up and flew away. But here as many birds seemed to be coming as going, and the explorers had pushed into the forest to see why. Guided by the birds they found, deep in ferns, a very small pool, at which the parrots were drinking. There was no stream from it. The water seemed to soak away into the sand. But they could see that a trickle of water was coming into it all the time out of a crack in the black rock high above it. It was easy to climb along the rock to the place where this trickle came out, and Nancy had caught some in the palm of her hand and tasted it, though she had not allowed her men to do the same, until Captain Flint had tried the water and said that it was all right.

"It's as good water as we've got on the other side," said Captain Flint. "Well done, Nancy, and you two. We shan't die of thirst, anyhow, but you'll have to be careful to take it from up here, where it comes out, and not from the pool. There'll be other things besides parrots drinking at that pool. Look there, now!"

The others were climbing on the rock beside him, but now they peered down through the ferns into the tiny pool, about six feet below them. A green snake, mottled with black, was lying beside the pool with its head in the water. It lifted its head, then slipped into the pool, bathed there for a moment, swimming round, and then slipped quickly up out of the water and disappeared.

"Safe enough if you always get your water from up here," said Captain Flint, "but look where you're going, and make a noise."

After that they went back to the digging. Looking at Nancy's spring had been a bit of a holiday for everybody. They dug on now until it was time for dinner. It was very hot. The new wooden spade, though it looked as if it had been made by prehistoric man, was a good deal better than the one that Peggy had broken, but the two tin spades from Cowes were the only spades that were the slightest good at digging ground that had not first been loosened with the pick. So, after dinner, Captain Flint kept hard at it with the pick until the evening, and the others kept at it, too, working along, taking turns with the good spades and doing as well as they could with the others. But not one of the diggers found anything. Some of them began to doubt if there was really anything to dig for.

"It may be just like the crabs," said Peggy. "They seemed big to Mr Duck when he was a little boy, but you said yourself they probably

grew a bit when he was telling the story. These
crabs are nothing" (she picked one up that was
sidling after a fallen bit of biscuit, and threw it
away) "and the treasure may be just the same."

This was at the evening meal, when the trade
wind had dropped and dusk was falling, and digging was over for the day. Captain Flint rolled
over to look at his younger niece, and found that
Susan was looking at him as if she, too, felt that
he could have nothing to say to that.

"Of course it may not be much," he said unhappily.

"It's jolly good fun looking for it," said John.

"But what if it never was there at all?" said
Peggy.

"Or taken away long ago."

"Shiver my timbers!" said Nancy. "What's all
this? Here we are in a fine camp. Anybody can
see that Black Jake did his digging in the wrong
place. We've only been digging for one day and
part of that was tent-making."

"We're going to dig until we find it," said Titty.

"What do you think, Roger?" asked Captain
Flint.

"I'm going to dig with Titty," said Roger. "And
so is Gibber."

"Then we're bound to find it," said Captain
Flint. "Look here, you two mates," he added,
"we haven't really given it half a show. The
stuff's here all right. None of the digging's wasted.
Every bit dug is so much that we needn't dig
again. It's like mowing a field with a hare in
it. The hare may jump up any minute, but, if
he doesn't, in the end there'll be just a tiny

patch of long grass and the hare'll be sitting tight in the middle of it. Anyway, as soon as half of us want to give up, we'll go back to the schooner."

When supper was over he nearly ruined the blade of his pocket-knife, trying to smooth the rough handle of the new spade. Then he lit his pipe and went off for a stroll in the dusk while the fireflies were dancing in the shadow under the trees and the diggers were settling down in their sleeping-bags in the improved and larger tent.

"He'll be most awfully sick if he doesn't find it," said Nancy, sitting up in her bag in the dark. "Not just because he wants it, but because he won't like coming back without it after bringing us all this way."

"But if it isn't here," said Peggy.

"If it isn't, it isn't. But it isn't only Uncle Jim who thinks it is."

"And what if it's nothing when we find it?"

"What a galoot you are," said Nancy. "Whatever it is, it'll be something to have found. To put in the British Museum, perhaps, or some place like that. 'Presented by the Captain and Crew of the *Wild Cat* Expedition to Crab Island.' Like Roger's pirate knife ... We've simply got to help him to find it. He's failed again and again. Finding just one thing like that would make him really happy."

"We've got a week's food here," said Susan. "We'll dig until it's done, anyway."

"We may just as well do that," said Peggy. "Nancy's probably right."

"We may find it tomorrow at the very first dig," said Titty.

"Nobody's let me have a go with the pick," said Roger. "It's my turn to start with it in the morning."

Captain Flint came back from his prowl along the beach, still a little worried by the talk at supper. He killed a lot of invading crabs to get peace for the night while they were being eaten up by their cannibal friends. Then he lay down to sleep across the doorway of a tent which, though he did not know it, was once more crammed with determination and good will.

*

Next day the digging went on.

Roger had first whack with the pick in the morning, but its point did not plunge deep into a bag of gold as he had thought it might, but only into sand, and not as far as it should have done if it was to be of any use. He had another whack or two, and then was glad to hand over the pick to Captain Flint and to take to the broken spade that suited him very well.

The digging today was more regular and business-like. Yesterday everybody had kept on having good ideas and deciding that the right place must be under this tree or that, going straight there, and having a dig to see or even getting Captain Flint to come along and to see what happened when he used the pick. Today, by general agreement, people dug along lines carefully marked beforehand.

"It stands to reason," Captain Flint said, "that

when those two scoundrels buried their bag under a young coconut tree, they had some way of their own for knowing that tree again."

"They probably blazed it," said Titty, looking up at the tall trunks of the palms.

"Sorry, Able-seaman, but that's just what I think they wouldn't do. A blazed tree all by itself would start anybody thinking. No. They probably chose some tree that didn't need blazing. All they wanted was a tree they would be able to find in a year's time, or two years' time, or whenever it was they meant to come back."

"But all the young coconut trees are as like as belaying-pins," said Roger. "Peter Duck said so. I heard him."

"That's just the point," said Captain Flint. "They'd have to choose a tree that they would recognise by something else . . . These rocks, for example. A tree in the middle of the forest would be no good to them. Too many others all round it. They'd choose one right on the edge. And there's another thing, too. So would Peter Duck. Remember, he'd chosen the very same tree, and bolted up it out of the way of the crabs. He wouldn't bolt farther than he needed. Everything shows that he chose a tree near where he was thrown up, and that they chose a tree they could tell again, on the edge of the forest. It might be the first tree north or south of where the rocks come down on the shore. It might be the second or the third one way or the other. But one thing is clear, and Peter Duck says the same . . . It must have been a tree very close to where we are standing."

"Sitting," said Roger.

"Shut up, Roger," said Titty. "You may be sitting on the hoard at this very minute."

Roger got up in a hurry. Captain Flint went on talking.

"The big tree I took for a mark coming in, is exactly above Duckhaven, where Mr Duck was washed up. That's why I started there. We'll go on digging both ways, beginning at that tree. We can't miss it if we do the thing thoroughly."

He set up two sticks in the sand in front of the trees and scraped a rough furrow between them. "That marks out our claim. We shall find the stuff all right, if we dig under all the trees along that line."

"It's a longish line," said Susan.

"Makes it all the surer that we shan't miss the thing. It's not as if we were Black Jake and digging in the wrong place to start with. We know we're starting right, and that's the main thing."

By evening of that day, all the ground between that scraped furrow and the trees at the edge of the forest looked like a bit of ploughed field. Stones dug up out of it had been laid aside and built by Roger into a row of little cairns. The digging went up to and behind the nearest trees. Nothing had been found, but before dark Captain Flint, working till the sweat poured off him, had cleared the whole of the ground round the trees that grew immediately behind these outer ones, to make ready for the next day's digging.

"You see," he said, while they were sitting round the camp fire, having their supper, and battling with the crabs who were as bothersome as horseflies, "it never struck me this morning.

The wind's mostly easterly, and the shallows are on this side of the island. It may well be that in these sixty years the sea's gone back a little, or piled up the sand, and the earth and the forest may be gaining on the shore. Perhaps all those trees at the very edge of the forest weren't there sixty years ago, and we'll find the stuff a little further back, where the edge of the forest used to be."

"Well, we've got lots of time," said Nancy.

Captain Flint looked hurriedly out over the darkening sea.

SWALLOWS·AND·AMAZONS·FOR·EVER!

CHAPTER XXVI

THREATENING WEATHER

DURING the morning of the third day of the digging hopes were falling low. The cairns of stones along the edge of the ground already dug stood there as memorials of one disappointment after another. The clink of iron pick on buried stone had long ceased to bring everybody on the run expecting to see the treasure brought to light. Everybody had by now too often seen a lump of black stone tenderly dug out of the ground by hands that were nervous with fear lest they should damage something valuable.

At middle-day dinner, John had been all but ready to give up. Even Captain Flint had begun to feel that perhaps, after all, there was nothing to be found. But a change of another kind had come over the feelings of the mates. Susan, by now, was settling down at Duckhaven, and, for the moment, wanted no more house-moving. The discovery of Nancy's spring had made the camp much easier to run than she had thought it would be. Captain Flint had said it was good drinking water, and this, after all that time in the schooner, carefully rationing the water, made Susan want to stay where she was. Peggy agreed with Susan. The two housekeepers had made up their minds to camp at Duckhaven till the food ran out. That, in itself, was enough to put heart into the doubters. Just before dinner, Roger had been asking Titty whether it wasn't nearly time to start back to the schooner, and John had been thinking that it would be good to be at sea once more, but when they saw that Susan took it for granted that they would be digging on for at least another four days, John somehow forgot his doubts, and Roger said: "Of course, we could stay a whole year if we ate some of the crabs." Captain Flint, naturally, was ashamed to give up while everybody else seemed ready to dig on, and after dinner all the diggers set to work again, almost as keenly as if this was the first day. They worked steadily on through the afternoon in the shade of the outer trees until something happened that, for a time, brought digging to an end.

"What's the matter with Gibber?" said Roger suddenly, and Nancy, who was digging close by, looked up to see the monkey shivering as if he had had a sudden fright.

"What's gone with you, Gibber?" said Nancy. Only a few minutes before she had seen him busily scratching away with a bit of stick, pretending he was digging, like his master.

The monkey whimpered. Its lips drew back from its chattering teeth. It clung to Roger and tried to hide its head in Roger's shirt. It shivered so violently that Roger himself shook.

"Uncle Jim! Uncle Jim!" called Nancy. "Gibber's going to have a fever."

"Not he," said Captain Flint, who had thrown down his pick and come on the run at hearing Nancy's call. He took the wrist of the monkey as if he were a doctor feeling a patient's pulse. "He's

had a fright. That's what it is. Seen a snake, perhaps. What was he doing?"

"He was helping me to dig," said Roger. "But
there weren't any snakes. I didn't see any. And
we'd been digging in that hole for a long time."

"He's frightened about something or other,"
said Captain Flint.

And just then there was a strange loud noise, so
loud that everybody heard it in spite of the steady
roar of the surf along the beach on either side of
sheltered Duckhaven.

Everybody had heard the screaming of parrots
and chatterers before. There was nothing strange
in that. But this time it was as if all the birds on
the island, from every part of the forest, all at
once rose screaming above the trees. There was a
shrill, ear-splitting din. It seemed to last for about
three minutes on end. Then it stopped dead, in an
absolute silence, except for the noise of the surf,
and the sighing of the wind in the tops of the trees.

"What on earth made them do that all at once?"
said Nancy.

"They're frightened, too," said Captain Flint.
He looked out to sea almost in the way he used
to look whenever anything reminded him of Black
Jake.

A moment later everybody was startled by a
sudden breath of cold wind. It was gone again
in a couple of minutes, but during that short
time, all the explorers, hot as they were with
their digging, shivered like the monkey. Then
once more came the warm trade wind, but it
died suddenly away as if it were late evening
instead of afternoon, and again they shivered in

the cold breath that on this hot beach seemed
icy.

"Something's wrong with the weather," said
Captain Flint, and ran down the beach to Duckhaven, where he had hung his coat over the end
of the long ridge-pole of the tent, out of the way
of the crabs.

He came slowly back, looking first north, then
south, then north again, then over his shoulder
out to sea, and glancing down every other second
at the pocket barometer that he had gone to fetch.

"Dropping like a stone," he said. "It'd gone
down nearly an inch. No wonder the monkey
was upset. He knew. And so did the birds."

"What? What?"

"There's something pretty bad coming. Dash
it all, I wish I knew what to do."

"What about?" said Nancy.

"The ship," said Captain Flint.

"We've got her well pulled up," said Titty.

"*Swallow*'s all right," said Captain Flint. "But
if we get the *Wild Cat* smashed up we shall be
in a pretty fair mess."

"She's in a jolly good anchorage," said John.

"In good weather," said Captain Flint. "She's
all right there with the trade wind blowing all
day and dropping every night. Couldn't be better. She's sheltered by the island. But those cold
breaths mean a shifting wind, and more than
that, too. What if there comes a buster, swinging
all round the compass? What if we get a circular
storm? We're in the tropics, mind you." He was
talking as much to himself as to the other diggers. "What if it blows up from the south-west

or north-west? *Wild Cat*'ll be on a lee shore and
with the sea that'll come in there no anchors on
earth'll hold her. I wish to goodness I'd had the
sense to look at the glass before."

"What do you do when it comes on like that?"
asked John.

"Get an offing first of all. Get away from the
land and heave to, maybe, when you've got the sea
room, and come back again when things quieten
down."

"Won't Mr Duck do it?" said Nancy.

"I don't know that he will," said Captain Flint.
"And if it comes a proper snorter he'll need more
than Bill to help him."

"Do you think it is coming a snorter?" said
Roger.

"Sure of it," said Captain Flint. "You can't
have a surer sign that those cold breaths. And
then the barometer, too. Sure of it. Gibber knew
it, too."

"He's all right again, now," said Roger.

"I'd never forgive myself," said Captain Flint,
"if the *Wild Cat* got smashed up and we were
marooned here for good."

"To wait for Black Jake to take us off," said
Titty.

Again Captain Flint glanced out to sea and
round the horizon.

"Look there," he said, and everybody looked
away to the south in the direction he was pointing.

It was not a vessel he had seen, but something
that meant very little to his crew. Far away to the
south, low over the sea, was a long line of bright,
copper-coloured cloud.

"And the wind's northerly," said Captain Flint. "That cloud's coming up from the south. Against the wind. There's no time to lose. The trouble's coming at once, whatever it is. Never mind about the digging. How long will it take you to pack?"

"In *Swallow*?" asked Susan.

"We can't put out in *Swallow* till the wind drops," said Captain Flint, "and by that time it'll be too late. We'll have to leave everything we can't carry."

The cloud in the south was visibly rising. It was the colour of a bright copper kettle. As it rose, it ceased to be a mere line of cloud. Its base narrowed while its top widened. It was as hard-edged as a thunder-cloud, but no one ever saw a thunder-cloud of such a colour.

"We can't leave everything," said Susan. "Half the things are things we can't do without. And if we've got to hurry it's no good thinking Roger and Titty can go as fast as John and Nancy."

"What about our sleeping-bags?" said Peggy. "We'll want them when we get back to the *Wild Cat*."

"What about *Swallow*?" said Titty.

Captain Flint looked this way and that, away up to the north, where those strange cold breaths had come from, and away south to this great, hard-edged copper-coloured fan that was spreading up over the blue sky as if it were cut out of sheet metal.

"The thing's coming at once," he said. "There isn't a moment to lose. There may be only just time to get across."

"Don't waste any of it saying goodbye," said

Nancy, firmly taking command. "What's the good of talking about it? You've got to go. How are we ever going to get home if anything happens to the schooner? Go on. We're all right here. Nothing can possibly go wrong with us. Duckhaven's right as rain. We've got food. We've got water. We're on land."

"If I could only be sure that Mr Duck would take her out to sea," said Captain Flint.

"But he won't," said John. "He'll be waiting for you to come because you said you'd slip across if the weather looked like turning nasty."

"He won't go at all," said Titty. "He'll be remembering what he felt like when he was wrecked here and couldn't get away."

"I believe you're right," said Captain Flint, bothered beyond anything by the thought of the coming storm, and fear for the schooner that was, after all, their only means of getting home. "Look here, Nancy, you've got a lot of sense if you care to use it. So has John. I can trust you both. Susan has more than enough to spare for the rest of you."

"When you come back," said Susan, "please don't forget to bring some more matches. We've got plenty for a couple of days, but we'll want more after that."

"And some more chocolate," said Roger.

There was a breath of hot air from the south, air as hot as if it had been puffed out of a furnace door, as hot as those earlier breaths out of the north had been cold.

Captain Flint hurriedly emptied out his pockets. There were three boxes of matches, all half-empty, in the pockets of his coat. There were two almost full boxes in one of his trouser-pockets, and another, empty but for one match, in the other.

"I might have guessed it," said Susan, laughing. "I almost did." She gave him the empty box, putting half a dozen matches into it. "That'll last you till you get across. But do hurry up."

"We'll be perfectly all right," said Nancy.

"Give my love to Peter Duck," said Roger. "And Gibber's too."

"All our loves," said Titty. "And to Polly."

"And to Bill, of course," said Nancy.

"Just remember one thing," said Captain Flint, looking hard at that copper cloud that was now covering nearly a quarter of the sky. "If it really comes on to blow, and we may have a hurricane before night, keep out of the trees. The less shelter of that sort the better. Trees are all right, but you don't want them blowing down about your heads. Stick it out in the open and you'll perhaps be better here than aboard ship. Anyway it looks to me as if the wind's going to swing round to the south-west. You'll be all right here, but the sooner I get the *Wild Cat* clear of the land the better for us all."

"Don't go on hanging about, Uncle Jim," said Nancy. "You can't be in two places at once. We've said goodbye to you."

"Swallows and Amazons for ever!" cried Captain Flint, flung his coat over his shoulder instead of putting it on, and hurried off into the forest.

"Swallows and Amazons for ever! Goodbye! Good luck!"

The others shouted after him, but he was already disappearing among the trees and though at that moment there was another of those strange hot breaths from the south, and a lull in the trade wind from the Atlantic, the surf was so loud on the beach that he probably did not hear them.

"Do you think it's going to be a really bad one?" said Susan.

"Giminy, how do I know?" said Nancy. "Anyway, it isn't our first hurricane. Remember being hove-to in the Bay. And just remember the hurricane we had our last night on Wild Cat Island."

"I wish he hadn't gone," said Peggy. "It feels almost thundery."

"Thundery!" said Captain Nancy. "What if it is? Do try to remember you're an Amazon. I don't know why it is my mate's no blessed good at thunder. But she'd be quite all right if it was guns," she added.

"Do you think he'll have time to get out of the trees before it comes?" said Titty.

*

"What's become of all the crabs?" asked Roger suddenly.

They looked about them. There was not a crab to be seen, even by the fireplace on the beach, where, usually, it was almost impossible to move without stepping on one.

"They're afraid, too, like Gibber and the parrots," said Titty.

"It must be going to be pretty bad," said Peggy.

"All the more fun to remember it afterwards," said Nancy.

CHAPTER XXVII

GREAT GUNS

It was lucky that Susan thought of getting tea over before the storm broke.

"Remember what happened last summer," she said. "If the rain and the wind had come a bit earlier that last night we couldn't have had anything to eat. Nothing hot, anyhow. Let's have tea at once."

"Let's cram supper in as well," said Nancy. "Then we'll be ready for anything."

"All right," said John, watching that strange coppery cloud that still seemed to be coming up against the wind. "And what about firewood? Hadn't we better store some in the tent?"

"I'll take some in," said Peggy. "We've got a good lot stacked by the fire. Enough for another cooking besides this one."

"Good," said John. "And let's go on digging up to the last minute. Captain Flint didn't say anything about it, but he'd be awfully pleased."

"Why not?" said Nancy. "But he'll be pretty sick if we find it, just after he's gone."

"He won't really," said Titty. "He'll be pleased whoever finds it. I wonder how far he's got by now."

"He can keep up a pretty good trot when he wants," said Nancy.

"Well, come on, the diggers," said John. "Sing out, you mates, when you're ready with a real stodge."

"Aye, aye, sir," said Susan. This was like old times. John and Nancy in command. It was like being back on the island at home. "Come on, Peggy. The fire only wants opening up and feeding. And thank goodness there are no crabs about. There's a lot of red embers underneath left from dinner. Out of the way, you fo'c'sle hands. Go along and dig for treasure while you can. We'll call you when we're ready."

"You can't really be very hungry yet," said Peggy.

"We can," said Roger.

"Well, there's no chocolate going now," said Susan. "We're going to have tea and supper, and then you can have some chocolate when the storm comes. If it does come . . ."

"And if it doesn't?" asked Roger.

"Bother you," said Susan. "Skip along. You'll have chocolate just the same."

"Well, it's only fair," said Roger, and hurried off after Titty to join the diggers. Gibber ran after him, whimpering again, and wanting to be comforted.

For half an hour or so, while the mates were busy round the fire, and the copper cloud was creeping up against the wind, and Captain Flint was racing across the island to put the *Wild Cat* in safety, the diggers at Duckhaven dug as busily and as keenly as if they had only just begun and had not already been tempted a dozen times to give it up and to do something else instead. Captain Flint was not there to see them, but John and Nancy, taking turns with the makeshift pick, and Titty and Roger shovelling the loose stuff away with the best of the spades, worked as if they were racing with the storm. Even Gibber, watching all this eager business, scrabbled in the sand and seemed to forget his fears.

They deserved to find something, but they did not, though time went so fast in this racing, desperate kind of digging, with the sky growing darker and darker as that cloud spread over it, that all five of them were startled when Peggy ran up the beach and shouted at them.

"Can't you hear?" she shouted. It was a meal-time and she was one of the cooks. "We've yelled at least twice."

The diggers had not been listening. Even if they had, they might not have heard, because of the noise of the surf and the water breaking on the reef.

"Come on, John," said Nancy.

"Well, we've done our best," said John. "Hi! Roger, do carry your spade over your shoulder. You'll get it mixed up with your legs if you don't."

Supper and tea all in one usually means the happy end of an adventure that has kept people from starting home in proper time. But today it was not like that. No one was chattering about what had happened. Hardly anything was said. Everybody was wondering how far Captain Flint had got on his way, how soon the storm would break, what was happening on the other side of the island. Everybody was disturbed by knowing that Captain Flint himself, who was not one to make a fuss about nothing, had been really worried about the *Wild Cat*, though she was lying in what had seemed to them all the most peaceful anchorage in the world, there, off Bill's Landing and under the shelter of Mount Gibber.

"Bill's awfully lucky," said Titty, when the meal was over. "He'll be in the *Wild Cat* when they take her to sea, and we're just sitting ashore."

"We couldn't all have gone," said John. "The storm may be here any minute, and Captain Flint wouldn't be down at the Landing for ages if he'd had to wait for us. As it is it looks as if he'll only just be in time. We've got *Swallow* to look after. Come on, everybody, and lend a hand. We'll haul her farther up, just in case."

Almost without talking they hauled *Swallow* a few yards higher up the beach at Duckhaven, using rollers made from the spare bits left over after the cutting of the ridge-pole for the tent. Captain Flint had put them aside on purpose, ready for *Swallow*'s next launching. John was not pleased with the way he had stowed the sail, that evening when they were busy with the tent. He made a neater job of it now, rolling it up along the boom and using the mainsheet as a lacing round it to keep boom, yard, and sail all together.

Susan climbed up out of Duckhaven on the northern side of its sheltering rocks and had another look at the old wreck embedded in the sand. It was a queer thing. Not a crab was to be seen, even there, where, usually, three or four were crawling in or out, and hundreds were scrambling one over another inside. Every crab had disappeared. She came slowly back over the rocks and joined the others by the tent.

"What's up, Mate Susan?" asked Nancy.

"I was just wondering how much wind this tent'll stand," said Susan.

"It'll stand a good deal," said Peggy.

And just then the copper cloud closed over them. The trade wind from the sea suddenly fell away to nothing. Then came a hot breath as if the cloud were throwing heat before it, a hot breath along the beach, from the south, where, already, the feathery green palms were fading in a ruddy brown haze as if they were behind a veil of coppery silk.

Roger was the first to cough. A moment later everybody was doing it. They tried not to breathe. But you cannot live without breathing, and it was impossible to breathe without filling nose and throat with the fine red dust of which that cloud was made. It settled over everything. It put the fire out at once. A plate, a white enamelled plate that had been left by the fire with a biscuit on it belonging to Roger, dulled and turned copper coloured.

"I c-c-c . . . can't . . ." choked Roger.

Susan saved them.

"Stick your heads in your sleeping-bags," she cried. There was a rush into the tent, and everybody burrowed head first into a sleeping-bag like a crab going into a burrow. Roger stuffed the frightened monkey headlong into his little bag and pulled the string tight so that Gibber could not get out. "It's no good trying to explain to him," he said to himself as he burrowed into his own. The woolly sleeping-bags were stifling, but they worked as filters, more or less, and let air through while keeping out most of the dust.

And the dust was falling all the time, a fine dust, soft and yet heavy, suffocating. Every now and then someone put a head out, red-faced, with starting eyes, unable any longer to bear being smothered inside a sleeping-bag. But instantly, eagerly, the head went back to get, from inside that smothering bag, a cleaner breath of air than was to be had outside. Even being slowly smothered in one's own sleeping-bag was better than filling one's nose and throat and lungs with that red dust.

The cloud passed. Nancy, putting her head out for the third or fourth time, found the air still full of dust but not quite so thick and choking as it had been, though there was not a breath of wind. She could see about her once more. The trees along the edge of the beach were no longer hidden in a thick copper-coloured fog. They seemed to have turned dark brown. Nancy called to the others, "Come out, you ostriches!" She dug a finger into Peggy's ribs. Heads came out of all the sleeping-bags. John jumped up. As he did so he shook a cloud of dark red dust into the air, dust that had settled on him while he had been lying there with the others.

"Look out," said Susan. "Don't stir it up again. Get up as gently as you can."

But, no matter how careful they were, they could not move without filling the air once more with the fine dust that had settled over them all like a thick, ruddy brown blanket.

"The beastly stuff's everywhere," said John, through his teeth, keeping his mouth as nearly closed as he could. "By gum, Susan, if you hadn't thought of the sleeping-bags we might all have been choked. Look at the roof of the tent! Look at the beach!"

The beach had changed colour. The bright sand they knew was now dark. As for the old staysail from the *Wild Cat*, that made the roof of their tent, it was no longer weather-beaten grey but ruddy brown. It might have been made out of thick felt.

"What on earth's happened?" said Nancy.

"It must be one of those volcanoes somewhere," said John.

"Like Mont Pelée," said Titty. "Hundreds of miles away, probably. Perhaps a whole mountain has been blown into the air."

"Into dust," said Roger, "and this is it coming down again."

"It must be something like that," said Nancy.

"Just look at *Swallow*," said John.

The thwarts of the little boat were copper-coloured with the dust that had settled on them in that still air. Her bottom boards were covered with it. Dust seemed to have raised her gunwales.

"Do help with Gibber's bag," said Roger. "He's in an awful hurry to come out."

"You've tied a granny knot," said Nancy.

"Oh, bother!" said Roger. "Anybody might."

Nancy unfastened the knot. Gibber came whimpering out. He sniffed at once at the carpet of red dust that was stirring round their feet, and got a lot of it in his nose. Sneezing and chattering he jumped up on Roger, and clung to his neck.

"What do you think we ought to do about sleeping?" said Susan doubtfully. "It won't be safe to let them lie and breathe this stuff, and they'll never go to sleep if we make them keep their heads in the bags."

But that question was almost instantly answered for her.

"There's wind coming," said John. "From the sea this time. Look!"

"Listen to it," said Titty.

With a loud hissing noise, that they heard above the roar of the surf, a line of white foam was rushing at the island from the Atlantic. The wind was upon them in a moment. They turned and leant against the wind as if it was a wall. For one half-second the air was again thick with the red dust, and then it was gone. The beach was once more bright sand. The wind had lifted the dust blanket from everything and blown it up into the forest.

"Look out, the tent's going," cried Susan, as the squall rushed at them with new force. Roger, trying to balance himself against the wind, was blown forward on his face. Gibber lost hold of Roger's neck and was blown helplessly up the beach.

"Lie down," shouted Nancy, dropping on her hands and knees.

There were three or four loud cracks and the noise of ripping canvas. The old patched sail that had made their tent tore itself free from its fastenings, flung savagely round, swung the ridge-pole sideways, tossed away the supporting oars, and then rode up into the air, whirling like a scrap of thin paper, and was carried high up, over the tops of the trees, and out of sight. It was gone. They never saw it again.

"Save the sleeping-bags!" cried John, throwing himself down on them and hanging on to all he could reach.

Nancy, Susan, and Titty tried to save what they could of the camp from being blown away. Peggy had flung herself full length on the sand and was hiding her head in her arms so as not to see what was happening. Thunderstorms at home were bad enough. And this, though not a thunderstorm, was more than she could bear.

"There's one gone," said Susan, "and THERE'S ANOTHER."

No one heard the first part of that sentence, but everybody heard the last, and Susan was herself surprised to find that she was shouting at the top of her voice. The squall had stopped as suddenly as it had begun. They could hear it in the distance, driving away over the tops of the trees, but here, on the beach, there was silence again, except for the surf, and after the savage shrieking of that wind, the noise of the surf seemed nothing at all, and it was as if Susan, for no reason at all, was shouting in an empty room.

"Is that the end?" asked Peggy breathlessly.

"It's only the beginning," said Nancy. "Have you got your bag?"

"I don't know where it is," said Peggy wretchedly.

"Come on and look for it," said Nancy. "We'll find it if it hasn't blown up to the top of Mount Gibber with the tent."

The camp was a ruin, but, even so, Susan was grateful to the wind. Anything was better than to have to deal with that red dust. Four of the sleeping-bags were safe, five, counting Gibber's, which Roger had hold of when he fell down. Two, Peggy's and Titty's, had been blown away. But, though dusk was now falling fast, it was still light enough to see and both were found about a hundred yards away, close to the edge of the forest. John and Nancy brought them back. John found his hat, half full of sand, in the diggings.

They came back to what had once been a neat, trim camp, to find Susan shaking the old riding-lantern, which she had found on its side, some way up the beach.

"Stick some more oil in, quick," she said. "It'll be dark in no time now. The little tin of oil's in *Swallow*. It'll be safe enough. But there's hardly a drop in the lantern. Come on, you others. Each bring your own bag."

"I've found the box with the chocolate in it," said Roger.

"Trust you," laughed Nancy. "What are you going to do, Susan?"

"We'll get into the wreck till morning. All the crabs have been frightened away. It may be a bit smelly, but we can't have Roger and Titty lying out in the open if there's going to be a real storm."

"It's going to be real enough," said John. "There's something altogether wrong. Something really big must be happening somewhere."

"Hurry up, you two," said Susan.

They made a hasty move from the wrecked camp in Duckhaven to the old wreckage that lay half-buried in the sand on the northern side of the rocks. It was already growing dark on the beach, and not even Susan herself would go through the hole between the ribs of the old wrecked boat until John brought the lantern. Susan had seen that there were no crabs in the wreck earlier in the evening, but that was before the coming of the cloud and the dust, and before the coming of that great squall off the sea that had blown the dust away and the tent with it. Besides, the crabs might easily have come back with the dark. But it did not take John more than a minute or two to pour some more oil into the old lantern, light it in that breathless air in which the match-flame burned without a flicker, and scramble over the rocks with it after the others. He put the lantern through the opening into the bows of the old boat and held it up inside. It lit up nothing but the grey ribs and dry, splitting planking of what had once upon a time lifted proudly over the seas. There were no crabs.

"It's all right," said John, and climbed in. "Not a crab. There isn't much room," he added, bumping his head as he tried to stand up.

"Stow yourselves down somehow or other," said Nancy, taking command once more. "In you go. Better wriggle into your bags right away. There's no point in poking our elbows into each other's eyes, and we shall, if we all get in and try to settle down afterwards. Look out, Titty. That starboard elbow of yours is as sharp as a needle."

"Then there must be some point in it," said Roger, but nobody laughed or tried to squash him. This was no time to bother about words.

The lighting of the lantern seemed to bring the

dark down on them like a curtain. John crawled out of the wreck again, to leave more room for the others while they were settling in, and found he could already hardly tell where the forest ended and the sky began. But presently he heard a new noise of wind, not, this time, coming over the sea, but from the other side of the island.

"There's another squall coming," he said as he crawled in, blinking in the light of the lantern at the five mummies who had stowed themselves along the ribs of the old boat. The boat was deep in the sand, and her bows, all that was to be seen of her, were cocked up at an angle, making a queer sort of shelter in which no one could lie down, though everybody could rest, on a slant, leaning against the planking with feet firm in the sand. The smaller of the diggers had, of course, been given the places farthest in, because the narrowing bows left less room there. The lantern, on the sand inside the wreck, lit up the monkey squatting beside it, Nancy's jolly grin, and the anxious faces of Susan, Peggy, Titty and Roger. None of the faces seemed to have a body of its own, for all grew out of the sleeping-bags, and there was so little room in the wreck that it almost seemed as if instead of five sleeping-bags there was only one big one with five holes in it and a head out of each hole.

"Come on in, then," said Susan. "And you two had much better make up your minds to get to sleep."

But there was little sleep for anybody during that wild night. John had hardly had time to turn himself into a mummy like the others before the new wind swept down on them across the island.

"What's that noise?" asked Roger. "Breaking."

"It must be trees," said Nancy, "but it sounds like someone tearing calico to pieces in a rage."

The wind came in furious gusts, rushing down from Mount Gibber across the forest, stopping altogether for a moment of almost frightening quiet, and then coming again from the opposite direction, from the sea, with a shrill hissing and the noise of the blown spray slapping on rocks and wreck. They never knew where the wind could come from next, and every squall seemed stronger than the one before it.

"It's blowing a lot harder than it did that day when we were hove to off Ushant," said John, in a lull between two gusts.

"They must be having an awful time in the *Wild Cat*," said Susan.

"It's a good thing Captain Flint went off in such a hurry," said Titty.

There was a low chuckle from Nancy.

"What is it?" asked John.

"I was remembering Bill and the bacon fat," chuckled Nancy.

"Don't," said Titty. "Not even on land."

And then the wind came again, whistling through the planking of the old boat, and bringing with it the tremendous crashing noise of falling trees.

It stopped, and there was a lull lasting for so long that the six treasure-hunters, stowed away in the wreck, began to believe that the worst must be over.

"Well," said Nancy to Peggy, "it wasn't really

much worse than it was on the island at home. And, anyhow, there was no rain."

"Or thunder," said Peggy, as cheerfully as she could.

But, as she spoke, they heard a new noise, not so much like thunder itself as like the slow, echoing rumbles when thunder is dying away. Only, instead of fading into silence, like the echoes of a clap of thunder tossed from cloud to cloud, this rumbling began low, and grew swiftly louder and louder until it became a deafening roar that went on and on, minute after minute, a tremendous chorus of noises in which the breaking of great trees seemed no more than the cracking of matchsticks in the overwhelming clangour of rock crashing against rock.

Suddenly, with nobody touching it, the hurricane lantern fell over on its side. The monkey screamed. A violent tremor shook the old wreck like a bundle of sticks. Titty and Roger, up in the bows, bumped against each other. Nancy nearly fell sideways. John, stooping hurriedly down to pick up the lantern, hit his head against one of the timbers on the opposite side of the boat. That dreadful noise of splitting rocks and great stones rattling together came now from Duckhaven itself, not thirty yards away. In the light of the lantern that he had picked up before it went out, John saw startled faces and Roger's hand reaching out.

"Susan," shrilled Roger. "Susan, is everything really all right?"

Susan grabbed the reaching, frightened hand, but in that terrific din John could not hear her speak. He saw that Peggy had buried her face in Nancy's sleeping-bag. Captain Nancy herself seemed to have larger eyes than usual, though she was comforting Peggy and the monkey both at once. The monkey had refused to go into his bag, after being tied up in it during the falling of the dust. Nancy looked at John. She was speaking. He could not hear her.

"Is it an earthquake?" her lips seemed to say.

"A big one," yelled John at the very top of his voice.

They felt one more violent shaking of the beach beneath them, and, after that, the noise began to lessen and change its character. It was as if from different parts of the island there came smaller echoes of that first tremendous roar. And then, once more, the winds flung themselves at the island and the noise of stone on stone was drowned altogether as a million trees creaked, broke, tore their roots from the earth and crashed headlong. A curious chemical smell came with the wind, and for a moment John feared that they were once more to be choked with that red dust. But the smell was blown away and, for the first time, almost gratefully, they heard heavy raindrops splash, like cupfuls of water thrown from a height, on the old cracked deck-planking of the wrecked boat.

A few moments later, the water was pouring in on them through the seams of deck and sides, and they were desperately trying to keep it out of their sleeping-bags. This was so much less frightening than the earthquake, the feeling of the shaking ground, and the noise of rocks crashing against rocks, that they found themselves laughing at each other, not for any real reason, as they pulled up their bags, and burrowed their heads down, and turned the mouths of the bags into hoods to keep the water from running down their necks.

The rain stopped at last. There was a strange quiet. That great downfall of water had flattened out the sea and all but silenced the surf. John put his head out through the door of their refuge.

"It's too dark to see anything," he said. "But there's very little wind."

"Is it all over?" asked Roger.

"I don't know," said John.

"It's the first real earthquake we've ever had," said Titty. "Not like that one that just rattled the washing-basins at home."

"Have some chocolate, Roger," said Susan.

Everybody had some chocolate and then, unexpectedly, tired right out, they fell asleep just as they were, neither lying nor sitting, hunched down in their wet sleeping-bags, in the old wreck, leaning against each other, or against the dripping planking. The monkey had found a new place for himself and slept curled up between Roger and Susan.

*

It was already long after dawn when John, waking, startled to find a lantern burning on the sand at his feet, surprised for a moment to see where he was, wriggled out of his bag and crawled out on the beach. He straightened himself stiffly and looked about him, and then banged on the outside of the wreck to wake the others.

"Susan!" he called. "Nancy! Something's happened. Mount Gibber's disappeared."

CHAPTER XXVIII

THE FINDING OF THE TREASURE

THE others, stiff, cramped and sleepy, tumbled one by one out of the old wreck and stared up the beach to the forest where, only the night before, at dusk, they had seen the black summit of Mount Gibber rising up above the trees.

Mount Gibber had not disappeared, though John had thought so, on first seeing the strange, broken shape that was left where only yesterday had been that lofty peak. Those black, precipitous rocks were gone. The whole top of the hill had slid sideways and crumbled down into the forest. And of the forest itself only a wreck was left. It was as if a thousand giants had been at play, pulling up trees like grass. Far inland, there were still palms here and there, waving above the wreckage, but in wide stretches of the forest, between Mount Gibber and the eastern shore, not a tree was left standing. They had fallen, some one way and some another, as if they had been twisted up, torn out of the ground, and flung aside.

"It really *was* an earthquake," said Titty.

"Jibbooms and bobstays!" said Nancy. "I should just think it was."

But strange things had happened even nearer than the forest. Susan, as soon as she came out of the wreck, blinking in the light, and only half awake after sleeping for so short a time, and so uncomfortably, had made straight for the old camp. Mount Gibber might have disappeared or changed its shape, but Roger and Titty were still there, and breakfast had to be made and pitched into them at once. But she had hardly taken two steps towards Duckhaven before she saw that there, too, things looked somehow different. The rocks had shifted. There were deep clefts between them. They no longer seemed to be growing out of the sand.

"John, John," she cried. "Everything's been changed."

"What about *Swallow*?" said John. "Come along, Nancy."

Titty heard that, and ran after the others, who were already climbing over the big rocks, every one of which had been stirred in its place. Peggy, Roger, and Gibber came too, but not so fast.

Things were not so bad as, for one moment, John had feared. Duckhaven was still there, and still a harbour, in spite of the shifting of the rocks. *Swallow* was still there, and unhurt, though she had been lying on her starboard side before the earthquake and was now heeling over to port. John, Nancy, and Titty went over her anxiously, looking for serious damage. They found none, though all along the starboard side there was a wide strip of bare planking, from which all the new white paint had gone as if it had been rubbed off with sandpaper.

"Wind and sand," said John. "I wouldn't have thought they could have done it."

"Lucky it's no worse," said Nancy. "It might have been if we'd left her leaning up against a rock. What about the sail? My hat, it's a good thing you stowed it properly. It would be flying over America with the tent if you hadn't."

John was already casting loose the mainsheet which he had used in stowing the sail.

"It looks all right," he said, "but we can't tell without opening it. Anything may have happened." In his mind was the thought that the flying sand in one of those great squalls might have rubbed a hole somehow, even in the rolled-up sail. But when the old brown sail was spread out on the sand they could see that it was none the worse. The bit of it that had been outside was still wet, but the rest of the sail was dry. Indeed, as they unrolled it, little puffs of that red, coppery dust flew out from between the folds, driven in there, perhaps, by the wind, instead of being blown away. Titty looked at it curiously.

"Doesn't it seem ages," she said, "since we were all hiding our heads in our sleeping-bags?"

And indeed, it was hard to believe that it was only yesterday afternoon that they had noticed the first signs of something wrong, and had watched the copper cloud creeping up against the wind, and had seen Captain Flint race off into the forest to get across the island in time to help with the *Wild Cat*.

"I say," said Roger. "Just look at the place where we were digging." He pointed up the beach. There, yesterday, had been the row of feathery palm trees, and that giant palm that had been a landmark for the *Swallow*. There, yesterday, had been the neat little cairns that marked the trenches of the explorers. Today all was chaos, and the fantastic roots of the trees stuck forlornly into the air, still clinging to the stones and scraps of earth that had been torn up with them.

But it was Susan who had the worst news. She had gone straight to the place where the tent had been. The ridge-pole, broken, lay on the other side of the rocks. The two oars, still roped together, were twenty yards away up the beach. The stores had come off badly. One of the biscuit tins in which they were packed had been close under a rock and the rock had fallen on it, crushing it and all that was in it. Another, that had been half empty, had been bowled up the beach by the winds. Its lid had come off. It had left a trail of sardine tins behind it. The rest of the stores had disappeared altogether. Worst of all was the accident to the water-breaker. The little barrel had been neatly chocked up on stones, so that water could be drawn from its tap. The bung in the top of it had been left loose. And now, in the earthquake, the chocks had been shaken out, the little barrel had rolled along the beach, and had come to rest with the bunghole undermost. Every drop of water had run away.

"We can't have breakfast till someone goes to Nancy's spring."

"I'll go," said Nancy.

"So'll I," said Peggy. "What are we going to carry the water in?"

"Oh, bother, bother!" said Susan. "The kettle's gone, and so has the saucepan."

"There's the kettle," said Nancy, "wedged under that rock."

It was indeed the kettle, but when Susan pulled

it out she found it had lost its spout, which was crushed flat and was hanging on the body of the kettle by a little strip of torn metal. Somehow this misfortune seemed to Susan much worse than the loss of the tent. She was slightly comforted by the finding of the saucepan. It was dented like an old hat. Its handle was bent double, but it would still hold water.

"Come on," said Nancy. "We'll take the breaker with us and fill it there. Come on, Peggy. Let's have one of those oars, and we'll borrow *Swallow*'s painter to make a sling. Captain John won't mind. There's no point in carrying just a saucepanful at a time."

"It wouldn't be a very full saucepan by the time we got back," said Roger.

"Not if you had the carrying of it," said Nancy. "But, anyway, we'd better fill the breaker at once and get it over."

In two minutes they had slung the barrel from an oar, and John and Nancy scrambled over the rocks with it, and marched off along the beach with the ends of the oar resting on their shoulders.

"Come along, Roger," said Peggy.

"Yes, go along," said Susan. "Get your legs stretched after being cramped up all night. Titty and I'll have the fire going before you get back. Some of the wood looks fairly dry."

"It's all very well," said Nancy, as she and John marched along the beach, "but how are we going to know where to turn into the forest. I'd blazed a tree, a twisted one that looked as if it had been broken and mended again. And now,

with all these trees down, everything looks alike.
I'm sure we hadn't gone much farther than this
when I saw all those birds and went up into the
forest to see what the fuss was about."

"We'd better walk along the edge of the forest," said John, and they moved up well above
high-water mark though it was tougher going
there than on the hard sand lower down. It was
a dismal sight, the forest that only the day before
had been rich and green, with tall palms overhead,
and ferns as high as Captain Flint himself, and
flowering trees, and the long, twisting tendrils of
the climbing plants. The trees had been tossed
this way and that, and in their fall had crushed
the ferns, and brought down with them all those
gay curtains of flowers round which so lately had
hovered the busy hosts of tiny humming-birds.
Not a bird was to be seen. They had vanished
like the crabs. Even the parrots were silent, and
cowering somewhere among the wreckage.

"It's no good trying to carry the breaker through
that mess," said Nancy. "Nobody could do it. When
we find the place, we'll leave the breaker outside."

"Isn't this your tree?" said John.

Nancy looked. So many trees had been twisted
and broken in their fall. But she knew this one.
"There's my blaze," she said, "but everything else
is different. Where's the black rock above the
pool?"

Over the tangle of fallen trees they could
see into what had once been green, shady forest. There, only yesterday, had been the rock on
which they had climbed to catch dripping water,
and to look down into the little pool among the

ferns. Now, there was nothing of the sort. The great rock had been split into a hundred pieces. Trees and ferns had been smothered in earth, sand, and stones. It was as if Nancy's spring had never been.

"You'd better stay out here," said Nancy to Peggy and Roger.

She and John put down the water-breaker, and struggled into the forest, climbing about over the wreckage, looking for that trickle of water. It had found some other way to earth. Even after that tropical rain not a sign was left of it, not even a damp patch on a stone. The two captains, searching this way and that, lost sight of each other, and both at once called out, each the other's name. "John!" "Nancy!" It was horrible, even for a moment, to feel alone in such a wilderness. They scrambled out again, over the fallen trunks.

"You've spilt all the water," said Roger, looking at Nancy's empty saucepan.

"There isn't any water to spill," said John.

"But what about our breakfast?" said Roger.

"You'll have to do without drink," said Nancy.

They looked back along the beach. There were the grey, weathered bows of the old boat in which they had spent the night, sticking up out of the sand, and the black rocks of the long reef that sheltered Duckhaven, and there, beyond Duckhaven, was the blue smoke of Susan's fire. Already, they knew, she must be wondering what was keeping them, and what was the good of making a fire if they went off with the only saucepan and did not bring it back with plenty of water for the most important part of the most important of all meals?

It was a sad party that carried the empty water-breaker back to Duckhaven.

Titty came running to meet them.

"Susan says, 'Hurry up!' We've got a grand fire."

"We've got no water," said Roger.

"Nancy's spring isn't there any more," said Peggy.

Susan took the news calmly.

"Oh, well," she said, "we'll want the fire anyhow, to get those sleeping-bags dry. Come along and eat sardines. I've opened three tins. That's half a tin for each of us. And some of the biscuits out of the tin that got squashed are still eatable. We'll be all right till Captain Flint comes back, and then he'll take *Swallow* round and fill the breaker from the stream."

"What if the stream's gone too?" said Roger.

"It won't have gone, and if it has, there's all the water we've stored in the *Wild Cat*."

"But what if the *Wild Cat* isn't back?"

"There's your tin," said Susan. "You share with Titty. One fork between you. Sit down and tuck in."

Susan shared a tin with John. She had found only two of the forks, so she had given one to Nancy and Peggy, and the other to Able-seaman Titty and the ship's boy, whom she could not trust to eat with their fingers without getting into a mess. John and she could manage well enough. And now, picking a sardine from the tin, leaning forward so that the oil should drip on the sand instead of on herself, getting the sardine neatly into her mouth, and licking the oil from her fingers, she was thinking things over.

She was thankful that they had come through the night so well. Anything might have happened to them, with the whole island shaken by earthquake and landslide, and with the forest mown down by those wild squalls that had come from all points of the compass. Anything might have happened to them, and, after all, nothing had. Here they were, all of them, sitting round the fire eating sardines. (She took the tin from John and, holding it at arm's length, pulled out another sardine.) A bit damp they certainly were, but, thanks to that old wrecked boat and the sleeping-bags, she did not think they would be much the worse for it. In this heat things dried at once even though there was no sun. It would be pretty bad, though, if the weather grew worse again. And then she thought of Captain Flint. How far to sea had he taken the *Wild Cat*? How soon would he be back? Anyhow, there was nothing to be done but to keep Roger from getting nervous. But this water business was serious. Who could possibly run a camp without water and without tea? Sardine oil was not much of a drink, and there wasn't enough of it, anyway. For some minutes she hardly heard what the others were saying. They seemed as cheerful as usual.

"Until he comes back it'll be just like it was for Peter Duck when he was wrecked here," said Titty. "Nothing to eat and nothing to drink."

"Coconut milk," said Nancy. "He lived on coconuts and crabs."

"We can't eat crabs," said Peggy.

"Where *are* the crabs?" said Roger. "I haven't seen one since yesterday."

"They must have known the earthquake was coming," said Titty, "and all got out of the way together. You know. Just like cows all looking the same way when it's going to rain."

"Well, I couldn't eat them even if there were any," said Peggy.

"Not crabs," said Nancy with a shudder.

"We'll have bananas and coconut milk," said Roger. "It won't be half bad. And there's enough chocolate left to last till Captain Flint comes. He promised to bring some more."

"He's going to have a horrible time getting across the island," said Nancy. "It'll take him hours and hours. It was all we could do to move while we were looking for the spring."

"He may have sailed miles away in the *Wild Cat*," said John. "In weather like last night's they'd want to be as far from land as they could get. And there's not much wind now, so it may bother them a bit to get back."

"Let's lay in a good store of coconuts," said Roger, "and there were some bananas in the forest just behind the big tree."

Everybody glanced up the beach. Great tangled roots waved in the air where once the gigantic palm tree had served as a landmark to show the way into Duckhaven.

"Nobody would think it was the same place," said John.

"Nobody would think it was the same island," said Titty. "What do you think of it, Gibber, now that your mountain's lost its head?"

But the monkey was busy with some nuts that Roger had found in his pocket. It had cheered up by now, and was no longer the whimpering, frightened thing of yesterday. Now that the earthquake was over it did not seem to mind what sort of changes had been brought about in geography.

The last drops of oil in the sardine tins were poured down thirsty throats. Fingers were licked for the last time, and, as there was nothing to wash up, the whole party moved together up the beach to look for bananas and coconuts among the fallen trees.

"Captain Flint'd be awfully pleased if we went on with the digging," said Nancy.

"Digging," said John. "The earthquake and the winds have done more digging in one night than we could do in a whole year. Just look at the mess."

All along the edge of the forest, where the palms had stood above the beach, there was now nothing but ruin. Not many of the trees had been broken, but not one was standing. It was as if the earthquake had loosened the hold of their roots and made it easy for the winds, blowing in hard squalls first one way and then another, to twist them up out of the ground. The trenches of the diggers, the work of their makeshift pick and feeble spades, seemed shallow scratches beside the gaping holes left by the uprooted trees. Close together the trees had stood. And the great pits they had left were joined one into another, open to the beach in places, and elsewhere screened by a melancholy tangle of torn roots, fallen trunks and feathery tops that would wave in the trade wind no more.

The diggers of yesterday stood looking at this tremendous digging of the night. Without knowing it, every one of them must have seen, under the roots of what had yesterday been the landmark of Duckhaven, the thing that, suddenly, Susan and Peggy noticed at the same moment.

Peggy could not speak. Not a single word would come to her lips. She just pointed.

"What is it?" said Susan. "Is it –? Is it –?" She could get no farther.

"What?" said the others, and then, following Peggy's outstretched arm and pointing finger, they all saw the thing at once. Brown and sandy, in the brown and sandy earth, they saw the corner and a bit of the side of a box.

Everything else was forgotten in a moment.

What could it be but the thing they had crossed the world to find?

John and Nancy jumped together down into the hole and began scraping the earth away with their hands.

"What's this?" said John, as the sand, trickling through his scrabbling fingers, left a small, flat, metal ring in his hand.

"Here's another. And another."

Nancy found one, too, and looked at it carefully.

"We've got it," she shouted suddenly. "Of course I know what they are. Remember the eyelet holes round the mouth of your kitbag. Mr Duck said it was a bag they buried. These are all that's left of it. The box was inside, just like Uncle Jim said. The bag's all rotted away, but these are the eyelet holes where they tied it up. There ought to be more of them."

"There are," cried John. "Look here." On the top of the box, that he was now clearing from sand, there were half a dozen of the little metal rings all close together.

"Can't we come down?" said Roger.

"Better not," said Susan. "And don't go too near the edge. The sides might cave in."

She spoke too late. The words were hardly out of her mouth before the ground on which she was standing slipped from under her, and she, Titty, Roger, and a very startled monkey found themselves, half covered with sand, beside John and Nancy, under the roots of the great fallen tree.

"Look out, Susan," said John. "We've lost half those rings."

"Never mind," said Nancy. "They don't really matter."

"I bet Captain Flint would like to see them. No. Don't try to climb out again now you're in. Hang on to the rings while Nancy and I get on with clearing the box. It's fairly wedged in among those small roots."

"I'll hold them," said Roger. "No, you don't, Gibber! Botheration! He's got one."

"Do look after the others," said John.

Titty and Roger took the eyelets and handed them up to Peggy, who alone had not fallen in. They scraped about in the sand for themselves and found one or two more. Gibber had climbed out of the pit and was biting the one he had stolen, and wondering what all the fuss was about. It was only metal, after all.

THE TREASURE FOUND

"Susan, will you hang on to this root and hold it out of the way," said Nancy. "Now then, John, haul away on that side, and I'll give it a bit of a boost downwards. That's done it."

The box was free.

"It isn't so very heavy," said John.

"It's a very little box," said Roger.

"Anyway, it's it," said Titty. "We've found it. At least Peggy did, and Susan. They saw it first."

"Swallows and Amazons for ever!" cried Nancy. "And three cheers for Peter Duck! If Captain Flint isn't busting pleased he ought to be. Heave it out. Carefully, Peggy! Don't let it drop."

Peggy took it from them and carried it quickly a little way from the pit, while the others pushed Titty and Roger up, and then, slipping and scrambling in the loose earth and sand, struggled out themselves.

"Let's have a decent look at it," said Nancy, shaking the sand out of her hair and dusting her hands against her shorts.

Peggy put it on the ground and blew at it gently to shift the sand from it.

"It'll stand more than that," said John. "It's all right, Susan," he went on. "It's worth a handkerchief." Taking his own from the pocket of his shirt, he carefully wiped the dirt away. Everybody crowded round to look at the thing.

It was a small, teakwood box, with brass bindings at the corners of it, and a brass clasp and staple to hold the lid down, fastened with a rusty padlock. John took the padlock in his fingers, meaning to flick away the dirt round it, and, rusted right through at the hoop, it came away in his hand.

"It ought to have been brass," said Nancy, "but I suppose they hadn't got a brass one handy. Or they'd lost it."

"Will it open now?" asked Titty.

Gingerly, John freed the hasp from the staple, and lifted the lid. Heads bumped together as the lid went up. Inside, the box was lined with lead. In it at one side were four small leather bags, with bone or ivory tags fastened to them with strips of leather like bootlaces. At the other side of the box was a small leather wallet.

"What's written on those labels?" asked Roger.

John was reading.

"'Bonies,'" he said. "'Mallies.' What on earth can that mean? 'Niggers.' 'Roses.' Shall we look in the bags?"

"Let's wait till he comes," said Nancy. "Let's shut it up. The main thing is that we've got it."

CHAPTER XXIX

SPANISH GALLEON

Stately Spanish galleon coming from the Isthmus,
Dipping through the Tropics by the palm-green shores,
With a cargo of diamonds,
Emeralds, amethysts,
Topazes and cinnamon and gold moidores.
                                    MASEFIELD

THEY had no difficulty in finding coconuts, some
of them full of milk, and bunches of bananas
not altogether crushed by fallen trees. But the
discovery of that brass-bound teakwood box had
changed all their plans. There could be no possible doubt that this was the thing that Peter
Duck had seen buried under his bedroom tree
sixty years ago. Digging was over. There was no
longer any point in staying in Duckhaven, except
that Captain Flint would presently be coming. He
would know what to do. Neither John nor Susan
nor even Nancy liked the idea of trying to take
a land party across the island so soon after the
terrific upheavals of the night. And then there
was *Swallow*.

When the council was held on the beach, with
the little teakwood box there on the sand, no one
suggested that they should do anything but wait
until Captain Flint should come back to take
command and to see exactly how it had happened that the failure of the diggers had been
turned as if by magic into complete success. At

first they were expecting that at any moment he might come struggling out on the beach. But later they began seriously to wonder how far to sea he and Peter Duck had taken the *Wild Cat*, and they began reminding each other how long it would take anybody to force his way across the landslides and the tangled ruin of the forest. "It took us a jolly long time," said Nancy, "when everything was all right and we had the blazed trail to follow, but now it'll be like getting through miles and miles of solid hedge."

John looked at *Swallow*. The rain had flattened out the sea. What wind there was was off-shore. There would be no difficulty in sailing round. But what if Captain Flint were already on his way across and were to come out there and find no one on the beach, and *Swallow* gone. No. The only thing to be done was to stay where they were.

"But I vote we start back the moment he comes," said Nancy.

"Let's run *Swallow* down, so that she's all ready to launch," said John. "It's no bother. The rollers are still there, and we can easily haul her up again if he doesn't get here before dark."

"Before dark?" Susan looked at him gravely. Already Roger had been saying that coconut milk only made him more thirsty. There was no tent. And no one looked forward to a second night crouched up inside the old wreck. Titty and Roger, at least, ought to have a proper sleep. Besides, the crabs were coming back. Susan had found the first of them, making a meal of some broken biscuits in the crushed tin, when she had gone to see

if anything there could be saved for midday
dinner. Soon after that Roger and Gibber had
found another. Then Titty, who had gone to the
old wreck meaning to crawl in and remind herself
of what it had been like in the night, had come
hurriedly back to report that the wreck was once
more crawling with crabs. "I don't know where
they've come from," she said, "but there they are."

"Anyhow, that means there's no more earthquake coming," said John.

"But we can't sleep in there with the crabs,"
said Peggy.

"Don't be a galoot," said Nancy. "We won't
have to." But even Nancy was feeling rather
glum at the thought of the darkness, with no
tent, no hot tea or cocoa, and the eatables almost
at an end. She liked thinking about coconut milk,
but she had to look the other way and try not to
taste it while she was actually drinking it.

· Bananas and coconut milk were all very well,
but even those who liked them were pretty hungry and thirsty by the time the morning was over
and the afternoon had begun and still there was
no sign of Captain Flint.

They had done all that could be done. They had
dried the sleeping-bags by the fire. They had tak-
en *Swallow* down the beach. They had collected
the oars, that no longer had a tentpole to support,
and put them into her with the sail. They had been
very much tempted to open the box again and to
see what was in that wallet and those little bags.
But Nancy had stopped that. It was only fair that
Captain Flint should share in the final triumph.
They had even hooked the rusty padlock into the

staple again, so that Captain Flint should see it
just as it had been when they found it. A good
many times some noise had made them think he
was coming. But there were too many noises of
a likely kind, as the fallen timber settled down
where it lay. In the end they had hidden the box
in *Swallow*, for a surprise, so that Captain Flint
would not see it the moment he reached the camp.
They were sitting on the rocks above Duckhaven,
talking of home and of Mrs Dixon coming down
from the farm with a bucketful of hot porridge on
the morning after that other storm that seemed
now so long ago. The sky was overcast and low
banks of cloud moved over a leaden sea. Gone,
since yesterday, was that clear, brilliant weather they had had when first they came. Suddenly
Peggy leaped to her feet and pointed away to the
north of the island. Everybody else jumped up,
too, at the sight of a schooner, under all lower
sail, heading south-west.

"The *Wild Cat!*" shouted John.

"There she is," cried Nancy. "You *are* a lucky
one, Peggy, always being the first to see things.
It must be because you're never thinking about
something else. I'm always looking the other way
when anything turns up."

The schooner disappeared in a bank of haze.
She showed again just for a moment, and then,
though she was still far away, she was hidden
from them by the north-east corner of the island.

"That settles it," said John. "If we buck up
and start now, we'll be round at Bill's Landing
as soon as she is. That'll save Captain Flint
struggling across all that beastliness. Can we

cram everything in, Susan? There's nothing of a
sea, and the wind's off-shore and not too strong
. . . Oh, come on, Captain Nancy!"

"There isn't much to take," said Susan. "We've
lost nearly everything."

"What'll Mr Duck say when he sees what we've
got?" said Titty.

"Captain Flint'll be the one to be really pleased,"
said Nancy.

"Bill, too," said Titty.

"It'll be lovely to sleep in bunks tonight," said
Peggy.

"No crabs," said Nancy.

Susan looked at Roger, who, in spite even of the
excitement of seeing the schooner, was rubbing his
eyes.

"If you're sure the sea's all right," she said.

"It's the best it's ever been," said John, and
he and Nancy slipped down from the rocks,
grabbed an armful of sleeping-bags that had
been spread on the rocks to dry, and raced for
the *Swallow*.

*

Stowing the cargo was easy.

"It's a good thing there's been an earthquake,"
said Roger, who had cheered up altogether now
that it was certain they were going back to regular meals and unlimited chocolate. "It leaves us so
much more room in *Swallow*."

"It found the treasure for us, too," said Peggy.

"Nothing took so much room as that old sail,"
said John, "but of course it came in handy in
keeping the other things dry," he added, looking

out to sea. "But there was more swell then. There's practically none now."

"Put Peter Duck's box amidships," said Nancy. "Easy with that barrel. I know it's empty, but fix it so that it can't bump about."

"Stick a sleeping-bag under the box," said Titty. "Let's pack it round with all the rest of them. Nothing else really matters. *Swallow*'s a Spanish galleon with a hold full of treasure from the Indies."

"Keep Gibber down in the bottom of the boat," said Susan. "Don't go and get wet again, cramming in before the mast."

It was a pretty close fit for the six of them and the monkey, and for a moment Susan feared that they were too heavily loaded. But she thought again of Roger, and the empty water-breaker, and of how impossible it was to leave anybody behind. So she said nothing about it, but was careful over the mate's job of getting everything as well stowed as it could be.

Nancy hoisted the little brown sail while they were still in Duckhaven. John, paddling beside his vessel, climbed in over the stern when he had her pointing seaward and beginning to move. With the wind off-shore and the reef sheltering them from what little was left of the swell, *Swallow* slipped out of the harbour.

*

They looked back to Duckhaven. It had been hard to find it from the sea, when John had sailed along there with Captain Flint, and they had been glad to see the smoke of Nancy's fire rising from the beach. Now, it was all but invisible as soon as they had left it. The tall palm tree that had been a good leading mark when they were near enough in to see it against the sky instead of against the green background of the forest slopes, had gone for ever. The very shape of the hills had changed. The green island had turned a dusky greyish brown, with the ruin of the forest and the falling dust of the earthquake and the landslides. There were still three hills, but no one could have recognised Mount Gibber from out here, at sea, if he had not known what had happened. It was now hardly higher than the others. The tremendous landslides caused by the earthquake had carried the whole of that precipitous black peak headlong down over its wooded lower slopes. Where the green forest had climbed more than half-way up the mountain-side, where the old track from Bill's Landing had wound across above that earlier landslide, already rich with trees and giant ferns, there was now nothing but a dreadful chaos of raw earth and rocks.

"I'm sure we were right to sail," said Susan, with a good deal of relief in her voice. "It'd take anybody ages to get across all that. Roger could never have done it. And anyhow, another night . . ."

"Cheer up, Susan," said Nancy. "Everything's as right as ever it could possibly be. Of course we were right to sail. And she's making first-rate weather of it."

"Isn't she?" said Titty. "Stately Spanish galleon. That's what she is. Well, she was built for a sea boat."

"She's a jolly good one," said John. "I say, Nancy, would you like to steer?"

"Go on," said Nancy. "I'm all right. You know her better than I do."

This was child's play, John thought, compared with the steering he had had to do, when sailing her round with Captain Flint in the great swell left by the trade wind. Gone, now, were those mountain ranges of water, Andes, Pamirs, Sierras, rolling in from seaward in the evening sunshine. They were gone, but the sunshine was gone also. The sea was somehow slack and sulky. It was grey, like the sky. It was like a sea stirring in its sleep, troubled by some uneasy dream. It had been hard sailing that other day, but it had been sailing done in the clear glow of healthy weather. Today the sailing was easy, but John was in a hurry to get it over. There was something wrong. This was not the end of last night's storm, but a lull in it. Something else was going to happen. He looked out to sea at the low clouds that hid the horizon. He looked at the ruined island. There was something in the weather that was not to be trusted, and, child's play though the sailing seemed to be, John put his mind to it to get the best out of his ship, to get round the island, and to have the *Swallow* safely lifted up once more on the decks of the *Wild Cat* without wasting a minute. He had felt it only fair that Nancy should steer her if she wanted to, but he was glad that she had refused, that she was sitting there amidships, ready for anything that might turn up, but leaving him to do the steering, and meanwhile keeping Titty and Roger busy talking, thinking of treasure-ships sailing homeward from the Indies, and keeping still instead of moving about. Nobody moved about except the monkey, and, as they came out of the shelter of the island and began to tack towards the southern point, a little spray flew aboard and fell on him, and Gibber, after that, kept as still as anybody else, cowering on the bottom boards beside his master.

Slowly the island shores slipped by as the *Swallow* tacked along, out to sea and in again. From far out they could see the desolate ruin that had been made of the island, but, when they came nearer in again, it was hard to believe that so much damage could have been done. The trees had suffered less in the southern part of the island. The hills may have sheltered them from the worst of the squalls. The palms were still standing along the beach, and if there had been some sunshine, and if the green of the leaves had not been dulled by dust, John might have thought that there had been no change since the day when he had sailed past here with Captain Flint. But then, when he tacked out to sea once more, the upper slopes began to lift into view and betrayed the dreadful havoc of the night.

A last, long tack took them well clear of the southernmost point of the island, and John eased the sheet a little as the *Swallow* reached northward for the anchorage. They peered eagerly forward every time the boom lifted, watching for the first sight of the *Wild Cat*'s masts in there behind the palm trees.

"What luck if she isn't in yet?" said Nancy. "We'll anchor close in and let them find us there."

"We'll sail out again to meet them," said Titty.

"Or we could get the barrel filled," said Susan.

"She's back all right," cried John, as they neared the end of the spit, and could see over it and past the trees into the anchorage beyond them.

"Only just back," said Nancy. "They haven't properly furled the sails."

"They wouldn't," said John. "They'd leave the sails loose. I bet they got jolly wet last night. Hullo! . . ." He was so startled that he brought *Swallow* up into the wind. "Sorry!" He recovered himself at once. "There's another schooner. Two of them. It can't be . . ."

"It's the *Viper*," said Titty. "He's come after all."

"Black Jake!" said Nancy.

"Well, he's jolly well come too late," said Titty, her hand on the old brass-bound teakwood box that was safely stowed under the middle thwart in a nest of sleeping-bags.

"He's had a pretty tough time," said John. "He's in a worse mess than we are. Look at that jib down in the water. I wonder why he didn't take it in? All his sails are anyhow. *Wild Cat* hasn't stowed hers, but she's done better than that."

It was true. The green schooner lay there, looking neat enough, with the boom of the mainsail resting in a crutch, and both gaffs lifted clear, and the sails loose and drying. The black *Viper* looked altogether different. Her mainboom tipped drunkenly downwards and rested on her bulwarks. Her gaffs had been lowered right to the deck and left there, while the halyards swung loose about the masts. A jib, the halyard of which must have come unreeved, trailed in the water under the bowsprit.

"Perhaps they've only just got in," said Nancy.

John looked at her. "Perhaps it was her we saw coming in from the north and not the *Wild Cat* at all."

"Golly!" said Nancy, "but where are they? Why aren't they doing something?"

"If they've just got in, they'll be having supper, won't they?" said Roger. "Or tea."

"Anybody'd want a good tuck in if they'd been out all night," said Nancy.

"But wouldn't they have had it this morning as soon as things got quiet again?" said Susan.

"And where are our lot?" said John.

"I do hope they haven't gone ashore to come across for us," said Susan. "Perhaps we ought to have waited, after all."

"They wouldn't all go," said Nancy. "Mr Duck'll be aboard, and probably Bill. Giminy," she added, I'd like to see Black Jake's face when he sees Bill looking over the side."

"Someone's ashore," said Titty. "Look. There are two dinghies by Bill's Landing."

"I wonder how many the *Viper* had," said Nancy. "She lost one that day with Bill in the fog."

"One of them's probably ours," said John. "Can you see anybody ashore?"

"No," said Susan, "but do look after your steering."

"Sorry," said John, with a glance at *Swallow*'s wake, which showed by its waggles that he had been thinking of more things than one.

The *Swallow* slipped on, past the spit now, and into the bay. There was not a sign of life on either of the anchored schooners. Nothing seemed to be moving on the beach, where two dinghies were pulled up clear of the water. Of the schooners, the *Wild Cat* lay the nearer, the water lapping along her green topsides, while beyond her the black *Viper* tugged at her anchor-rope.

"Do you see that?" said John. "Black Jake must have lost his chain cable. He's got a warp out instead."

"Perhaps he's only put his kedge down," said Nancy.

The *Swallow* slipped nearer and nearer in the light, unsteady wind from the west, the water now silent, now lapping under her forefoot. There was no other noise but that of the water on the beach, and that, too, was not as loud as the surf had been on the other side of the island. It was more like a whisper than a roar. The colour of the island had faded, and it seemed that its noises, too, were hushed.

"They'd hear a hail now," said John, speaking, for some reason that he could not have explained, much more quietly than usual.

"*Wild Cat* ahoy!" shouted Nancy in her clear, ringing voice.

"*Cat* ahoy, ahoy! . . ." echoed back across the anchorage from the hill behind the landing-place. But no red head showed over the bulwarks of the schooner, and no old seaman came out of the deckhouse to welcome them.

"*Wild Cat* ahoy!" shouted John. He did not know why he had not wanted to be the first to shout.

"*Cat* ahoy, ahoy! . . ." the echo came back from the shore.

"There's no one stirring on the *Viper* either," said Nancy. "What's gone with them?"

"Our Jacob's ladder's down," said Titty. They all saw the old rope ladder dangling down the green side of the *Wild Cat.*

"Stand by to grab it," said John, luffing up sharply. "Lower away the sail, Nancy."

"Aye, aye, sir," said Nancy. But now even she was feeling her throat trying to close behind her words.

The brown sail came down. The *Swallow* slipped up alongside, Nancy grabbed the rope ladder. Roger brought the painter round clear of the mast. John clambered forward, took a turn of the painter round his wrist, and gripped the ladder with both hands.

"Let's give them one more shout," he said.

"*Wild Cat* ahoy!" they all shouted together.

There was a moment's silence, and then the echo came back to them over the water.

"No answer," said Roger.

"Did you hear anything?"

"No."

"Well, they must be asleep," said John, took his chance as the dinghy lifted, got both feet on the ladder, and climbed aboard the schooner.

CHAPTER XXX

DIRTY WORK

THE first Bill knew of the coming of the *Viper* was the bump of a boat alongside the *Wild Cat*.

There had been no time to rest from the moment when Captain Flint had hailed the *Wild Cat* from the shore. Long before that, Peter Duck had been saying that, in the sort of weather that looked like coming on, the schooner would be better at sea. Bill had tumbled into the dinghy, rowed ashore and fetched the skipper aboard. Ten minutes later they had had the sails set and were getting the anchor up, making harder work of it than when there were half a dozen active sailors to go walking round the capstan. They had put to sea and made all the offing they could to the south-west, for it was from that quarter that Captain Flint was expecting the storm. They, too, had been suddenly shrouded in that copper-coloured cloud and choked with the same red dust from which the diggers had taken refuge in their sleeping-bags. It had been a desperate night. Again and again, even under her much shortened canvas, the *Wild Cat* had been flung over on her beam-ends by the savage squalls that leapt upon her first from one side and then from another. They had hove her to, only to have the wind swirl round on her quarter and send her burrowing into the confused steep sea before they had had time to bring the headsail once more

a-weather. They had felt, far out at sea, blows
that shook the timbers of the ship and made them
fear for her masts, strange blows that could only
be given by some explosive upheaval of the ocean
floor. Not one of the three of them, Captain Flint,
Peter Duck, and Bill, had had a moment's rest,
and all the time Captain Flint had been saying
that with squalls like these, anything might have
happened to the camp at Duckhaven.

"I ought not to have left them," he said. But
Peter Duck would have none of that. "They've
solid earth under their feet," he said, "and where'd
they be, where'd we all be if we'd waited while the
Wild Cat was drove ashore? And drove ashore she
might easy have been. The anchor's not made as
would hold her in such weather."

But with the first of the morning light, Captain
Flint had clapped on sail to hurry back. He had
clapped on sail too soon, in his hurry, and a foresail had been split, two jibs had been blown clean
out of their ropes, and both topsails, that Mr Duck
had begged him not to set, had burst the moment
he had them aloft and drawing. "Hang it all," Bill
had heard him say, "it isn't even as if they were
my own." For a moment Bill had been puzzled, till
he guessed that Captain Flint was talking not of
sails but of children.

Anyhow, with the first signs of a lull in the
weather, they had been hurrying back to the
island, hurrying all the more when, from far
away, through the telescope, they saw that something had happened to change the shape of Mount
Gibber. From that moment Captain Flint had not
said another word. He had stood there, grimly

looking forward at the island, and hardly stirring, until at last, in the late afternoon, they
had made anchorage. Then, the moment staysail
sheets were let fly, and the anchor was down, he
had helped in lowering the dinghy overboard, had
taken Bill with him and had rowed like a madman
for the landing-place. There he had jumped ashore
and pushed the dinghy off again.

"Back you go, Bill. You've worked like a man
last night and I shan't forget it. Row off now
and lend a hand with the sails. I'd not have left
Mr Duck to it if it hadn't been for the others." And
with that Captain Flint had run up the beach and
disappeared among the trees.

Bill had rowed back to the *Wild Cat*. Peter
Duck and he had lowered the sails and left them
to dry. Then, tired right out, they had dropped into
their bunks just as they were, Peter Duck in the
deckhouse and Bill down below in his cabin, and
had fallen instantly asleep.

They had never seen the black schooner, herself
tattered from the storm that had helped her the
last few miles of her long voyage, slipping down
on the island through the low banks of haze to
the north. They had never heard her anchor in
the bay. Perhaps it was because he did not want
to be heard that Black Jake had lowered a kedge
on a silent grass rope instead of dropping his
heavy anchor at the end of a few fathoms of
noisy chain.

In any case, the first news that Bill had of
the coming of the *Viper* was a bump somewhere
outside his cabin and yet close by.

*

Sleepily, Bill stirred in his bunk. A boat that was. Captain Flint back again. Must have forgotten something. Bill turned over. Hardly a muscle in his body was not stiff and aching after his hard work during the storm. Ouch! That hurt him. He stretched out one leg, carefully. But how had the skipper come aboard? Why, Bill had brought the dinghy back himself. Of course it wasn't the skipper. But what was that dinghy doing, bumping against the ship's side, knocking off the paint, instead of swinging astern. Change of wind? Another? That was what it must be. He supposed he ought to go on deck and see if all was well, and warn Mr Duck if the schooner was swinging over her anchor. But what was that? The boat was being handed along the ship's side. Perhaps it was them children back again. But how on earth? Bill waked up suddenly and altogether with the noise of steps on deck. Heavy steps. Men's voices. Bill had a leg out of his bunk. Yes. Mr Duck was stirring in the deckhouse.

Suddenly he heard the old man's voice.

"What are you doing there? Off this ship before you're thrown off!" And then an order shouted to an imaginary crew: "All hands on deck there!"

Bill was out of his bunk in a moment and bolting barefoot for the forehatch. This was no time to wait to put on the shoes he had kicked off as he rolled into his bunk. Up the ladder he scrambled and out on deck.

Three men were on deck at the after end of the vessel. A fourth, with a knife in his mouth, was climbing over the bulwarks. Bill knew him

THE VIPERS COME ABOARD

at once for Black Jake's brother, who was wanted by the police. He knew the others, too; Black Jake himself, Fighting Mogandy, and the ex-convict, Simeon Boon.

"Drop that knife, you fool," Black Jake was saying. "We want no killings, yet."

Mogandy, with clenched fists, was crouching by the deckhouse.

The man with the knife was on deck now, and the scarred face of the bruiser from the "Ketch as Ketch Can" showed above the bulwarks.

"Close the forehatch, one of you," said Black Jake.

But just then Bill heard the old seaman's voice again. "Come on, now. All hands on deck! Off the ship, you scum!" And the next moment the old man came round the corner of the deckhouse, as if he had a score of men to help him.

"What are you doing here?" he said, but at that moment the crouching negro shot forward and upward. There was a thud as his fist caught the old seaman's chin.

"I'm coming, Mr Duck!" cried Bill, and hurled himself, head down, into Mogandy's stomach. The big negro doubled up with a groan.

A terrific blow caught Bill on the side of the head. Black Jake's fingers seemed to be meeting through Bill's shoulders as he twisted him round and lifted him off his feet.

"I reckon I'll kill you for that," groaned Mogandy.

"You've put the old man out for good," said Black Jake angrily.

"Let me have a hold of that boy."

"I'll deal with the boy," said Black Jake. "What's the good of killing ... before they've done some talking." He held Bill's head against the deckhouse and banged it with his fist.

"You, now. Speak up! And sharp. That's where you went out of the dinghy that day. You wasn't drowned. You'll wish you was before we've done with you. Speak up, now. Where's the skipper?"

"Dunno."

The word was hardly out of his mouth before Black Jake's fist swung round again, and Bill's red head crashed into the side of the deckhouse. He dropped, stunned, to the deck.

Someone kicked him fiercely in the ribs.

Dimly he heard voices.

"Who's done it now? If I knocked out the old man, you've killed the boy."

"Heave 'em over and be done with 'em," came another voice.

"I want to kill that boy ..." Mogandy again.

Bill's head was pounding like a pile-driver. Up, up, up, up. Bang! Up, up, up, up. Bang! Drowning, he seemed to be, in waves of red mist. Closing over him. For some minutes he knew nothing at all.

He came to himself again with a violent pain in his ankle. Someone had stepped on it and slipped. A heavy boot caught him in the back. What had happened?

"Give him a rope to chew." That was Boon's voice, with a grunt at every few words. What was he grunting about? Bill very cautiously looked out from eyes that he kept all but closed.

He found he was lying on the deck by the galley door. Simeon Boon was close by, grunting as he

pulled a rope tight and made it fast, grunting as
he hove up a heavy body and let it fall, grunting
again as he took a new turn with the rope, pulled
it tight, and again made fast. The body was that
of Peter Duck, and Boon was binding it round and
round from head to foot. Black Jake was tying
a large loose knot in a stouter piece of rope. He
forced the knot into Mr Duck's mouth, and tied
the ends of the rope behind his neck.

"If you won't talk for me, you won't for yourself,"
he growled, letting the unconscious head fall on
the deck.

"What's the use of all this," said another voice,
that of Mogandy. "Heave 'em over and have done.
We know all we want. Ain't we seen the smoke of
their fire? North of your old diggings you said it
was. Stands to reason the old man's told 'em where
to dig. While we're talking here, they're a-digging
up the stuff."

"We've got the guns now," said the voice of
Jake's brother. "Good 'uns, too."

"What are we waiting for?" said Mogandy.

"Right," said Black Jake suddenly. "We'll wait
no more. You, Mogandy, and you, George, come
with me. The other two'll stay to guard the ships.
There's a lot of stuff in here we'll want before
we sink her. And beyond that there's no sense
in sinking her in shallow water. Three's enough
to go across the island. Put it there's six of 'em.
These is all the guns there was. I know that, for
I'd a good look at 'em in Lowestoft harbour that
time when there was no one aboard. They may
have revolvers? What's revolvers against guns?
We can pick 'em off from far away as easy and

as safe as shooting squabs in a rookery. Pick 'em
off we must, and then, if they haven't done the
digging for us, why, we've still got the old man
here, if Mogandy hasn't killed him. We'll make
him talk . . ."

"Easy, there." This was a new voice. Bill knew
it at once, though he could not see the man. It
was the bruiser from the "Ketch as Ketch Can".
The voice was cunning, and suspicious. Bill saw
Simeon Boon look up sharply at the first words.

"Easy there. Boon an' me's to let you go off with
all the guns. We can't sail the ships an' well you
knows it. We lets you go off with the guns. And
then you gets over the other side, an' how're we
to know what you does there? A bargain, likely,
to save trouble, and us knowing nothing of it. Stay
here? Not much. We'll know what's said, and we'll
know what's done. Eh, Simeon?"

"Sense, and I says the same."

Black Jake gave in at once.

"Right," he said. "I'll stay here with George,
and you three . . ."

"No, you don't," said George. "Not me. I'm
for the stuff."

Not one of them, except Black Jake, was willing to let the others land on the island without
him, and not one of the others liked the idea of
leaving Black Jake with the ships. Perhaps they
feared some trick or other that would leave them
at his mercy or helpless, without a navigator.

"Wasting time, we are," said Mogandy. "We
sticks together. These two won't run away with
the ships. Have you got the old fool properly
roped?"

At this moment, while the others bent over the body of Peter Duck, bound and helpless as a bale of cotton, Bill staggered to his feet and bolted forward along the deck. Why he did it, he did not know. It was the instinct of a mouse, caught and hurt by a cat, and making its hopeless bid for freedom when the cat lifts its paw.

"Stop him there!" roared Mogandy.

Steps thundered behind him along the deck. Bill dropped on hands and knees down into the forecastle. Someone landed heavily on the top of him. Bill scrambled from under. A terrific grip closed on his shoulder. He was shaken violently. The cat had the mouse again. Bill grabbed at the bars of Gibber's cage. The door swung open. Black Jake lifted Bill clean off his feet and shook him till he felt his teeth were going to be shaken out of his head. One, at least, had been knocked out already, when Black Jake had banged his head against the deckhouse.

Bill suddenly heard himself shrieking, shrieking at the top of a voice that hardly seemed to be his own. He shrieked and shrieked.

"Yell, will you? We'll cure that." Black Jake picked up a great hunk of soap that was lying handy, crammed it into Bill's mouth so that it all but choked him, and tied a handkerchief across that, so tightly that it forced the soap against the back of his throat, and pulled his lips back almost to his ears.

Bill gasped for breath. He had no time to use his hands. Simeon Boon had come down the ladder after Jake, bringing some rope with him. Bill felt his arms seized, twisted, forced together

behind his back, tightly lashed and then held fast
while turn after turn of rope was taken about his
helpless body.

He was picked up and flung headlong into
the straw at the bottom of Gibber's cage. The
gate clanged to. The padlock snapped.

Mogandy's head showed in the hatch.

"I'm going to kill that boy."

"Time enough," said Black Jake. "He'll be
asking you to kill him before I've finished with
him. Come on, Boon. We've the shore gang to
settle first."

Steps went up the ladder. It was suddenly
dark. The forehatch closed with a bang. For
a few more minutes there was a noise in the
saloon. Then slamming of locker doors, steps on
deck, and voices. "Both boats. We're short of one."
"Easy with those guns there." Boats bumped and
scraped against the ship's side. There was silence.

*

Bill, an aching bundle in the straw at the
bottom of Gibber's cage, managed with a great
effort to turn on his face in time to save himself
from choking. Soap filled his throat and his nose.
The hard lump of it kept his mouth agape. He
dribbled soap and blood into the straw. That, at
least, was better than swallowing it.

This, he thought, was the end of everything.
What had they done to Mr Duck? Was Mr Duck
dead? He tried to shout, but he was so well gagged
that he could make no noise at all. He lay silent,
listening. There was not a sound from the deckhouse. They had not thought Mr Duck dead or

they would never have roped him up like that. He, too, was lying somewhere, alive, and waiting, like Bill himself, until Black Jake and the crew of the *Viper* should come back to pay off old scores. And Captain Flint? And them children? What chance had they against men who could not safely leave them alive? The skipper was afraid of nothing. Bill was sure of that. But what could he do against desperate men with guns? And Bill saw the little party of diggers happily talking together on the beach at Duckhaven, while Jake, Mogandy and Simeon Boon, armed with elephant-gun, shotgun, and rifle, stalked them in perfect safety from the cover of the forest. Again he gathered all his strength, as if to shout a warning to them. But in the dark fo'c'sle of the schooner, flat on his face in the monkey's straw, he knew that he could make no sound, and that even if he could, it would not reach them. He choked again, and tears mingled with the blood and soap that still dribbled from his mouth. He forgot the threats of Black Jake and Mogandy about what they would do to himself, and thought only of what might at any moment be happening to them children. The able-seaman he thought of, and Cap'n Nancy, whom he had made seasick with that old tale of the bacon fat and the bit of string. They had always stood his friends. And what would happen to them now if those cut-throats laid hands on them? Down in the dark fo'c'sle Bill lay helpless and fairly blubbered into the straw.

*

It seemed to him that he had been lying

there for ages, though it can hardly have been much more than an hour, when his thoughts were brought sharply back to his own peril. He heard a faint shout, not so very far away. Had the pirates changed their minds? Were they coming back already? Had he slept? "Worse than killing," Black Jake had promised him, and, in such things as these, Black Jake, Bill knew, was one to keep his word.

There was again a bump against the side of the ship.

Bill shivered, and, clenching his bound hands so that his nails cut into his palms, he made up his mind to take what was coming to him and to shout "*Wild Cat* for ever!" when they killed him.

And then, close by, he heard the shout of "*Wild Cat* ahoy!" That was Cap'n John's voice, and Cap'n Nancy's and the others. It was them children back again. He must warn them . . . He must. He must. And Bill choked and spluttered with the soap, and, doubling his knees, jerked his bruised and aching body again and again as hard as he could against the iron bars of the cage.

SWALLOWS·AND·AMAZONS·FOR·EVER!

CHAPTER XXXI

THE ONLY HOPE

"WHAT about the treasure box?" said Nancy. "Shall I bring it up?"

"Fend her off a bit. Let's get the crew aboard first. Come on, Roger. Now's your chance. All right, Gibber. Who said you could use my hair?"

Roger, grabbing the ladder with both hands, while Susan hove him up, had let go of the monkey, which had leapt from his shoulders to the ladder, taken a firm grip of John's hair, and pulled itself up on the bulwarks. It was now running gaily along them towards the bows of the schooner.

Titty saw her chance just as John was pulling Roger over the rail. She slipped up after him, and went off on tiptoe to peep into the deckhouse, where she thought that Peter Duck and Captain Flint were lying asleep, not dreaming that a Spanish galleon with treasure aboard was lying alongside. Peggy came up the ladder. Susan threw the sleeping-bags up one after another. The treasure box lay on the bottom boards of the *Swallow*. Nancy was carefully fending off whenever the *Swallow* threatened to bump into the *Wild Cat*'s green paint.

"Go on, Susan," she said, "and we'll send the box up in a sling."

Susan scrambled up, and, at that moment, Titty called out that she could not get the deckhouse door open, and there was an impatient shout from Roger, who had gone forward after his monkey, and had found the forehatch closed, and a strange clanging noise going on below.

"Do come and get the hatch open," shouted Roger.

"They're hammering something down below. I banged on the hatch but they didn't hear me."

Peggy and Susan hurried forward. John went round to the deckhouse door, where he found Titty shaking at the handle.

"What a donk you are, Titty," he said. "The key's fallen out. There it is on the deck. You're nearly standing on it."

"What did they go and lock it for?" said Titty.

There was a sudden chorus of shouts from the forepart of the ship. "Help! Help!" Titty and John rushed along the decks. For the first time John noticed a patch of blood close by the galley door. But he did not stop to look at it. There was no one on the foredeck. Susan had opened the hatch for Roger, and they had all gone down into the fo'c'sle. Susan's head appeared through the hatch.

"John! John!" she shouted. "Quick! Come quick!"

John flung himself after her down through the hatch, to see, in the dim light of the fo'c'sle, that everybody was staring into Gibber's cage, while Gibber himself was angrily rattling from outside the bars that he had often playfully rattled from within.

"It's Bill," said Susan. "He's all tied up. Roger, where's the key of the padlock?"

"Hanging round my neck," said Roger. "It always is."

"Get it out. Don't waste time."

Roger struggled with the neck of his shirt, found the string, pulled it up, got the key and fitted it into the padlock. Susan pulled the door of the cage open and bent over Bill.

"Bill! Bill!" she said.

Bill, with a great effort, rolled himself round and tried to smile at her. The effect was horrible. He choked again on his soap gag. Susan and John had their knives out at once, and were wasting good rope by cutting it to bits, not caring at all so long as they did not cut Bill.

"Don't try to unknot the handkerchief, Titty," said Susan.

"Let me get at it." She cut through the handkerchief. Bill tried to spit the soap out of his stiff, cramped jaws. He was suddenly sick.

"Mr Duck!" he coughed, and groaned with the effort of moving. "Quick! In the deckhouse!"

"I knew there was something wrong," said Titty.

Susan, Titty, and Peggy ran through below decks and up the companion steps. John, followed by Roger, climbed up out of the forehatch and raced aft to unlock the deckhouse door.

"Hi! Hi!" called Nancy from down in the *Swallow*, "what's gone with you all? How long am I to stay here, fending off?"

Nobody heard her.

Below decks, as they rushed through, Susan and the others had seen that everything was in disorder. In the deckhouse it was much worse. The lockers had been emptied on the floor. The guns were gone. On the floor, partly covered with things from the emptied lockers, lay the body of

Peter Duck, roped round and round, helpless as a parcel. One of the locker drawers lay across him where it had been thrown. He had not been able to move even enough to shake it off.

"Is he dead?" asked Roger.

"Of course he isn't. Look at his eye," said Susan. "Poor Mr Duck. Be quick, John."

There was more desperate cutting of good ropes.

"Black Jake must have been here," said Roger.

"Oh, yes, yes," said Titty, "but why did he go away again? Where is he now? And where . . ." Her voice suddenly shrilled. "Susan, John, where is Captain Flint?"

Peter Duck's first words asked the same question.

"Where's the skipper?"

John, Susan, and Peggy, between them, helped the old man to his feet. He staggered a step or two, leant against the chart table, and put his hand to his head. "Mogandy fetched me a fair clip," he muttered. And then, sharply, as if it were once more his watch at sea, and he was in charge of the ship: "Where's the skipper? And young Bill? Where is he? And how did you come aboard?"

"In *Swallow*," said Titty.

"We sailed round," said Peggy.

Peter Duck pulled himself together, and limped hurriedly out of the deckhouse.

"They'll have killed young Bill," he said.

But Bill was coming along the deck, stooping low. In one hand he held the cake of soap that had been used to gag him.

He opened his mouth at seeing Mr Duck,

opened it in a wide, red grin. Three of his teeth were missing.

At that moment Nancy, out of all patience, came climbing over the bulwarks.

"What are you all doing? Why! What's happened? Where's Captain Flint?"

"Skipper's on the island," said Peter Duck. "Gone across to your camp, and Black Jake and the rest of them are after him with our guns. That's their boats at the landing."

"But he'll never get across the island," said John. "Half the trees are down on the other side, and there's been an earthquake."

"Nothing'll stop the skipper," said Peter Duck. "Nor Black Jake neither," he added.

"What's been happening here?" said Nancy. "Whose blood is that on the deck?"

"Mine," said Bill, grinning wider than ever.

"Bill," said Nancy, "where are your teeth?"

"There's two of 'em in the soap, Cap'n Nancy, and t'other one must lay somewheres about here."

"There's only one chance for the skipper," said Peter Duck, "and only one for us, now they've taken them guns. And that's to sail round to meet him and take him off before the others gets there. He'll be there before them. He was in a hurry right enough."

"It'd take anybody half a day at least to get across," said John. "The whole forest's down on that side, and there've been landslides as well."

"It'll take more'n that to stop him," said the old seaman. "He was half-crazed with thinking what had come to you last night."

"We were all right," said Roger.

"We didn't know that," said Peter Duck. "Now, then, Cap'n John, and you, Cap'n Nancy, will you lend a hand with getting the mainsail up again? Foresail's split. Be heaving the anchor short, the rest of you. Where's that boat of yours? Let's have the mast and sail out of her. Shift two pigs of ballast into the stern and we'll tow her. Need her later. What's that you've got in her?"

"It's your treasure," said Nancy and John and Titty all together.

Peter Duck stared.

"Did you find it in a bag?" he asked, but hardly heard them answer. "I'd be glad you've found it," he said, "if skipper's to know of it. Main pleased he'd be. But if that Jake gets him I'll be sorry I ever came aboard this ship." He quickly made a running bowline in the loose end of the painter and dropped it down to Nancy, who had already half flung herself back into *Swallow* to shift the ballast and send up the mast and sail. "Make this fast about that box," he said, "and we'll have it safe on deck. Skipper'd never forgive us if we lost it now. Be quick, now. There's maybe no time to lose."

Three minutes later the throat of the mainsail was up and John and the old seaman were hauling up the peak. A shout from Nancy, who had run forward, told them the anchor was a-trip. The staysail was up. A moment later the *Wild Cat* was moving. The hurry and bustle had turned into a breathless sort of peace. The anchor was at the bows. *Swallow*, after one impatient jerk at her painter, was towing quietly astern. People were coiling down ropes and each of them, as the deck

grew tidier, came after where Peter Duck was at
the wheel, steering to clear the southern point of
the bay, and glancing almost angrily at the little
teakwood box with its verdigrised brass binding,
resting there by the deckhouse door.

"I dare say that box has cost more lives than
one already," said Peter Duck, "and I hope it ain't
going to cost another. Take it inside there, one of
you, and stow it in the skipper's bunk. I don't like
to look at it."

The wind was still from the west, but there
was little of it. It came in short puffs that heeled
the *Wild Cat* suddenly over, to rise again as she
slipped ahead with the noise of foaming water
under her bows. And then there would be all but
no wind at all, and she would be on an even keel,
moving more and more slowly until, without warning, another puff would heel her over again and
Swallow would be hauled along with her forefoot
well out of the water.

"I don't like the weather neither," said Peter
Duck. "There's another packet of dirty weather
to come. We're not out of it yet."

"What are we going to do now?" asked John.

"Come as near in as we can with the schooner,
and be ready to take him off as soon as he comes
down on the beach."

The others were busy asking Bill about what
had happened aboard the *Wild Cat*, and Bill was
telling them as much as he knew about it and
perhaps a little bit more.

"And when did you lose your teeth?" asked
Susan.

"I ain't lost 'em," said Bill. "I found that

other one, right again' the galley door. Wear 'em
on me watch-chain I will, when I got a watch. If
you wears a tooth what's been fair knocked out,
knocked out proper and not drawed, you'll never
have no bad luck and you'll never have no rheu-
matics neither."

"And they came over the side just like pirates,
with knives in their teeth?" said Titty. "It must
have been a real fight."

"I done my best," said Bill modestly. And
indeed he had.

"Aye," said Peter Duck. "It was Bill did the
fighting. I got mine as soon as I was out of the
deckhouse door."

And then there was the story of the night,
or rather two stories, to be exchanged, one for
another, one about the happenings at Duckhaven,
and the other about the *Wild Cat's* adventures at
sea, and of how, when at last she had reached
the anchorage again, Captain Flint had set off to
fight his way across the island to see what had
happened to the diggers during the earthquake.

All eyes were turned to the island. Somewhere there among the new landslides, with
their treacherous loose earth, somewhere there
in the ruined forest, struggling from fallen tree
to fallen tree, freeing himself from one climbing
plant only to be caught by another, Captain Flint
was hurrying to the rescue of the diggers, while
they were already safe aboard the little schooner.
Somewhere there, more real to Bill and to Peter
Duck than to the others, were Black Jake and
his savage crew, armed with the very guns that
Bill had welcomed as a protection against them,

and ready, as they had already shown, to stick at
nothing. If one of these men were to see Captain
Flint, Peter Duck and Bill knew well enough that
the skipper stood a good chance of being shot down
by a bullet out of one of his own guns.

And there lay the island, silent, secret in the
fading light of the evening. What was happening
there? Had Captain Flint reached Duckhaven,
and, finding the diggers gone, turned back? Was
he now, all unknowing, hurrying headlong towards his enemies? Or was he still fighting with
the thousand clinging arms of the fallen forest,
in frantic effort to get to Duckhaven before dark?
Had the others seen him? Were they stalking him,
closing in on him with their guns? Had he seen
them? Was he, even now, dodging from one bit
of cover to another? They could get no answer by
looking at the island. It might never have known
the footsteps of man, so indifferent, so desolate it
looked to the watchers on the deck of the *Wild
Cat* as the little schooner slipped along its eastern shore and they strained their eyes into the
twilight.

"Take the wheel, will you, Cap'n John," said
Peter Duck at last, and took the telescope and
looked through it along that shore, where, sixty
years before, he had been washed up, fastened to
a spar.

"The big tree's down," said John. "You won't
find Duckhaven."

"I've found it," said Peter Duck. "There's only
that one place where the rocks run down across
the sand. No, there's no one on that shore. That
'quake's stirred things properly, that and the

storm. Matter of six hours it might be, crossing, where it wasn't above one before if a man was in a hurry. Well, I daren't bring her much nearer. Shallow far out it'll be this side."

He took the lead and sounded, swinging it well forward and feeling the bottom as the *Wild Cat* slipped on. "Aye, I thought so. Less'n five fathom. Too near in. Port your helm, Cap'n John. So . . . That'll do. Let fly staysail sheets there, Cap'n Nancy. Hard down now and bring her to the wind."

He went forward. The *Wild Cat* brought up in the wind and lost her way. Down went the anchor. Peter Duck came aft.

"Now," he said, "someone's to be waiting ashore with the boat, ready to pull off with the skipper sharp the moment he shows up. There won't be no time to lose. If the wind shifts there'll be nothing for it but sheering off. He may show up any time now, but, by the look of things, he couldn't have been here before, not without flying. Well, who's to go?"

Everybody wanted to go, but Peter Duck chose John and Nancy.

"Best pullers," he said, "though maybe Mate Susan's got the more sense." Grim though they were feeling, John and Nancy laughed.

Bill hauled in on the painter of the *Swallow*. John climbed down into her as she came alongside. Nancy followed. Peter Duck went forward, dropped down into the fo'c'sle and came back with the big hurricane lantern, bigger than the one they had with them at Duckhaven, the same lantern that was usually hoisted on the forestay when the *Wild Cat* was anchored at night.

"Darkening," he said. "You'd best show this as soon as you can't see the trees. We don't want him looking for you in the dark. Don't go ashore. Lie afloat in her ready to pull off, and douse your light if you doubt it ain't the skipper. But I reckon he'll be a long way ahead of them others. And if the wind changes and there's nought for it but to make sail, I'll give you a call on the bull-roarer."

"Aye, aye, sir," said John and Nancy together.

Old Peter Duck started. "Aye," he said. "That's so. I'm in command. But not for long, I'm hoping. Now, then. Lie afloat, and don't stir till he gives you a hail. It'll be dark now in less'n no time."

They were well away from the schooner's side before anybody thought of saying goodbye to them. Everybody was watching. Then Bill ran forward and shouted, queerly, because of the gap in his teeth, "Go it, the cap'ns!" Then everybody shouted. A cheerful call was blown back to them over the water. *Swallow*, bobbing up and down over the waves, was already beyond talking distance.

"Lower the peak there, Bill," said Peter Duck. "And you two mates, lower the staysail, and put a bit of yarn about it, so's we can hoist in a jiffy if we want to. There's something gone clean wrong with the weather in these parts, and it may come away again from the north-east and find us on a lee shore."

"Oh, Mr Duck," said Susan, a few minutes later, as she came aft, "we've sent them off without anything to eat, and they're thirsty already."

"Maybe they won't be long," said Mr Duck.

"And the skipper went off without taking a bite with him. How'd it be if you was to be getting something ready?"

He gave everybody something to do but, himself, never left the deck. For as long as he could see the white line of the sand, he was sweeping the beach from end to end, to and fro with the telescope. And then, as it grew dark, and far away there the light of the hurricane lantern sparkled out in the gloom, the old man had no words for anyone, but kept moving, now to one side, now to the other, keeping his eyes always on that distant flicker.

CHAPTER XXXII

WHOSE STEPS IN THE DARK?

Nancy and John, pulling short, hard strokes, and lifting their oars well clear of the water between them, drove the *Swallow* shorewards. There was very much less swell than on that evening when he had sailed round here with Captain Flint, but there was still enough to break on the low reef outside Duckhaven. As they came nearer, John, when he glanced over his shoulder, could see the white splash of the spray over the rocks, and was glad to see it, because it gave him something to steer for. He was rowing with the bow oar and keeping time with Nancy. Now giving a harder pull or two, now easing a little, he was able to keep *Swallow* heading for the end of the reef. Nancy left the steering to John. She set herself only to pull as steady a stroke as she could, and did not allow herself even once to look over her shoulder.

"Is he there already?" she asked breathlessly, for they were putting all they could into their rowing.

"I can't see anybody," John panted back.

They plugged on. Even for Nancy's lurid taste things had been happening too fast. Besides, it was all very well to be the Terror of the Seas, but real pirates, like Black Jake and his friends, were altogether different. Bullies. Cowards and bullies, five of them together going for an old man and a

boy. Nancy clenched her teeth and dug in so hard
with her oar that she all but made John get out
of time with her. She did, indeed, feel his oar just
touch her back.

"Sorry," said John.

"My fault," said Nancy.

They would have said just that if they had got
out of time while rowing together on the lake at
home. They said it now, though they were rowing
in at dusk to an island of landslide and earthquake and half-mad pirates roaming about with
stolen guns. Still, some things were the same as
usual. Wherever you were you said "Sorry" if you
bumped "stroke" in the back with the bow oar, and
you said it was your fault if you had happened to
change the time unexpectedly because you were
thinking of something else.

They plugged on.

"Easy a bit," said John. "We're close to the
reef now."

Nancy resolutely looked straight before her at
the *Wild Cat* anchored out there, dim in the
twilight. She would not turn round. She rowed
steadily though the noise of breaking waves was
not more than a few yards away.

"We're in," said John.

A rock showed in the dusk on the starboard
side of the boat. Nancy, steadily rowing, saw it
on her left, with a white splash of spray flying up
it. Another rock swam into view. Another, higher.
Already they were rowing in water sheltered by
the reef.

"Mr Duck said 'Don't land!'"

"We won't," said Nancy. "We'll keep her afloat

in the harbour, ready to pull out the moment he comes. If only he hasn't come already and found nobody here and turned back."

"He can't have done," said John. "He'd have seen the *Wild Cat* if he'd come out on the beach. So he wouldn't think of turning back."

They brought *Swallow* carefully into the tiny harbour from which she had sailed so proudly only a few hours before, a Spanish galleon with treasure in her hold. Everything seemed just as they had left it and yet altogether different, because they could no longer think of the island in the same way. It was no longer their island and theirs alone. Earthquake and landslide had not been enough to make this kind of difference. It was the coming of the *Viper* that had changed the island for them. Somewhere in the dusk among those fallen trees and lifted roots there were the men who had come aboard the *Wild Cat* and left Peter Duck roped and helpless on the floor of the deckhouse after one of them had all but killed him with a blow. Somewhere on the island there was the man who had not been ashamed to knock Bill's teeth out, and to leave him gagged and choking in the bottom of the monkey's cage. Who could think of the island as the happy place it had been? Worst of all, Captain Flint was still there, thinking only of his crew, and knowing nothing of the danger at his heels.

It was still light enough at first to see their old camp. Little was left of it. The broken ridge-pole of the tent, a crushed store-tin, Susan's old fireplace, their own footprints leading down to the water's edge, and the marks of *Swallow*'s keel in the

sand, showing how they had come down there
and launched her to sail away, as they supposed,
for ever. The crabs were coming back. They saw
several of them, wandering uneasily about, lifting
themselves from the ground, slowly waving their
pincers from side to side, as if they were feeling
their way in a fog.

"Hullo," said John, "there's one of Susan's
spoons. There's no harm in hopping ashore for
that."

"No. We'd better get it."

The spoon was sticking up out of the sand,
its handle buried. John jumped ashore, ran to it,
picked it up, looked this way and that along the
beach and came down again to the boat.

"There are lots of crabs round the wreck," he
said. "Hullo, why are you turning her round?"

"Jump in," said Nancy, who had taken both
oars and turned *Swallow*'s stern towards the
beach. "Better this way. We can pull out at a
moment's notice."

John scrambled in and sat down in the stern,
while Nancy pulled offshore again and kept the
boat in the middle of the little harbour.

"It's a horrible place to be alone in," said John.
"I don't wonder Mr Duck didn't like it when he
was small. Listen!"

They listened. Tonight there was no noise of
wind in trees, for there was hardly any wind,
and on this side of the island hardly a tree
was standing. Far away they heard the cries of
startled birds. There was no other noise except
the water breaking on the rocks and the sand,
and that was quieter than usual, for the regular

swell sweeping in from the east had somehow
been flattened out by the storm, and instead there
was an undecided sea, sulky and petulant. It was
very hot, but though the dusk turned quickly to
such darkness that they could only just see the
shape of the land against the sky, there were no
cheerful fireflies where the ruined forest met the
beach.

John, in the stern sheets, was busy with the
hurricane lantern. He lit it, and the moment it
was lit neither he nor Nancy could see anything
at all outside the boat, unless it was so near that
the lantern showed it to them. It showed them,
when they drifted that way, the side of the rock
that sheltered Duckhaven. It lit up the yellow
oar with which Nancy gently fended off. It lit
up their faces, oddly white, as they looked at
each other across it, and then, as John turned
towards the shore and held the lantern at arm's
length, it seemed to Nancy to turn him into a
monstrous flickering shadow between her and the
light.

"He ought to see that all right," said John.

"They'll see it, too," said Nancy.

John peered into the darkness, but there
seemed to be splashes of light everywhere, from
the dazzle in his eyes.

"Well, it's no good our seeing, anyhow," he
said. "We don't need to."

"I can't even see the *Wild Cat* now. No. There
she is. There's the light in the deckhouse door.
She's an awful long way out."

Away out to sea in the pitch darkness of a
clouded night the schooner was invisible, but now

and then a light in the galley or the deckhouse glimmered and died and then shone out again as the *Wild Cat* swung to her anchor.

"I'm going to turn her round again," said Nancy. "It'll be just as easy to work out stern first, and easier if the *Wild Cat's* showing a light. You'd better come back to the bows, so there'll be less shifting about when he comes."

"All right," said John, and clambered forward with the lantern.

They were speaking in whispers now, though they did not know why. Sometimes Nancy spoke out loud, on purpose, but she did not keep it up. Whispering seemed easier.

"I wish he'd hurry up," said Nancy, after a long wait in silence.

"I say," said John, "you don't think they've got him?"

"Of course they haven't," said Nancy. "There'd have been a fight. They've got guns. We couldn't have helped hearing if one of them had gone off."

"He's been an awful long time," said John.

"Well," said Nancy, "just think what it was like just going into the forest a few yards to look for my spring."

"It would have been quicker to come round by the shore."

Nancy caught her breath.

"Uncle Jim started straight across. Bill saw him start, and he wouldn't turn back whatever it was like. Not once he'd started. But if the others came round by the shore . . . they might easily get here first."

IN DUCKHAVEN AT NIGHT

They stared at each other in the bright glare of the lantern, and looked out of the light into the thick darkness that shut them in.

"If they'd been coming by the shore they'd have seen the *Wild Cat* and rushed back to look after their beastly *Viper*."

"Or hurried on," said Nancy. "Bill heard them say they'd seen the smoke of our camp."

"Are you awfully thirsty?" asked John, after a long time.

"Yes," said Nancy. "Empty, too. Don't let's talk about it."

Empty, thirsty, more tired than they knew after the wild night of storm and earthquake, the excitement of finding the treasure, the shock of what they had found on getting back to the schooner, and the horror of knowing that Captain Flint might be at the mercy of the pirates, they almost drowsed with open, smarting eyes.

Suddenly John started up.

"It's him," cried Nancy.

Both of them had heard at last the sound for which they had been waiting, the cracking of branches, the brushing of leaves, the uneven sudden noises of someone struggling over rough ground in the dark.

"It may not be," said John.

Nancy's eyes widened. "What do you mean?" she said. "One of *them*?"

"Listen," said John.

There were no wild beasts on the island to make a noise like that. Only a man would push at boughs until they creaked or broke or swung back, one against another. And then, those sudden crashes. That could be only a man forcing his way through the tangle of the fallen forest and falling every now and then into the holes left by the uplifted roots of the trees.

"Pull in, Nancy, pull in!"

"What are we to do if it isn't him?" said Nancy.

There was a noise of stumbling and of stones striking against each other somewhere up the beach.

"He's tumbled into the place where we found the box . . . He's coming straight down the beach. We'll see him in a minute. Have the oars all ready to back her out . . ."

John stood up, holding the lantern before him as high as he could.

Steps, stumbling, uneven, hurrying, were coming nearer in the dark.

"WHO GOES THERE?" Nancy suddenly called out in a high voice, unlike her own, stirred by a memory of some old tale of sentinels and war.

"Friend." A voice came back out of the darkness, and a moment later Captain Flint limped into the glow from the hurricane lantern. His face was scratched, his shirt hanging in ribbons, one of his knees, red with blood, showed through a great cut in his flannel trousers. He was helping himself along with a big rough stick from which twigs and green leaves were still sprouting, and anybody could see that he could hardly bear to put his right foot to the ground.

"What have you done with the camp? Is anybody hurt? Where are the others?"

"Hurry up," said Nancy. "Everybody's all right. They're waiting for you in the schooner."

"The schooner?"

"She's anchored out here. Everybody's in her and quite all right."

"What about the camp?"

"Packed. Oh, do get in. The others may be here any minute and they've got all our guns."

"Who? What?"

"Don't stop to talk, Uncle Jim. Get in!"

"I'd have been across ages ago if only I hadn't sprained my ankle between a couple of rocks. But what a bit of luck P.D. thought of bringing the schooner round . . ."

"Do get in."

Captain Flint climbed painfully in over the bows of the *Swallow*. John splashed overboard into the shallow water to get out of the way.

"What was that you were saying about guns?" Captain Flint asked, as, leaning heavily on Nancy's shoulder, he stepped over the main thwart and sat down in the stern.

"Black Jake," said Nancy. "He's here. The *Viper*'s here. They're all on the island. They may be anywhere by now. Go on, John. Push her off . . ."

"What? What? But . . ."

"They captured the *Wild Cat* . . . All right. We've got her again. They landed on the island and went after you. Won't she go, John? Too much weight aft?"

Nancy stood up and pushed at the bottom with an oar. John put the lantern down on the forward thwart. He wanted to use both hands and all his strength. *Swallow* slid off. John got a knee on the gunwale and gave a last kick at the shore. They were afloat. And at that moment there was the sharp crack of a rifle away to the south, a crash and tinkle of broken glass, and the lantern toppled down from the thwart and went out.

"*Now* do you understand?" said Nancy.

Captain Flint understood well enough.

"Lie down, both of you," he said.

"Rot," said Nancy. "They can't see us now the light's gone. They've got nothing to shoot at. Keep still while I paddle her out. Don't let's bump those rocks. Reach out over the stern to fend her off."

"Oh, what a mess I've gone and got you all into," said Captain Flint. "I ought never to have brought you here. The whole island's turned upside down. Anything might have happened to you last night. And now these scoundrels ... We're sailing at once, if we get out of this. Hang the treasure! Let them have the stuff if they can find it! I'm through. I ought to have known better than to start. I'll never forgive myself if anything goes wrong now ..."

"But we've got the treasure," said John quietly. "That must be the end of the reef," he added. "Turn her round and let me have that bow oar."

"You've got it?" said Captain Flint. "Got it? But where is it? Not on shore?"

They could not see him in the dark, but they could feel the boat give a bit of a lurch as if he had suddenly half stood up.

"In your bunk in the deckhouse," said John.

"Gosh!" said Captain Flint.

CHAPTER XXXIII

ALL ABOARD ONCE MORE

THE others were very unwilling to begin without the three captains, but in the end the sight of the meal that Peggy and Susan spread out on the saloon table was too much for them. They were very hungry. They had been taking sips of water and bits of biscuit that happened to be broken, and small rations of chocolate while the kettle was being boiled. That sort of thing is all very well on an ordinary day, but it hardly counts when people have had practically nothing to eat since the day before. What was wanted aboard the *Wild Cat* that night was a meal that should be breakfast, dinner, tea, and supper all in one. At last Susan asked Peter Duck what they had better do about waiting, and he said the skipper would be none too pleased to come back and find his crew all hanging about with empty bellies. So they sat down and fell to, Roger, Titty, Peggy, and poor Bill, who had to cut everything up into small bits, because, with a bruised face and three teeth gone, he could not do any serious biting.

As for Peter Duck, he said he was on anchor-watch and could not leave the deck. But Susan cut a big hunk of pemmican, and, instead of vegetables, made a sandwich of two ship's biscuits with a lot of butter in between them. Before sitting down with the others, she took the beef and the sandwich and a huge mug of boiling tea and

carried them up to the old sailor, who thanked
her for it, but never for a moment took his eyes
off that dim, shadowy shore.

Down below, the first few mouthfuls and the
first round of tea made a tremendous difference.
The meal had begun in silence, almost as if each
one of them were alone or not able to see the others
very well. The silence suddenly turned into loud,
eager talking. There was still so much to say. Bill
had not heard half enough of how they had found
the treasure. The others had a hundred things
still to ask about the *Wild Cat*'s adventures in
the storm, about the boarding of her by Black
Jake's pirate gang, and about the short, disastrous
battle on her decks. And Bill untied the knot in his
handkerchief, into which he had put his teeth for
safe-keeping, and passed them round for the others to see, and told how he had run his head into
the middle of Mogandy, and how the big negro had
said that he would kill that boy. "I reckon he'd like
to," said Bill, and, for a moment or two, felt almost
as if he had driven the pirates off the deck instead
of being collared and bound and tossed into Gibber's cage. Then he remembered other things. "I
thought he'd killed Mr Duck," he said.

Titty looked at Susan.

"Susan," she said. "Susan, is it all right about
Captain Flint?"

"He started before they did, and he'd go much
faster," said Susan. "He's sure to be all right."

She was going to say more, but she caught
Peggy's eyes on her, questioning, afraid. She fell
suddenly silent. Was it all right, really? Susan
swallowed something and looked away.

"I wish he'd come," said Titty.

"It's as dark as dark, outside," said Roger.

Peter Duck, on deck, stared through the darkness towards the island. Darkness had fallen fast. They had been only just in time. The riding-light those two had taken with them to Duckhaven was glimmering away there on shore. The wind was still out of the west, but so little of it, so little indeed that he doubted if it would last the night before it came again from the east. There was a dreadful heaviness in the air, even at sea. With this weather anything might happen. "If it comes east we must be away out of this," he said to himself, munching his pemmican and his biscuit sandwich and drinking his hot tea. Why was the skipper so long? He should have been across by now. If those others were to catch him . . . Peter Duck thought angrily of the little teak box lying in the bunk in the deckhouse. Ah, he should never have told that yarn. If he'd had the sense to keep his mouth shut they'd be cruising in the Channel now, or looking into Strangford Lough, or in some of them places up the Clyde, or away there in the Baltic, or lying in Lisbon or Vigo, anyway in some sensible place instead of here on the wrong side of Crab Island, with the skipper ashore, and half a dozen cut-throats loose from gaol and after him with guns. And just then he heard the crack of a rifle, and that light on shore was gone.

His mug dropped to the deck and broke there. Peter Duck hardly noticed it. He listened. No other shot. But the light? Had they put it out for fear of showing a target? But how was the skipper to find them in the dark? Had they rowed off without

him? They would never do that. But what could
they do? If he had thought for a moment that
Black Jake and his gang could get across the
island before the skipper, he would never have let
those two go in alone. Sound the foghorn to bring
them off? He went into the deckhouse, and found
the old bull-roarer, one of the few things still in
its place, slung up under the roof. He heard Bill's
mumbling, toothless talk going on below. What.
could he say to those children if . . . ? He went out
again with the bull-roarer. He put it to his lips,
and then leant sharply forward. What was that?
He could not be mistaken in that noise anyhow.
The creak and knock of oars somewhere between
the *Wild Cat* and the shore.

*

Yes. There was no doubt about it. Somewhere
out there in the dark there was a rowing boat
without a light, coming out to the *Wild Cat*. For
one moment Peter Duck was for getting the lantern out of the deckhouse to show more of a light
than came through the deckhouse windows. Then
another thought came to him. That rifle shot?
What if the two captains, John and Nancy, had
gone ashore and been surprised there, and the
boat coming off was full of the cut-throats from
the *Viper*? Or could it be one of the *Viper*'s own
boats? Well, they had boarded the *Wild Cat* last
time easily enough, while her crew were lying
asleep. But not again, anyhow, not unless they
had more than one boat. Even children could use
a belaying-pin on pirate knuckles as they showed
along the rail. He hurried round the deckhouse

and called down the companion, "All hands on deck!"

*

"All hands on deck!"

Peter Duck called down quietly enough, but there was something in his voice that stopped spoons full of tinned pear half-way between plate and mouth, and even cut a sentence of Roger's off short in the middle. For one second, down in the saloon, there was a dead silence. In the next second, everybody was rushing for the companion.

Bill was on deck first, with Titty and Roger close after him. Susan and Peggy had been just a little more careful not to sweep things off the table as they got up. They were last, but even so they came tumbling up on deck almost on Roger's heels.

"Boat coming off," said Peter Duck. "Don't know who's in it, but we're not going to be caught twice. Don't go showing yourselves with the light behind you. Aye, that's right. Close that galley door. Get hold of a belaying-pin apiece, from that rack by the starboard shrouds. And don't think about the paint when you bring them pins down to pulp the first hand you see getting a grip of the rail . . . Where's Bill?"

"He was here just now," said Titty. "What is it? Not the pirates?"

"They ain't coming aboard here if it is," said Peter Duck. "Not twice in one day. They can't, neither. Not without they've two boats. And I can't hear but one out there. Listen!"

Just then the light from one of the deckhouse

windows lit up Bill's toothless grin, as he came aft trailing with him one of the capstan bars which he had gone forward to fetch.

"This'll do proper for one of them," he said.

"Less lip," said Peter Duck. "Listen!"

"'Sh, 'sh," whispered the others.

It was coming nearer now, and everybody could hear it, the sharp knock as the oars swung across the rowlocks at the end of each stroke, and the squeaking of a rowlock that needed oiling.

"It sounds awfully like *Swallow*," said Peggy, speaking very low. "John said he meant to give some oil to the rowlocks, but I don't believe he did."

"Why don't they show their lantern?" whispered Roger.

"Aye. It's *Swallow*, all right," said Peter Duck. "But who's in her?"

"You don't think anything's gone wrong with John and Nancy?" said Titty. ". . . And Captain Flint?"

Peter Duck grunted. The crack of that rifle-shot was still in his ears, but he did not want to tell them of it if he could help it. "Best be ready for anything," he said.

But just then, from close by the bows of the schooner, as she lay across the current, in the wind that was still coming light off the shore, there rose a loud, eager shout.

"Ahoy there, *Wild Cat*! Show us a light!"

Peter Duck straightened himself in the dark. He had been stooping to listen, a little, bent old man, bowed down perhaps by the weight of his fears. Now he threw up his head with a cheerful

"Aye, aye, sir!" "It's the skipper," he said, bustling into the deckhouse for the lantern. He was back with it in a moment. "Throw the ladder over there, Bill. Now then, Miss Susan, have you got a cup of hot tea for him? Ladder's over on the port side." He was shouting now, swinging the lantern to and fro above the rail. Already it lit up the faces below, and everybody aboard the *Wild Cat*, peering eagerly down into the darkness, had seen that all three captains were there, two at the oars, and another in the stern. Bill dropped a rope over and carried it forward to the main shrouds, while somebody below there in *Swallow* made it fast. A moment later Captain Flint, ragged, bruised and scratched, was coming up the ladder one rung at a time. He flung a tired leg over the rail.

"Well, that's that," he said. "And better luck than I deserve after getting you all into this mess."

The others were not in a hurry to come aboard.

"Hi! Mr Duck," called Nancy, "do just pass us down that lantern."

"Where's your own?" asked Peggy.

"We'd be using it if we had it," said Nancy. "Thanks. Are you sure you've found it, John?"

"I can feel it all right. Have you got the lantern?"

The next moment the two of them, down there in the boat, made sure, with the lantern to help them, and the little group on deck heard Nancy's delighted yell. "So she has. Do you hear? *Swallow*'s got a bullet in her. John's found it. We'll never take it out."

"But how?" said Roger.

"The bullet that smashed the lantern," said John.

"When?"

"We never heard any shooting."

"Didn't we?" said Peter Duck. "Well, better the lantern than what I thought it might have been. Come along with you now, and let's have that lantern. We're in the dark up here."

Nancy passed up the lantern. Then she and John climbed aboard, and John took the rope from Bill, and carried it aft and made fast there, to let the *Swallow* lie astern.

"Have you told Captain Flint about the treasure?" asked Titty, following Nancy into the deckhouse.

But Captain Flint would not look at the treasure at that moment. He just glanced across the deckhouse at it, where it lay in his bunk. "A box," he said. "I thought it would be. Did you find the bag?" And then, before they had time to tell him about it, while Roger was still feeling in his pocket for one of those old greenish metal eyelet rings, Captain Flint had turned away, almost as if he were ashamed. He would not look toward his bunk again. "No, no!" he said. "We must get out of this first. A dozen times today I've wished that treasure at the bottom of the sea. What anchor have you got down, Mr Duck?"

"Only the kedge," said Mr Duck. "I thought to slip it if the wind changed sudden."

"That's good," said Captain Flint. "Let's have it up and be off. If we can we'll put Crab Island hull down before dawn. I never want to see the place again."

"My way of thinking," said Peter Duck.

And so, while everybody was bursting to hear

something or to tell something, while the story of the taking of the *Wild Cat* by the pirates from the *Viper*, and the story of the rescue, and of the finding of the treasure, and of Captain Flint's crossing of the island, and of *Swallow*'s wait at Duckhaven in the dark, and of the rifle shot that had smashed the lantern and left a bullet in the gunwale, were still waiting to be told, the whole ship's company turned to. Capstan bars were fitted, sails were set, mainsail and staysail, an old spare jib instead of the one that had been blown away, a trysail instead of the foresail that had been split from top to bottom in the storm, the anchor was raised, and the *Wild Cat*, in the light wind that was still coming fitfully out of the west, sailed away from Crab Island in the dark.

"There's very little wind," said Captain Flint. "I'll have a go at starting the motor."

"You'll never do that by lantern light, sir," said Peter Duck. "And you may make him worse. Leave the little donkey to sleep and maybe you'll have him running in the morning. But it's a donkeyman's job and not a sailor's to be working them things."

Susan had a fresh lot of tea going in the saloon, and Captain Flint, John, and Nancy sat in there hungrily eating and drinking. The others finished their own supper, and then leaned on the table, watching them. There was so much to say that they could have talked all night, or rather they thought they could. But Roger's head fell slowly forward, and Susan got up and hauled him off to bed. When she got back to the saloon she found a strange scene. The whole lot of them were sleeping, some pillowing their heads on their arms among the supper things, others hunched down where they sat. Captain Flint sat up with a start, stared at Susan, tried to take a drink from his empty mug, and staggered across the saloon to the companion ladder.

"Well, I don't know what to do," said Susan to herself. "Perhaps I'd better not wake them."

She left the others sleeping as they were, and went quietly up the companion ladder.

"North-east it is," Peter Duck was saying. "We'll not do better than that. If we want a quick passage we must work up north till we get into the westerlies. There's no sense butting into a trade wind. No, Cap'n, there's nothing wrong with me. Knocked out I was, and maybe I was lucky. No, no. I can carry on till dawn, and then we'll see better what's coming to us."

Susan heard the faint slop slop of the water on the bows of *Swallow*, towing astern. The *Wild Cat* was sailing. She slipped quietly down below once more, in time to see Titty moving, more than half asleep, across the saloon and into her cabin. The others were still sprawling about the table. Titty, groping in the dark, found her berth and fell into it. Susan listened to Titty's even breathing. She then climbed as quietly as she could into the upper berth, and a moment later was as fast asleep as Titty.

CHAPTER XXXIV

WATERSPOUT

THE sleepers round the saloon table were roused by the noise of tinkering with the engine. It was broad daylight. They stretched stiff arms, yawned, and rubbed eyes that did not seem inclined to stay open. They got up and wandered aft, like sleep-walkers, to find Captain Flint crouched below the deckhouse in the hole that served as an engine-room, trying to free the choked engine from some of the oil that Gibber and Roger had lavished upon it. There were smudges of grease now, as well as the scratches on his face, and his torn shirt, as Peggy said afterwards, might just as well have been an overall, it was in such a state. He did say "Good morning" to them, but that was all, and he went on at once with what he was doing to the engine.

"He's jolly bothered about something," said Nancy, as they went sleepily up the companion steps. As soon as they came out on deck they knew why.

There had been hardly any wind during the night. Crab Island was still in sight on the horizon. But that was not all. Soon after dawn Captain Flint and Peter Duck had seen a tall black schooner creeping round the northern headland. There she was, with topsails set on both her masts. The *Viper* was after them again.

That, in itself, was enough to set Captain Flint tinkering at the engine. But it was not the thought

of Black Jake alone that kept Peter Duck, who
was at the wheel, looking uneasily about him.
Anybody could see that there was still something
altogether wrong about the weather. Where was
the steady trade wind of the last few weeks? What
did they mean, these little cat's-paws that ran
across the water, now from this side, now from
that, under this heavy metallic sky, orange and
purple in the east, black and thunderous in the
west? There was something wrong with the sea,
too. With the ordinary trade wind of these parts
there should have been a steady swell rolling down
from the north-east. There was nothing of the sort,
but tossing, aimless waves.

But on that morning, not even the sight of
the *Viper*, or the look of the weather, or the
grim faces of Captain Flint and Peter Duck could
cloud the happiness of the crew. There they were,
all together again in the *Wild Cat*, homeward
bound, with the treasure, whatever it was, safely aboard. Nothing else seemed to matter. They
hurried below again to get into their bathing
things for washing decks, as on the old, happy
mornings of the outward voyage. Susan, Titty,
and Roger were on deck and ready when the two
captains, followed by Peggy and Bill, clambered
up through the forehatch. They soused each other
with bucketfuls of salt water, and took turns in
driving the water along the deck with the long-
handled mops. They crowded round to look at the
purple spreading bruises on both sides of Bill's
right shoulder where Black Jake's fingers had
held him in that cruel grip. Tenderly they felt
his swollen face. Bill wished the bruises would

last for ever, like tattoo-marks, because John, and Roger, and Nancy seemed to admire them so much. But at least he would always have the teeth to show. They would last as long as he would. And then, while the others swabbed the water into the scuppers, Peggy and Susan hurried into the galley to make breakfast. It was a pity, said Peggy, that nobody had thought of bringing aboard a really large stock of bananas. They dressed while the kettle was coming on the boil. Titty brought the parrot up on deck. Roger let loose the monkey. Everybody, except Captain Flint and Peter Duck, was in the highest spirits.

"Come along here, one of you cap'ns, or you, Bill, when you've done washing down the decks, and take the wheel," Peter Duck called out at last. "Just you come here and do the best you can with her. I want to see what canvas we've got in the locker, and the skipper's busy with the little donkey down below."

But just at that moment Captain Flint came up the ladder into the deckhouse and put his head out of the door.

"It's a donkey that won't go, Mr Duck. I'll take the wheel for a bit, while you see what you can do in the way of more sail."

"She'd carry all we could put on her," said Mr Duck, "but we've nothing to put. Now if only I'd the foresail mended, or a bit of topsail to set over her main . . ."

"Uncle Jim," said Nancy. "You'd feel a lot better if you went and had a go with that bucket, and got some of the dirt off."

Captain Flint looked round over his shoulder

at the far-away schooner. Then he laughed, in spite of his worries. "You've been taking lessons from Susan, Nancy," he said. "But I believe you're right. You can take over, you three, just for a minute." And he went forward up to the capstan, and pulled his ragged shirt off, and poured bucket after bucket over his head. He came aft again, looking cleaner and much more cheerful, just as Peggy began hammering at the breakfast bell.

Neither he nor Peter Duck would come down to the saloon for breakfast. They had theirs brought to them on deck by Titty and Bill. Captain Flint was steering, and Peter Duck was already desperately stitching at a sail. He did not believe in engines, anyway.

After breakfast it was clear to everybody that the *Viper* was gaining on them, very slowly, because of the fitfulness of the wind, but gaining all the time.

"Why not let me start the engine?" said Roger.

"Didn't you hear me trying to start it?" said Captain Flint. "That wretched monkey of yours has fairly choked it with oil and grease. There's nothing to be done with it until we take it to pieces and put it together again."

"It's not really Gibber's fault," said Roger. "He did his best, and he worked very hard."

"Yes, I know that," said Captain Flint, "but laziness, in monkeys, is a virtue."

All the same, when John, Nancy, and Bill were all free to look after the steering, Captain Flint took Roger down with him under the deckhouse, and they spent the morning in taking the engine to pieces. Gibber would have liked to join them, but Roger had to agree that just now the monkey would be better in his cabin.

Once or twice during the morning Captain Flint came up to glance astern from the door of the deckhouse.

"The little donkey'll not help us," said Peter Duck.

"It's something to do," said Captain Flint. "I'm no good with a needle."

When Nancy struck eight bells, one two, one two, one two, one two, on the ship's bell at noon, Crab Island was just disappearing below the horizon.

"Goodbye," cried Titty suddenly, and waved her hand.

"Who are you waving to?" asked Bill. "Black Jake? We're not leaving him, seems to me."

The island was disappearing, but the *Wild Cat* was not alone. There was the black schooner sailing after her, and it was easy to see that she was drawing nearer.

It was dreadfully hot. There was no sun. A black cloud spread from one side of the sky to the other.

"There's trouble coming for both of us," said Mr Duck. "We're not through with that storm yet. Now a capful of wind'd be welcome. She's faster'n us, is the *Viper*, in light winds, but in a bit of a blow we'd be showing her our heels while they'd be dowsing her sails. But there's something more'n a capful coming."

Everybody had dinner on deck.

Nobody felt much like talking.

Roger did open his mouth to speak, but even he, when he saw Captain Flint's face, knew without being told that this was not the time to remind him of the treasure box in the deckhouse.

All afternoon the *Viper* crept up. The little wind there was blew this way and that under the heavy sky, and sometimes died altogether and left both schooners idly drifting, rolling, rolling, and swinging their heavy gaffs and booms from side to side in the uneven sea.

"There's not a chance of getting that engine going before dark," said Captain Flint at last, coming up on deck.

"If it would only come on to blow now, so that the *Viper* couldn't carry her topsails, we'd slip away from them yet," said Peter Duck, stitching away as hard as he could, to get one topsail ready to set on the *Wild Cat*. Both of her topsails had been torn to shreds in the squalls that had come after the earthquake, while Captain Flint was hurrying to get back to the island, not knowing what might have happened in Diggers' Camp during that terrible night. "There's something pretty bad coming," said the old seaman, "but it'll have to be bad indeed for us to mind it now."

And still the wind freshened and died away, freshened and died away without ever blowing hard enough to worry Black Jake, who was crowding on every bit of canvas he had, and with every hour was making the distance less between the *Viper* and the *Wild Cat*. The little green-hulled schooner that had slipped out of his clutches once was not, if he could help it, going to escape him again.

Nearer the *Viper* came and nearer yet. The little company about the wheel of the *Wild Cat* could see, even without using the glasses, that there were men looking forward from the black schooner's bows. One of her jibs had gone and had been replaced with a smaller one, but that hardly mattered with a slack wind that swung from south-west through west to north-west and back again. Her topsails alone, high aloft, were enough to give her the mastery over the *Wild Cat*, which, even with all sails set, had never been a match for her unless in half a gale.

At last Mr Duck's topsail was ready. "It's a poor job," he said, "but it'll be better up there than a bare pole. Come on, Bill, and let's have it up. And will you lend a hand, Cap'n Nancy? Cap'n John'll look after the wheel."

"She's going better already," cried Titty, as the topsail spread and stiffened between the mast and the gaff of the mainsail. "Oh, if only we had another for the foremast!"

It was just then that Peter Duck first saw the waterspout. He was walking aft, looking astern to the *Viper*. Crab Island was already out of sight.

"Where are them glasses?" he said.

Titty handed them over.

"I was thinking there was some dirty weather still to come," he said. "Look away there now. Call up the skipper."

Far astern, right away on the horizon, where the sea met the sky, a narrow band of light showed under the black cloud that stretched above it, hard-edged as a bar of iron. And across that narrow band of light a thin black thread seemed to join the cloud to the sea.

Captain Flint came up in a hurry when Nancy shouted down to him.

"Do you know what that is, sir?" asked Peter Duck.

"Looks like a waterspout," said Captain Flint. "I've seen them in the Indian Ocean. Let's get the telescope on it. Yes. It's a waterspout, all right. That may mean a bit of wind. By Jove, it's moving pretty fast."

"Coming up this way," said Peter Duck.

Roger was busy with the little telescope, so busy that he had not seen what the others were looking at. He was trying to get the little telescope properly focused on the *Viper*.

"What are they doing on the foredeck?" he said.

"Look at the waterspout, Rogie, and then let me have a look." Titty had parted with the glasses to Peter Duck.

"They're awfully near," said Roger, "and they're doing something on her foredeck."

"I say, Uncle Jim," said Peggy, "if the *Viper* does catch us up, what can they really do?"

"They can't do anything," said Captain Flint. "Not anything that matters."

Bill opened his mouth and shut it again. Peter Duck looked oddly at Captain Flint, and then glanced round the horizon ahead of them.

"We're not anywhere near the regular shipping routes," he was saying to himself, but Titty heard him.

"Why should we be?" she said.

Peter Duck looked at her without smiling.

"Company," he said.

Captain Flint looked astern at the *Viper*.

"Yes. I wouldn't mind falling in with another vessel just now."

But there was not a ship in sight, besides the *Wild Cat* and the *Viper*, and the distance between them was steadily growing less.

"The waterspout's going to pass quite close to us," said Nancy. "It's coming along at a tremendous lick."

That thread of dark colour between cloud and sea was thicker now. The cloud itself seemed now to roof the sky. The waterspout was changing its shape with every moment. It was like a tremendous indiarubber tube joining sky and sea. It widened at the top where it met the cloud, and the bottom of it spread out like a base of a candlestick.

"It's twirling like a corkscrew," said Titty.

"They do that," said Peter Duck. There was something in his voice that startled Captain Flint.

The thing was now near enough to hear. A wild, shrill, rustling noise swept over the sea. The grey waves were white with foam under this twirling, swaying, monstrous pillar that was coming nearer and nearer, dancing as it seemed across the troubled water.

"That'll give them something to think of," said Captain Flint. "That thing's got wind with it, and the *Viper* won't stand topsails in a wind, you said, didn't you, Mr Duck?"

"Aye, sir," said Peter Duck, and still his eyes were on the waterspout.

They saw the white spray leap from under the

bows of the *Viper* as a gust of wind stronger than
any they had had that day suddenly lifted her
on her way. A moment later they felt the wind
themselves, and Captain Flint glanced up at the
newly mended topsail.

"It looks to me as if we'll be glad to have
our own topsail down again in a few minutes,"
he said. "There's a real wind coming."

But Peter Duck said nothing. He was watching
the advancing waterspout, twirling towards them
across white, wind-whipped water.

"It's coming right at us," said Peggy, and her
voice rose with the words until it startled her and
she wondered if the others had heard the fear in
it.

"Close all hatches!" Captain Flint suddenly saw
how very near the waterspout was going to pass
them. "Close the forehatch, will you, Bill? Shut
down the skylights."

"If that thing hits us it isn't hatches'll save
us," said Peter Duck quietly. "Smashed to match-
boarding we'll be, with that weight of water on top
of us."

But Bill had already darted forward.

A moment later something happened which,
for a moment, startled them so much that even
the waterspout was forgotten.

"We must have that topsail down again, Mr
Duck," Captain Flint was saying. "There's more
than a summer squall coming with this thing . . ."

CRACK!

What was that puff of pale smoke by the stem
of the black schooner that was driving after them
with the white foam flying from her bows?

A shrill whine passed close between Titty and Mr Duck. There was a sharp thud and the noise of splintering wood somewhere right forward.

John and Nancy looked at each other. Again! They remembered last night. The *Swallow* was not the only vessel to get a bullet in her.

"They're shooting at *us*," said Roger. "I wondered what it was they were getting ready to do."

Captain Flint took the wheel from John.

"Go below, the lot of you," he said. "The drunken scoundrels! And us with children aboard!"

"It was no drunken man fired that, I'm thinking," said Peter Duck, and still his eyes were on the waterspout, not on the schooner.

CRACK!

A bullet whined close over their heads. There was a rending noise aloft. The newly mended topsail burst at the leech. The gaff came down with a run, and swung against the mast. The boom dropped, and would have crashed down on the rail if its fall had not been broken by the topping lifts.

"Think of that fellow," said Captain Flint, "having the luck to cut the peak halyard with a bullet."

No one had stirred of the little group about the wheel. All, except Roger, who still had the telescope focused on the *Viper*, were looking up at the wreckage that a single shot, cutting a single rope, had made of the *Wild Cat*'s mainsail.

"Done our reefing for us," said Peter Duck grimly. "And there's a day's work in that topsail. Well, it's no great odds. Look at that!"

The crippled *Wild Cat* was losing her way,

while a tremendous wind was hurling the *Viper* along in a smother of white foam, her topmasts bending like reeds. But it was not at the *Viper* that Peter Duck was looking.

There were new deafening noises in the air, the sound of great waterfalls, the sound of a hurricane over the sea. The waterspout, now a whirling column of dark water, thicker than a house, and many hundred feet high, was rushing upon them. The sea about its base was churned white, and out of the white the dark pillar twisted up and up until it spread again into the roofing cloud.

"It's coming right over us," said Peggy.

And then, suddenly, they saw that it was not.

"Look! look!" shrilled Roger.

Both masts of the *Viper* broke off short, one after the other. Almost in the same moment the waterspout was upon her, seeming at once to suck her up into itself and to tear her to pieces. Of them all, Roger was the only one who was quite sure what he had seen. The others had seen a waterspout and, close beside it, a schooner suddenly overwhelmed and dismasted by a mighty wind. Then they had seen a waterspout and no schooner. Then, before their eyes, the whirling column of water began to narrow in the middle. It grew narrower, still narrower, until it seemed to twist itself in two, and the upper part, still whirling, was drawn up into the cloud, while the lower fell thunderously back into the sea. They saw a mass of water leap up again into the air, and drop, and then there was a gigantic whirling hollow in the sea, as if the water was being run off after a

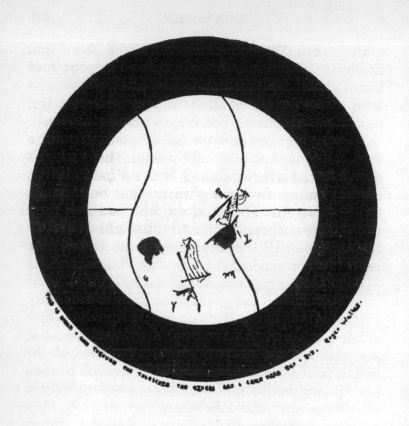

giant's bath. The hollow filled up, and there was nothing left to show where the waterspout had been. There was no waterspout, and there was no longer any *Viper*. The *Wild Cat* was alone, tearing along under nothing but trysail and headsails.

Everything had happened so fast, from the firing of that shot that had brought the mainsail down, to the overwhelming of the *Viper* by that colossal mass of whirling water, that no one had had time to stir. The children, who had been told to go below when the first bullet whistled past them, were still on deck, staring at each other as if to make sure that all of them had seen this monstrous thing. For a few seconds Captain Flint and Peter Duck were as silent as their crew. Then, as the *Wild Cat* was caught in the outer edges of the whirlwind that had made and carried the waterspout, Peter Duck rushed round the deck-house, to the mainmast, lowered away the throat, and, as the heavy gaff swung outwards, brought the whole tangle down on deck.

"Haul in on the trysail sheet," yelled Captain Flint, "and get the staysail off her."

"What are you going to do?" asked Nancy.

"Go back to pick them up," said Captain Flint.

But the best sailor in the world is hampered when his mainboom is lying over the side, and his mainsail is useless, his peak halyard gone, and he tries to come to the wind in a hurry with a small trysail on the foremast and two big headsails. The man who had fired that second shot from the *Viper* had made the *Wild Cat* all but unmanageable. And yet perhaps the *Wild Cat* had reason to be grateful to him. Perhaps that sudden loss of topsail and mainsail had saved her from losing a mast as the *Viper* had lost both of hers. In that first fury of the wind that had come with the waterspout the *Wild Cat* had run on safely under her shortened canvas. But now that Captain Flint wanted to bring her about and go back to pick up the *Viper's* crew, time was lost because he could do nothing at all until Peter Duck had brought the swinging gaff of the mainsail safely down on deck. As soon as that was done Captain Flint tried to haul his wind and come about to cruise over the place where only a few minutes before there had been a black schooner and men with no other thought in their minds but murder and revenge.

Peter Duck hauled in on the trysail sheet, and shouted for help.

"Bill," he shouted, "lower away the staysail! Bill, lower away there! Stir yourself!"

But poor Bill was sitting by the forehatch, leaning against the capstan and holding his left arm in his right hand. As the vessel came round to the wind and heeled over, his head slipped sideways, and, full-length now, he slid across the deck in a faint.

Nancy and Susan at the same moment had seen that something was wrong, and were running forward. John was hurrying after them.

"Lower away that staysail!" shouted Captain Flint, wondering what was happening there to prevent the staysail coming down, as the *Wild Cat* slammed suddenly into a wave and a great cloud of spray lifted over her bows and soused Bill and those who had come to help him.

"Lower away now!" said Peter Duck, shoving the staysail halyard into John's hand. "Ship comes first. Lower away, now, and I'll smother the sail." The wild thrashing of loose canvas added itself to the noises of the wind and of the *Wild Cat* thumping into short, steep seas.

The spray brought Bill to himself. Now he opened his eyes to see Susan and Nancy bending over him.

"What's happened?" asked Susan.

"They've shot him," cried Nancy.

"What's ado?" said Peter Duck.

Bill smiled happily through his pain.

"Less lip," he murmured, and then, trying to move, turned very white.

"It was the forehatch," he said. "That first shot. Broke my arm . . . All right . . . I saw the waterspout. I saw 'em go." And he fainted again.

"His arm's broke all right," said Peter Duck, tenderly turning back the sleeve when he saw how the arm was hanging. "Broke, but there's no bullet here."

"Look at the hatch," said John. A piece of wood had been knocked clean off it. Bill had been closing the hatch in fear of the waterspout, and his arm had been snapped, either by the blow of the bullet on the hatch or by the knocked-off bit of wood. No one would ever know for certain how it had happened, for Bill himself had known nothing but a sudden, violent blow on the forearm.

Peter Duck said no more, but picked Bill up in his arms, and carried him aft to the deckhouse. Susan hurried below for her First Aid box.

"What's happened to him?" asked Captain Flint.

"That first bullet broke his arm," said John.

"He's wounded," said Nancy.

"Oh, Bill!" said Titty.

"It might have been a lot worse," said Peter Duck, coming out again, after laying Bill in his own bunk. "But those fellows that did that don't deserve no picking up."

"It doesn't look to me as if they're going to get any," said Captain Flint grimly. "No human being could live in the sea there was here when that spout broke. We must be pretty near the spot. There's a bit of wreckage, but no sign of those scoundrels. Not now. If they'd left our mainsail alone and not done that bit of fancy shooting we might have been a bit quicker."

"It's my belief," said Peter Duck, "that if they'd not done that shooting the waterspout would have missed them, same as it did us. Those fellows in that ship, they was fairly asking the Devil to take his own, and he's done it, and I think the better of him. Shooting like that at a ship full of children!"

To and fro Captain Flint sailed the *Wild Cat*, under trysail and jib, to and fro over that wind-tossed water where the *Viper* had last been seen. They saw fragments of deckplanking, a painted lifebuoy, a broken mast in a tangle of rigging, and other flotsam. But though they cruised there until dusk, and though all hands, except poor Bill, and Peter Duck, who was very busy, were carefully searching the water, they saw no sign of any living thing, no sign even that there had ever been a living thing on the schooner that had come to so sudden and so terrible an end.

CHAPTER XXXV

"BONIES" AND "MALLIES"

PETER DUCK had not been sorry to have no chance of picking up Black Jake and his friends. They had been aboard the *Wild Cat* once, and it would be a week at least before he stopped feeling the bruises on his jaw and the back of his head. One visit from such folk was one too many. He did not want another. Anyway, he said, they could not have lived long in that swirl of heavy water. If the skipper thought he must look for them, well and good, but the old seaman had hardly glanced over the side. He had plenty to do clearing the wreckage on deck. The moment that was done he had set to work to cut a couple of wooden splints for the setting of Bill's broken arm. That was the next job that mattered. He had lit the lamp in the deckhouse. He had finished roughing out the splints, and now he spoke to Captain Flint.

"The sooner we sets about that doctoring job the better, sir."

Captain Flint called John and Nancy to take the wheel.

"If there's the least hint of another squall coming up," he said, "give me a shout. Peggy, Titty, and Roger will help to keep a sharp look out. You'll hear a squall before it comes. Anyhow, she's got no sail to speak of. I want Susan in the deckhouse to help Mr Duck and me with the bandages."

Not a word was spoken by the others to the two

captains as they steadied the wheel, watched the compass through its little window, and kept the *Wild Cat*, under small jib and trysail, reaching away northward in the dusk. Not a word was spoken by the captains. Everybody was thinking of the deckhouse as a hospital, an operating-room. They had seen Bill's white face when he had fainted with the pain of his broken arm, and now, though they did not want to listen, they could not talk, and every moment were afraid that from inside the deckhouse would come some groan or sigh or other sound that would show that the pain was more than he could bear.

But, for all the noise he made, Bill might not have been in the deckhouse at all. They heard Peter Duck talking of the way a broken arm properly set is often stronger than it was before, and they heard him telling of how he had had both arms broken at once when he had been carried off his feet and thrown into the scuppers by a green sea coming aboard. And then they heard Captain Flint's voice. "Steady. Keep just so. It shouldn't hurt now. Next bandage, Susan. Get the end unrolled. Pins." But they never heard a word from Bill. And then Captain Flint's voice came again, louder, more confident. "Good lad, Bill. I couldn't have stuck that without squeaking. You'll be right as rain now if you don't get those splints shifted. But you'll have to eat with one hand for a bit. And you'll have to sleep up here. No climbing up and down until that arm's set. You and I must swop cabins for a few days."

Captain Flint came out of the deckhouse, followed by Peter Duck, with a handful of scraps of bandage and bits of wood, which he threw over the side.

Susan came out with her First Aid box, which had been very useful, after all. "All right, Bill, I'll tell them," she was saying over her shoulder. And as soon as she was through the door she told them.

"Bill grinned all the time, except just one moment when they were getting the bones to fit."

Titty felt sick and so did Nancy, but Roger changed the subject, and, for once, nobody minded.

"Captain Flint," he said.

"What's that?"

"When *are* you going to look at Mr Duck's treasure?"

Captain Flint glanced round and looked up at the sky. The wind was steadier now, but not strong, not nearly enough for the *Wild Cat's* storm canvas. Stars were showing in patches of clear, deep blue. That overhanging roof of black cloud had broken up at last.

"It looks better," he said.

"Aye," said Peter Duck. "Quick up. Quick down. We've had what was coming. We'll maybe get fine weather in the morning."

"Yes, but when *are* you going to look at the treasure?" Roger was not to be put off once he had made up his mind to ask.

"Well," said Captain Flint, "as we've got it aboard, we may as well look at it. We can't leave it in my bunk for ever. We may as well look at it now."

"Uncle Jim," cried Nancy indignantly. "Don't talk as if you wished we hadn't found it."

"I'm taking the wheel," said Mr Duck, and took it as he spoke.

Captain Flint went back into the deckhouse, and the others crowded after him.

*

Bill lay propped up on a pillow and a roll of coats in Peter Duck's bunk, his left arm, a monstrous bundle of white bandages, resting in a sling across his chest. The others hung on where they could, and were thankful that the motion of the ship was so much easier than it had been. Under the light of the cabin lamp, on the chart-table, resting, indeed, in the middle of that big chart of the Atlantic on which the trail of red crosses had marked their progress on the outward voyage, was the small teak box that had brought them so far. Captain Flint had set his heart on finding it, and yet, during these last dreadful days, he had wished a thousand times that he had never come to look for it. Now he was going to know what it was that all those years ago Peter Duck, the little boy hiding from the crabs, had seen buried in the sandy earth at the foot of his bedroom tree.

"Of course, there may be nothing in it after all," he said. "Nothing worth anything."

"But there is," said Nancy.

"Bags with labels," said Roger.

"Bonies and Mallies," said Titty.

Just as John had done on the beach, Captain Flint took the rusty padlock from the clasp. It was on the point of falling to bits, and, gently though he moved it, a trail of rusty brown powder fell from it on the chart. Susan was just going to blow the dust away when Captain Flint tried to flick it off with his hand, and smudged the broad Atlantic.

"Indiarubber'll take it out," said Susan.

A lurch of the little ship tilted the deckhouse, and half a dozen hands were put out to save the treasure-box from sliding across the Atlantic into Europe or even off the table. But it did not stir. Captain Flint's hand had been the nearest, and rested firmly on the lid. He waited a moment in case another lurch was coming, and then opened it. There, untouched, just as they had been when first the diggers brought the box up from under the roots of the fallen tree, were the wallet and the four leather bags, each with its label.

"Whalebone, those labels," said Captain Flint, and read, just as the children had read: "Mallies," "Bonies," "Roses," "Niggers."

"But what do they mean?" asked Nancy. "Why couldn't those galoots write sense, whoever they were?"

Captain Flint picked up the little bag labelled "Mallies." It was the best filled of the four. He felt it between his fingers.

"It might be dried peas," he said, "but it might not."

He unfastened the leather lace that closed the mouth of the bag. Inside the bag was a little parcel of soft leather.

"It isn't peas," said Roger.

"Not likely," said Bill, from his place on Peter Duck's bunk.

"Don't try to sit up, Bill," said Susan.

Captain Flint opened the little parcel, and

from it poured into the palm of his open hand a
stream of little white beads, or things like beads,
only that they had no holes in them. They were
not very white, and there was a sort of faint glow
in them as they trickled out of the little leather
packet into the pile in his hand. He knew at once
what they were.

"Pearls," he said, "and a pretty poor lot.
'Mallies,'" he said to himself thoughtfully. "Let's
see if the 'Bonies' are better. There's no fortune
for anybody in that lot."

"They're very pretty," said Peggy.

But Captain Flint had poured the little dull
pearls back into their parcel, and put it in its
bag, and propped the bag in a corner of the box.
He now opened the bag that was labelled "Bonies."
There was not so large a packet in this bag, but
the moment its contents rolled out into his hand
everybody knew they were something altogether
better. Clear, glimmering things, as big as peas
some of them, and not dried peas at that.

"Of course, it's easy to guess what he meant
with his 'Mallies' and 'Bonies,'" said Captain
Flint. "The chap that wrote those labels had had
the things from a Portuguese pearl-fisher. Or a
Brazilian, perhaps. One of these South Americans
with a lot of Latin at the back of their own lingo.
Mallies . . . yes. Malus. Bad. And a rotten lot they
are. Bonus . . . Good. I remember that much. And
sure enough the 'Bonies' are a lot worth looking
at. I only wish there were more of them."

"What about the 'Niggers'?" asked Titty.

"'Niggers.' Negritoes. Niger . . . Black. If they
had black pearls in there there's no wonder they

took some trouble over them. And the 'Roses''ll be
pink pearls, worth a tremendous chunk if they've
got the real colour in them."

With quick, eager fingers he undid the "Niggers." There were very few of them. Not more
than a score or so of the sooty little things. But
three or four of them he seemed to think very good
indeed. There were a good lot of the 'Roses.' There
was just the faintest glimmer of pink about them,
and Captain Flint said that maybe sixty years ago
they had been fine pearls enough, but faded now
beyond recovery.

In the leather wallet that was in the box with
the little bags of pearls there was nothing except
two old, stained, folded pieces of parchment. They
almost fell to pieces as Captain Flint opened them
out. He spread the first on the chart-table, close
under the light of the lamp. In the top left-hand
corner was a crown, and the emblem of the Board
of Trade beneath it. Captain Flint began reading
aloud:

"By the Lords of the Committee of Privy
Council for Trade. Certificate of competency
as First Mate. To Robert Charles Bowline.
Whereas it has been reported to us that you
have been found duly qualified to fulfil the
duties of First Mate in the Merchant Service
we grant you this certificate of competency.
Given under the seal of the Board of Trade,
this Thirteenth day of February 1859. By
order of the Board, etc."

Captain Flint went to the door of the deckhouse,

and spoke to the man at the wheel. He had a good
excuse.

"Mr Duck, what was the name of the captain
of the *Mary Cahoun* who took you off Crab Island
and piled his ship on Ushant?"

"Jonas Fielder," came Mr Duck's voice, prompt
and sharp out of the darkness.

"And what did you say were the letters he
had tattooed on his wrist?"

"R.C.B."

"I thought so. Well, Mr Duck, we've something
here well worth taking a look at."

"We're not likely to meet any shipping," came
the voice of Mr Duck from outside, quiet and
businesslike, "but there'd be no harm in having
all shipshape and rigging our sidelights, if you'd
tell one of my watch to get them lit."

"That's one for me," said Captain Flint, coming
back into the deckhouse. "You, John, just light
those lamps for him . . . No . . . I'll do it myself."
And Captain Flint left the crew to look after the
treasure while he lit the two big sidelights, and
went out to set them in their places on the
shrouds.

The others read through the certificates. The
second parchment was like the first, but had a
different name in it.

"But why did they leave the certificates with
the pearls?" John was saying when Captain Flint
came hurrying in again. He answered the question
at once.

"That's a bit more of Mr Duck's yarn," he
said, "a bit we can't be sure about. But I wouldn't
mind betting that Jonas Fielder was out of this

life and in Davy Jones's locker before Mr First
Mate Robert Charles Bowline made so free with
his name, took command of his ship, and sailed
her across to wreck her on Ushant. I suppose he
thought a time might come when he'd want his
own name again. Well, they're all dead now and
a long time ago, and we shall never know if First
Mate Bowline and his friend took the pearls from
Captain Fielder or from someone else unlucky
enough to come in their way. I wonder how many
lives that boxful of beads has cost already."

"And broken arms and teeth," said Bill, grinning
from the bunk where he lay propped up.

"You've certainly earned your share," said Captain Flint.

"Are they worth an awful lot?" asked Roger.

"I don't know about that," said Captain Flint.
"Anyhow, it's the first time in all my life that I've
ever gone anywhere to look for treasure and laid
my hands on it to bring it home. And of course
I'm jolly glad you found it. But even with that
box lying safe in this deckhouse, I'll tell you now
there've been a dozen times in the last twelve
hours that I was wishing I'd never heard of it.
Bringing the lot of you right over here. You just
don't know what might have happened."

"But we'd have wanted to come anyway," said
Titty.

"You ought to be jolly pleased now," said
Nancy. "Think of the chapter you can put in
the next edition of *Mixed Moss*."

"It's much more of a treasure than just an
old book," said Roger, "and you were very pleased
about that."

"It's what you've always wanted to do," said
Peggy, "and now you've done it."

"And we had a grand voyage," said John.
"We'll remember it all our lives."

"And it isn't over yet," said Nancy.

"And nothing's really gone wrong that can't
be mended," said Susan. "Not even Bill's arm.
Of course, there's his teeth. Were they second
ones or first ones, Bill?"

"They ain't wasted," said Bill. "Not they."

"Well," said Captain Flint, "tomorrow we'll
have to begin regular watches again. And the
sooner we get some sleep the better."

"And supper," said Roger.

"I'll boil up some water right away," said Peggy.

"Get along out, all of you," said Captain Flint.
"And I have a word or two to say to Mr Duck."

But of all the crew of the *Wild Cat*, Peter Duck
took least interest in the treasure. He would not
leave the wheel to go into the deckhouse to have
a look at the pearls. It was not until after supper,
when most of the others were going to bed, and
Captain Flint took the wheel for the first watch
from eight o'clock till twelve, that Peter Duck
just glanced through those old certificates, reading them word by word under the lamp on the
chart-table.

"Yes," he said, for Captain Flint had told him
what he guessed. "Yes. I reckon there was no
Jonas Fielder aboard the *Mary Cahoun*. I wonder
what happened to him. Scuppered, likely as not,
and his mate, too. There's been a heap of trouble
about these pearls."

"Ain't you going to look at 'em?" asked Bill.

"Pearls," said the old man. "Pearls. Pearls'll keep till morning. What I wants now is sleep."

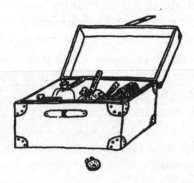

CHAPTER XXXVI

"SPANISH LADIES"

Farewell and adieu to you fair Spanish ladies,
   Adieu and farewell to you ladies of Spain,
For we're under orders for to sail to old England
   And we may never see you fair ladies again.

So we'll rant and we'll roar like true British sailors,
   We'll range and we'll roam over all the salt seas,
Until we strike soundings in the Channel of Old England:
   From Ushant to Scilly 'tis thirty-five leagues.

The first land we made, it is callèd the Dodman,
   Next Rame Head off Plymouth, Start, Portland and
     Wight:
And we sailèd by Beachy, by Fairlight and Dungeness,
   Until we brought to by the South Foreland Light.
                  SEA CHANTY

With the passing of the waterspout the strange, violent weather had come to an end. A breeze from the east smoothed out the aimless tossing of that disturbed sea, and ploughed it with the long, even furrows of a steady wind. There is little more to tell.

Peter Duck put right the damage that had been done by storm and enemy. Up at the mainmast head he rove a new peak halyard to replace the one that had been cut through by that lucky shot from the pursuing *Viper*. At dawn next day he was at work with needle and palm, patching and mending the sails that had suffered in the storm, and John, Susan, and Nancy gathered round to watch him, learning the stitches that are best

for canvas, and how many there should be to
the inch when putting a rope into the luff of a
flying jib. There was more than one day's work
to be done before he began to be ready to think of
other things. Day after day he sat stitching in the
sunshine, and all day long he kept singing quietly
to himself the old songs of the homeward bound.

"You sound almost as if you were in a hurry
to be back," said Captain Flint one morning, after
hearing for the hundredth time that it was time
for Johnny to leave her.

"It's a poor seaman as don't wish a good passage home," said Peter Duck, looking up aloft,
where once more topsails were helping her along,
patched, grey, second-best topsails, unlike the
clean, creamy canvas of the voyage out, but still
topsails, drawing well, doing their full share, as
the *Wild Cat*, with a bone in her teeth,[1] swayed
on her way in the sunshine.

A good passage they had, too: one of those
passages that come once in a hundred, and make
up for the other ninety-nine. They kept the trade
wind well up into the Sargasso Sea, where they
found a flat calm, and this time were able to get
the engine to do some work, much to the delight
of Roger, who had learnt by now that a bundle
of cotton-waste to wipe the oil away is sometimes
much more useful than an oil-can. Gibber, copying Roger in wiping and cleaning, did far less
harm than once he had done by slopping oil all
over the place. But in the end the trailing green

[1] This is what they say when the white foam spurts from under
the bows of a vessel sailing really fast. – CAPT NANCY.

weed, stretching like tracks of green foam across
that smooth sea, wound itself round the propeller
and clogged it. Captain Flint went overboard with
a rope round his middle, while Peter Duck and the
rest of the crew stood by ready to scare sharks and
to haul the skipper out of harm's way if necessary.
He cleared the propeller, but it soon got clogged
again, and this time, after clearing it, Captain
Flint said they would keep it clear and use it no
more until they needed it for coming into harbour.
After all, he said, a few hours more or less would
make no difference now. At this Peter Duck was
very pleased, and nobody bothered with the little
donkey again. Instead, they fished and collected
some of the green sargasso weed, and found small
crabs in it, just as Columbus had found them more
than four hundred years before. And Peter Duck
showed them the way the old-time sailors used
to put some of the weed with a crab or two in
a narrow-necked bottle, and cork it up with a
well-greased cork, and seal it if they had any
sealing-wax, and take it home for a curiosity to
give their wives and sweethearts, or to swop for
a drink or two in a longshore tavern where they
liked to have such things hanging up to show that
theirs was a proper port of call for sailormen.

And soon after that the wind came again, out
of the south-east, stirring the long lines of green
grass across that oily sea, and the *Wild Cat* held
on her way, heading north and a little east, but
not too much, for Captain Flint was looking for
the real westerly winds that he would find farther
north, to give them a good passage. And then, one
evening, between sunset and dawn, the southerly

wind dropped, and there came a steady breeze out
of the west and the *Wild Cat* squared away for
home.

From the first they had been keeping regular
watches, and the days slipped by fast and easy,
as days do when everything goes by the clock.
Long before they were half-way home across the
Atlantic they were beginning almost to forget the
wild turmoil of those last two days on the island,
earthquake, and hurricane, and landslide, and the
coming of the *Viper*, and the horrible hours when
they knew that Captain Flint and the pirates were
on the island together. Even the horror of that last
day of all, when the *Viper* had crept up on them,
and the pirates had brought down their mainsail,
and they had thought that all was up, until the
waterspout that they had feared themselves had
suddenly made an end of their enemies, seemed
now like a dream or something that had happened
not to them but to somebody else.

One day, when the whole lot of them were
on deck together, all sitting about in the sunshine while Peter Duck was steering, and Captain
Flint was reading aloud to them out of one of the
volumes of Hakluyt that made part of the little
library in the deckhouse bookshelf, he came upon
a passage about another homeward voyage in a
little ship. It is printed in the report of Master
Thomas Masham, who sailed with Sir Walter
Raleigh to Guiana, in a pinnace called *The Watte*,
in the year 1596. Here is what Captain Flint read:

"Between the Isle of Barbadoes in the West
Indies and England we had three mighty

stormes, many calmes and some contrary
windes. And upon the foureteenth day of
June, 1597, there being divers whales playing
about our pinnesse, one of them crossed our
stemme, and going under, rubbed her backe
against our keele . . ."

"Oh," said Titty, her eyes lighting up at the
thought, "why don't things like that happen to
us? Exciting things, I mean . . ."

Captain Flint looked over the top of the book
at her in great surprise, and then at Bill's broken
arm, still in its sling, but setting quite nicely. It
seemed to him that they had had all the excitement they needed.

"Oh yes," said Titty, "but not whales!"

"Well, you can't have everything," said Captain
Flint.

They carried the westerly winds with them
to the mouth of the Channel, and then, as if to
laugh at them, the wind came out of the east, a
contrary wind, and they had to beat against it
the whole way up Channel, until they came to
the Wight. But even that had its good side. If
they had had the wind with them, they would
never have seen the stone cross on Dodman Point,
and seeing the Dodman was like coming home for
John and Susan, for sailing out of Falmouth with
their father, they had once passed close under it,
between the point and the wild water over the
sunken rocks outside. And then another tack
brought them in towards Plymouth and they had
a good look at Rame Head, and at the brave pillar
of the Eddystone Lighthouse rising out of the sea.

"And the first land we made, it is callèd
    the Dodman,
    Next Rame Head off Plymouth, Start, Port-
land and Wight . . ."

Titty was singing to herself, and Peter Duck
heard her.

"Aye," he said, "you can tell that them chaps
in the song had the wind against them. What for
else should they be singing about the thirty-five
leagues between Ushant and the Scillies? They
wouldn't be thinking of the Scillies if they'd raised
Ushant light, and were coming from Spain with
a fair wind. No, and they wouldn't be poking
into Plymouth Bay neither. Not they. They was
plugging up Channel against a north-easter, and
that's how they come to be there. They was looking for the Dodman and Rame Head and the rest
to show them what they'd made on each tack. If
they'd have had the wind with them they'd be
looking for nothing before St Catherine's."

John and Nancy saw the Start Light, for it
was abeam at four in the morning, just when
they changed watches. John had seen it coming
nearer and nearer, and Nancy watched it fade
astern, weakening in the morning light, while
Captain Flint steered for the buoy in the middle
of Lyme Bay. Everybody was on deck to have a
look at it, with its black and white stripes and its
name, "Lyme Bay," painted round it. And everybody heard it, too, tolling its melancholy bell. As
for the long, low wedge of Portland, it was about
three in the afternoon when they came nearest

to it, and four hours later they were nearing St Alban's Head. That night they were within sight of the flashing light on St Catherine's Point, and then, some time after the watches changed at four in the morning, the easterly wind slackened, and then worked away round to the north-west, and at eight bells, when Titty, and Roger, and the two mates came hurrying on deck, the *Wild Cat* was bowling along on her course for Beachy Head, with a fine breeze off the land, and the Owers Lightship plain to see.

"And we sailéd by Beachy, by Fairlight and Dungeness," sang Titty. "I wonder if we're going to see them all."

Nobody could bear wasting time on meals in the saloon that day. Mate Susan and Mate Peggy filled people's mugs and bowls for them on deck. They sat in a row with their backs against the deckhouse watching the English coast. They passed by Beachy with its seven white cliffs (eight, Roger said), and ran through a regular fleet of small fishing boats that deeply stirred Bill and set him talking of the Dogger Bank. Then there was the *Royal Sovereign* lightship, and then, high on its hill, the church of Fairlight, a square, dark tower, rising out of dark green trees. Dungeness, long and low, they saw in the late dusk, and then, passing by Dover in the very early morning, they did indeed bring to, not exactly off the South Foreland light, like the sailors in the song, but not so very far from it, off Deal, because the tide was hard against them, and the wind weakening and not strong enough to carry them over it.

"Between us, we've really seen the whole song now," said Titty.

They sailed again a few hours later, with the wind round at south-west, that suited them well, but made Captain Flint talk of bad weather. They passed once more the remembered lightships, marking the way home for them as they had marked the way out. That night there was mutiny aboard. Not even Roger would go to bed in proper time. They stayed up counting the flashes of the lights, running in and out of the deckhouse to see on the chart just where the lightship was, or the lighthouse, that made just the number of flashes they had counted. Titty and Roger fell asleep for an hour or two in the saloon, when they had been bribed below decks by hot cocoa, but they were out again to see the lights of the Rotterdam steamer out from Harwich. After that Susan did get them to bed, but they went only because they heard Captain Flint say that he didn't want to bring his ship home with all his sailors good for nothing because they could not keep their eyes open.

And then, at last, in a grey, cloudy morning, the *Wild Cat* headed in for Lowestoft pier-heads. Bill, his arm still in a sling, but really better, stood by to lower away the jib. Susan was ready with the staysail halyard in her hand. As they shot through the pier-heads the orders rang out. John and Nancy gathered and smothered the headsails as they came flapping down. Peter Duck was at the wheel. "Lower away the foresail!" "Lower away the main!" John, Nancy, Susan, Peggy, Titty, Bill, and Captain Flint brought the great sails down for the last time. The engine was already working, chug, chug, chug. Roger was standing by the clutch waiting for the word. He got it, and the noise changed as he set the lever to "Half Speed Ahead," and the engine settled down to its work. The *Wild Cat* moved slowly in towards the inner harbour. The swing bridge opened before her. Foot passengers, held up by the opened bridge, looked down on the little schooner as she passed through. They looked down at her busy, sunburnt crew, at the parrot in his cage, at the restless monkey, who hardly knew which way to turn, torn between his loyalty to Roger (who never left his post by the engine lever) and his natural interest in the wharves and the harbour, so different from the open sea, Crab Island, or the quiet Caribbean anchorage. They stared down at the old brown sailor at the wheel, who did not think it worth while to waste a single glance on any one ashore until he saw his friend, the kindly harbourmaster, waving the *Wild Cat* towards an empty berth, the very berth she had left when she slipped away in the early summer morning, little knowing what high adventure was before her.

The voyage of the *Wild Cat* was over.

After that, of course, the Swallows and Amazons had to hurry back into ordinary life, and to make up for lost time. "Though you can't really call it lost," as Nancy says, "because of all we learnt." The treasure turned out not to be worth such a tremendous lot, after all, but Captain Flint did not mind. He had been to look for treasure a hundred times before, and now, for the first time in his life, he had not had to come back without it. He had a grand new chapter to add to his book

(*Mixed Moss*, by A Rolling Stone), so that he could very well do without the treasure itself, and gave most of his share to young Bill. Peter Duck had a pearl necklace made up for each of his three daughters, and gave a new coat of paint to the *Arrow of Norwich*. Young Bill he took with him, up to Acle, and to Potter Heigham, and to Beccles. Bill liked the Beccles daughter best, and she liked him, and Bill went to live at the farm with her and her husband while he was getting a bit of schooling, and weekends and holidays and any other time he could get away he spent with Peter Duck in the old wherry, going here and there with one cargo and another along these inland waters, and doing a little fishing. As for Black Jake and his friends, no questions were ever asked about them, so none were answered.

ADMIRAL PETER BUOL

THE
ARTHUR RANSOME
SOCIETY

The Arthur Ransome Society was formed in June 1990 with the aim of celebrating his life and his books, and to encourage both children and adults to take part in adventurous pursuits – especially climbing, sailing and fishing. It also seeks to sponsor research, to spread his ideas in the wider community and to bring together all those who share the values and the spirit that he fostered in all his storytelling.

The Society is based at the Abbot Hall Museum of Lakeland Life and Industry in Kendal, where there is a special room set aside for Ransome: his desk, his favourite books and some of his personal possessions. There are also close links with the Windermere Steamboat Museum at Bowness, where the original *Amazon* has been restored and kept, together with the *Esperance*, thought to be the vessel on which Ransome based Captain Flint's houseboat. The Society keeps in touch with its members through a journal called *Mixed Moss*.

Regional branches of the Society have been formed by members in various parts of the country – Scotland, the Lake District, East Anglia, the Midlands, the South Coast among them – and contacts are maintained with overseas groups such as the Arthur Ransome Club of Japan. Membership fees are modest, and fall into three groups – for those under 18, for single adults, and for whole families. If you are interested in knowing more about the Society, or would like to join it, please write for a membership leaflet to The Secretary, The Arthur Ransome Society, The Abbot Hall Gallery, Kendal, Cumbria LA9 5AL.

SWALLOWS AND AMAZONS FOR EVER!

ARTHUR RANSOME

Great Northern?

'I was wrong,' said Captain Flint. 'He's not mad but bad. Rotten bad. It isn't only eggs he wants. He wants us to take the credit for it. You're quite right. It's up to us, it's up to the ship, to see he doesn't.'

Dick's birdwatching discovery turns the cruise of the *Sea Bear* into a desperate chase. Not only do the Swallows and Amazons have to prove the facts of the case but they also have to dodge the savage natives and evade the ruthless pursuit of a fanatic egg-collector, determined to kill a pair of rare birds. Fortunately, Nancy has a few plans...

By the winning author of the first Carnegie medal.

ISBN 0 09 942726 5

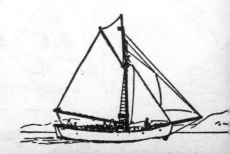

ARTHUR RANSOME

Missee Lee

Miss Lee looked at John.

'Were you coming here when you lost your ship?'

'No,' said John.

'We jolly well would have been if we'd known,' said Nancy.

'Why?' asked Miss Lee.

'Well, pirates,' said Nancy. 'Who wouldn't?'

Nancy Blackett, the terror of the seas, has finally met a real pirate – the tiny, pistol-carrying Missee Lee, who has rescued them after their shipwreck off the coast of china. The only trouble is she wants to keep them…forever.

By the winning author of the first Carnegie medal.

ISBN 0 09 942725 7

ARTHUR RANSOME

Secret Water

'You'll start with a blank map, that doesn't do more than show roughly what's water and what isn't. You'll have your tents, stores, everything we'd got ready. You'll be just a wee bit better off than Columbus. But you'll be marooned, fair and square.'

John, Susan, Titty and Roger, the crew of the *Swallow*, take on the job of mapping the mass of small islands round Pin Mill while living on the biggest one. But who are the mysterious savages who lurk in the islands – and is the tribal totem they find in their campsite a threat of attack…?

By the winning author of the first Carnegie medal.

ISBN 0 09 942723 0

ARTHUR RANSOME

Swallowdale

'There was nothing of Swallow to be seen, except a couple of floating oars and one of the knapsacks, drifting in between Pike rock and the island.'

John, Susan, Titty and Roger return to the lake for another summer camping on their island with their old allies, Nancy and Peggy, otherwise known as the Amazon pirates. But immediately disaster strikes when the Swallows find themselves marooned ashore by the shipwreck of their boat. But if they can't have the island, there's always Swallowdale, the secret valley, hidden from the world and containing an extra secret concealed within it...

By the winning author of the first Carnegie medal.

ISBN 0 09 942715 X

ARTHUR RANSOME

Swallows and Amazons

Titty drew a long breath that nearly choked her.
"It is ... " she said.
The flag blowing out in the wind at the masthead of
the little boat was black and on it in white were a
skull and two crossed bones.

To John, Susan, Titty and Roger, simply being allowed to
use the boat *Swallow* to go camping on the island is
adventure enough. But they soon find themselves under
attack from the fierce Amazon
Pirates, Nancy and Peggy.
And so begins a summer
of battles, alliances, explo-
ration and discovery.

*By the winning author of
the first Carnegie medal.*

ISBN 0 09 942733 8

ARTHUR RANSOME

The Big Six

'But who are the Big Six?' asked Pete.
'It's the Big Five really,' said Dorothea. 'They are
the greatest detectives in the world. They sit in
cubby holes at Scotland Yard and solve one mys-
tery after another.'

It's great detective work that's needed now. Bill, Peter
and Joe are falsely accused of setting boats adrift and the
whole river is against them. Only Dick, Dorothea and
Tom Dudgeon are there to
stand by their friends and
they soon set to work to
investigate the crimes and
trap the real criminals.

*By the winning author of the
first Carnegie medal.*

ISBN 0 09 942724 9